GHOST
OF THE
MOUNTAIN

SHAD B. KING

MILTON & HUGO L.L.C.
4407 Park Ave., Suite 5
Union City, NJ 07087, USA

Website: *www. miltonandhugo.com*
Hotline: *1- 888-778-0033*
Email: *info@miltonandhugo.com*

Ordering Information:
Quantity sales. Special discounts are granted to corporations, associations, and other organizations. For more information on these discounts, please reach out to the publisher using the contact information provided above.

Library of Congress Control Number:		2025912143
ISBN-13:	979-8-89285-553-2	[Paperback Edition]
	979-8-89285-554-9	[Digital Edition]

Rev. date: 06/16/2025

Chapter

1

From factory after factory, altogether spewing in harmony, a dark cloud fluttered toward a gray-clouded sky and drifted through a lantern-lit city. It smiled and cropped its brass-like towers, the smog then driving to crowded sidewalks filled with rain-prepared civilians scurrying to their jobs and home, to work and errands. It enshrouded the common folk with hard-to-see glances directed at one another, causing clenched pressure around personal bags and a passive paranoia that indulged every man and woman who walked along the sidewalks of Haze. Upon every face latched a lifeless gas mask, black and clear-lensed goggles, along with thick filters pressed against their mouths, anything to help against the smoke. No man or child were without one. Along the sidewalks, the cloud dispersed into the busy road where honking cars, buses, and taxis all at odds and shouted at one another, blaming each other for slow traffic and missing the lights. A gust then diffused toward the west sanctum of the city, following the grid-like roads and the funnel of the buildings rolling ever right angle into the next, until it whirled the limits of its stretch and reached a long, wooden building, the only one in Haze to not have two stories, and faded into the constant mist of the providence.

The building had no metal, save its bolts and screws, despites its youthful flow of hundreds of feet leaving and entering the front doors, creating two channels of people marching in lines. It was composed on an elevated platform, a timely arch, and a silver bell enticed at the center of the roof, with an embolden sign just below that read, "CAVALRY STATION."

Among the channel of faces attempting to enter the station stood a girl looking up at the sign. The folk navigated this troublesome obstacle, and like water, bodies passed around her. But the girl still stood, and through her dark mask, a glint of her emerald eyes shined through, and her charcoal hair curled around the back of her neck to her breast, protected by her leather jacket. She held along behind her a large black briefcase, a similar sight for those funneling into the station. The girl breathed heavy and blended with the channeled, heading inside.

Bella Tomson, this was her name. She raised her hood so the lifeblood of Haze could not recognize her, as the mask wasn't effective enough. She zipped through the entrance with little time wasted and stepped onto the creaking elevated platform. It was then a second before she crossed into the entrance and saw hordes of souls facing the locomotive half of the station, an open panel that revealed the distant fields of brown grass and the sloping foot of the Giant mountain range. Their hatted heads dotted the scene, and their coated bodies blocked her view of the tracks she longed for, placed there so long ago. Bella walked toward the waiting crowd and glanced back at the entrance. She wondered at the masterful architecture that composed the walls and ceiling of the station. She had never seen an old structure before and in such great care as well, a fresh sight in a poisonous city. She followed the wooden walls as she turned toward the tracks but stopped and marveled a painting of rugged man wearing to what Bella understood as halo hats, on top of horse whirling loose rope on a dusty plane of earth, lit only by the wide open widows that attempt to gift the interior with as much light and smog-drawn air that it could. She then faced the direction she wanted and reached the stalling group in front of her, stopping before she hit the back of a tall man wearing a slick blue suit, his mask latching uncomfortably tight on his skull. She scanned the crowd. They stood a fair bit taller than her, most of them being men, but even the women made her look small, their children being her only saving grace. Bella directed her attention to the bottom half of the station, trying to catch a glimpse at the railroad tracks through a maze of pant legs, angling right and left to try and peer past the first tall man in front of her. But it was impossible; the huddle was too dense. She would never ask him to move. She was always too nervous to ask anyone to move. Bella wanted to see the track. She had never seen them before, only in history books. They were an absolute in her youth to be mentioned and too scrutinized in college to hold a conversation about, all while still being very much needed. They were a way out.

Countless banter and small talk were being tossed back and forth, friends jeering at each other, apprentices laughing over stark comments and their masters rolling their unseen eyes, and families arguing and smiling in warm manners—all behind masks. The uptake in voices filled the station with loud chatter that made it hard for Bella to focus on any one particular conversion. But she found some words:

"How do you do?"

"Good."

"Did you buy bread?"

"There wasn't any."

"How's your day going?"

"Did you remember to pay the gas bill before we left?"

"Let Charlie get down."

The chatter was a constant noise to which Bella disliked, but endured the interaction between person to person with a hard-to-hide smirk, even behind plastic, able to guess the convection being held of a gas-masked society.

Then out of the corner the station boomed a man.

"Stand away from the red line! Two minutes! Stand away from the red line! I told you, back up!"

The crowd deafened for a moment, then rose back into their volume, the people shifting back in sections, layered in their timing, keeping engaged in their matters. The tall man in front of Bella almost stepped on her brand-new sneakers as he moved. Bella quickly understood the motion and stepped back as well. She looked at the man to see if he noticed if she was there. He didn't check behind him and simply turned his head to the right. She then heard it, a clamor of chugging metal sounds in the distance that could be heard through the station's commotion. She realized what the sound meant.

3

Bella rose on the tips of her toes in an attempt to view the upcoming clamor of chugging and heavy steam. She could hear it getting louder and the noises of the crowd dimmed. The girl heard a child roar: "It's coming! The train is coming!" She heard another yell: "Mom, it's here! Mom!"

Although embarrassed for she wasn't a child, Bella herself couldn't help feeling excited as well for the train's arrival. Her calves eventually grew tired, and she succumbed to fall flat- footed again, but Bella still listened to the crescendo chugging of the approaching train.

It grew and grew until it reached a climax, and the train rolled in from the right, strolling into the station, then screeching like a pig. The locomotive passed her, but she caught sight and wondered at its almost square-like body with red-black frame and tan body. Next came the travel carts, all an elegant brown; tight, taunt gas lantern on the sides, slowly rolling until they made a complete stop. The girl counted the light until the trail sighed an exhausted hiss.

Bella stood motionless. The cart of the train seems to go on eternally but ended so suddenly. She was both intimidated and intrigued at the age-old vessel that spanned out in front of her.

"Back up!" voices on the cart yelled. "Back up!"

Thereafter, the doors of the travel cart in front of her folded open, and a river of trouble-faced folk bleed out of the cart. The waiting crowd, as if by slow command, divided into rough chunks and provided slight cracks in their foundation enough for the approaching people to squeeze through. The leaving commuters, eager to reach Haze, fumbled on their masks, bumping into standing others that shook their heads, or even barked. Bella, fearing she will be swept away by this new current, wedged herself right behind the tall man in the blue suit, doing her best not to get bumped.

The standing crowd waited patiently for the current of comers to trickle out. Bella felt as if she would be stuck behind the blue-suited man forever at the current rate of people pouring out from the train. But, as soon as the girl felt her contempt, the current grew small enough, and a man's voice boomed again.

"All right slowly! All aboard! All aboard to Refuge!"

Then, as a mass, the waiting crowd moved toward the traveling carts, sliding past the remaining people and stepping onto the train. The sudden movement left Bella behind by a few feet, but she quickly recovered, dashing to the blue-suited man and treading stealthily behind him. The progressing formation then began to funnel into the travel crates. Bella was coming closer and closer to the excitement. People were still hurrying and exiting the train. The crowd quickly diminished, and while waiting for the horde to fill into the train, now near the front, Bella spotted a thick red line on the edge of the station. And four feet below, squished by metal wheels, were the mighty tracks of the Union railroad. Bella smiled, but was pushed along by those in back of her.

"All aboard! All aboard to Refuge!" a male voice boomed.

Bella turned and saw those hurrying her along. She saw that there were a fraction of people in front of her as compared to the back. She quickly reclaimed her pace so as to not get run over by the others and found her spot and set her foot on the first step of the travel cart, then a second, then a third, and lifted herself up by the base hand railing, then carried herself onto the train.

"All aboard! All aboard to Refuge!"

The interior was furnished with light oak booths that could seat three people. The wall that sheltered were connected by a diamond pattern and lit by yellow glowing lamps, the same texture from the exterior. A walkway separated in the middle the columns of booths and appeared to run almost the entire length of the train. Rectangular windows accompanied every pair of booths, positioned between each other was a compartment for luggage. The floor was well laid with compact carpet, which Bella was hurried onto.

The passengers scurried to their seats with Bella, filling in the booths they could. Family and friends went together, coworkers and acquaintances, and the girl quickly realized that she may not get a seat to herself. She rushed down the walkway in search of one, to get at least a window seat, and after appearing no doubt as an idiot, she discovered that the track companies were larger than she expected, and she found less and less where she thought would be filled to the brim. She then spotted her heaven, a section devoid of any consulates, and crossed to the opposite side to where she entered. Bella walked over, passing others who were figuring their sitting arrangements, taking her place by the window. She slipped to the clear window, setting her luggage on the seat next to her.

All the passengers had taken their seats, save a few still settling on. Bella was surprised at the fact that nobody had to come sit by here, bracing for this problem for the trip. It didn't bother her. She preferred to be on her own, that no one was around, but considering the sheer volume of people, it baffled her. She had to share at least one person in her booth. She nevertheless smiled, riding her first train in peace.

She heard in front of her a passenger consulting his partner, "Getting less crowded, eh?" And his coworker replied, "Yeah, a bit, but that's just the way these things go. It'll all be gone in a year or so."

The train's doors then folded shut. The people sat waiting. Bella leaned her head against the window and looked out toward the empty station platforms, save for a few pedestrians filling in for the next train. There a man with a beard dressed in black trench coat flung out a golden watch that was linked by chain to a vest pocket. Bella heard him shout through the carts wall in a muffled boom, "Refuge leaving! Refuge leaving!" He then stopped, checking the playroom, and peered back to his watch and then to the locomotive. The man nodded and brought his free arm strength up, then down in a sending motion.

Three whistles then filled the air, one after the other, and the train began to move. All the travel carts rocked as the locomotive tugged, and the locks all heaved in unison. Bella watched as the bearded man, waving a hand to the leaving train, faded into irrelevance compared to the size of the station and then how the station similarly grew into only one building compared to the labyrinth of towers that composed Haze.

Finally, thought the girl, watching the brass colored building shrink from view. She took off her mask, noting others that have done so.

The girl tilted her vision toward the brown and yellow fields and the blotted cattle that graze them, black dots as they passed in the window frame. Cheap barbed wire kept the farmers herds separated and from the cows throwing themselves onto the track, causing a disturbance in everyone's schedule. These fields were all Bella could see, along with a few that the girl would deem Lucky Homes and a fast-approaching mountain on the right side of her vision.

Bella then slipped her hand into her coat pocket and produced a thin rectangle phone with no buttons. It had on it a silver case with a clear back; and a Polaroid photo of an emerald-eyed girl celebrating in a dorm, drink in hand, with a taller girl, was wedged between phone and the case. The girl had red curly hair that hung down past her breasts, and a plaid jacket with jeans covered her. Bella swiped up on the phone's surface, smiling, and tapped it a few times before bringing it to her ear.

"You gone yet?" a voice asked.

"Yes, ma'am," replied Bella in a laugh. "I'm just on the train now."

"Oh my gosh, oh my gosh, do you like it?"

"Yeah! It was like going back in time!"

"It's somethin' different, ain't it?" asked the voice, a hint of honey in her voice.

"Oh yes! It's so old and rustic. It really is a time machine. There was people everywhere, but like I still got a booth to myself."

"Well, ya, that's not unusual. The rest of the country doesn't use trains anymore."

"But there were so many people, Molly!" said Bella. "You should have seen it. How could they throw them out?"

"It's not within their policy anymore," replied Molly. "You should have seen the station when I went. It was an army! But don't get used to crowds, now that Refuge is just right around the corner. You're gonna freak! It hasn't changed one bit since I was a girl."

"Yeah, then Heartlake a few miles east," said Bella.

"But ya get to see it!"

The girl sighed. "Clear skies?"

"The clearest," said Molly.

"I won't mind that for a while."

"Well, on bad days you can see Haze's smog kinda bleed through," admitted Molly.

"Oh."

"But in Heartlake you won't!"

"Well, anything is better than Haze," replied Bella.

"Oh yeah, you'll love it," said Molly. "Complete night and day. You can actually breathe air all year, no mask mandates. That was the worst at college. I felt groggy all the time. It was the worse."

"I remember. You took sleeping pills every night."

"Yeah, yeah, I did," Molly stumbled over her words, recalling memories. "It was a godsent test for sure. I know ya don't believe that, but I do. That place is the devil. But I got through it!"

"Yes, you did, Molly," replied Bella. "Yes, you did."

"And now you're free too! God, we're gonna have so much fun."

"As much fun as nurses can have," said Bella, rolling her eyes.

"No. Where gonna have even more fun than nurses."

"We're not doctors."

"No, those crows do nothing fun," said Molly. "What I meant is that we're gonna actually do stuff!"

Bella sighed and leaned her head against the glass. "If you say so."

"I'm serious!" Molly sensed the dissatisfaction. "The day, the first instance we have off," she snapped through the phone, "we're hitting the town."

"Why?" Bella asked. "Why would we ever do that?"

"It'd get ya around more people."

"Just what I need." And the girl pressed into the window.

"And who knows," Molly continued, "there's always a chance you'll find that fancy lil' gent."

"What are you even going on about?" Bella laughed. "You know we're both dying alone."

Molly snickered. "Not me. I'm dragging someone with me, and he better be cute."

"Well, he better be as horny as you are."

"It's not a sex thing!" Molly cleared. "It's endearing. And I don't fancy my deathbed surrounded by cats. I just want someone to hold me, is that too far?"

"I'm just teasing," said Bella. "You'll get married. A girl like you should have no problem."

"Well, it won't be before you, that's for sure, ya man snatcher."

"Whatever, ya hag."

"Excuse me?" Molly drew out her voice. "Who had a boyfriend in the ninth grade and didn't tell me, hmm?

"Oh my god, it lasted a month!" Bella defended.

"Oh, okay, sure. Still has his jacket."

The girl looked down to the leather. "He didn't ask for it back!"

"Well, it obviously meant something."

"It's a nice jacket," said Bella. "It's comfy."

Molly giggled. "Yeah sure, punk. Listen, I gotta hurry and run some errands, but I'll be there to pick ya up."

"Yep."

"Wait by the station if I'm not there. I shouldn't be too late if I am."

"Sound good, I'll stay put when I get there. See ya there!" said Bella.

"Yep, yep, b-bye!" And Molly ended the call.

The girl took the phone from her ear and placed it back in her pocket. She released a heavy exhale and stared back out the window at the moving scene. The train had just reached the foot of the mountain where the tracks began to bend around the Sleeping Giant, looping to fresh land. The girl had never seen the range up close before, and now at the forefront of the Giants, she felt minuscule. Bella saw smooth and gradually steepness at the mountain's base, where oaks still grew and sagebrush. It was there the girl noticed something strange: a massive chain-linked fence, hurls of wicked barbed wire lining the edge, and it stretched for miles and miles, as far as she could see, staying on course with the base of the mountain. The girl thought this queer, believing the mountains to be free, but reasoned that someone had to own it. Then she raised her gaze up past the ugly fence. The higher the mountain ascended toward its peak, the more jagged and unforgiving rocks and cliffs became, the majority appearing as primitive knives, sticking out toward the sky. Among the creases of these crowns grew dense columns of green pines that varied in length. Bella panned to where the mountain joined another, and another, and another. This was the common look for range, standing cruel, standing proud.

Bella grew comfortable on the booth's leather seat, watching the scenery pass her by. She was rocked back and forth by the rumble of the tracks and the train underway. The weight of her eyelids started to exceed her strength, and soon she began to nod off into a void of conscious thought.

She fell asleep; however, rest did not last for the girl. A minute or so in slumber, Bella was shaken awake by some unseen force. The girl opened her eyes, startled. She turned to her left, feeling someone's touch on her shoulder, and glancing a hand she recoil to attention, there stood a man in a black uniform over a blue collar with a silk tie lying upon gold buttons on his vest. In his other hand, the man held a metal object that possessed small jaws with one having a single circular tooth and the other with an open lip.

Bella's body cinched at the sight of the stranger.

"Sorry, ma'am," he said, his eyes friendly. "I didn't mean to scare you. Just need to click a ticket." He brandished the metal trinket in his grasp.

Bella figured he must be a conductor and flung to her coat and dug on the inside compartment.

"Y-yeah," said Bella, seeking for the ticket within. Bella kept her eye directed toward the floor and extended her hand toward the man. She felt an ice-piercing wave clutched her heart when she struggled to find the ticket, but pursued her way down and retrieved a crumbled up slit of paper.

"Thank you, young lady," said the man, grabbing the ticket. He looked down at the ticket as he brought the metal object. "Refuge, ay? Looking to become a fisherman?"

"No, sir," she replied in a flat voice. "I...I'm a nurse."

"Ha! I know I know. Ladies don't go stay in the swamp, they go up to Heartlake."

Bella nodded.

The man exposed a toothy grin. "Good to see ya on the train. Ain't nothin' like it."

"Yeah," said Bella. She shifted her gaze back and forth. "My friend wanted me to see it for myself." She turned to the passing mountain outside her windows.

"Oh yes, they're quite gorgeous," said the man. He angled himself away. "Travel safely, ma'am." And the man continued along his way, opening the door leading onto the next travel cart. He twilled the metal object around his finger and slipped through without so much as a sound.

Only when the man's attention wasn't to her that Bella glanced at him leaving. She returned her attention to the mountains looking from the pristine glass. She thought that conversion could have gone better. She wanted to say more and stutter less.

"Oh well," she said to herself. "It's over." She closed her eyes again, and the rumbling of the track once soothed her yet again. She drifted and found herself falling into unconsciousness.

But the train kept along its tracks. It traveled with constant speed and strength, unearthing dust in its wake. It continued to the side of the Sleeping Giants and left miles of prairies behind. After the grasslands, the dirt beneath lost its texture and became mud, and soon lost all durability, becoming puddles that dotted the territory, reflecting clouds in the clear sky. Life began to appear among the yellow-wanned fields. Cattails and lily pads cut through the mud, and far-spread trees stood frozen as if caught tiptoeing on mangled roots. A hint of green gave rise to water fowl. Ducks, herons, and geese flew and floated throughout the expanding ponds in search for bugs, bass, or small minnows that sought shelter in the water.

And past the threshold of this marsh, the tracks were thought of and were bolstered on erected gravel compacted in equivalent mounds. The swamp stretched and became the dominant terrain, save the range and the massive fence along it. Passengers soon saw boats on the water and patches of captured swamp with moldy wood and rusty wires. The consistent riders prepared themselves, and few readied to leave their seats.

The train began to slow itself with slight braking, screeching its wheel on the metal track. A settlement became discernible, along with fields of corn, wheat, and more unusual pens among the swamp. Its buildings are more toward the center composed mostly of stone and timber, some larger, some smaller, but nothing compared to the city of Haze. However, some showed signs of brass.

The train slowed even more, and the screeching became more apparent. The buildings were close; and the unpaved road that put together, seemingly at random, the town, all leavyed on a patch of earth that rose enough to where the swamp could not reclaim. Evidently, there was no perfect layout within Refuge, and fields and aquatic ranges far outpaced the town boundaries.

Eventually, the train slowed until it stopped. Outside was a quaint station with the common composition of Refuge architecture. Bella, still sleeping, felt a nudge from the train's halt, but it did not fully wake her. She shifted and looked to see three of the passengers in her cart stand up. Her brain was foggy. The conductor then burst into the cart in a yell.

"Arrived at Refuge! Arrived at Refuge!

Bella sprang up. Startled, she understood now what was happening and looked around to see the conductor descending down the walkway. She then spotted the few men exiting the station, and she grabbed her luggage. She scurried through the alley and stepped down the steps one by one.

It was a draft in the air. There wasn't any pressure in it, and Bella could see everything. She had the instinct to fit herself with her ventilation mask, but instead, the nurse lifted her head and roamed around the station, taking deep breaths. There wasn't anybody boarding the train, and no one that needed to be off was still on. Soon enough, the loud man sounded from the side of the train.

"All aboard to Molly-Mason! All aboard to Molly-Mason!"

Bella took a last look of the relic there on the tracks, then walked to where she assumed the entrance to be. The conductors sounded off again, and the train left in a hurry.

Bella wandered into the covered portion of the station. There were no lights within the building, and the only radiance piercing the shaded interior was through simple square windows that were plastered throughout. On the far side of the wide room was the outline of a door, a crack of light displaying through it. Bella noticed the other passengers who had left with her directing toward it, and she followed. Unlike Haze, there were no paintings, and the only furniture of note was a wooden table and two chairs, a deck of playing cards on it.

There was a man dressed in an overcoat and shiny shoes who held the door for Bella. She smiled and thanked him as she passed underneath the frame. He smiled too and walked out behind her, not a word spoken as he navigated to one of the buildings there.

A few steps from the door, Bella stopped and watched the unpaved street. The air was filled with dust and the noise of a truck running in the distance. She scanned around her. She was shocked how less dense it was compared to Haze. Bella then saw what she believed to be a resident: a woman in a well-knitted skirt and cotton fleece. Walking up to the side of her was a man in an overalls and a short-sleeved shirt who took her arm. The lady appeared happy about it and switched to join hands instead. It stranged the girl out how openly they showed affection. She spotted a few others going about their day's business, many men carrying fish and corn, all dressed in similar fashion.

She then saw a woman, hair braided in an unusual manner, which left a design on her upper back. By her breast, folded with her collar, there was a soft piece of fur, red with a tip of black; and a strange necklace hung near it. The rest of her seemed normal, her clothes appearing old- fashioned, but it didn't seem out of place for her, yet Bella focused on these slight details.

The woman passed from the girl's sight, and Bella tried not to watch, the attire still so bizarre to her. She figured she should go find somewhere Molly could get into and found what she believed to be the station's dirt parking lot. She stood at the cusp of it, leading against the old wooden wall of the building. The girl then noticed the murmur from a truck engine moseying in her direction, along with a satisfying crunch of the road.

Bella turned to her right and waited for a minute or so. Soon at the end of the road, a beat-up and dented vehicle with a single cab approached, and in its driver seat sat a curly redhead with the widest of smiles.

Bella smiled too.

And the redhead whipped into the parking lot in a not-hard-to-find open spot and flung her door open with a metallic spring.

"Bellz!" she cried, rushing the girl. She opened her arms wide and seized Bella.

The girl reciprocated but visibly didn't like the touch, however the exception being close friends. "Been a while, huh?" she said.

"I can't believe it!" Molly pried her arms and looked at the girl, still touching. "It has been a while! This is gonna be so much fun!"

"I bet," said Bella. "I might just end up having to go back to Haze if we don't."

"That's a fib. Who in their right mind would go back to Haze after seeing this!" Molly gestured to the town.

"Yeah. " said Bella. "Our Planned Home isn't here though"

"Well, I know. But imagine if they were. God, that'd be great."

"Why aren't they here?"

"No money," said Molly. "Not even a clinic down in these parts."

"Oh," said Bella. "Well, it's still lovely. I'm pretty sure I'm gonna throw my mask away."

"Oh, I threw it out the first day," said Molly, shifting a little. "I have to admit that Heartlake's got even fresher air than here."

"That's good to hear."

Molly dug her heel into the ground. "Everyone who needs medical attention got to drive up to Heartlake. Most people don't even bother."

"Surely they got to have some medicine down here."

"Yeah, well, we have some. Over the counter and what not. But most people rely on more taboo methods. I…I remember as a kid my parents were teaching me how to ride a horse. I was about eight or nine and pretty tall for my age, but the horses still rocked me off. My pa came to my side and found out my leg was broken. Oh, it hurt, but lucky it wasn't bad break. My folks took me to a house, an ol' wooden shack, and this old man whipped up something and gave me a splint. I don't know what it was, but it wasn't all ulterior mambo. But it cost us nothing. The old fella didn't even charge! Lord knows we didn't have the money to get hurt." Molly struck the ground again. "Dirt poor."

"That's terrible," said Bella. "Why would ya family ever trust someone like that?" She didn't know what else to say.

"He knew what he was doin'." Molly smiled. "Anyways, wanna see more of the town?" The redhead started for her truck.

"Take pride in it?" Bella laughed, following and towing her luggage behind.

"Of course, I do. It's the gem of the state."

"That's Molly-Mason's slogan."

"Well, it fits Refuge better," said Molly, hopping into the rustic truck.

Bella set her case into the back of the truck. She then grabbed the passenger side's handle and attempted to open the door, but it didn't budge, not so much as an inch. Bella looked up at Molly through the dirty glass.

"You gotta yank it," she said.

The girl jerked the handle twice, and it gave way. The door creaked open, and Bella stepped up into the cab.

"I kinda wanna go up to Heartlake, if ya don't mind." Said Bella. "But if ya wanna drive a round, I'm all for it."

"Ya don't wanna tour?" replied Molly. "That's fine." She slipped a key into the ignition, a lanyard with many other trinkets were connected to it. "We can go straight up." She twisted the key, and the truck roared to life.

"You say," said Bella, scanning the interior of the cab. "I don't wanna choose." Her eye fell to a window crank lever next to her, then to the screenless radio between the redhead and her.

Molly shifted the truck into reverse, placing one arm in the back of the dotted-skinned seat and turning to view out the rear window. "Well, you say, you're the newcomer."

The truck swung its back into the dirt road, then accelerated forward, toward an intersection with no stop sign and overgrown brush-like trees blocking sight of coming traffic. Molly rolled her truck forward and checked several times, left and right, before accelerating and hooking a left turn.

"I don't wanna seem rude," said Bella. "I'm just tired."

"You know," she said, "they ought to cut those pickles." Molly then acknowledged the girl. "Ya only sat on a train."

Bella defended. "It wasn't only that, I had to pack and get, ya know, mentally ready for everything. You know I have trouble with people."

The pair continued along their path. The truck now headed east toward the Sleeping Giant and traveled on the closest road one could consider Refuge's main street.

"Getting ready to be a nurse?" Molly then asked.

Bella nodded.

"It's okay, I understand."

And the truck passed by many fruit stands on the dusty sidewalks selling a plethora of berries, melons and corn. Her stomach growled at the sight of them, she had nothing to eat in Haze She soon spotted the row of small stores that enamored the road and shaped the town to the vague mold of a city. There were some that sold clothes; others, labor; and other, metal parts that reminisce merchandise of village tinkerers. Most, however, had paper on a thread that read, "Close." Discouraged at the lonesome hanging signs, Bella looked down the street though the windshield and spotted some cars on the road, but mostly big diesels carrying some sort of produce in their beds. She saw above the streetlights that dangled on wire over the many intersections interlocking the road. Beyond them was the mountain range and a turn that obviously connected to a turn that would lead to a winding highway that snaked around into the canyon. The large fence, appearing more like a wall, could be seen still, following the interstate.

"They're beautiful," said Molly, "aren't they?"

"Hm?" Bella sounded, caught off guard.

"The mountains," Molly referred. "Aren't they beautiful?"

"Oh, well they're something."

"What?! Come on, they're majestic."

"They look dangerous."

"Nah, they aren't dangerous," explained Molly.

Bella studied her friend. "What about that barbed wall?"

"Well"—Molly gripped the steering wheel—"there's just there to keep us out."

"It's all state property, right?"

"The old timers told me that they all once belonged to the people and that the state took it all away."

"Right." Bella rolled her eyes. "That sounds like what happened."

"It's true!" exclaimed Molly. "It was all privately owned before the state took it."

"Why would they do that? It doesn't make a lot of sense not to use it, like a national park."

"Ha, they just want more land to keep poor folk off it. I bet they still use it. They hate the Locals."

Bella's ears pricked at the word. "Molly, come on, they wouldn't do that."

"Ya sure?" The redhead grew more hostile. "Who says?"

"They're good people."

"Says you!"

Bella sighed. "They wouldn't be in their positions if they didn't have some idea. Now come on, you know who you're sounding like."

Molly scuffed. "I'm not trying to be. I just don't see the reason."

Bella turned again to Molly. "I've never seen you so cynical about something."

A stoplight had turned red, and Molly obeyed. A massive truck rolled past them. "I'm sorry, Bellz, I don't mean to be. I just know there are good things those Giants hid."

"That's loony talk." Bella laughed. "There's nothing hiding up there, besides a mountain lion."

"You'll see," said Molly, not wanting to argue any longer.

The light turned green. The truck accelerated past the light, and the pair continued along the dirt road. Eventually, the building soon dissipated, and the farmland was all behind them. The road became paved, and the longer they drove, the more developed it became. Bella looked further, and that road soon merged with the winding highway and up into the Sleeping Giants.

Chapter

2

Molly's rustic truck weaved through the busy traffic of the canyon 77. She traveled at a mediocre pace, having to stop and go to avoid unnecessary legal battles, but the pair made good pace nevertheless, singing popular songs on the radio and insulting other drivers in front of them.

Molly then spied a line of steady semitrucks that stalled the flow of quicker cars in line with them. Molly sighed and rested her elbow on the hide of the door and brought her fist to her cheek, preparing for a long trip to become longer.

"This is gonna take a while, Bellz," she said.

"That's fine. It's a good thing we left when we did," replied Bella. The girl was in no rush, and spied out the truck's window the variety of vegetation growing off the mountain slopes. There were outstretched vines and lily trees tangled into deadly pines and into hard oak, scarce among the wild. There grew renewed blossoms of vigor, with plump bushes and sages that dominated the duffs with young grasses beneath them, all recovering from the harsh winter. The girl saw the flora behind and, above, a tall steel-locked fence that kept, as far as Bella could tell, along the length with the road, keeping its spiraling roll of barbed wire along its top.

"When do you think we'll get there?" asked Bella.

"I don't know," answered Molly. "Maybe twenty five minutes?"

"How long does it usually take?"

"Fifteen, if ya drive like a grandma. I can make it in ten."

Bella was taken aback by the exact answer. "In this old thing?"

"Ah, well, ya know, she may be old but she's fierce," said Molly. "And she's used to it. Heartlake has things, but I'm never content with just city dwelling."

"How'd you ever live in Haze?"

"I died there." The redhead laughed.

Bella smirked and turned her head to view the traffic in front of her. They were still moving but passively. Bella looked at the dull-faced passengers in their mirror, men and women alike, most of whom looked middle classed or lower.

"So," she broke in again, "Heartlake is more of a city, right?"

Molly nodded. "Way more than the lil' dust ball. There are some areas that are kinda open, just kinda. Everything scrunched together. I hope ya like that fence."

"We're right next to it?"

"That was where they built the Home. But we have a wonderful look at the mountain. And this field in front of it—it's beautiful at night."

"Oh, joy."

"Planned Houses." said Molly. "Gotta love 'em, though it's just kinda the porch size that bothers me."

"It's better than nothing," her friend replied.

The truck continued on. Though slowed by the excessive number of vehicle plying on the highway street, it was a comfortable ride, as far as Bella was concerned. But then the canyon eventually parted away from the artificial construction, giving enough space not to breathe, and another line emerged from the road.

Traffic began to flow faster, and a few more miles in, the pair spotted a dotted white line and a ramp that veered off in an arch away from the highway. It was the exit, and Molly whipped through the staggered line and sped past the vehicle in front of her. As Molly did so, Bella looked to the right and saw where the wall had followed the hooking, then Molly turned and maneuvered around a passing sign that read, "Heartlake."

From the exit, the road rose, and the rustic truck climbed a slight hill next to a woody ditch. It blocked the view of everything, save the surrounding mountains curving almost as the perimeter of a bowl. Then the pair reached the hill's top and travel leveled to the ground, and as soon the woody ditch reached its end, both girls saw the city ahead.

It was clearly larger than the land provided for the province. The outskirts of the town had edges inches from the barbed wall that bars the city from the exact ascent of the mountain. Among the cramped area, it appeared that the city bore signs of divided quadrant, a clear main street being the city's equator, a grid-like structure much to its sister's provinces' stature, cutting most, if not all, of the branching random roads. The quadrants' lines were more or less blurred between them, but what was more reliable was the architecture of the constructions found in each quadrant. There in the southwestern side erected skyscrapers, some to which revealed Haze; and other, meager office buildings. The eastern areas, closest to the girls, were humble rural suburban houses mixed with more stores, malls, and bars in the area with Planned Homes constructed anywhere they could. And then the northwestern quadrant, where a multitude of wooden cabins sat with an encroachment of Homes and a reservoir that reflected sunlight off its clear waters, adopting a vague shape of a human heart.

Over toward the western half of the city, the highway continued up higher into the canyon. The steel-gated French doors formulated around this and the city as well, with the highway cutting all the way to the Brass City.

"Here it is," said Molly. "Home away from home."

Bella glared through imposing sunlight. She was surprised by the size of the city, thinking it would have been far smaller and less tight. The roads looked barely able to hold two cars. It was peculiar that the chain-linked wall had determined the shape of the city, rounding out the borders and making the province appear as liquid in a bowl. It provoked images Bella didn't understand.

Molly glanced at her friend. "What do you think?"

"I think it's pretty," said Bella, eye drawn on the southeastern quarter.

The redhead nodded. "It's nice, grumpy people though."

"There all squished probably!"

"Yeah, and we're gonna be squished."

The tuck carried on. It reached the outer areas of Heartlake, but unlike her siblings, the Mountain Gem had little to no farmland surrounding its outskirts. Most of the outer houses were log layered, but like the northwestern quadrant. At closer sight, the girl could she varieties of markings carved into the wood, always near the front doors. Bella noticed this and took special interest in the cabins, having once again never seen anything like it, and the deep glass within the window.

"Are these lodges?" asked Bella.

"No," replied Molly. "There from the old hunters and trappers of the area. Locals. They have roots here since the lake."

"Before the lake?"

"Yeah. The whole thing was man made. And old as dirt too, which says something about these damn cabins." Molly ended her sentence with a smile and glanced over at Bella and saw her confused expression staring out the dirty truck windows.

"So it's a reservoir," said Bella in a clad of resolution.

"I guess so," said Molly.

The emerald-eyed girl turned to face the windshield. Out of the corners, she could see no person about except for some strangely dress kid in a mix of modern attire: brand T-shirt and brand jeans, but with a pin of fur on his collar. She thought he looked ridiculous.

"I never knew that," she said. The girl glanced back at the passing houses. "What's a trapper?"

Molly sat thinking for a moment. "Someone told me it's a man who plants cages for critters and catches them inside."

"That sounds awful," says Bella. "That's cruel. Why would they do that?"

"I don't know," said Molly. "It's an outlawed skill though, how they got their little fur things."

"How do they still get fur?"

"There just dividing them up now. They used to all wear animal skins all the time, but as the city grew more, well, civilized, they wore normal clothes. It's only until a couple years ago they started wearing them, following the hunting ban. Kinda like a protest, but also kinda like a remembrance thing."

"I remember that," said Bella. "There were a bunch of chips circulating about it. I just wanted them to get over it."

"Yeah?" said Molly. "You have to remember that it's a way for people to get food. What happens if the store goes out? Can't expect any meat. I can't imagine how brave those first folk were."

Bella shifted her weight. "I sound like they go through hell every year. I could never do that. I don't think I could hold a gun!"

"Ha!" Molly chuckled. "It's not that hard. Ya just point and shoot and try not to hit anyone."

"That's the part I'm afraid of!"

"Well, if ya know ya target, know what's behind the target, and know ya can hit it, it's not all that bad! Recoil can be a bitch."

"Where'd ya go shoot?"

Molly took her eye off the road and scanned a biker in the opposite lane. "It was for a date."

"Oh?" said Bella. "A date?"

"Yeah. It didn't go very good. I'm pretty sure he could barely hold on. Which ya know, I can't really blame him for that."

"Who was he?"

"A fellow coworker."

"You know," said Bella, "I thought guns were banned too."

"They are," said Molly. "But you can go fire the ones at a range though. For fun. I've done it a couple of times, but it's way too expensive."

Bella went back to staring out the side window. "Interesting."

The truck was beginning to cross in the suburban area, which looked similar to the cookie-cutter designs, in a dull shade of white floor and dark tile roofing. But passing the blurred boundaries, Bella saw in the distance the tall skyscrapers that inched toward the blue sky. Bella thought, then wondered. She turned to ask her friend another question, but stopped herself. She figured she just asked later when she wouldn't come across as too weak. The girl brought her knees unto her chest and hugged them, watching the city zoom by.

What she saw next to an inn and a gas station, a grocery store and a pub; and in her opinion they appeared as what she expected. However, all were built so close together. Cars had been passing by the pair; and out of her peripheral, well, she swore some were going to collide. Bella then spotted a police car arriving at a scrunched home with its lights off and thought how even the Heartlake officers looked alike in harshness but a tad bit brighter than those serving in the Brass City.

Now placed firmly in suburbia, the out-of-place truck waited behind the lingering fleet of smooth cars, arriving and sending from the many houses. There wasn't any room for more than two lanes. When one of the vehicles would cut out in front, Molly avoided them without so much as a stop, carefully weaving into the other lane and back for a crash record. It became second nature to her, much to the dismay of her passenger, who thought the pair was set for an accident, and let out a loud cry.

"It's what ya gotta do," claimed Molly. "We're fine."

Bella remained on edge as Molly drove in her sporadic ways until the pair reached a light of a slightly more spacious street running horizontally to the towers. Molly flipped into the left lane and turned north toward the reservoir.

"We're getting closer," said Molly. "Ya ready to move it?"

"Yup," replied Bella. She patted her suitcase. "All set."

Molly rolled her eyes. "I never understood how minimal you live."

"I guess I don't really need a whole lot."

"You're telling me."

Molly kept her attention toward the road, and her friend spotted the metal street sign that read the name "Meadow Lane." She laughed to herself and thought how so many streets had similar dumb names. The truck rolled past several more houses and stores. One tall building caught Bella's eye. It possessed a synthetic look, as if it had been made from plastic. The building was rectangular in shape and was taller than it was wide, with straight and level windows in perfect pattern. Bella looked worried; she didn't want to be stuck in another apartment.

"Hey, chill," said Molly, catching where her friend was looking. "Were staying in a Planned Home. It's only half as bad."

Traffic had slowed to a crawl. Apartments surrounded them, and Bella remembered before, all her life in the little boxes.

"We got a Home, Bellz! Don't worry."

"It's gonna be small still."

"Bigger than what you used to. It's just the outsides that are all close together. Inside you'll be surprised."

"If you say so."

They continued, a little past the apartments, and the girl kept her head low until she was met with the sight of earth uncovered. She sought further to this miracle and noticed a small incline in the land, with grass and river stone, that stood uncluttered for a distance before curving backward. Just a bit further was a bridge on the elevated land and a stream of water that followed down to a large pipe in the ground and surrounded by a cage. On top of the dike, Bella quickly spied the barbed-wire barrier that aligned with a path that followed the bend of the incline. In the center of this, near the bridge, was an outline for a hinged entrance, and beyond that, a muddied terrain scattered with boulders that gave way to polarized clear water, surrounded by willows and cattails.

Bella's eyes lit up to the sight. She recognized the reservoir in an instance. Molly sat content in her seat, letting the girl revel in the sight of such beauty, recalling her first time seeing the inviting waters.

And just beyond the bridge, on the path that the barrier stood, congregated a group of people. The nurse saw these folks and observed they had a strange formation about them. Two individuals stood away from the group and faced outward, almost as lookouts. A bit close stood a line for five that held queer sticks or herbs. At the center were four, all hunched over and in brown robes with directive twigs protruding from their hoods. Up against the fence was a man, his beard knitted in the same way the woman from in Refuge had her hair, and brandished a black fur vest, with what appeared as medieval clothes under them.

"What are they doing?" asked Bella.

Molly spotted them. "Oh! Just watch!"

The four in the middle kneeled as well as the man against the fence. They performed a pattern that touched their chest, their forehead, and their lower sternum. They seemed to have been reciting something. One of the four stood, a different formation of twigs in his hood. He carried a silver-headed axe. This weapon had strange symbols down the handle of it, and the one holding the tool was gifting it to the kneeling man. He received it, then stood up. The other then bowed and did the same pattern again. Where they stood positioned, the water encroached closer, and from where he stood, the man with several braces tossed the axe back, over the barrier, and into the pristane water. They all then knelt in silence, save the two looking out to the world, guarding. They kept the reverence as the pair eventually passed them, towing behind slow-moving cars.

Bella turned to Molly. "What was that?

The redhead smiled. "They're arming the Ghost."

"What?"

"Ya see. There's a myth about a man that lives in the forest. They say he's a giant, or at least the locals do. They give him weapons as a means to help him, they even bless them too."

"Wow. It's super common here?"

"It feels like I see more and more."

"Is that a good thing?"

"I think so. They're getting more religious."

Cars departed onto the many avenues and side roads. The pair grew quiet. The truck made a couple more turns before reaching the border of Heartlake, to which they made a right heading east, following the invasion of Planned Home to the different batter of home structure. Molly began to slow with nothing in front of her. To her friend's side, Bella spotted a different type of house: a two-story structure in a square block format, somewhat like the apartments. Others in dark wood could be seen and in square marble blocks. The roof was jagged and slanted to one side while the windows were few and centered in the corner block parts. The front door was dark and had two columns of marble to which a single step led to, followed by an angled cement walkway that connected to the driveway. A single garage door was left open with enough space for two vehicles, one gray car taking up residency already. A small chunk of lawn had been placed. The neighboring houses nearly brushed against one another.

"Kim left the door open again," said Molly. She turned and pulled the truck into the garage. "Goddamn it. Well, welcome home!" She looked to her friend to see if she had arisen a laugh, but saw that she hadn't.

Bella looked backward out to the driveway, then back at her friend. She didn't know what to think, other than the fact it reminded her of school buildings, but still better than an apartment by the looks of it. She wondered if the graduating engineering class developed this place.

"So ya like it?" broke in Molly, concerned at her friend's silence. "I probably should show ya around first for asking, huh?" And she jumped out of the vehicle.

Bella was made self-aware of the lack of noise. "It's lovely! From what I can tell." And she followed the example of her friend, struggling a moment with the handle.

"You do?" Molly didn't look convinced.

"Yeah, I do. It's got a garage, doesn't it?"

Molly glanced around. "I probably should have parked outside. Let me just show ya the inside first!"

To the side of Bella, Molly walked past and saw the door that led inside. The redhead fumbled the keys as she tampered to open it. The girl went to her side and waited.

"It's kinda hard. Wait." And the redhead jiggled the handle and found that it was already lose. "Goddamn it." And she opened the door. "I was gonna say it was kinda hard but nope, apparently Kim does everything."

Bella peered from behind her friend and analyzed the interior. The first thing she noted was the light-gray carpet floor that, to the side, channeled up at flight of stairs to where she stood diagonally toward, accompanied by a pair of monotone white walls and a cheap hand railing. To the right she saw another door, which she expected to be the front entrance, and left after the stairs, she saw a hallway filled with paintings of obscure shapes and colors.

"We'll check in the kitchen first," said Molly.

Bella stepped behind her. "I think…" She spun around to absorb the full picture, spotting a potted fern she couldn't see from outside. "I think it's nice." She turned to her friend.

"Just nice?"

"Yeah, nice."

"You don't find anything wrong with it?" asked Molly.

"No?" said Bella. "Then again, I haven't seen all of it." The girl stopped for a moment. "Is there something wrong with it?"

Molly pretended to look around. "I mean no. There's nothing. It covers ya needs."

"It is similar to my apartment. But that doesn't mean—"

"Is that bad?" Molly interrupted.

"No, no!" said Bella. "It probably made by the same company. I already feel a lot better than my old home."

Molly led the way down the hallway and to the table with the four chairs. Bella tagged close behind, towing her luggage behind her.

The pair crossed the monotone walls.

"I hope it's better," said Molly. "And the dining room's here. If ya ever can't find me, I'll be in here." She laughed and folded her arms.

Bella looked around and noticed the tile floor beneath their feet. She looked up from there, followed the legs of the table up to the face and the four chairs surrounding it—all with plain seats. She turned more toward the kitchen and saw a bright countertop reflecting the rough ceiling pattern of the kitchen, to which led to the far side of the room with a tap-sensor sink; a microwave above an electric stove; and a dishwasher with a not that read, "Gonna get fixed,"—all spaced appropriately with cupboards of various sizes and girths. A chrome refrigerator stood opposing them. Atop of it sat a string-like plant. In the middle of the wall, to the right, was another hallway, its interior in shadows but its frame guarded by two flowers.

Through the window, Bella realized it was a sliding door. She saw the fence, near inches away from the sliver of patio they rented and the two planked privacy shade that stopped the neighbors from peeking. The girl tugged away from the fence, sick of the metal wall, and drew away from it, noticing a plant near the corner of the screen door. Bell then found lines between all the different plants scattered throughout. Above the sink was a windowsill with many small cacti in pots of proportional sizes. And near the oven on the counter, she rested on a plant that appeared to have a vibrant mouth with leaf stem teeth.

"Are all these plants Kim's?" she asked.

"Yep," Molly replied. "She got wild with them." The redhead walked over to the sink and picked up a cactus. "Ain't these cute? I told her to get them."

"They're cute," said Bella, rejoining her friend by the window seal.

"I know, right! I might set some of these myself, or better yet, a sage bush!

Bella squinted at Molly. "Why on earth would you get a sage bush?"

"They're pretty!" she replied.

"If you say so." Bella smiled at the ridiculous thought, ending up again on the toothy plant by the stove. The question intrigued her enough to ask, "What kind of plant is that?"

The redhead followed her sight. "Oh, she just told me its name a while ago. But it is one of Kim's favorites. I think it eats bugs."

"Really?"

"Yeah, I've seen her feed it."

"I like this plant too."

"I heard it can even munch on wasps!"

The floor then creaked as muffled feet stepped toward the kitchen. Bella looked behind her and saw another hallway that went down to two rooms. A figure emerged from this shadowed tunnel-like hall and into the light. A woman came out covered in loose night robe. On her exposed sleeves and to her ankle and her knee were spiked blazing tattoos in black ink. Her face, elegant yet pained, captured a controlled fury that inscribed warning to whoever saw. And Bella saw, and her sight fell to the floor.

"You said you were gonna keep it down." She spoke in a restrained voice, leading to one side, and eyes skipping to this new person, then back to her roommate.

The redhead flung a glance toward the top of the over where a digital clock read the time: 12:25.

Bella's eyes fell on Kim's tattoos. There were all vines that covered her entire body, with flowers throughout. She was a canvas.

"Good afternoon!" said Molly. "I keep forgetting you're on night."

"Yeah, I am," said the tattooed woman. Her eyes flicked between Bella and Molly. She motioned back to the hallway. "Just keep it down."

And she turned back into the darkness, taking several strides before being interrupted.

"Wait!" yelled Molly.

"What!?" shouted back Kim.

"Aren't you gonna say hello?"

Bella shook Molly's arm. "It's fine. Stop it."

"We'll talk later," Kim yelled.

"You have no manners!"

"Don't need any!"

"Molly, it's really fine," Bella exasperated.

The redhead looked at her friend. "Will you at least tell us what this plant's name is?"

"What?" Kim's voice sounded confused.

Bella hid her face.

"Stove plant!" said Molly. "What's its name?"

Kim poked her head back into the kitchen. "The flytrap?"

"Yeah!"

Kim walked back toward the pair. "What about it?" She peered toward the plant through them.

Bella looked up at the approaching woman. She stood taller than her, but shorter than Molly. The girl then changed to looking at the flytrap.

"Well," said Molly, "can we feed it?"

Kim looked down at the plant, analyzing it. She sighed. "Sure."

"Can you show us?"

Kim looked at the time, then to Bella. "Do you wanna?"

"Oh, no, no, no," Bella squeaked.

"Yes," exclaimed Molly. "Have her feed it!"

The tattooed woman smiled, as did the redhead. Bella wanted to scream, "Come on, I don't want to feed it!"

Kim folded her arms and headed in the direction of the hallway. She walked with patience, and the girls watched her step into a shaded hallway and vanished behind its wall, the floor creaking.

"I can't feed that thing!" Bella nearly yelled.

Molly laughed. "It's gonna be fine. It'll put Kim in a good mood. Plus you'll have squeezers. It ain't a bit deal."

The girl groaned.

Molly laughed some more. "It just a little cricket."

"Not a bug anything but..." Bella paused.

The hallway creaked one more, and Kim appeared at the cusp of the hallway, her hand erect and pinching something between her fingers Kim then walked toward the pair and the plant, the dot becoming distinguishable as a spine-legged cockroach squirming to break free.

Without a word, Kim held out the vile critter. Bella recoiled, trying not to vomit at it spindled its legs.

Molly, disgusted, refused to move. "Look at the lil' devil. He's a hottie."

"Ewwwwww," sounded Bella.

"Hmhm," sounded Kim. "He did not want to be caught." She hovered closer to the girl. "You ready?"

Bella stayed no way out. "I guess..." She stepped close enough to see the flytrap.

"Yes, ma'am!" hollered Molly.

Flipping the insect, she altered to where she pinched its legs and can expose the Carapa enough to be grabbed. "It's not gonna bit you. Just pinch it right there and drop it in a mouth."

Kim checked to see if the new roommate was truly ready, then pushed it further.

Bella shuddered but lent her finger, seizing the cockroach's shiny shell, its tickling limbs reaching around, tapping to be set free. She panicked. But Kim would not let her drop the insect, keeping the nurse's fingers tight around it. The tattooed woman guided her over to the plant.

"What do I do?" Bella squirmed. "What do I do?"

"Drop it."

And the girl let the insect go. It was in the mouth of the flytrap within a second. It landed its forelimb, between the vine-like teeth and on the vibrant section of the plant. Its antenna searched the air, and the roach moved forward. One of the six legs tripped a translucent wire, setting the leaf jaws of the flytrap spring halfway closed, closely processing to be fully shut, baring the vine teeth to which the jailed insect could be seen struggling.

"Look at that," said Molly.

"It's kinda anticlimactic," replied Kim.

Bella examined the unfinished flytrap. "It didn't close all the way."

"That's to allow small prey items to leave," said Kim. "While trapping anything big enough for a good meal."

"Oh," responded Bella, feeling a bit childish.

"Once it's like this, the plant will slowly shut. You can kinda see it close right now. The two leaves will soon fully touch, making an airtight seal." Kim raised her hands, clawing them and closing them if they were the leaves. "Like this. Then will produce enzymes to digest it. Then in the next couple days, it'll open up."

"You are such a nerd," said Molly.

The tattooed lady scoffed. "Girl's gotta have a hobby." She turned once again and crossed to the hallway. "You got yours."

Molly went silent.

"Mhm, right." She stood by the threshold of the shaded walkway. "Well, it was nice while it lasted." And she descended into the hallway without a reply, the floor creaking like it had arthritis.

Molly sighed and looked to her friend, who was still staring at the clamping jaws of the flytrap, its victim in its maw. "It was nice she showed us, at least. You'll be friends in a second."

"Or we won't," said Bella.

"Nah," replied Molly. "You will."

Bella glanced at friend. "We don't need to be friends. We just need to tolerate each other."

"You guys should at least try," she muttered. "Let go up to see your room." Molly started for the queerly drawn paintings on the monotone white walls past the corridor to Kim's room. Bella followed, towing her suitcase behind.

The stairs mimicked the murmur of the roommate's hallway. Molly and Bella strode to the second floor. There, at the top of the flight, in a tight connecting stripe of a carpeted corridor, were three open rooms, one with polished finishes and the others appeared to Bella to have nothing at all. The girl wondered why there were two empty rooms and not only one, but the second thought overruled, and she followed still, all while Molly led her to the closest room.

"Here we are," said Molly, crossing into the empty room.

Bella peered beyond the frame. It was a renovator's dream: bare; white, like the rest of the building; a single closet; and two curtain-empty windowsills with full sight of the Sleeping Giants, the barrier peeking from the bottom of the glass. There was a bed on a flimsy metal frame, in the corner near the closet across from a window. Bella was relieved.

"It's nice," she said. "I don't have to sleep on the floor."

Molly frowned. "Just nice?"

"Yeah."

"Hon, you can put anything you want in here! You can buy as many decorations as you want! Isn't that a bit exciting?"

Bella shifted herself to look around. "Yeah."

"Just 'Yeah'?"

"What do you want me to say? I like it!"

"Well, I'm glad, I'm glad. Ya just don't seem that excited," said Molly. "Wasn't it fun when we decorated our dorm?"

"It was!" Bella lowered her head. "But that's just we were messing around the whole time." She then lifted to her friend. "How about you help me decorate this room?"

Molly smiled. "I was gonna do that. But I'm giving ya no freebies. You gotta be the one to pick things out."

"I don't really care." Bella laughed. "I would like a nightstand though."

"All right" The redhead motioned to the exit. "Let's get going."

"Now?!" exclaimed the girl.

"Yes, now! We got all day. Plus we can grab some chow."

"With what money?" Bella paused for a moment, thinking and scheduling a delay. "Let me hang up my clothes first."

"We'll just get some small stuff," said her friend. "And nightstands aren't that bad." She stepped into the hallway. "I'm gonna grab my card."

"Are you serious? Where are you going? We just got here."

"Yes." And Molly slipped out of sight of her room.

The girl shook her head. "A better life," she said to herself, then dropped to her knees and opened her suitcase.

Chapter

3

Rays of sunlight warned of morning piercing through newly hung curtains. Specks of dust fluttered, drifting in holy radiance, dancing between the lines of visibility, from shine to cold shadow. A once empty room, now furnished with a nightstand and wall light, and cheap trinkets polished and perfected to the liking of Bella's eye. The room was proper and, though bare, was in order, all except a corner by its closet where a nest of blankets dangled and touched the carpet from an old and forgotten bed, touched by her faint breathing.

She lay in comfort, surrounded by her new possessions. She stirred none, moving little, appearing as if in stupor to retain one's strength for unforgivable winter. She dreamt little, no elements, no troubles, no problems to conflate her mind into useless torment and suffering. She thought little. No more are her days of examinations and classes, studying to the martyrdom of intelligence. And to this life she graduated, the girl found rest. Deserved rest.

Yet time holds no accomplishment forever. The sunlight stretched from the edges of the blinds, capturing more ground in warm light. Ignition of automobiles echoed from outside, along with rumbling wheeling on insulted roads. Birds screamed not-so-humble songs, pausing the new sun that beckoned to Heartlake of the new day. Life grew back from the night, and knocking came from the far side of the room. It stirred Bella, but she did not wake. It came again, louder and followed by an irritated voice. Still the girl lay in slumber, until finally the voice boomed from behind the door.

"Bella! Wake up! Breakfast is almost ready!"

The girl's eyelids sprang open.

"Okay. I'm coming."

The girl slugged her legs out of the many covers of her blanket nest. She stretched out her arms, then her back, twisting her torso, until she heard a pop. Then off the bed she hopped, and into her closet she went, to which she closed and stared into the oval mirror hanging from a cheap plastic hook. Bella scanned over herself. She wasn't in the slightest bit presentable: the baggy T-shirt she wore to bed was wrinkled, her charcoal hair was all tangled, with dark lines underneath her eyes to complement. But her face was nevertheless still fair and presentable to her long-standing friend, and she figured Kim would be out. She was confident she could slack and left the closet unchanged. She searched for her phone and found it, then headed out of the room.

Bella entered through the doorway and onto the narrow platform connecting the other rooms of the second floor. The smell of bacon and eggs lingered in the air. The girl passed the vacant room on her right, and just before turning into the stairway, she stopped and gazed into the unshut room of Molly. It bore many signs similar to the constructions of the outer home of Heartlakes, her bedframe and desks sharing the same dark log structure. The girl panned further and saw a tractor configuration and tiny toy horse sitting on the flat head of a thin desk. Next to them, Bella noted, sat a bright-colored boxed with impeccable artworks covering it, far outpassing the items by the front door. She felt like she saw too much and began turning for the stairwell. Curiosity turned her head back, catching another glance at the box. She knew she stayed too long and went down the steps.

The girl walked through the hallway where she judged the artwork. She peered into the kitchen as if nothing had happened. First, she spotted Molly, rubber-tipped spatula in hand, standing next to the electric stove, playing with the components of a stainless-steel pan. Next to her was a plate filled with bacon, crisp and ready to be devoured. The wonderful smell caused Bella's stomach to growl.

She walked over to the dining portion of the mixed-unit kitchen. She looked over toward the table and saw Kim wearing hospital scrubs and elastic long-sleeved shirt that covered her tattoos, her arms folded and resting on the back of her seat with shut eyelids. Bella stopped. Next to her, a man with a clean-shaven face rubbed her thigh, not a drop of ink on him, and hair that waved like the sea, dressed in a button-up shirt, loose tie, and slacks. Bella panicked. She felt so sloppy, too gross and unprepared. Her weight shifted, wanting to go shower and become presentable.

"Good morning!" called the man, discovering the girl. "You must be Bella."

The girl nodded and smiled, dropping her sight to the floor. She stood there and turned to Molly, who was watching her and greeted with a wave.

The man beckoned. "Come sit! Molly offered to cook breakfast!"

The redhead motioned to her, and Bella turned to face the man. Feeling, she continued to the table and pulled out a seat across from the pair, believing to be a slug. She saw the man's coffee mug and stuck-out hand.

"Derrick," he said. "Or Mr. Nelson if you want to be formal about it."

Bella shook the gesture. "A pleasure," she said.

Kim lifted her head from the chair rest. "Morning."

"Good morning," the girl said back. She protected herself from their pleading eyes, staring lonesome at the salt and pepper shakers, then to the dolly they stood on.

Molly turned from the stove, hoping a conversation would break out.

"I heard you're a nurse," said Derrick at last. "Following the program?"

"Yes." Bella smiled.

"That's grand," said Derrick. "We always need more nurses."

Bella nodded.

"And a whole house full of nurses! We need more 'em. Hell, it needs a lot more of everyone! City's barely managing to operate."

"You just want to build more houses," said Kim.

"Well," replied Derrick, hoping to ward off a fight. "You're not wrong."

Bella noticed a gray suit coat across the man's seat.

"We're already crammed enough in this shit hole," said Kim. "I don't know how long you can keep building homes."

"People will always need houses. And if we run out of room, we'll build up. And up and up until we hit space." Derrick looked around the room. "But I heard better options."

"Like what?"

"I was gonna tell you this later." He looked to Bella. "And don't tell anyone you hear this from me." He looked back at Kim. "But there's talk about extending the city's boundaries."

Molly's ears perked up. "Who told you that?" she echoed from the kitchen above a sizzling pan.

"A couple of trustees," Derrick said back. "And some friends in city hall. They say the city is gonna make a push for it."

"I doubt it," said Kim. "They'll talk about it, but then it'll never get done."

Derrick smirked. "Not unless a special someone keeps hounding their asses for it."

Bella thought to ask a question, but did not.

However, Kim shared the same impulse. "Like who?"

"I'm making friends," the man replied.

Kim glanced at her partner, a certain dread rooted in her dark eyes. She then stared at the same shakers, then dolly, as Bella.

"Tell them to extend it past the peaks, Derrick!" Molly howled from the stove.

"Ha!" The man laughed. "They won't ever give that much land! But hey, it's worth a shot."

"How do you know them?" Kim questioned.

Derrick sipped from his coffee mug. "Well, ya meet one person, and they lead to more and eventually, you're part of the inner workings, brushing coats with bigwigs."

"They're not your friends." Kim looked at him. "Please never think that they're your friends."

Derrick turned to her, a bit taken aback. "I know. It's just a business term. Ya know, when you're expendable."

The tattooed woman took his hand. "Could we change topics?"

Bella looked up from the table for a split second. She saw in Derrick the lines of rebuttal cinched in his brow, but they ultimately fell flat, as if mannerism hijacked his action and deemed it improper to argue. "All right," he said. "How was work?"

"It was good," said Kim, noticing a contrast to her partner's tone and body language. "I'm glad I'm back home. And expressly glad for movie night, Mike Reslistate." She leaned her head on the man.

Derrick dissolved and smiled. "Me too. Which one are we watching?"

"You'll have to choose, babe. I forgot which series we were on."

"Ha, well, I know what that means."

"Reruns of *Can't Help Myself.*"

Bella wanted to retire herself. It wasn't so much the act of placing her head on his shoulder, but it was the matter that it was being done in others' view, or at least while she sat across from them. The girl fell back to the doily and realized that they must have thought she had disappeared. She based the conclusion like it was fact and sat there not making a sound.

Any absence of sound became apparent. The girl clenched on the inside, feeling her own heart tick. She almost turned over to Molly, noticing a lack of sizzling from the stove, but her attention was brought back to the table.

"Bella," said Kim, retracking from Derrick, "are you always this quiet?"

She wished the conversation death. "Yeah, usually."

"Molly more of the talker between you?"

The girl nodded. "But it's not like I can't talk. I just got nothing to say."

"That's fine, I guess. But it's a good skill—"

A sudden pan slammed down on the table. "Eggs are ready folks!" Molly yelled, placing a "Hope ya'll like scrambled."

Kim jumped. "Jesus, Molly!" she shouted. "The hell is wrong with you?"

What? Eggs are ready." Molly looked back to the kitchen. "Lemme go grab the bacon."

"God," the tattooed woman rested a hand to her head. "I was gonna say it's a good skill."

Derrick laughed. "To what?"

"Oh, talk—oh, shut up."

A bending swirl of steam rose from pan, and the three looked inside, Bella first and Kim last, and gazed upon the golden bounty of eggs mixed with peppers and onions, the smell hitting the party and antagonizing their hunger.

"I'll grab the plates," said Derrick. He stood up to walk to the kitchen.

Molly intercepted him. "Here we are." And she grabbed plates instantly.

Derrick set the bacon next to the pan. She moved over to the vacant seat next to Bella. The girl caught a glimpse of her attire. She half expected her friend to be already dressed in light-blue scrubs, but no. Instead, Molly had on shorts and a jacket tied around her waist, her hair in a bun and sweat on her face. The redhead's shirt ran low, and most strange to Bella, however, was an emblem: a dainty spiraling knot that seemed to begin where it ended and end where it began. It merged with whatever material connected it to her neck, a beautiful spiraling fray all the way around, seeming impossible to remove. She focused on the necklace. It reminded her of the woman in Refuge.

"It smells great, Molly," said Kim.

"Yeah, it really does," confirmed Derrick.

Bella thought, *How could I have missed that?*

The redhead grinned. "Oh, thank you. It's just a Refuges recipe, nothing too special. Shucks, y'all are too kind," she said.

Bella shook herself to attention. "Yeah, it looks amazing."

Now all seated, the group reached for their plates and began serving their food plates. Molly was the last one to dish her plate, wanting to make sure everyone had enough before she took her fill.

"Thank you, Molly," said Bella, fork in hand, ready to experience her first bite.

"Wait!" the redhead stopped the girl.

The nurse nearly dropped hers. "What?"

Kim and Derrick stopped as well.

"Well, um, before you start." Molly swallowed. "I was thinking maybe—and y'all might think this is corny or weird or doesn't belong in a place like this—but well, I think is appropriate and important. And so maybe could we say a prayer."

Derrick and the girl were baffled.

"A prayer?" asked the man. "Like what the Pelts do?"

Kim simply began eating.

"Yes, a prayer," said Molly, spying the tattooed woman munching on a strip of bacon she detested. "Kim, stop it. Can't we just try it? You know, um, for the hell of it!"

"It's a load of hohaw," replied Kim.

"It might be worth doing."

The tattooed woman took another bite. "Are we gonna practice magic next?"

Molly appeared visibly hurt. "Why do you say that?"

"You don't believe in a god."

Molly bit the inside of her lip. "Maybe I'll start believing."

Derrick cast a concerned look on his girlfriend, but she kept herself collected, keeping focus on the food. Bella was watching her too.

"That's not how it works," said Kim.

"How do you know? It's not like you're the least bit religious."

"I grew up in that crazy cult." Another bite in. "Wanna tell me more?"

"It's not a cult!"

Kim put her fork down. "Look, I'm not trying to be a bitch. I'm just saying you have a Yudaku around your neck and I don't. I grew up in it, and you didn't. It's beyond crazy."

Molly looked down at the knot. "It doesn't mean anything bad. It means nothing bad!"

"Not the point I'm making," said Kim, raising her hand to halt the redhead. "I don't mind it. I know the sisters who gave you it." She looked at the others at the table. She pointed to her boyfriend. "You probably know what I'm talking about." She pointed to Bella. "You have no idea."

"It's about belief," said Molly.

"No, it's not. It's indoctrination."

"They tied it around my neck. You can't tie a Yudaku by yourself, Kim. You should know that."

Kim palms her face. "I know, I know." She straightened herself. "The least they could do is teach you to untie."

"Why not just cut it?" asked Bella. "I mean, they could always retire."

Molly shot a glance at her friend. "It's for your future husband to untie after marriage."

Kim bolstered. "I cut mine off."

Derrick peered out the screen door, sipping his hot coffee.

"At sixteen."

"That's horrible," said Molly.

"It's better than having a target on my chest," said Kim.

"Wh-what do you mean by that!" Molly spat. "I'm not gonna sit here and have you insult me like that. I know your belief died long, long ago, and that fine. But don't stop me...don't stop me trying to get closer to God!" She looked down at the table. "You...you don't know what you're talking about."

Bella's shoulders dropped, and she ate in avoidance of the argument. Having no clue as to what or when the conversation turned, she thought it best to remain silent. It'll blow over.

The tattooed woman looked into Molly in the eye. She pressed her lips together, and the redhead reciprocated the gesture, staring into Kim with the same loathsome stare.

"You know, Molly," said Derrick. "Some men will perceive ya differently."

"It's not a bad symbol!" yelled Molly.

"No, that's not. What I mean, you know what the reputation of this town is. I mean, let's just say that keeping that necklace exposed is not the best choice."

"I'm wearing it, and that's that. Ain't no one gonna tell me what to wear."

"I'm not gonna keep arguing with you," said Kim in a dead voice. "It never does any good. It is your call."

"You're damn right it is."

"But," added the roommate, "you're walking in a dangerous line. When you eventually attract the wrong attention, don't say I didn't tell ya so." She continued into her plate.

Silence took room. Bella dared not look up. She didn't understand why the two couldn't just be okay. The girl, attempting little awareness, kept chewing, hoping to finish and leave, feeling glued to the chair. It then occurred that this argument must be common, and her roommate's bitter feelings were rooted in a well of carless comments and assumptions and would replenish every time they'd be corralled. The next thought became a warning: *Get used to this.* She just wanted to move on.

"I just thought it was a good idea," admitted Molly, and she began to eat.

The only noise, therefore, created was the raking of plates, sharp squeaking and clunking, muffled chewing and crunching bacon. They finished their meal—all wanting to get on their way. Kim and Derrick promptly decided to go into the tattooed woman's room, carrying their dishes to the sink, rinsing them, and claiming to help later. The remainders were left to pick up. Derrick, however, did thank the chef for the meal.

Without a word, they got up and gathered the remaining pan and plates. When they gathered all the dishes and silverware, the pair stood side by side in front of the sink, peering through the fence. Molly scrubbed with soap and water, and vapor mist settled on the glass. Bella dried what her friend gave her, picking up paper towels in the corner. The girl could only guess what troubled her mind.

"I'm sorry." Molly broke the silence.

"For what?" asked the nurse. She knew.

Molly gave a small cheery smile. "You shouldn't have been exposed to all that."

"It's all right. I wasn't bothered by it. I...I didn't mean that you should cut it by the way. I just spoke when I shouldn't."

"No, no, it's okay." Molly lifted her Yudaku. "I hope you don't think this thing is bad. It's not, and they're lying when they say it'll bring me bad luck."

"It's cute. I don't really understand what Kim's problem is."

"Well"—the redhead passed a plate to Bella—"I don't either. I think she has a hard time seeing something so prevalent in her past. She grew up a Local. Guess she's still mad at them."

"Why?"

"We won't ever say. I think when ya grow up a certain way, ya just rebel from it. Call it lame and stupid. She'll never know how lucky she was."

Bella eyed the necklace and her friend touching the twine that made it.

"The knot is special," she continued. "It can only be untied in a certain way, and the men only learn how right before marriage. The Locals have spent, I don't know, how many years creating it."

"You believe in it," said Bella.

"Not at first. But then I started to wonder, and it seemed right." She held the amulet. "Do you want the full explanation? I'm kinda a nerd for this stuff."

"Sure!"

"Ha ha, okay, okay. So you see, way back when, Local girls received Yudakus after the baptism—I think that's what they're called. And they never take it off, not even to wash. They wear it until after their wedding, until the groom ties it off. Then, of course, he learns from the older men, who learn from their fathers, and so on. But then he wears it around his wrist until the day he dies! Isn't that beautiful?"

Bella was taken aback. "Well, it's romantic! But…" The girl thought of a way to not be offensive. "How do you get one?"

Molly handed her friend another plate. "It's like what Derrick said, friends of friends. Some gals at the hospital are Locals, and they led me to meet these sweet old ladies who tied this on to me."

"You never mentioned this before." Bella finished drying a plate.

"Okay, good." The redhead laughed. "Well, I met these old ladies and became friends with 'em. They're real wise and very protective of their art." Molly's voice grew quiet. "They allowed me to learn how to tie it! Maybe I can even do it for my daughters."

"So you're basically converting," said Bella.

Molly shoved the last dishes of the sink and shrugged. "Yeah," she said with a glance. "I don't like how I lived, Bellz. I felt like every damn kid that college shits out—and I don't mean to cuss—but it is just that. I wanna go somewhere when I die. I don't want there to be nothing. There can't be nothing." She raised the Yudaku again. "And I won't be alone. I'll have a man, and he'll be with me."

Bella pondered what her friend said, then gave a careful response. "I don't think it's bad wanting a family. But it can't be the only thing to a good life, can it? I mean, I wasn't raised by my mom or dad."

"Would you want to have been?"

"I don't know."

"Well, I didn't mean it'll solve all my problems. It would just give me something to strive for, and my kids watching them grow. Hey, maybe if you started a family, you could actually be there for them. Would ya like to meet the old ladies?"

Bella dried the last dish and stacked it. "Not likely."

"Not likely you'd have a family or not meet them?"

"Both. I probably won't do both."

"Oh." A downdrop of sadness presented within her. "Then I'll just have to name one of my kids after you. Keep your memory alive."

Bella laughed, surprised by her friend's choice of words. "Don't do that! No girl wants to be stuck with Bella."

"Too late. Bella is going straight to the top of my names list."

"You got a name list?"

"Had one ever since high school."

Bella giggled. "You're a pure dreamer."

Molly smirked. "I hope that's a good thing." She then stared that the pile her friend had accumulated. Molly grabbed a handful of the stack. Bella followed by grabbing some but appeared lost as to where to put the dishes, and then the redhead instilled, "In this drawer." Molly opened a lower cabinet with her foot, inside rattled short columns of glass plates to which the pair sat her load upon. "I don't know why we have so many," she said, putting the pan in a section lower.

Bella put what little she had, then both put the silverware in its place.

Molly faced her. "Are you serious about going out?" she asked.

"What?" Her friend's question took her off guard.

"I mentioned about going out on the phone. Are you really down?"

"I mean..." Bella didn't want to seem weak. "When we have time. Sure."

"Great. We have the weekend off."

"What? I'm just barely starting!"

Molly laughed. "Maybe you should look at your schedule."

"It can't be that soon," said Bella.

"Sorry, that's how it crumbles. And too late, you already said yes."

"I said sure!" Bella clarified.

Molly laughed and glanced across the shiny surfaces and to the electric clock on the stove. It read 10:30. "We better start getting ready. We don't want to be late."

Bella spun around to check the clock. She turned back. "Molly! We're not done!"

"Best you shower first," said Molly. "I take too long."

"I can't go out tomorrow!" She turned back to the dreadful recognition of the time. "God. Where's the bathroom?"

"Ha! " Molly pointed down Kim's corridor. "It's down the hallway to the right, opposite to Kim's door."

The girl turned. "I can't believe we don't have one upstairs." She exited out of the kitchen. Bella paid no mind the paintings and stepped up the tight stairwell to her room. From her entry door, she crossed to her closet and flickered through her hanging wardrobe until she found light- blue scrubs, identical to every other nurse at the hospital. Bella then released the uniform and walked back into the room to her suitcase leaning across the bed frame. She dug inside and found a stout leather bag. The girl hurried back down the stairs, not wanting her friend to wait, despite the fact she believed herself quick.

Again, Bella passed the modern corridor, still paying no mind to the ugly art, and hooked right, hugging the wall. The girl approached the shaded entryway with the two ferns as guards and spotted Molly gazing at the flytrap.

"I'll be quick!" she said, passing into the hallway.

"You're fine!" replied the redhead.

Bella walked further down the hall, dim but distinguishable. There were no paintings here but rather more potted plants near the bases of opposing doors. As the girl neared the end of the hallway, the wilting bodies and the browning leaves became apparent, along with an earthy smell. Muffled voices chattered in Kim's room.

Responding to the voices, she perked her ears. She soon reached the door on her right and placed a meek hand to its handle.

"I thought you would be happier," said a male voice.

"I've always been fine with less money," responded a woman.

It was Kim and Derrick. Bella believed them to be in argument.

"I'm thinking of our kids here. I don't want them growing up in one of these houses!"

"We already have enough money to move."

"But if I inquire more, I could give you and them the best possible life. They won't have to grow up knowing, well, any of this!"

"But is it worth losing your life over?"

"What are you talking about?"

"I'm saying that these people are dangerous, Derrick! When you're working with snake, you're gonna get bit, and…and then what? You're going to leave your child fatherless? Your wife is a widow? What would your parents say? Please, you can't do that to me. Please."

Bella slipped into the bathroom. She found and flicked the light switch, zipped open her bag, and began getting ready."

"No, no, they're not gonna kill me," said Derrick. "They're assets. They need houses, and I can supply them."

"But if you don't cut the corner they want…if you make them spend more money…"

"God, it's the government, not the Mafia."

"Same thing."

"Stop with the nihilist stuff. No one wants to hear that. It's gonna be fine, all right?"

"And when it's not," said Kim.

"You won't stop, will you?" Derrick grew impatient.

"They knew something about Mason, okay. They lied about right to my face. I know they did. No white collar went and looked for him!"

"Keep it down."

"All they do is take it!"

"Kim, please."

"I won't let them take you too!"

Chapter

4

They were quick. The rustic truck bounced along on a busy road and not-fast-enough drivers. They passed convenient stores and barber shops, ran through yellow stoplights and followed sudden road sign stops, throughout it all remarking at potholes, redhead cursing under her breath whenever a bad bump was felt. Molly sat, one hand on the wheel, the other prompting up her head, staring at the vehicle in front of her, but every so often peeking up to the towering mountain range who drafted all of Heartlake. Both girls wore their uniforms.

Bella peered out the passenger side window, watching the rows of pressed facilities pass her by. She spotted in front of the homes, tending to their gardens, retired folk, lines deep in their faces, and what Bella must assume to be grandchildren running and playing on the connected properties and lawns. There were more boys than girls out; and for the most part, they appeared modern, civil. But around the scarce young ladies, a swirling knot Yudaku hung. However, he didn't have the necklace and nonetheless appeared the same. It occurred to her that her friend had told the truth about the necklace.

The girl couldn't see her friend wearing it forever, deeming it a hobby rather than a lifestyle, and speculated there on the semitorn bench, she would abandon the necklace one day. Because, of course, no one held to their interest for long. This Bella swore the empty sky knew. She hoped that sense would come and Molly wouldn't be devastated for long. They should know better.

They traveled toward the southeastern quadrant of the city, and all suburban sites vanished, replaced with heavy steel buildings, save a last local structure being a church on a corner of a bend. Blocking even the mountains now, towered skyscrapers with shining glass, symmetrical frames, and vandalized bases. More stores and bars littered the streets, filling anywhere they could between the offices and the hotels. The streets were in an ordered frenzy. Annoyed honking persisted throughout the quadrant, with lights blazing red and cars still escaping through. People flooded across the crosswalk, some in suits, others in casual means, but normal, thankfully normal.

The rustic truck was one of the vehicles fleeing red lights, scaring her passenger completely. In her defense, it was yellow when it crossed the crosswalk; however, her friend didn't believe her.

"Were fine," said Molly. "You gotta be aggressive here."

"Just don't hit anyone," pleaded Bella.

"Everyone knows the name of the game here." Molly stuck her elbow to a comfortable spot. "Its people who don't get in wrecks."

"Just don't kill me!"

The redhead laughed. The girl didn't.

"What do you think?" Molly asked, hoping to move on from the subject.

"What, about the buildings?" Bella asked, still peeved from the light.

"Yeah."

"Well, it's as big as Haze. But I feel right at home."

"Ew." Molly squished her face. "That's a bad sign right there."

"Well, it's got big skyscrapers. What do you want me to say?"

"Nothing," said Molly. "But believe me, once the sun goes down, these people turn into animals."

"Oh." Bella turned to her friend. "How's that not like Haze?"

"Well, I mean, like party animals," said Molly. "Haze, you'll have a couple of drinks. A conversation or none, but here, Heartlake knows how to have fun."

"Well, that's good."

Molly glanced at the girl. "And, of course, you're gonna become one."

"I am?"

"Yeah! We gotta meet some people. Get out there."

"Yeah." Bella just went along with it and noted her friend peered ever so overtly to the encompassing buildings. "But you know there's always dating apps."

"Tried those," said Molly. "Didn't like them."

"All of them?"

"No. I don't like the idea of scrolling to someone. Not at all romantic. And it isn't the best way to find a man."

"You don't have to get outta bed though."

"Um, well." Molly twisted her brow. "You eventually have to. You'll get up a date, if you find a good boy to go out with, and then ya go on more until you are married."

"Who said anything about setting up a date?" The girl laughed.

"You're content with just talking."

"Not even that. Just looking.

"But you've got a boyfriend, haven't you?"

"Yeah...nothing short of a miracle though."

Molly shot a worried glance. "Don't fret. I'm sure you'll find one again. You just gotta keep trying, and one will turn up. Hell, I'm still trying."

"That's not the issue." Bella paused. "I wasn't raised good like you. I'm not a good talker."

Bella's language troubled her. "Well, sure you are," Molly said. "You talk to me just fine."

"Yeah, but I know you. I can't with strangers."

"We're gonna get that out of your mind. Work's gonna help a ton."

Bella shrugged. "I'm honestly terrified."

"Ya look fine." Molly looked over unnerved. She saw in her friend a stillness. "Something to work on again and again until you don't even notice you're getting better. You're gonna do good! The doctor is gonna have me show you the ropes. Plus you only gotta worry about one patient."

Bella shifted to the window. "I'm glad."

The onset of cars littering the street eventually gave way to a route that lead down many intersections. Signs directed to the community hospital, and Molly took a left to turn onto the facility road. Facing east, and glimpses of the woodland that barrier the north, the pair navigated to the entrance of the community hospital. However, it wasn't so simply a spacious parking lot but diverged into separate paths in some sort of artistic manner that then curved and wined through another intersection and ended at complete opposite parking stalls at the hospital. A sparse image came to Bella's mind, and in guilty humor, she imagined a man having to complete his trail before arriving at his checkup. The path, in good conscience, had arrows to indicate the correct way to the emergency room, somewhat lessening the confusion. But beside patients, the design would be hard for her to traverse if she didn't have Molly to take where she needed to be. Along they went through a path next to a fresh lawn and rolled right into the parking lot, which the redhead did as if she was blind.

Bella stared up at the massive structure, taking in the full sight of the community hospital. It was a grand building, protected by the city's most abundant materials, only in a hue of brown and red. It appeared as a hybrid structure of the common constructions in the southeastern quadrant, a giant block-like structure, possessing more than enough stores, in a bulkier, greedily spacious design. Close to them, the visitor entrance was extended out from a carefully designed tube-like continuation, held up by granite cylinders.

Molly checked the time on the radio as she shut the door. Bella, intimidated by the scale of the hospital, did the same, staring at the building. It looked due for a renovation. After the redhead started in a direction, Bella ran up next to her.

They started for the tubelike protrusion. Molly strolled as if not a care in the world.

Bella kept looking up at the facility. "Oops, forgot my bag." She laughed.

Molly side-eyed her friend. "Don't worry," she said with a smirk. "We'll give you a new one."

"Great." The girl was in tempo with the redhead. "Will I have to talk to Nelson?"

"Probably."

"Lovely."

They carried on to the tubelike protrusion and crossed the first granite pillars. Such material must have been picked for fun. Soon the girls crossed an automatic door that opened for them. They walked in, and Bella noticed that the interior of the structure did not match the harsh outside. Smooth rays graced the reflective tile and brightened the space with a cream-like color, vibrant foliage bloomed out in almost all corners with credence to Kim's opposition in their home. Along the fake planets, many advertisements of conversions were pinned on the wall of which were children, speaking to medical personnel with mouths full of white teeth.

From the entrance, an overweight woman sat behind a counter. Molly went to her, and Bella carried on behind. She saw her friend wave to the information behind the clear desk that contained a yellow box of face masks, hand sanitizer, and a stack of papers that the woman worked on.

Molly hollered, "Hey, Amber!"

The woman's attention toward her. "Hey! Back already?" She chuckled.

"Of course." Molly smiled. "Ya can't take a break for too long."

"Oh, yes. There's always something to do." Amber picked the stack of papers.

They reached the desk. "How's your mom doing?

Amber's grin dropped. "Oh, you know, still won't take her meds. But she hasn't gotten worse so far, so there's hope in that at least."

"That's good."

"But still, not any better. I mean, she's so old I hardly blame her. Death's yanking on her arm, and she don't care."

Bella stood behind her friend. She waited, keeping her eyes fixated on the light hospital floor, not intently but paying attention to the conversation.

"I'd keep trying," said Molly. "Maybe she'll come through."

"I don't think so," said Amber. "She'll never, not after Pa died. You know she was never the same, and you know she got a right. They wouldn't give him the care he needed. But that doesn't mean you can't take some pills they give you." She sighed and pointed her finger at Molly. "Don't become a Pelt like that. It's frustrating."

The redhead nodded, rolling her eyes with a smirk.

The lady spotted the lingering girl. "Who's this?" she asked Molly.

Bella felt uncovered, a quick smile and a wave to her defense. She noticed the deep lines in Amber's face. The lady waved back.

Molly nodded as if she was proud of the girl's ability to introduce herself. "This is Bella. She was my dorm mate in college."

"Oh, really? Ha! It's good to meet you," said the woman. "I'm Amber. I actually have something for you." And at that moment, the woman reached into a drawer along her feet. She flopped a name tag with Bella's information on it and a little slip of paper with log-in codes. "Now don't you go losing this," Amber joked and extended the items to the girl.

Bella reached over and snatched the name tag and log-in, catching a hint of tobacco on her breath.

"Thank you," she said.

Molly nodded in pride. "We better head off. Tell your mom I said hi though."

"Oh, I gotcha. Nelson's a peculiar fellow, weird rules. Weird he's actually working on the floor."

The redhead began to walk away. Bella followed.

"Maybe he actually likes his job."

"He can't do that." The women waved goodbye to the nurses. "You have yourself a pleasant day now."

"You too, Amber," said Molly, and the pair crossed into the main hallway of the facility.

The two walked side by side. Molly smirked and repeatedly glanced at her friend, hoping to pivot her attention. Bella paid no mind, analyzing the soft throne chairs and the end tables that accompanied every department and every waiting area they crossed. Her nerves clenched getting closer to her first day.

Molly kept trying to get her friend to look at her. At last, she said. "Name tag?"

Bella turned to Molly. "What?"

"You got a badge! Log in? It's happening!"

The girl rolled her eyes. "That doesn't help."

Molly took several strides before responding. "It's exciting."

"I guess. I'm just really feeling it now."

The redhead appeared puzzled. "The nerves?"

Bella shrugs. "Yeah, I guess."

"Just keep going. It'll be fine."

The pair shedded their conversation. A family passed them, a sense of dread on their faces, a lack of a matriarch in the group. There was a steady hum of clients and professionals disputing prices and information, along with the air conditioner's murmur.

Bella peered to the sides, on the receiving points to the many different laboratory or clinic offices, many patient waiting their turn to see a doctor, some had children with them. Bella's heart stirred whenever she catches a glimpse of an acting family, but despite her heart's nagging, she ignored and persisted through with a concerned awe. The people were dressed in all sorts of manner; some even glared at the pair as they walked by. No child wore a pin of fur, and the only sign of local influence was with some of the old, and Molly. There were no Yudakus, except the one that dangled off the neck of Molly.

Leaving behind the density of patients and many sights of informational posters and "can do" saying, the nurse continued. The hallways were oddly wide, considering the rest of the cramped city. Plenty of room for the body traffic and a relief from not being so close to everything. She realized the hospital must have been made long before the rest curled in on itself, hogging the delicious land from its close neighbors. An odd admiration grew within the girl for the facility.

"This looks nice," Bella said.

"Yeah," replied Molly, walking on. "We don't work here though."

"I know, it's just so wide."

"Different, huh? Its gets busy on the floor though, lots of moving parts."

Bella studied her friend's face. "Think I'll make it?"

"You'll get the hang of it. It's just hard sometimes." The redhead repeated, "It's just hard."

Her tone was alien. Molly tried to mask it, but she could tell Bella could find the slight miss-mannerisms in her vocals. However, this new angle of fixation did not last in her friend, and it faded into a smile. Molly pointed up ahead.

Bella looked straight to see what they were walking toward. Close, about ten yards, an elevator sat ingrained in the wall.

They soon reached its door, the transportation appearing worse for wear. It did not look the age of the rest of the interior, and the girl recounted seeing identical metallic doors lint collecting in college buildings, even its plate that clung to the walls shared a wilting hue. The naked, unclaimed wall exposed the cement muscle. Bella began to worry about stepping into the machine.

Molly didn't seem to mind the condition and pressed its beckon. Then came the echo of rattles and vibrations, next a series of bangs and clicks, ending with a ding. The doors of the elevators parted and revealed a slick cab with the logo of the community hospital: a dove carrying a wreath with thistle to its wings stamped the back wall.

The two then crossed the slight gap between the elevator and floor tile and stood patiently as the metallic door closed.

"Press 3," said Molly.

"Oh." Bella pushed the corresponding number. She didn't know she was the one standing closest to the terminal. Her friend seemed happy, but she couldn't help but feel that Molly was discomforted. She wondered as the doors folded close and the pair was carried up like a bucket on a string.

After another ding, the two stepped out into another hallway void of posters, replacing it with the true bleakness of the building. Scarce was the color, save the light-blue uniforms who occasionally passed by. Little conversion could be heard between personnel. There were a pleatna of stained oak doors dotting the hallway.

Molly hooked around and went down a corridor near the elevator. At the end of this corridor was a dual entrance, which another nurse stepped out of as the pair made their way toward it. Bella staggered behind and was quick to recover, careful not to lose her guide.

Thereafter, entering on the outswing of hinges, they stepped into a sector filled with employees. It was by far more condensed and what Bella imagined. She saw nurses sitting in front of all the closed rooms, going ballistic on the keyboards of the computers in front of a rectangular slit of glass that nurses occasionally peeked through. In the middle the fray, erected an oval-shaped counter encircling many screens and facing off personnel manning behind them, also typing away at their keyboards but as well monitoring and studying what the computer showed. Carts were parked where they needed to be, nurses pushing them along. The sight made her blood race, veins pumping as a release to the nausea she felt.

Bella turned to Molly, which she believed planned to cartwheel onto the floor and go about her job, but no, the redhead stayed at her side. A somber grin stretched Molly's face, and she motioned to the girl to follow her. Bella did so.

Bella watched Molly's shoes closely. From her angle, a few pairs of legs crossed the border of her vision. She followed her, turning unexpectedly from where she thought she was going, spotting the bottoms of counters and what she thought to be the lower compartments of a refrigerator. The redhead suddenly stopped. Bella spied in front the legs of a large table with five chairs around it. There Bella's eyes glazed to a pair of sneakers in front of her friend, with scrub pants legging up to a nurse's shirt.

"Hey, Kade," said Molly.

"Hey," said the nurse.

Bella's eyes climbed to face. He had a runner built, a face full of stubble, and no hair on his head. The man anchored an elbow on the table and held his coffee with the same arm.

"I was about to say good morning, but it's not really that."

"I hear you." Kade laughed. "I've said good night to something this morning. I once said good morning in the evening. It's just getting all mixed up."

The redhead nodded. "Is that your fourth or fifth cup?"

He looked down at his cup. "Probably my sixth." He set his mug down on the table. "How have you been?"

"Eh. Good enough," said Molly.

Kade's eye met the girl, and she withdrew them back to the floor.

"She looks like she needs a first cup," asked Kade.

The redhead laughed. "That's Bella. She's a close friend of mine."

Bella gave a short wave to the man, meeting his stare again, then back to the tile.

"Well, it is good to meet you, Bella." He didn't care enough to ask for a last name. He switched his attention. "So when are you two on?" Kade asked.

Molly glanced to the microwave clock. "Soon. Nelson wants to talk to her before she's on."

"Customary," he replied. "He likes to keep the machine well oiled. Gotta put the fear of God in you."

"Well, it's a pep talk," said Molly.

"Doesn't come across as a pep talk."

"For me, it did."

"For me, it didn't."

Molly snickered. "It's caffeine. Ye brain is all jittery."

"I think it's fine," said Kade, taking a sip from his cup. "I've never seen him talk to a doctor like that though."

An inhale from Molly suggested a reply, yet it was snuffed, and she quickly looked behind her. Bella tracked her line of sight. Right to where they came from, an opening with no closure, was a brown board with charts and directions plastered all over it. It possessed the time and patients of each nurse and what time they should get there.

"Something important?" asked Kade.

Molly looked over her shoulder. "Oh no, I just forgot to check something." She then walked over to the board. She delivered the line and found hers and Bella's name. "Yes! They actually got some common sense." The redhead spun around. "You'll be with me in room 390."

"Cool," said Bella, and she saw the full surrounding of the room she was in.

Personnel loitered in the quiet hub.

Kade checked the time. "God, Nelson's gonna make you late."

"He's a busy boy, ya know," said Molly. The nurse then looked at Bella. "I gotta at the room at noon."

Don't go, the girl thought. *Don't leave me here.*

"Is that okay?"

"Yeah, sure," were Bella's words. She couldn't be terrified.

"Ya sure?"

"Yeah, 390."

Molly smiled. "Great, I'll see, yeah over there." She stepped to the side and turned out the open exit.

Kade waved to her goodbye, but the action wasn't seen. He shifted to the girl still standing. "How long have you known her?"

"Oh, um..." She thought to sit but was too scared. The girl bridges her hand together, thumb over top another. "Four years."

"That's a long time."

"Yeah, it feels like a long time."

Kade squinted. "Your came from Haze right?"

Bella nodded. "Ya from the College of Haze too."

"Well, ya that's the only school there."

"Yeah, yeah." Her insides squirmed.

"No, I didn't mean." Kade pause. "Never mind. I'm guessing you've lived there all your life."

"How can you tell?"

He checked the girl out. "You don't look like you've seen the sun for years."

She, all of a sudden, became self-aware of what she must look like.

"Ah." The man stood up, stretching his back. "From what I heard about the place, it doesn't seem like it gets much light to begin with." He grabbed his mug from the table and walked over to the counter nearest to him. "You'll get plenty of sunlight here." Indented in the counter, he found a sink, and the man placed his mug, stealing one last sip, in the stainless container.

Bella kept her appearance up.

The microwave clock read 12:05, and Kade took notice. A grin Bella felt was fake cracked over. Kade left out into the corridor without a word, leaving the girl stranded in the center of the room. She watched him leave, seeing him being succeeded at the bountrie of corridor and the medical ground. A short man walked in, holding clipboards and studying its components. He wore a lab coat and fine-collared shirt with a tie. His hair reminded Bella of storm clouds, but storm clouds that divorced and fumed at opposing ends of his head. Kade knew this strange man and hugged the wall to avoid him. Despite his efforts, the man looked up and spotted the nurse eluding him. He shook his head and continued in.

"Bella Tomson?" he said, reading the clipboard. "Is Bella Tomson in here?"

The nurses scattered in the room looked among themselves. The girl then raised her hand.

"Ah," he said. "You look different from your photo."

"I used an old photo," said Bella, realizing to whom she spoke. "I'm sorry if that's not okay."

"It's not, but I can kinda see it," said Nelson, looking down at the board, then at her.

Bella observed his square head and frame.

Nelson took the same chair Kade had sat. "Have a seat, please."

Bella instantly sat.

"I'm pleased that you were able to find the faculty okay. We spoke over the phone, I think, or we should have." He reached out his hand. "I'm Dr. Peter Nelson."

She took the hand with her flimsy grip. "Thank you, sir," said Bella. "Thank you for the opportunity."

He looked beyond bored with the interaction. Nelson bobbed his head and stored something in his clipboard. "It's good to see you found your way here. I know Heartlake's road is brutal. But again some of the best roads in the state."

"Agreed, sir."

"Very good." And he wrote something down. "Now, since your introduction into the nursing program at…Haze, I believed." He checked his paper once again, and when failing to find what he sought, he turned up to the girl. "You are pale. Don't worry, normal pigmentation will be gained within a few months away from the smog."

Bella pretended to know what the old doctor meant and nodded.

"But regardless, I wanted to inform you that many things since your introduction at the College of Haze have become outdated in the time of your training. Nevertheless, new education is on its way, but it never can be fast enough, you know. I wanted to ensure that you don't bicker with any of your superiors about medical protocols. I don't like arguments. I don't like fights. I've had to make sure the employees trust us who steer the hospital, that every doctor here knows what he's doing, and you just have to listen. Nursing has become such an easy job, with the new train. Lower occupations have had trouble with these new regulations, but they need to adapt. And if not, I'm sure others would be glad to take their place."

Bella believed that the other nurses were staring at her. A question to what this "information" or "education" boiled up from within her, but heeded the doctor's word.

"Do we understand one another?" he asked.

She suppressed it, knowing it be for the greater good. "Yes, sir."

The doctor smiled, or something similar. "I can already tell you'll go far here. You know the first time I talked to you, I had a feeling we were going to be an excellent hire. We do things differently here, but I'm happy that you'll be a part of our fight against disease." He held his hand out again.

Bella shook it.

"I won't keep you any longer. You need to be places."

"Oh, yes, sir. Room 309."

"Amazing. You're already one of my favorites." Now the doctors leaned back in his seat, writing another note to himself. "You can go. I'm sure you have already met your partner for the next couple of days. She'll show you what's to happen here."

Blood rushed through the being of the girl, and she stood up with eagerness and started for the exit.

"Have a good day," Nelson said.

And the girl left the room, feeling the eyes of her peers glued onto her as she entered into the open space of the medical bay and turned the where Molly had prior.

She could see just about all the patients' quarters. Beeps and clicks flooded her hearing. Almost every nurse were away at their tasks, their fingers quickly pecking away at their plastic keys below their chests, keeping conscious watch over their clients as others entered in and chatted.

After passing several, she overtook the oval counter center and received belligerent glances from its attendants. Bella almost had the courage to wave to one, but dismissed the idea after performing maneuvers evading other nurses. Exiting the oval counter, and a little red in the face, she checked the rooms for their appropriate number.

Upon center of the nesters, she observed the brass labels: 385, 386. She was getting closer.

The on-duty nurse stationed out of 386 whipped around her stool and asked, "Did you need anything?"

Bella pretended not to hear her. She kept her sight focused on the labels: 387, 388. She counted to more gapes and scurried to where she believed was the right door. She found next to it an empty stool and black computer screen. She panned to the brass label: 390. Bella then spied through the observation window and found the redhead tending to what she assumed to be an old man. The girl was relieved, knocking on the glass. Molly turned around.

Footsteps sounded from the other side, followed by a handle clank and sudden pull. Molly greeted the girl with white toothy chuckle and motioned her in. The room strayed not too far from the standard layout from what she thought of hospital rooms. A sink and an array of cabinets sat against the left wall, visiting chairs were placed against the window, and bleak monitors stood next to the fluffy hospital bed. In it was a man, a cast nearly on every part of his body. He faced a black TV screen, something she thought would be surely on.

"About time!" she said. "I wonder if ya gone home."

Bella stepped forward. "No, Nelson's just long-winded."

Molly closed the door. "What he say to you?"

"He said that he had a problem with people not listening to doctors or something like that."

"Huh, that's nothing new."

Molly positioned herself by the bed. He was an old man, rough and wrinkled, shorter than average in height, and sour. Draping from his scalp was long silver hair that was in steep decline and a salt-and-pepper mustache. It was true, most of his limbs were in casts, strung up in bandages and harnesses, that kept them straight, the only free extremity being his right arm, the string being an intravenous drip. A bag of pretzels lay on a tall cart next to the bed, along with a dull pencil and blackened eraser.

He'd seen the girls enter out of the corner of his eye, but didn't acknowledge her. He kept his nose in a coverless, titleless book, to which he kept very close to himself.

"Evergreen," said Molly in a cheery way, entering the room. "This is Nurse Tomson and you'll be helping me help you out today."

Bella recalled preparations on the board and stepped forth. "Hello, Mr. Seager."

"Hullo," he said, keeping his eyes on his book, then glanced at the two girls. "I guess I'm little more than a practice dummy now."

Molly laughed. "No, you're not. You're too ticklish."

The old fella chuckled and set his book next to his pretzels, a sticky note kept his place. His laughter soon turned into spurts of coughing, and he began cursing under his breath.

"You all right?" asked Molly.

"Fuckin' hell," he said the last of it. "I'm fine, I'm fine."

Molly rubbed his shoulder. "It's going away."

He returned with a breath. "Aaah. But isn't it about time for medication?"

"I'm sorry but not yet. But these bandages are gonna go." The redhead studied the gauze around the man's lifted leg. "Yeah, we better get on it."

Bella lowered to assess the leg. "Well, what does the doctor think?"

"Bastard doesn't even know I'm here," announced the old man. "I haven't seen his face in days."

"Doctor Hale is real busy," said Molly.

"Should we at least check first?" asked Bella.

"It's on the regiment to change them at least every day." She walked over to a drawer by Evergreen's head. On top was a monitor plus a mouse and keyboard and below were a column of drawers. Molly opened up the first compartment and withdrew a crate of bandages.

"Are you sure?" asked Bella.

"Yes!" said Molly, returning to her friend's side. "Didn't ya check outside? There should have been a paper."

"I didn't see any."

"There shoulda been. Maybe it fell."

"I just wanna make sure we're doing what we need, ya know. Should we go ask someone?"

"Bella," said Molly, surprised. "I've done this almost every other day. Technically, I'm higher than you, so Nelson's talk should apply to me."

Evergreen chuckled. She turned back to him.

Bella looked at her friend. "It's just, are you sure?"

"Yes!" said Molly. "Why're you so unsure?"

"I'm sorry, I just…" She paused.

"Don't let the doctor's talk discourage ya from basic medical care. The bandages need changed. So we're gonna change them, once every day." She turned back to the patient. "I'm sorry, we'll get started now. You gotta feel clean, right?" Molly looked down to find something she didn't possess. She then motioned for Bella. "Could you grab the Listers from the first drawer there."

"Sure." Bella walked to the same drawer her friend did prior. Looking down, she saw and assortment of scissors, bandages, and eventually grabs two listers. She closed the compartment and joined the redhead to the side of Evergreen, extending the tools on her palm and expecting her friend to pluck one of them. But Molly didn't do this; instead, she seized the wrist and pulled with surprising strength to speak in her ear.

"Try to make conversation."

The girl's heart sank, and the redhead let go of her, now grabbing one for the listers with a friendly smile to show support. Bella knew she was right, but for the life of her, she wanted to remain silent.

Molly then started removing the old gauzes on the man's right leg, suspended in air with a cable. Molly carefully cut through the linens and pulled off from Evergreen's legs. Bella stood to the side of her and watched.

"Please don't move them," said the man, worried under his breath.

"We won't," assured Molly. "I know it hurts."

Evengreen moved his free arm and lifted his book from the cart. "Thank you.

As the redhead worked, Bella moved to the other side of the bed. She almost began cutting, but as she moved in to position, she felt something bump her toe. It was decently heavy, and she looked down to investigate.

"Leave it alone," came from the old man.

Bella saw a worn briefcase angled against the bed, a strange hole on its exterior.

"Sorry, sir," she said, and she did her best and began cutting through the cast set upon Evergreen's left leg.

Molly worked on the left arm. After breaching the cast, the girl unwound the wrapping around an exoskeleton-like sleuth of many pins embedded along the old man's scabbing yellow skin.

Bella looked away for a brief moment, unexpecting the condition of this flesh.

She turned back and spied the book in the Evergreen's hands. She saw an image within the corner of a page: a strange written and mangled food. This intrigued the girl, and she found something actually interesting to ask. She braced herself.

"What's in your book?"

"Pardon?" said Evergreen.

Bella returned to working on the shattered leg. "What's in your book?"

The old man looked down at the pages and broke the book closer to his chest. "Nothing. Just notes."

"What for?" Bella added. She saw him searching for an answer.

"It's not worth sharing." Another jolt came from within him. "Dammit. Argh. It doesn't matter to you."

"I'm sorry, sir," said Bella. "It really looks interesting."

Molly popped her head from the other side of the bed, having almost completed wrapping the arm, cleaning a little of the ooze that befell him. "She's good at keeping secrets, if ya worry about that."

"I don't dare. ."

Bella kept rewrapping his leg.

The redhead put her hands to her hips. "You told me."

"You've been baptized. No one says I can trust her."

"I say you can trust her."

Bella kept wrapping. She hand graced one of the pins.

"You may wear a Yudaku, but you're still not a—Ah!" He stopped the sudden pain.

Bella froze.

Evergreen shouted in reaction, agony from the fragmented bones being stirred in the fleshy soup of his leg. The girl made a locked step backward from the patient.

"I'm sorry. I'm sorry!" she said.

Molly sets aside the spare gauze she held by the sink. There was nothing to be done, but the redhead went to the old man's side. She rubbed his shoulder again.

"It's okay, it's okay. It's going away." She turned to Bella. "How badly did you hit it?"

"I didn't know I even touched it!" she responded.

The old man stared at his leg, his teeth still gritting. "Just get me my fucking drugs."

A sigh escaped Molly. "I guess that's fair." She motioned to Bella.

Molly headed toward the cabinets on the other side of the room, and Bella hesitantly followed. The girl knew his harsh eyes were upon her, and she sought the floor. Molly located the correct medicine. "This is for his cough. And this is for everything else. It's morphine." Her friend gave her the persecutions.

Bella continued to look at the floor. She didn't believe Molly wanted her to proceed. "Are you sure?" her voice was just above a whisper.

"You oughta. It just might warm him back up to you."

An exhale escaped the girl, and she nodded, accepting the responsibility. She walked with both pill containers to the old man, whose body languages shunned her. Remembering a glass of water, Molly came close behind, filling it as Bella strode toward the bed.

"I'm sorry, sir," she said, dropping the appropriate amount of pills for the old man. "I really am."

Evergreen brandished his palm without a word, to which Bella understood and gave him the drugs.

Molly approached with the glass of water. "I got you water right—"

Within a second, the patient flung the pills into the back of his throat. "You can leave it on my cart," he said.

Molly did just that. "Were going to be outside for a little bit, Evergreen. You remember which button to press when you need us?"

"Yes."

"Great! Well, we'll be right outside if you need ups." Molly then turned to her friend. "It's smart to get a head start on your logging." She acted if nothing happened, then once again signaled Bella to follow. They exited the room. Bella a few paces behind her friend.

Bella looked to Evergreen. She fathomed what he must think of her. She knew this would happen, something like this. Possibility was always against her.

Outside the room, Bella looked to her left and saw Molly prepping the computer.

"You should be able to log in now," said the redhead. "This is gonna be where ya spend most of your time.

Bella nodded, keeping her head angled at the floor.

Molly noted the expression. "Hey," she said. "It was a mistake. I've freaked out a lot of times."

Bella bit her lip. "No, I'm all right."

"There ya go!" she said, standing up and beckoning her friend toward the seat, and once the girl sat, she continued, "Listen, I gotta go. I will switch with another nurse for a bit. I'll come get you though once I'm done. It should be at the end of the day, if I remember right."

Bella tapped her foot.

"Hey, but you got this. It looks like old Evergreen won't be too much of a trouble, so just keep an eye on him and look busy. Oh, and also give the medication again after dinner. All right?"

Bella nodded and boosted a fake smile.

"All right! See you in a bit. I think I'm running late." She forced a frown, then smiled again. "I'll see ya around." And she went off toward the oval counter.

Bella watched Molly walk away. After a sigh and triplet from her tapping food, she turned back to the computer. She could do this, no problem, but she would have to chart what had happened. Every little detail must be written out. It unsettled her. The girl couldn't sit comfortably. She remembered the way he cried out. It chilled her as if her own bones were exposed. She retreated, peering through the graded window, shame controlling her. He might catch her, and she was prepared to duck down. The old man who wore a sore look held her pity. She held only a guilty conscience. Bella caused him pain. She was mortified by that fact.

Tormented still, the girl typed away at the black plastic keys, performing the mundane medical work of the community hospital, mirroring every other nurse as far as the rows excelled. She reported every movement, every yawn, every moment he spent reading his dumbfounded book, as per what was required in her job. She charted the exact second his eyes drooped and when they fell closed. She didn't mean to hurt him. She never wanted to hurt him. She never thought she was capable of the infarction.

Through each glance, a thought increased. *How could you do that?* it said. *How could you really do that?* This voice she said in her own, and it would not wash away so easily, not without distraction. The clamor of the hospital, the talking, the stepping, the beeping of queer equipment, the plastic smell paid no aid to the girl. Her heart beat rose. *How could you do that?* The glorious reason to become a nurse, to serve comfort to dying men, and she did the opposite. She tried to not think, tried to reassure herself it wasn't worth all the fret, tried losing herself in her mundane work. Unsuccessful, her mind circled again and again to the fact that she caused pain to his old man. Tears filled her eyes. *How could you do that?*

At last, she couldn't take it anymore. The pale girl flung both hands from the computer, baring herself into her palms. She tried not to cry. *Have you lost all sense?*

It could have been five or ten minutes that the pale girl was left alone. Nurses and medical personnel walked by, casting judgmental sneers and continuing with their day, to which most doctors did the same, all but one. Heavy breathing, paired to together with the smell of sweat, was made known to the girl. Bella then felt a strong tap on her shoulder. She spun her head around to see a short stout man glaring down at her.

"Is there a problem, Ms. Tomsom?" Doctor Nelson puffed.

Bella's mind turned to jelly. She spun back to her computer and hammering away at her logs. She replied with a crack in her voice, "I'm fine."

The stout man raised his brow. He made a single stride to the side of Bella, his hands folded behind his back, pacing his strides, taking examination of her. He could only be taller than her while she was sitting.

"Were you sleeping?" he asked. "Were you dreaming?"

Bella shrank in her seat. "I wasn't sleeping, sir."

"Oh? Then what were you doing?"

"I…I was just overwhelmed. I'll…I'll get back to it now. Th-thank you, sir." She continued her typing.

"I don't want you to feel stressed."

Bella feared. "N-no, sir. I'm fine."

"Splendid," said Nelson. He bent down to examine her screen. "Let's examine your work, shall we?"

Bella's stomach dropped one hundred feet as the doctor reached over to her mouse and scrolled up. His face was a stone. "Disappointing." He then pushed the mouse aside and straightened his back. "I thought you knew how to format correctly. This is all just lazily done now, is it? Your time stamps aren't even in the right place."

Bella stared at her mistake. "I'll do better."

"I expect you to. Or are you too stressed? I can have someone else fix your notes if you can't."

"No, I'll do it. I'll do it. It won't happen again."

"Good answer. See now I'm starting to like you again. But I don't desire to have this conversation again. I still hope that my estimation of you was correct, and you should too. Just be mindful of your work, Tomson, and you and I won't have any more quarrels." And gripping his arms around his back, he parted from the side of the girl. "Let's do better." Doctor Nelson walked along and spied another nurse, this one playing with her nails and parting in her direction.

Bella watched the square faced man leave. With a tremble, she returned to the screen and charted, redoing her work with special care, as to not be "lazy." She didn't even want to cry anymore; she just wanted the day to be done. *I'll be better*, she thought. *Have you no sense.* She took another look at Evergreen, asleep now, book on the metal cart, and pressed on with her logs.

Routine of the community hospital kept its cycle. Random tragedies occurred in all hospitals: people were born, others perished, but all remained the same on Bella's floor. Sunlight waned over the entirety on the horizon, seeping through the windows and to the cracks of the facility, passing the faces of men and women hard at work for those either in love or hate of their employment. Bella felt the latter.

Hours passed, marked by long shadows streaming from the geometry of the facility, until it began to swallow all, until the ceiling lights buzzed on, until the dark cloud formed halos of for the Giants.

Bella, having completed her log and resting her head, heard a rumbling behind her. She turned and looked and saw the dinner cart composed of multilayers of entrees on platters, with two men, one larger than the other, hailing it toward her patient's room. They stopped and greeted her.

"Hey!" one of them said. "Could you get the door for us?"

"Yeah," responded the girl, and she helped them enter.

"Thanks," said the larger one. He then squatted down to the dishes there on the car. "What is this one's name?

"Evergreen."

"Evergreen what?"

"Seager."

The male nurse screened among the plethora of plates. Bella wondered what he was doing, until she saw the tag with cursive names sticking out from the edges of the entrees.

"There we are." He found what he sought and lifted from a lower shelf, revealing a tray and a dish with a dry lab of meat, pale green peas, and a side of mashed potatoes with tan gravy. He stepped into the room and set the plate on the counters, near the sink.

"You better wake him up," he said, exiting the room and rejoining his coworkers. They traveled down, skipping several entryways before stopping again and conversing with the posted nurse.

Holding the handle still, Bella looked at the old man, his faint snoring filling the silence. She then moved inward and closed the door, wasting no time in grabbing Evergreen's piles and setting them to the side of his tray. She stepped forth with the components, watching the patient and preparing what she'll do to wake him. She fathomed a sentence and uttered it almost before rethinking it, then an action came to mind that a tap would be more effective. She decided to listen to her incursion, moving the other side of Evergreen to shake him on his good arm.

Upon reaching the metal cart where the empty bag of pretzels lay, Bella noticed Evergreen's book and its wide open leathery pages. She took the chance to satisfy her curiosity and drew close enough to read what was in it. Or she would have if the paragraphs were written in English. The words were written in dark lead and were composed neatly on the sheet, remarkable handwriting and fantastic details, possessing characters that she had never seen in a language like this. It appeared almost fake. Along with the paragraphs, there were diagrams and weather patterns, shown in Arabic numerals, that to which she could understand. Harsh lines were drawn also, and she thought these referred to the Sleeping Giants.

The girl looked over to the old man. It didn't appear foreign, just a Local. She hated this. She always hated a subject she couldn't understand. She was brilliant, despite not wanting more schooling. . The nurse knew the man wouldn't speak a word to her about the book. *But he's asleep*, Bella pondered, biting the inside of her lip, then deciding to set the tray onto the metal cart. She hovered over the pages, getting a better view of the strange characters. Then touching the paper, it felt meaty. Finally, she mustered enough courage and turned the page, excited to see what was next.

What greeted Bella is what she wished she never saw. There on the page was a sketch, and on the sketch was blood. Her intestines curled at the sight. There, on the page, though it possessed hands, the creature was bound to all fours with malicious elongated limbs with taunt skin peeling from the tension to keep the skeleton. No life inhabited its eyes, only void sockets with protruding bone. And a maw, a maw of humanlike teeth, a wide and ungodly jaw, like a canine, but sideways. Bits of fur dotted the monster, along with strip of clothing, almost as if it bursting from its clothes.

Almost out of instinct, Bella shut the book, not knowing it would make a sound.

Evergreen stirred and met Bella with a half-asleep look.

"What are you doing?" he asked.

"Ah." The girl prevented herself from jumping. "Sorry, I-I got your food."

"Mm, I thought I would go hungry." Evergreen looked at the tray. "What's in it?"

"Looks like steak with peas and mashed potatoes." Bella freed her hands and grabbed the dish.

Evergreen saw the girl put down his book. "Sounds good. You think you could cut up my steak for me?"

"Yes, sir." She moved to the dish, and with the flimsy silverware, she began cutting through the dry meat.

The old man watched her. "You're a weird one, aren't you?"

Bella kept silent. *Was he the author or just a reader?* she thought.

"Not in the joker's type of way, but just strange. You're a strange girl."

The nurse glanced over. "I'm sorry, I don't mean to be."

"No, you don't have to keep saying sorry for it. It's okay to not have your bearings yet. You're young, aren't you? It took me a while to understand folk. And hell, it's still a fifty-fifty chance."

"What about…bumping you."

"Bumping me?"

"Yeah."

"Well, that hurt like the devil," he said. "But I'm still breathing. Don't worry about it."

Bella sliced the last section of meat into squares. She was beyond relieved. "Thank you." The girl moved the cart within reach of the man. "It won't happen again."

"Well, it might." He took the fork from her. "Thank you for cutting the steak, my dear."

Bella nodded. "Let's give you your pills first."

"Ah, right." Evergreen reached to the side of the tray and grabbed both of the drugs. "No need for water, miss." And he swallowed them both, then smiled.

To the man's gesture, Bella took it as a sign to leave and strove for the door. "I'll be in the hallway if you need me, sir."

But as she passed just to the middle, Evergreen called out to her again. "Did you look in my journal?"

The nurse turned back and saw the old man's eye fixated upon the book. Fearing what he'd say if the truth was exposed, the girl lied.

"I didn't. It was on the floor, and I was just grabbing it."

"Hm, well no issue." the man starred at the object and pondered the girl's words. "Well, I swore I left it on the bed."

Bell shrugged. "Must have fell."

"Well, no big deal." He chuckled. "My age is just starting to settle then."

"No, it's okay." Bella smiled. And without another word, she passed the rest of the length of the room. She exited and returned to her chair. She waited for her friend to reappear, keeping an eye for Nelson. She found she had nothing more to add to the document before her, not wanting to add the image of what she saw into words. And she felt the time past her by.

Down the hallway, Bella spotted a redhead approaching, exhausted but still bearing a cheery grin.

Chapter

5

A tempest formed, followed by the low rumbling of thunder, violet whips of lighting striking the earth miles away from the city. Rain fell, not as a pour but as a drizzle, shining the concrete and asphalt under street lanterns and side lights. The rustic trucked squeaked to a halt. Molly unlocked her side and stepped out into the storm, stretching and sighing with a gurgle. She took in the wet atmosphere and embraced the heaven-sent droplets pecking her face, inhaling deep and exhaling slow. Bella slid out of her door next and shut it in one move. Her first reaction was to shield her eyes from the tapping rain. The cold reached her. She didn't know it was supposed to storm today.

Bella assumed they would go inside, but she stopped. "What are you doing?"

Molly didn't answer. Her eyes were closed, and almost as if she was led, she drifted to the drenched lawn. Her feet sunk in the wet grass, and she bent at the knees and controlled her fall toward her back. Molly lay there getting soaked.

"Molly?" Bella went toward her. She was confused. "What are you doing?"

"Relaxing," said Molly. "It doesn't rain that often here."

"But you're getting all wet!" the girl said, stepping nearer. "I'm getting all wet."

"It's cooling you off." The redhead arched her back into the swamped earth. "Come join me!"

Bella frowned. "Listen, can't we just go in?"

"Come here and lay by me. I promised it will help melt that bad day right off you. Just come on."

"This is stupid."

"Come on!"

Bella shook her head and marched onto grass, her shoes filling with water as soon as her weight compressed the blades. She slugged to where Molly was and sat down by her, regretting the instant her scrubs were flooded.

"Fully," said the redhead, her curls floating beside her in the creases of the lawn.

She did what her friend wanted and lowered herself till she hit the ground with a moist smack.

"That sounded fun. Now just close your eyes."

"We're gonna get pneumonia."

"We'll be fine. We're healthy, and this is helping."

"I feel silly."

"Close 'em!"

Bella did just that, rolling her eyes behind their lids. She felt the droplets peppering her body, causing her to feel even more like a dying corpse discarded on the roadside.

"Now breathe deeply."

"Water's getting in my nose—"

"Just try!"

The girl resisted the instruction at first, then complied, angling so her lungs will not fill with the manna and, instead, with the moist air. She exhaled giving it back into the cool world. She did this, again and again. Slowly, she focused more on the water than what had happened at work, a tense body slowly relaxing into control. She felt her strife evaporate, accepting the uncomfortable condition she was lying in, diverging all attention to the particles dropping from the sky to kiss her cheek.

"How do you feel?" asked Molly, rolling over.

"I don't know," said Bella, not wanting to admit its effect.

"Is it better or worse?"

"I guess, better."

The nurse rolled back. "I told ya."

The pair listened to the chorus surrounding them, the gentle rapping of the hard earth kept in time by shaking thunder. It somehow passed the point of discomfort and soothed them both. Molly yawned.

Bella wondered what she was thinking about, expecting her to be recalling when she discovered this practice, probably rooted with her newfound religion. But she found no crime in participating. *And she would tell me if something was wrong before.* But there shouldn't always be an ache to meditate.

Before Bella could ask, Molly said, "I'm sorry about today."

"It's okay. I feel better now."

"That's good. You'll get the rhythm down."

"Molly..." Now Bella rolled over. "When did you discover this?"

"Discover this?"

"Yeah."

Molly laughed. "Lying in the rain? Ha, I did as a kid. I found out it made me forget."

Bella was surprised. "I thought you learned this here."

"No, but it feels real nice to do it here."

A breeze whipped past the two and reminded the girl she was adapted for the smog and not for the cold. It no longer felt tolerable, and the girl shivered. Molly, then again, was fueled by her own assumption.

Let's go in," she said.

"Yes, please."

With a grunt, Molly got to her feet as did Bella. Both were drenched, the tips of their hair, leaking. They strode onto the porch and stood in front of the front door. The redhead pressed a key into the lock, the handle loosened, and they sagged into the Planned Home.

Warmth enveloped them. Water pooled at their feet from their clothes. Bella didn't want to get the rest of the home wet by walking up the stairs, and she stood there uncertain what to do. Molly stepped back onto the porch to shake off. Bella went out to do the same, bumping her as she tried to get rid of the water.

They weren't dry, but Bella wanted to be in new clothes. So did her friend, and she figured she just rubbed anything down with a towel when they got wet. Both took off their shoes and socks by the door and flew up the stairs and to their closest. Molly found a cute tank top to wear plus a pair of striped shorts. Bella was much colder than her friend and grabbed sweats and an oversized hoodie. She wanted to shower, yet she wanted to eat more. .

They reemerged from their compartments and joined together downstairs, with Molly quick with a towel to dry the puddle left by the front door.

There was a gleaming from the kitchen. Bella was the first to notice it. Molly flung the towel over her shoulder and made for its source. Bella did the same, right behind her guide. Her friend entered the dining room, but Bella stopped just before its cusp and looked behind the corner. She saw Kim, casual attire, stirring a rising steam pot, headphones in and hips swaying next to the flytrap. Bella almost said "Hi," but Molly brought a finger to her own lips in an order to be quiet. Her mouth curled, and the redhead crouched and began inching toward the tattooed woman. She stalked closer and closer until she was within arm's reach of Kim. Molly then stood up and pricked underneath her arms.

"*Dah!*" she shouted.

Almost spilling the pot, the tattooed lady jumped. Kim turned around. "What the hell!"

"Whatcha got cookin'?" Molly laughed.

"God, chicken soup! You almost made me spill."

Bella giggled.

"Ha-ha, want any help?" asked the redhead.

"No, I'm almost done. You could have given me third-degree burns."

"You wouldn't have spilled it." Molly walked toward the dish cabinet. "I'll grab the bowls."

"You better damn well," said Kim. She spotted Bella in the dime hallway. "And you!" She pointed with a wooden spoon.

The girl froze.

"You gonna cook the next one?"

"Oh," said Bella. "Yeah, I can"

Molly crossed the stove. "I'll put her on the chore list, ya stick. No sense getting a hissy fit about it."

"I just want to make sure we're all pitching in," Kim expressed. "There's no free loading." She stirred the pot. "Also, rent's gonna increase."

The redhead almost crashed the bowls she carried. "The hell it did! Where'd ya hear that?"

"Where do you think?"

"Can't Derrick do something about this? Like talk to Carlson for us?"

Bella chimed in, "By how much?"

"Two percent," said Kim, shaking her head. "And Derrick doesn't have any say on how landlords price their properties. He could maybe talk to him about ours." She turned off the heat. "But Carlson's a prick."

"There's probably a reason though for the increase," Bell said again.

"Come sit down." Molly motioned to her friend to sit with her, the bowls and spoons in order.

Kim hoisted the pot with rubber handles on its side. "Well...it's because of people, just us." She turned the table. "Many people want a house here. The Planned Homes are just filling up. I bet we have another nurse living with us by the end of the week."

"We don't have enough space if we keep going," Molly finished.

"Exactly," confirmed Kim, setting the pot on the table, taking her place among her roommates.

"You know," said Molly. "If you asked me, if it wasn't for that damn fence, we wouldn't be having this problem. Just get rid of it. I don't understand why we can't. It'd be too much land, too much to know what to do with."

"It's federal," said Bella.

"The state can share! Why are they hoarding it?"

"I don't know," replied Kim. "I don't follow politics."

"It's just not ours," said Bella.

"But it's so much!" said Molly.

"Maybe it's something with the wildlife."

"From the wildlife? Are you kidding me?"

"They don't tend to elaborate," said Bella. "But it's from the officials."

Kim grabbed her bowl and began pouring some of the soup in. "I just know groceries are next if rent is going up."

"Which is weird how they correlate," added Molly. "I just have a feeling the fence is cause of too much problems. Haze doesn't have one.

Refuge can expand as much as it wants into the swamp. Why can't Heartlake have her mountains back?"

"Beats me," said Kim. "It's a serious crime though, trespassing. I mean, just look at it. I bet they have some military bases on it."

Molly held out her bowl for Kim to pour into. "No, the forest is too thick. Plus we'd see air traffic."

Bella did the same.

"Well then, there are the disappearances," said Kim, and when she said this, Molly's demeanor changed.

"What do you mean?" the redhead asked.

"I don't know. I don't know what I mean." She played with her soup. "Something's happening though. And the police won't tell you."

"What disappearances?" Bella asked next.

Molly answered. "Well, we live around mountains, right? And well all over the world when there's towns and cities their tend to be disappearances. You can think most of them getting lost in the woods and such, and you know that'd be true and I'd believe it. But here, we can't do that, we can't even go to the woods. We can't go past the fence, I mean just look at it! And so when someone goes missing in Heartlake," she took a slight glance toward her roommate. "They tend never to be explainable."

"What? There's gonna be some explanation. How often does this happen?"

"It's rare, but there's a monument down at the police station for them. It's got their names and the last places they've been seen. Something for the families. But the police don't seem to have much power to stop em. They tend to blame the Pelt's though."

"That's horrible, Bella spoke. 'Why didn't I hear about this before?'

Molly sat up. "Well um. It's a-"

Kim cut her off. "I guess there's no point in worrying about it,it's not like they're gonna give much land in the future. Derrick texted me a diagram of how far they are planning on moving it, and that's if they do it. It's not a lot."

"Can we petition for more?" question the redhead.

"They never work. It's best to accept what we got and worry about tomorrow another time."

"I guess that's fine for you to say," said Molly.

"What do you mean?" Kim sensed an ounce of resentment in her roommate's statement.

"Well, you're all set if you stick with Derrick. He's a good man, with lots of money, mind you."

"Miss Pelt looking for a sugar daddy?" Kim snickered.

"I'm not saying that."

"Well, good," said Kim. "Because most of Derrick's friends are disgusted by Yudakus. They say they make girls look twenty years older."

Molly rolled her eyes. "Life would be hell with those folks anyway."

Kim nodded. "Some seem nice." She took a spoon's worth down her throat. "But yeah, they're despicable. I have no idea how Derrick can keep his soul. Maybe he'll sell it one day."

"Will you dump him?"

"Probably divorce by that time," she corrected. "But I don't know… you know." Kim sat in thought for a moment. "If what you want is a husband, you probably should ditch the knots."

Molly didn't look up from her bowl. "I'm not talking to you about this again."

"Okay. If you say so…if you say so."

Sneaking some bits in, Bella ate her soup, enjoying not feeling as the enemy and not the center of conversion. However, Kim caught sight of her, refreshing the tattooed woman on the existence of the girl.

"So does Bella have a boyfriend?" she asked.

Bella almost choked on the broth. "Oh no."

"Really? Why?"

"I'm not good with relationships."

"Like all of them?"

"Yeah. I'm okay with how it is now."

"You are?"

Bella nodded.

"You sure?" Kim asked again.

Bella nodded again. "It just complicates things, really."

"She had a boyfriend once," Molly interjected.

The girl scowled at her.

"Really?" Kim actually sounded excited. "When?"

"In high school. It was a fluke. It didn't even last a month."

"She still has his jacket," Molly cut in again.

"I forgot to give it back!" Bella almost yelled.

Kim laughed. "That fine, that's fine. But ya know how suspicious that sounds." She looked at Bella, but the girl would not meet her eyes. "But I get it." And she toyed with her soup some more. "Though I do know it's nice to have someone to come back to."

"It was nice," she admitted. "He'd wait before school started for me."

"Derrick waited until I got done with work."

"Aw, when did you meet?"

Kim pondered. "Well, we've known each other since high school. And through college we got to know each other better. He was always kinda there."

"It's always in high school," said Molly.

"Usually, you do marry someone you knew in there. I think there was a poll."

Molly stirred her bowl. "I sure hope that isn't the case."

"Why's that?" asked Bella.

Molly jeered. "I was home schooled."

"Gross," chucked Kim.

Bella laughed too. The room was left time to breathe, only filled by the clanging of spoon to bowls. The girl felt one with her peers, as if she'd been accepted into something that finally wasn't academically related. Her smile persisted. They all were happy, but Molly stared at her food, a grin waning. Bella caught her, wondering what was wrong.

Kim noticed her next and had to ask, "What's the matter?"

"Do you think we could say grace this time?"

The tattooed woman's brow bent. "We're already eating!"

"I know. But we haven't finished."

"That's not how it works." Kim took another bite.

"We can still do one," Molly defended. "It's the thought that counts."

"You honestly think there's someone poking around in the sky?" She finished her bowl, then went for seconds. "It's empty except for airplanes and satellites." Her vision intercepted the redhead, and she saw what she had said actually had an effect.

"You don't know that," stated Molly.

"I guess."

"But won't you join me?"

"No, I won't."

"What if I say—"

"No." Kim stood up. "But if you wanna pray, pray." And she went toward her room.

"All right." The redhead shifted to her friend. "Will you, Bellz?"

Bella watched the tattooed woman pass her corridor. "Oh, um… well, I don't know how."

"I'll show you!" said Molly gleefully. "Just fold your arms like this." She collapsed both arms onto each other. "And tuck your head in like this." She touched her chin to her chest. "And wait like that until I say, 'Amen,' then we can keep eating!"

The girl looked past Molly. "Why do you want to do this so bad?"

Dead air filled the room.

She then continued, "You can tell me."

"Well, it's for grace!"

"I just don't know if we should follow their tradition."

"It's a prayer. Anyone can pray. They say so!"

"But…" Bella tried to gather her thoughts. "But why start? I mean, we've never done this before. I just don't see why we need to start doing this."

"I've done it before," said Molly.

"Well ya, I bet. But I haven't. And I just felt like I had to stop you."

"Why?

"I don't know." And she felt instantly guilty, and she knew the word would sting. "It just all seems like we're pretending."

And Molly changed. Her eagerness changed into stubbornness, and she folded her arm and bowed her head. She stopped trying to convince Bella. She would prove herself.

"Dear Father in heaven," Molly began, "we thank you for this food laid before us and ask you to please bless it. We are grateful for this air, shelter, and water you so graciously made clear for us to use…"

"Molly," Bella tried to get her attention.

"And most of all, we are grateful that we all could be present here together among each other. Please bless us with good health and the strength to endure the trials you hath laid before us. We thank you for everything. And, in the name of Jesus Christ, Amen." And she ended with an uprise of her sight to Bella. She waited.

Bella stared back at her. "Well, do ya feel graceful?" She tried to be playful.

Molly didn't seem to care about the question. "I'm not pretending." She proceeded to eat.

Dinner had finished, and Kim came back out to help with the dishes and store the leftovers. There wasn't much said between the three. Bella kept in mind she had offended her friend. After bowls had been returned, Kim made the rounds to the several potted plants, a spray bottle in hand, watering her babies the exact volume each one needed before heading to her shaded room.

Bella lay on a missed bed not ready for sleep and expanded her arms and left across her sheets, multiple blankets folding in a jigsaw puzzle of no rhyme or reason. She stared at the dried paint above her. Some patterns could be discerned. Vague shapes could be connected into images of animals or murals of deformed people. Others, however, remained blots of lucid white splotches that possessed no character. But one, one did demand her attention. Not an intentional mark of ceiling, but rather willed itself together, its own creator. They all blended together, every spot. Then its eyes, that monster's eyes she saw, followed by its face.

The door flew open.

"Hey, Bellz," said Molly.

Bella sat up. "Hey."

"I just wanted to ask about what you wanted to do tomorrow."

"Um, I'm not sure." She looked back up at the ceiling. It was gone. "We could just chill here."

Molly leaned against the wall. "No, gotta do something fun. We gotta go out."

"You know, I was hoping you'd forget." Bella laughed.

"Maybe a bar," Molly said aloud. "Yeah, a bar would be good. We could chill a bit, then go to a bar."

"Don't we have work the next day?"

Molly shrugged. "We won't drink much. I know you won't drink at all." Then she chuckled. "Don't worry, it's really just a warm up. Get you outside."

"If I must."

"You don't have to be someone else. Just be you til you run out of things to say."

Bella looked at her. "I fully don't plan on talking to anyone."

"But if they talk to you, you're stuck then." Molly giggled.

"Maybe," the girl said, no longer smiling. "But just...just don't get your hopes up."

"Bellz," Molly held her head exasperated, "you need a dose of optimism in your life. I know you didn't get to experience a lot of life, but if ya never try to get out of that..."

"I'm fine not seeing it."

"How can you say that? You don't even know what you're missing."

"I saw it, it's just my day was hell. I don't want to see more of it."

"But it's all done now, isn't it?"

Bella nodded. "Yes...but it was hard, Molly. I don't mean to sound weak, but I..."

The redhead went to her friend's side. "You're not weak, Bellz. It's just that mentality. We gotta kick, then you see what you're missing!" She pulled Bella in tight. "Look, we'll get you talking to people tomorrow. Maybe even a date! Just try."

"I don't want to try," said the girl, a faint whine in her tone. "I feel bad that you have to tag me along everywhere."

Molly released her. "Don't! Don't think that!" And she gave her another hug, much to the dismay of Bella.

"I guess you don't mind..."

"Nope. I'm not gonna let you slack."

"Great," said the girl, and she released herself from Molly's grasp.

"But," the redhead retracted her friend. "Now you really don't want to go, you don't have to."

"No, I know I need to," said Bella, a smile returning to a straight face. "I'm just dreading it."

"You sure?"

"Yeah. I'll be fine."

Molly went toward the doors. "Great, I'll see ya in the morning."

"Good night," said Bella.

And her friend closed the door.

The girl watched the entrance. She half expected the redhead to burst back into the room, forgetting something in dire need to discuss, but she never did. Her guard went down. Gravity took back Bella's muscles and reframed back toward the ceiling. She lay there now, listening to the gentle settling of the house's acoustics. She wasn't sure if she wanted to remain stationary like this forever or slide to her pile of blankets and reinforce the nest once again. The seconds formed into minutes. Bella could feel them mature. She chose the latter and fell back into cover and positioned over the other, housing the plethora of folded blankets to her liking.

Bella didn't bother undressing. Her hoodie and sweats were all she wore to bed anyways. She didn't shower, but she could do it in the morning. She reached forth toward her chargers and pulled out her phone, inserting the metal tip into the phone's port. She sorted her blankets to the utmost perfect position, only her face and hand were exposed. Opening her phone and tapping into an app, she began to scroll. Through videos and pictures, she steamed past them, forgetting them all as she went. The awkward interaction with Kade; the mistake she made upon first patient Evergreen never seemed any less drastic; and the confrontation with Nelson never appeared to have even affected her. None of it mattered as she scrolled. She was occupied. She was full. What flicked upward could have been incredible passion, grand new scientific discoveries, or calls to ravish and destroy personal careers, softcore pornography, and the mindless attention-seeking individuals doing their bare minimum. It didn't matter what passed her; she gave the same reaction to all. The action was enough to busy her mind. And, satisfied, Bella sat there into the late hour of the night until she knew she should sleep. Her phone rested on her chest as the dark night gave way to blue.

Chapter

6

The birds didn't consider how much she actually slept. They shouted, they scuffled, they waged war with each other to the sun's return or just merely talking. Bella tossed back and forth, rattling her own nest at she turned as the foul fowls chatter. Usually, the morning meant extra hours to rest, but these creatures would not allow her another second. They weren't annoying, just too loud, and she found herself wishing she moved during winter.

Through the closed blinds, light creeped upon her face, coercing her to receive the day like all the others, entering on and adding to the racket of the streets. Her own mind even told her, *Get up*. It gave her no approval to say in her sheets. *Get up, you did this to yourself.* But she remained bundled in her blankets, her own way of self-rebellion, yet she didn't know it. The birds continued to sing, their own way of telling, "Get up." Bella stayed, not moving an inch.

Emerging footsteps added to the world. Bella thought it odd that someone was up and about, but she rationalized that Kim had an early shift and was preparing for it, rekindling her to a blank state. She heard a door open and close and didn't care. Most often she didn't care until she heard the ignition of a truck engine just outside. The girl sat up, the loud roar breaking her barrier and tossed her feet off the edge of the bed. Some blankets dropped to the floor, and she peaked through her blinds. She saw the driveway and Molly's truck where she left it, then she saw it backing out and pulling forward to the road. The girl first thought that her friend must have had a meeting of some kind, perhaps with those old women she mentioned, the second being a date, but Molly would have told her about that. Third was for groceries, something she knew she'd have to start pitching in for.

Bella stepped back away from the window, unsure the reason, and crossed back to bed. She sprawled over her covers, now knowing if she should start the day or waste more time. Bella aimed for the former and regretfully removed herself from her bed once more toward the exit of her room.

On the dimly lit corridor that connected Molly's room to hers, Bella looked past the hand railing of the stairs leading down beside her friend's wide open door. She had no intention to spy and coursed to the stairwell without so much as a glance toward Molly's private quarters. However, her curiosity wasn't contained and peeked into the room. The box, the tractor, and the horse were still in their place, the curtains granting them complete sunlight, Bella knowing that the first thing Molly did was probably open them. She noted thereafter a lack of equipment near the base of her bed frame. She dared a step inside the room and peered around the corner and spied a nightstand, an assortment of diverse rocks ordered in particle circular shape, being various different shapes of gray and red. Observing the stones, Bella dared another step, switching her gaze to Molly's moderate providence. There was a small dresser by the far wall, a bookshelf filled with magazines and thin novels, and closer to the girl sat a cedar chest. Bella wondered instantly where she would have gotten something of the sort. She turned to the walls, and on them, her paintings of wildlife, animals that Bella had only seen in textbooks and documentaries on the rare TV preview. Molly had one of a family of rabbits and, on this, deer and elk grazing. But oddly, one of a mountain lion near the bookshelf, its fangs were bared toward the viewer.

The girl expected most furnishings besides the chest, but they didn't really match the color of the room. What intrigued Bella though were the painting and how the brush strokes rippled the fabric of the canvases, and she checked back to the box and understood true art. A reason passed through her: *How could she afford all of this?* She believed her friend must have put nothing more than her whole paycheck into these decorations for the dark oak, and the painting didn't look cheap.

She took another step, keeping her gaze on the portrait of the lion, and walked closer to the bed covered in seamed sheets with a dozen or so pillows near its mantle.

Laughing to herself about how many pillows there were, Bella found it best to remove herself, not wanting to snoop too harshly, and left the room, shutting the door as she went. She descended down the stairs, like she intended, passing the hallway of modern art, laughing to herself even more.

Bella turned the corner and directed herself to the refrigerator. She opened it and found out how little food the food actually had, the appliance only possessing a roll of sausage, a meager block of cheese, and a quarter-filled gallon of milk sitting acutely in the corner. It affirmed the thought that her friend had gone to the grocery store, obviously knowing the lack of food before anyone else. An opportunity presented itself to which she took. Bella grabbed the sausage, the cheese, and the milk, setting them all on the counter and thought of what she could make of it. She felt ordained to fix a breakfast for her roommates. After all, they did and knew Molly would be hungry from whatever whereabout she'd stemmed back from. The girl would set aside a portion for her, but Bella had no idea the whereabouts of Kim or if Derrick had in mind to stop by. The girl looked down at their speculative breakfast, assuming the amount couldn't feed four mouths. However, there wasn't anything left in the fridge. Bella decided then to find the tattooed lady, not knowing if she was actually present in the home, to get an exact portion.

The girl could manage talking to Kim, but she wasn't excited about it. She would be brief. She would minimize the interaction. She then headed down the plant-guarded-and-shaded hallway.

Reaching the end, she recited what she would say, knuckle white and about to triplet the monotone wood.

Crying, she heard crying. Bella halted her motion, her trigger question fizzling from prompt concern. She stood there, hand still raised. She brought her ears to listen against the door. She didn't like tears. They caused her own, and she didn't like to cry. Her heels sunk in to retreat, wanting nothing more than to just leave her roommate be, yet it escaped her.

Bella knocked. "Hey, Kim?" Inside became mute. "Are you all right?"

Not a word was uttered, and the nurse stood there, regretting her words, anxious of the outcome she had set in motion. But she heard an approach to the door, and then the door itself moved back until a crack was created. Kim's eyes gleamed forth.

"H-hey, Bella." She smiled. "Y-yeah, I'm fine."

Pathos overwhelmed the girl. "A-are you sure?"

Kim nodded. "A bit at the whim of the world right now. But I'm okay."

Bella didn't understand what she meant. "Do you need anything?"

"No, I'm fine."

"What happened?"

"Nothing." And she paused for a moment, not sure whether or not to shut the door. "I...I just remember things. And...those thoughts take me back to where I was. I have these moments when...well, it's nothing to worry about. Derrick and Molly will tell you the same. There are a couple of times he got really worried, but I'm fine. I just have to get it all out, that's all." Kim wiped her face.

"I'm sorry," said Bella, taking her roommates words at face value. She instantly thought of a way to relate. "I sometimes think I'm back in the programs in Haze."

The tattooed lady sniffed. "You a trade kid. It must have been hard."

Bella nodded. "I kept to myself. It wasn't bad, just kept to myself."

Kim smiled. "Well, it helps to have someone check in on ya. Thank you."

"Oh no, worries," said the girl. "By the way, is Derrick coming for breakfast?"

"No, he's out of town for a while. He'll get back soon though."

"Great! We only have enough food really for three people right now."

Kim laughed. "I guess we should pool some money and head to the store."

Bella didn't quite get the tattooed lady's laughter. "Molly's not back yet. I'll wait a few minutes to get started."

"That sounds about right."

"Do you know where she went?"

"Beats me." She turned, signaling an end to the conversion.

"Oh, okay. Well, I'll get started in a little bit."

"Thank you," said Kim, and she shut the door.

Bella remained at the end of the hallway a bit longer. She was glad to be able to cheer her friend up, even if she didn't understand how she did so. The girl then turned and reentered the kitchen, perceiving herself as better than the version of herself mere minutes ago. It occurred to Bella that she might, in some small way, have helped her roommate. She was satisfied by the risk taken and gained more confidence for she agreed to tonight. Bella went by the table and sat down in an untucked chair, pulling out her phone. There, the girl took out her phone, until approximately seven minutes slotted by. Bella realized more time had passed than she would have liked and went to the kitchen, prepping the stove to the heat she theorized would be sufficient. She guessed a lawful medium heat and sought a flat pan to place the sausage roll, her search taking her to a cabinet right next to the stove under the marble counter. She reached down and extracted a wide enough metal slate, raising it carefully not to bag any edges. On her retrieval, she spotted the vibrant-mouthed flytrap gaping its jaws to her. Bella stopped at the sight of it, recalling the bug. She was unsettling to her that a plant of all things could eat an insect and digest an insect. It appeared that it was a devil with roots. But it had a cute pot, and Bella going about the task of cooking.

In no more than ten minutes, Bella rested the cooked meat on a plate. The girl was proud of herself, but she need to find a way to intricate a wedge of cheese and a pint of milk into the meal. She could melt the cheese, but didn't know if the others would like that as much as she would. She figured the two dairy products should be sides to the main dish and brought them all to the table.

"Kim!" she yelled, surprised by her own volume. "It's ready!"

And she heard back from the shaded hallway, a muffled response.

"Okay."

Bella waited, pressing the sausage into round bites. It didn't take her long, and she reached for her phone and performed the password. She filled the time; and before she knew it, Kim was by her side, taking a seat next to her, holding a glass of water.

"We really need to get groceries," she said, appearing cynical at the scraps of food on the table. "But the sausage looks good." She wore a cropped tank top that exposed most of her colorless ink, but shorter shorts that exposed beautiful vine-bone entanglement drawn down the length of her elegant white skin.

"Should we go after breakfast?" asked Bella.

"I guess. I have nothing better to do right now.

"What's the best place to go?"

"Full Cycle. Same place as everywhere."

"Oh, I should have guessed."

Bella scanned over the table, then gleaned to the front door. "When do you think she'll be back?"

Kim looked at the girl. "I don't know. Soon though." She checked the electric clock on the stove.

"Where is she?"

"There's a lot of places she could be. Probably out by the border somewhere."

"Why there?"

"She likes to look at the mountains."

Bella nodded, not wanting to press her further. She looked down and saw her roommate's leg. "Where did you get your tattoos from?" she asked.

Kim scanned her arm. "There's a place called Hot Steel in town. I got them a while back. It was a looooong process." She touched her bicep, recollecting the process.

"Did it hurt at all?"

"Eh, not much on the wider part of me. It felt worse on my wrists, but it still wasn't that bad. I want to get my hands done, but that's gonna be really painful." She panned up from her digits. "Are you planning on getting one?"

Bella scoffed. "Oh, no, no! I was just curious."

"Well, if you were to get one. What would you get?"

"I...I don't know." The girl looked to the floor. She remembers the painting in Molly's room. "Maybe a bunny or something."

"A bunny?" Kim's voice arched in disbelief.

"Yeah, or something like that."

"Not anything more capable?"

"Bunnies are cute."

Kim agreed. "Fair enough."

Another question reloaded in her brain. Bella fired without delay. "Is there a reason behind your tattoos?"

This was the first time Bella saw another person look toward the ground. Kim hesitated to speak. She took a drink from her water, still stalling on an answer.

"My son liked flowers."

The girl was taken aback. Her roommate was of age to have children, but she hasn't seen him once. She noted the distinction of past tense.

"Yeah." Kim stared motionless at the table. "It was something with the colors." She then, with a sudden push, got out of her chair and stood. "I'll make some coffee. You want some?"

"Oh, no. It makes me jittery." Bella watched her roommate tread behind the counter and to the coffee bean machine.

"Kim," said Bella, "where's your son?"

The coffee maker dripped a dark liquid into a glass container. Kim stood and idled, watching it slowly stemming to the pool of increasing volume. This was the only sound in the room—until the only word she could utter: " Gone."

Bella didn't have a chance to respond. She heard the front door unlock, a click that echoed through the home. She turned and saw the swing and the redhead step in, hands laced with grocery bags.

"I'm back!" Molly announced. She kicked the door with a slam. Molly marched thereafter through the hallway and stood and switched her fixation between both roommates, then the table not so full of food.

"Awww, y'all didn't have to wait."

Bella noticed that her friend had been sweating, damped sloths around her T-shirt top and shorts. The girl noticed a smooshed backpack she was bringing in and a long straw with a rubber tip that stemmed from one of the bag's pockets. Her boots here hardy, overqualified for the uneven roads and sidewalks of Heartlake, with a mild shine to them.

Bella, estranged by her appearance, asked, "Where have you been?"

Molly looked at her attire. She appeared back up with an easy response. "Getting groceries." She moved to place them on the counter.

Kim noticed Molly's shoe. "Off! Off!"

The redhead backpedaled. "Sorry! Sorry!"

"You better clean all this up!"

"I will, I will!" Molly stomped to the front door again and took off her boot. She reappeared in the room with an innocent grin.

"Just groceries?" Bella question.

Her friend turned. "Well, yeah. I might have been to one other place before that but…" She pointed to a plastic sack. "I got some great deals though! I saved so much money! Ha! I'm figuring this stuff out."

Kim checks the components of a bag. "Molly, these are all ingredients. There is not a precooked thing in here!" She then felt them. "And they're warm!"

"You save more money when you make it yourself."

Kim gave the redhead a villous glare. "Welp, guess I gotta go to the store."

"Why?!"

"Because I'm not spending two hours for a ten-minute meal. I mean, look at this. You have onions, tomatoes, lettuce, rice, flour, wh-why did you do this?"

Molly reared up a response, but Bella cut in.

"Did you buy this at Full Circle?"

"No, at the farmer's market," she rescinded and turned to the tattooed woman. "Now look, Kim, I got a bargain for all this. With everything being so expensive, maybe we have to put in a little more work."

"Would that make ya boots wet?" added Bella.

"What?" Molly turned to her.

"The processed shit is already cheap!" yelled Kim.

"It shouldn't be wet where you went." The girl pointed to the tile. There were wet bootprints shining because of the wandering sunlight.

Kim looked at Molly, and Molly at her. "Just tell her what ya do you freak."

"Freak?" the redhead protested.

"Ya you trespass on other people's property!"

"I'm there for a second!"

"You go to the backs of these homes. You follow the fence from yard to yard and pick up damn rocks!"

"You can do that!"

"You're trespassing!"

"I'm enjoying what I can," Molly spat back. "I'm just looking at the mountains! What harm is that.

"Oh my god." The tattooed lady retracted herself from the agreement, grabbing a bag and placing its components to the right location.

"I'll do it," said Molly. "You just go sit down. I'll do it."

Kim's fierce eyes lay on the redhead. "No, I will." She then turned back to her task and forced the food where it would have gone.

"Fine." Inhaling in preparation, Molly motioned to react to her roommate's word, but cut it off at the last word before. She decided against helping arrange the groceries and turned to her friend sitting on the chair waiting for her roommates to join her for her meal.

"Can we eat?" she asked.

Molly sat with Bella, staring out of the screen door to the backyard. She then looked at her friend with sadness in her eyes. "Yeah, let's eat." She looked behind her. "Kim?"

The tattoo girl knew she was hungry. "Fine." And she stopped what she was doing and sat across from the pale girl.

Molly gave a compliant smile. "I wish I could show you what it feels like. Everything feels so much fresher. And it happens out here, don't get me wrong." She motioned to the porch and the field before the mountain. "You can get closer though. There are closer places than just right here." Her eyes met Kim's. "I wish I could show you what it feels like to even be around them."

Kim took some sausage, some cheese as well. Bella did as well, starving.

"Someone will catch me, but I don't care," she continued. "I'll just go somewhere else to see them. It feels…wonderful." She paused at the word. "It feels wonderful to be so close to them." And she looked back out beyond the barrier.

Bella stared down at the floor. She munched on her cheese. She didn't care much for the conversion, only wanting to eat and maybe take a shower afterward, still deciding in her mind.

Kim saw her staring, yearning to be outside of the barbed-wire wall. She shook her head. "You know what happens if you catch someone crossing it."

"I know," said Molly. "I've heard all the stories from the Locals. But I don't know how they would have any way of catching me."

"That is dangerous thinking."

"Maybe," said Molly. "Or maybe it's what I need."

"All you need is a slap in the face," replied Kim.

The redhead smiled.

Chapter

7

Night chased away the day. Bella searched through her closet to find a perfect outfit. Molly already had one picked out for herself, and Kim pulled over her light-blue scrubs. It came to no surprise to her that the tattooed woman wouldn't join them, not after the arguments, but Bella wished she would go, only for the reason that she knew her and the nurse could have someone to talk to when her friend would ultimately be hunting for a date.

Bella didn't think she'd consume much alcohol, if any; however, it just might bolster some courage.

"Maybe just enough to look a bit longer," she said to herself. "That seems doable." Bella found herself staring goalless into her rows of clothes. If it be not work related, the item was either too soft or too big, and she wanted to look presentable, nice even. The thought of "what to wear" morphed into "what would people think of this," transferring a linear line into multitangent. She had no idea where to start, but black was more or less the safest choice he figured. She settled on a long-sleeve slim shirt and ripped black jeans and stole them from their hangers. The girl went downstairs to change in the bathroom.

Kim was lined up, the hallway light one, a rarity to be seen; and Bella snuck up beside her. She was in uniform, long sleeves covering her tattoos and collar close to her neck.

"Off to work?" asked Bella.

Kim looked at her. "Yeah. Grave shift."

"I wish you were coming."

"Eh. I'm no fun in public. I do all my drinking at home."

"Sounds a lot better." Bella grinned.

"No kidding," Kim studied the clothes folded over Bella's arm. "Those are cute."

"You think so?" Bella held them up to her chest.

"Yeah. Black always looks good."

"I hope it fits like how I remember."

Kim laughed. "You might need rubber bands."

The bathroom a door swung open. The redhead stepped out into the hallway, an open yellow jacket brandished a casual dress that hung about thigh high with a loose flounce, and a purse dangled beside her, daisies plastered all over the design. Her hair gleaned in the bathroom, all done up in a fancy bow. Her makeup was done to highlight her features, not done to drown her pores. The Yudaku hung low to her breasts.

"Any comments?" she asked.

Kim snickered and passed her into the bathroom. "Finally," she said, closing the bathroom door to her peace.

"What do you think?" she said to Bella. "Do you like it?"

Molly was far more beautiful than her. The way the redhead orchestrated her outfit, weighed the difference in pigment and came up with a combination that wasn't anything save stunning. Bella was put in shame, choosing a color to hide and blend in with the back. She didn't think she could compete with her.

"I like it," she said. "Especially the jacket. Where'd you get it?"

"Ha-ha, I just kinda acquired it. I don't really know. Maybe at a yard sale." She toyed with one of the zippers on it. "What about the perfume? Does it smell nice?"

Bella leaned in and smelled the aroma. "Smells great."

Molly smiled. "Good, good. Because it wasn't cheap! God, I thought gonna have to give an arm for it too."

"Mine was at a reasonable price. I'm not gonna tell you where I bought it from." She gave a small giggle.

"What is it?"

"I can't remember its name. But it smell like pineapple the last time I used it."

"When was that?" joked Molly.

"High school."

"Oh, use mine! That's way too old!"

"No, I feel bad. It's just gonna go to waste on me."

"It's not!"

"I'll just stick to my pineapple."

"It's okay, I offered."

"It's fine. I'm fine."

"Oh, please take some!"

The bathroom door then opened a second time. Kim stepped. Her hair was damp, and she was in the process of braiding it.

"All yours."

Their roommate passed the girls, Bella noticing no scent on Kim. She then crossed into the bathroom and shut the door. Molly must have stopped her while the tattooed woman went her way, she heard the muffled conversation.

"We can see if you want to do something tomorrow," said Molly.

"Nah," replied Kim. "Just watch out tonight. And be responsible for Bell too. Don't get her into anything stupid. And you're driving, so don't drink."

"I won't."

Kim shook her head, and continued to the kitchen before she was stopped again.

"I'm wiser than you think."

Kim sighed. "Change your shirt. Keep the Yudaku covered."

"Why the hell would I do that?"

Bella sprayed her perfume on and began dressing in her new clothes. She wanted to hurry, not wanting them to get into another fight. But she really wanted to do some light makeup work.

"You're not gonna find any local men there," Kim said.

"You don't know what bar where going to," said Molly.

"You're not going to a hole in the wall dressed like that. You want to impress."

Bella began adding eyeliner and some blush. She tried to be swift.

"You just hate to see me wear it," said Molly. "It makes your blood boil. But I have news for you—I'm not taking this off until the day I'm married."

"You're like a child! You really are. It's like your dad didn't set you down and really explained the world."

"Don't even mention my dad."

"Or maybe you choose to be this retarded," added Kim.

"You're a real cynic, you know that?"

The bathroom door opened for a third time. Bella stepped out to rejoin her party. She wore her dark wardrobe. They fit freely on her body. Her emerald eyes were highlighted by the eyeliner she used. Her hair was straight down and slightly curled at the tips.

"Look at you!" said Molly. "You look like a gothic queen!"

The dark lady panned down to herself. "Really?" she said, stretching her shirt out almost like a curtsy. The shirt possessed a white logo on the front in electric lettering that made it impossible to read.

"Yes, really!" exclaimed Molly.

Kim peered from the kitchen. "Yep, ya look single."

Molly glared back at her roommate. "Don't listen to her."

"Just being observant." And the tattooed woman moved from the line of sight. She sought something from the kitchen, settled on an apple she found, and came back. She passed them and went to her room.

"Still cynical," Molly said.

"Don't let me stop you at the door." She entered her account and cut the pair off.

"Come one, let's go," and the redhead lead the way.

Bella followed.

Now in motion, the girl's anxious heart could not believe what she was about to attempt, what everyone could. She felt awful, that she wanted to stay and maybe save herself some embarrassment. Her stomach tied in knots. But she couldn't leave now. Molly required her to go, and it wouldn't appeal to her if the girl was too weak. And it was strength to go along. Yes, strength.

"You excited?" Molly asked, leading to the garage.

"Yes," said Bella.

"You sure?"

"Positive."

The pair made their way to the truck. Molly clicked a remote pad that raised the garage doors. They jumped inside the vehicle, not wasting a second any longer, and the redhead started the engine, and she backed out into the driveway.

Staggering and jolting, Molly's tuck trailed the Heartlake roads. Bella rested her head on the passenger side window. She liked the town at night. It appeared peaceful, no crowds of people wandering the sidewalks. They had yielded at the stop sign, and Bella observed the vibrant red, and just below and at a paper poster, a hard to see figure and below it the emboldened word:: "Missing." She stared at the picture, not even thinking of bringing it up to Molly, and the rustic truck drove on. There was another just underneath it.

They headed toward the northeastern quadrant, traveling a similar course to her work route, hooking a left rather than driving through. The car in front of them directed to the same place, and shortly after another right, the pair arrived at a glowing neon sign, "Drop Inn." There were no parking spaced on the side of the street. Molly drove on.

"We just gotta find a place to park."

The redhead circled the block around the bar until she found a cement tower, to which she drove to the opening. A yellow-and-black striped mechanical arm blocked their way, and a machine similar to an ATM signed to pay. Molly rolled next to it, barely avoided the height limit bar millimeters from the top of the vehicle. She opened her purse and inserted cash into a slit. The machine beeped, and the arm retracted, and the girls carried on into the vicinity, desperate for a free spot. They ended up at the third story until Molly saw an open lot and shouted in glee. She sped toward it and turned sharply into the stall.

Bella still felt nauseous getting out of the vehicle, contemplating whether it was Molly's driving or the roads. It could have been for the unknown, to which Bella filled by seeking optic information of the parking tower's exposed pipes and wires.

Molly pointed out the stairs and crossed toward them. They descended each concrete slab, Bella spying how unphased the redhead appeared.

I'm a baby, she thought. *A true coward*. And she continued with them.

They joined on a sidewalk, merging with the slight stream of nightgoers. Bella clung near her friend, fearing getting lost, but if she ever did, Molly's height was sure to help her, standing taller than the average man. They didn't have to walk far to be in sight of the bar. Molly became ecstatic, bumping her friend to look at neon rays. It didn't look like a bar, being twice the size of one, and it had more decorations then it warranted. It appeared as a fast-food and bar hybrid. She didn't get the appeal. A line was in front of them. They halted. A generous number of people were waiting in the night.

A cold gust of wind cut through her clothes. The line moved slowly, and she pondered why there was even a line in the first place. Bella didn't want to go, but rather to be out of the chilling breeze. This building, connected to its siblings in a single mold, had a different smell to it, an oddity that unsettled her; but she ignored this feeling. She noticed from the warehouse-like doors, on the opposite lane they were waiting in. Some people were leaving, escorted by a fat bouncer. They appeared sick.

As the line stuttered forward, Bella noticed the individuals were being turned away, sometimes pointed violently to a direction, but resisting and parting words with the bouncers responsible. "Cocksucker" and "asshole" being the frequent words used. Bella couldn't hear much of the dialect used, but whenever a man was repulsed, he would walk away while saying these things, the bouncers daring them to come back. The girl didn't see any women being turned away.

"I wasn't expecting this," Bella said to Molly's ear.

"Yeah, so it's like a nightclub," replied Molly. "But don't worry! It's super nice, and it has a bar on the inside! It had good reviews."

Bella nodded. Her friend's assurance over the establishment calmed her. She felt her stomach shift somewhat back to a normal state.

Over many moments, the pair trudged closer to the opening of the nightclub, watching more people leaving and entering. Bella required more information. First was the smell of smoke alchemized with sweet and alcohol, second was loud music of an irritable kind that most people seemed to enjoy, and third was the bouncer searching each paid customer with his hands, presumably for weapons. Bella disliked the idea of him touching her. It made her skin crawl, but she kept silent knowing it was all part of the formula to get inside.

"Does he have to pat you down?" she asked her friend.

"Yeah, he's just to make sure you don't have something you shouldn't"

Bella bobbed her head. They were moving toward the building faster now. Whatever the problem was had been resolved. As she stood closer, she saw a paper in the corner of the glass. There was a photo of a man on it again with the word "MISSING." She thought nothing of it.

Before the girl could realize, she and the redhead were near the front of the line. Molly followed after the person in front of her, and the bouncer spotted her necklace. He patted her down, head to toe. The redhead almost laughed, then she slipped inside.

To which the bounce then beckoned Bella. The girl froze for a split second, then waited for the man to do his job. He told her to spread her arms out, and she did as instructed. She anticipated the touch and felt the palm of his hand pat around her ankles, then rise higher, searching her leg and up to her hip. She didn't like him around her pelvis, but he then went to her sides and up to her shoulder. It was over in an instant. The bouncer then hurried her alone inside the nightclub, and Molly stepped to her side, locking arms.

Vibrations reverberated through her skeleton. A cascade of beams of every color overwhelmed Bella's senses. It blinded her. However, she was being towed by the redhead, not affected by the splendor, driving forward, the girl having complete trust in her. Bella recalled bumping into several drunks and maybe some dancer, then stopping suddenly while feeling others moving around her.

Just barely, Bella heard her friend say, "Let's settle at the bar!" Then a resonance formed, and she responded, "Okay."

They began to move again. Bella being tugged along again, hitting several more dancing women that she felt sorry to touch. She decided to open her eyes then, wanting to knew her surroundings, and saw all around a cord of people dancing in every which way, and to the far side of the large room where a stage sat with current broad presentation was a man behind a throne desk with circuits and computers, disks and speakers that he alternated from. Molly pulled her on, and they zigzagged through the crowd, and almost-naked women in groups of threes moved toward them. A section of the club dialed down from the chaos captured them. There they broke free and emancipated themselves, stepping up, and wandered over to a velvet row of bars stools, mirroring those used in spy movies Bella remembered seeing. The actual bar was of dilated polished wood, a bottle of every imaginable liquor behind on shelves that reached and fused with the ceiling. And surrounding them were booths, fitted with more velvet and cushioned seats with friends, workers, and couples drunkenly expressing themselves with glasses of various volumes, some holding the desire to be taken back home with whom they spoke.

It was much more pleasant here. Bella noted the actual light sockets that dripped a cool amber on its customers. She could think here.

Molly led her to an empty bar stool, avoiding several other patrons standing about. Bella sat down, her friend next to her. The girl in the polished wood greeted her sight, her worried eyes reflecting back to her. The bartender, too enthralled in his work, didn't notice them at first. The redhead, with electricity in her spine, spun in the stool taking in the scene, and even into the dance floor that passed.

She then turned to Bella. "We're here!" she said, "We're here, we're here, we're here!"

Bella reared up. "Yeah. I hated the first part."

"I didn't expect that ether. But the bar is really nice!"

"What do we do now?" asked Bella.

"Hmm…" Molly turned back to the buzzing setting, then behind the counter. "I guess we'll get some drinks." She flickered to Bella's face and noticed a grim expression. "What's wrong?"

The girl's first instinct was to be dismissive. "Nothing. Nothing's wrong!" Her inside whispered their complaints.

Molly's face twisted. "You don't look all right. You sure?"

"Yes, yes! Now I wanna try some of this."

"Hell, yeah!" And she faced the bar and waited for the tender.

Bella knew she wasn't okay, but hid it. She wanted to be strong.

"Are sure you're okay?" Molly glanced back over to her.

"Yes!" the girl said quickly.

"Okay, okay." She raised her hand to be noticed. Molly readied a response, then saw the bartender.

Bella saw him move over in reply. He wore a collared shirt with a striped apron dangling from his neck. His sleeves were rolled, exposing many sea-life-related tattoos, more noticeable a lobster on his forearm.

"Hallo," he said to Molly. "What can I get ya?"

"Oh, uh." She paused for a second. "I like your voice." And then she turned to her friend. "What would ya like? I'll pay."

"Whatever you're getting," the girl responded.

Molly whipped back to the bartender with a smirk. "Two margaritas, please!"

The bartender reciprocated and left to fetch the right pump of inheritance for his customers. As he worked, Molly turned back to her friend.

"I think he likes me," said Molly.

"He's a bartender," Bella said gleefully.

"Well, don't ya always find a way to bring me down."

"Aren't they supposed to be nice?"

"Ha, yeah," said Molly. "But thanks."

"Oh, you're welcome."

"He's cute though," said Molly. "I like his tattoos."

Bella peered back to the man creating her drink. "Yeah, he's pretty cute." And the girl zoomed in on his left hand, a gold band fitting perfectly around his third finger.

"I see a ring though," she said.

"Damn it." Molly saw it as well. "Foiled again."

The girl scanned along the couples chatting among themselves, sleazy arms over each other's waists. They all appeared to be having a great time. She heard laughing all around. She forgot about her stomach in that instant. The girl began understanding this place.

Bella panned along the scene until she got to a group of men, mostly all in black, pints of beer on their table. There were boosting among themselves, jewelry chains around each of their necks. They seemed to have a fair bit of money, with their attire and the shape they were in. But she felt a stare unable to distinguish its origin. Thereafter, a morsel stubbed, prompted by a jeering jab, and gave way to a thin man, sitting on the group's branches, eye fixated upon the girl.

The bartender set two glasses filled with a smoothie-like texture of red liquids on the bartop. "Here ya go, miss."

"Thank you!" Molly reached for her card.

"Oh no, miss," said the bartender. "First drinks free for the ladies."

"Really? Since when?"

"Policy." He smiled again. "Just shout for refills." And he went along quenching others thirst.

Molly prodded her friend. "We need to come here more often."

Bella spun back around to the bar. "What?"

"I said we need to come back here more often. Here's your drink."

Bella grabbed the glass. She liked the fruit spewed on the edge and the petite umbrella that stood up at an angle.

The girl felt exposed, feeling the stare as she was too aware to look back. She saw Molly drink, and waiting a moment longer, she then had courage to try it herself and brought her lips to the skewered fruit. Her tongue greeted the mushed liquid and recoiled at the kick. But she knew someone was looking at her. That feeling never left her. Bella then forced the beverage down like a shot, trembling after the fact and swallowing.

Molly saw Bella struggling out of the corner of eye. "Are you okay?" she initially asked.

Bella smiled, attempting to remain calm. "Yeah, yeah, I'm fine."

"You might wanna just sip on it, Bellz. You don't just throw it down."

"I think I handled it…" And she gasped for air.

Even the bartender looked over. "Are you okay?"

Bella nodded, and her lack of color became pink. She didn't dare look. She'd become a mockery. The man and his friend, she predicted, were recoiling, slapping their knees from such an obvious display from a nondrinker. She felt no eyes on her. She knew she blew it.

The girl took refuge in the sight of the many bottle's behind the bartender. She tried to forget she was even in the nightclub, gently squinting to try and view the labels and which year they were brewed. She almost went for the device in her pocket.

A touch, a tap on her shoulder then made itself known. Bella turned with a burning on her tongue and a disillusioned mind. There stood the man who watched her across the room. Bella first witnesses his expensive shoes, then his sleek white pants, next a brand-designer shirt. His skin was well kept with strong cheekbones and jaw. His hair was dirty blond and was conditioned as much as a woman's. He wore square glasses that aided planning blue eyes.

"Hey," he spoke to Bella. "How's it going?"

Blank. The girl's mind mirrored blank. The sight of the man shoved her into realms and possibilities. *How could it be?* she thought inward. *Is he doing what I think he is?* She attempted to respond.

"G-good!" she squeezed out. "H-how are you?"

"I'm fantastic," he said. "You look amazing by the way. The plain black is stunning."

Molly looked over to the commotion. Complete glee was smoothed onto her.

"Thank," replied Bella. "You look good too."

"Thank you," he said. "What's your name?"

Bella saw past him. His posy watched, but two of which appeared frightened. She went back to the floor. "Bella. Bella Tomson."

"I like that name. I always loved names that started with the letter *b*." He stuck out his hand. "My name is Oscar, Oscar Dmitri."

Bella took the open palm, and his fingers almost wrapped around back to his knuckles. His skin felt tight, like something pulling fabric over plastic.

Oscar's eyes rolled to the empty glass. "I'll grab you the next one." He smiled.

"O-oh no, this will probably be my last."

He sat down next to the girl. "How will you ever hold your liquor if you never go hard?"

"The taste," she said plainly. "I don't like the taste."

"Why not?"

She struggled to find an answer. It felt like an audit question. "I don't like how it burns," she concluded.

"You're not really a regular here then, are you?"

"Yeah." Bella nodded, not knowing how to continue the conversation.

"What else do you drink?"

"Really just water." She laughed to herself.

"What about tea?"

"I'm afraid I won't like the taste."

"But you seemed to never had a margarita before."

Bella sought rebuttal. "I don't think I'll try anything new again."

Oscar stared at her. He kept his smile, but the girl knew he was thinking, perhaps on what to say next. Bella then began fathoming a way to keep talking. Her mind went a million miles a second. She then felt the man's stare migrate.

Molly chimed in. "She has other qualities though!"

In the instant the word left her friend, red flushed through the girl's pale cheeks. The man looked past the girl to the redhead, scanning her up and down. His eye fell on the Yudaku so close to her breasts.

"Don't you look like a model." He stood up and approached the redhead. "How the hell are ya?"

Molly smiled involuntarily. "Oh no, I didn't mean..." Her eyes darted between the man and her friend. "I-I'm good. I'm good. But Bella here is good too."

"What's your name?"

"Molly," replied the nurse. "I overheard. Oscar, right?"

"Ha! I knew you were eavesdropping."

"I didn't mean to. My friend here, see, is pretty nervous." She rubbed Bella's arm.

"Ha, well, no kidding." He moved his vision between her and the knots. "But you seem well enough though."

Molly laughed. "Well, it's not my first rodeo, buster."

"So you come here often? I haven't seen you before."

"No, I meant that I just come to bars often. I ain't never been to this one, but it's lovely."

"It is, ain't it? Not as much as yourself, of course, but still pretty."

Molly was confused for a moment, then realized the man's attraction. "Oh, oh! Why, thank you. You're so sweet!" She looked at her friend. Deep down she knew she'd stolen his attention.

Bella had failed to impress. She knew she wasn't cut out for this place or the task she was supposed to achieve. She pulled out her phone.

"You mind if I pay for your next drink?" Oscar asked.

"Oh, not at all!" exclaimed Molly, turning back to him. "Why would I mind? Come sit with us! We can make some room."

"I'm fine just standing."

Bella understood envy but was somewhat relieved she didn't have to fake a rhythm and make the beats presented by the man. What Molly did would always happen. It didn't sting as bad this time, for she prepared herself. Nothing could harm her, for she knew everything. Yet the girl's stomach twisted.

"Would you like to do shots?" Oscar asked.

"I have to drive home later." Molly giggled. "But I wouldn't mind a beer?"

"What kind?"

"Any!"

Bella glanced at the men in their booth. Majority of them had resumed their rowdiness, jeering, and guzzling; but the two who had seemed unpleased sat mute. They were fixated upon themselves. They reminded Bella of herself, scared to even speak. They unsettled her and carried on with her screen. Nevertheless, the feeling lingered, and she began to think about what they know.

"So you're a business guy?" asked Molly.

"Yes," answered Oscar. "I work for the Hedge Foundation. We meddle in stocks and such."

"That's wonderful! Does that mean you're rich?" she teased.

"I'm wealthy." He stretched a grin. "My folks are incredibly happy for me, considering their Locals and didn't have a lot to work with when raising me."

Molly looked at him with a discovered joy. "You're a Local?"

"Yes. That's why I had to come over to you." And he pointed to her chest.

"Where'd your parents live?"

"The house's been sold. They're gone now. But around the northeastern side."

"Aw, I'm so sorry." She stood up to hug him. "What was their name?"

He took her in his arms. Bella glanced at the scene, wondering how Molly was ever single to begin with.

There was a delay. "John and Sue Crawford," he said.

"I'm so sorry for your loss," said Molly.

"It's all right, but ya know, I'm moved by a Yudaku when I see them."

"Were you taught then?"

He nodded. And Molly blushed.

"None of them are Locals," Oscar continued, pointing to the mob he sprung from. "It's real sad to see how they treat them. You know, what's said behind closed doors. Sometimes they forget I'm one, and I have to remind them." He kept his smirk.

"I know. It boils my blood to see it happen. One of my best friends is an ex-Pelt, and she says the meanest things about them. It's hard to handle sometimes."

"But you do! And I can tell that you're tough. I like it."

Molly giggled. "Most men would disagree with you."

"Most men are pigs," he said.

"But you're not!"

Bella shot a concerned glance at Molly. The redhead ignored it. Bella felt something was off, but kept to herself. It would be a lie to say she didn't miss the attention.

"Thank you," replied Oscar. "I think I'm already falling in love with you."

"Really?" The redhead's eyes lit up.

The pit grew deeper in Bella's stomach.

The man nodded. He batted an eye to the commotion of the club and back to his men. "I didn't think I'd find someone like you in a place like this."

"Why?"

Oscar looked for the bartender. "I did to get you your drink. Are you sure you won't do a shot with me? Have you ever done them?"

"Yeah," Molly said. "Then shit faced in the morning."

The man laughed a bellow, and his mouth was so wide. Bella spied up from her phone the moment she heard his shrill and witnessed the uncanny. The proportions seemed all wrong to her. He appeared an almost monster, and it flung Bella past what was unknown. She turned to her friend. Molly wasn't the least bit aware.

"Will do one with me?" he asked.

Molly bounced her head. "Sure."

"Good call." He flagged the bartender down. "Excuse me, two shots of tequila, please. You know what I like."

The bartenders obeyed and placed several short glasses on the bar and began filling each and every one with a clear liquid. He didn't even charge Oscar.

"Shiny," exclaimed Molly. "You sure now have a night off."

"I know how to end it too." He smiled.

Over to the side, Bella hid her attention into the blaring screen. She overheard everything, but attempted not to. She was becoming sicker and sicker until the point of physical intervention, and she pressed her stomach. In her already-pale complexion, she sensed what little tint she had was drained. A wreck, but afloat, she needed to keep herself together and get through the night. She only wished that Molly would wrap up her conversation with her new boyfriend, and they could leave back home. And with the tone of their voices, she hoped it'd be soon.

"I like you, and I want to treat you with something," said Oscar. "Are you free tomorrow?"

"Oh," she shot a glance toward her friend. Bella didn't look at her, spending all mental ability to keep herself together. "Yeah, I think so."

"At one, would you like to go someplace?"

"Where?"

"Somewhere secret."

Molly's lips were to part with a sudden and enthusiastic, "Yes."

Next came a gargle and a sound that bubbled. A sudden chunky volume flooded the bar and onto the floor. They both recoiled in disgust. The bartender flinched to grab the mop and some rags. Others behind the counter dove in to help clean the mess. All eyes lock on the girl, an utter look of horror at what had just happened.

Chapter

8

The smell lingered in the truck. Molly kept steady at the wheel, trying to not mind the stench. She felt horrible. She couldn't imagine the shame, any stains of confidence lost.

Bella lay against the door, unbuckled. The girl watched the shroud cities escape her, wishing she was dead.

How could you? she thought. *How could you?*

The random jostling and bumping of the road paid no treatment. Her stomach still would have turned on its own accord, discounting the road, unable to find unity with the rest of the vessel. More than ever did she hate herself, more than the days alone where kids with no parents go, more than the nights secluded in her dorm room wishing she was someone else, more than when she had to say goodbye to the only boy who ever cared. She blamed it on the recency and tried to forget.

They merged onto main street and headed north to their accord.

Molly was tempted to drive home, anticipating it to be the right move. She noticed however the roads were hardly business, and main street wasn't the least bit in a rush. She spied thereafter, the opening of grass and the raised ditch and the curvature of the fence. The redhead had no right, expecting her friend to be fluid with contempt of her. But Molly knew the lake to be a great place that could heal. The Locals thought so, and so will she.

Tires crunched earth, and some grass folded. Molly parked the truck. The truck sat suspiciously off the side of the road.

"What are we doing?" questioned Bella.

"I want you to get some air," replied Molly.

"I feel fine. Let's just go home."

"No, there's a really good breeze here. Trust me. It will help."

"You keep saying that. But it rarely does."

"Only for a few minutes," Molly turned, the first serious tone Bella had heard from her.

The girl heard this and was baffled by the fact Molly wanted to do this. She was done with adventures and longed for her sheets and blankets, an isolated room separate from the world. But she too noticed the shrouded city around them. She looked onto the dike, then back, then in front of her.

Only for a few minutes," repeated in her mind. Her stomached shared some mercy. "Fine." she said. "Just a little bit.

Molly opened her door and was relieved from the stench, rolling her window down to air out the vehicle at the left. They were greeted by a fragrance of pollen and pine needles along with dense wind drifting aimlessly across the grasses. Bella spied there the embankment, a hill, and followed Molly up to the old hikers' trail that outline the reservoir, now split in half by the steel-gated gate. Wildflowers reached from the tan dirt. Bella hadn't seen one that wasn't in ink. Molly reached the gate. Bella stared through its interlocking hide and at the cascade of rocks and the swamp membrane that gave way to the glittering waters reflecting a silver moon's light back through the sky. Through the fence, there was a section of blank space where only the path, the rocks, and the mountain behind it could be seen. However, the booth's areas led to patches of forests distanced from the other woodland scabs on the Giant. There were instances of water-loving trees such as willow and river birch as well as normal wood of oak and pine and common plants: cattails, moss, and micro lily pads in masses that were visible. Water fowl inhabited close to the plant environment, settling for their bed, a higher variety then those seen in Refuge. Bella even believed she spotted an eagle's nest toward the left in the many willows. She was more taken aback by its awe rather than its aroma.

The redhead let her stand on her own.

"Take some deep breaths." said Molly, inhaling too. "Like we did on the lawn. Just look at the water."

The girl inhaled. She didn't believe a word her friend said. But she would rather focus on the lake. "It's stunning," she said.

"It is helping?"

"A little. It's beautiful."

"It is," agreed Molly. "You know it's funny, I forgotten how pretty the reservoir can be." She brushed a steel slot. "It'd be better without this damn fence. They could at least give us some water."

"It's still beautiful," said Bella.

"Yeah." And she looked like someone who longs to touch what couldn't. "I wonder how many swords and axes are in here."

The girl recalled the local performing their ritual. "Probably a lot. By the sounds of it."

"Unfortunately. I hope they get used." And she turned to the embankment. "Ready to go?"

"Just a few more moments."

The redhead smiled and faced the water again.

The girls stayed there for the undefined and unestablished span they set. They heard frogs croak poems to one another, crickets playing to fill silence, and the ever so often disturbance caused by a fish gulping down some unfortunate gnat or fly that flew too close gazing into their reflections. Peace, somehow from a human-made means created harmony. All these songs in all different keys structuring into one. A particular note caught Bella's attention: A crane near the right side of the reservoir standing in shallow water close enough to be seen but far enough away to be comfortable squawked and an unfortunate trill. It possessed a white plumage and a sharp needle beak. Hanging down in the water was a mangled leg, torn in some unbelievable way. Compassion flushed within the girl at the sight of the bird's disability, a reconnaissance she deployed, how a terrible act as such could happen in just a beautiful place to such a beautiful animal. She wanted to instantly help the poor creature for whatever reason she could not explain. And for whatever intention, the bird grew bored in its current environment and began to limp closer to the bank. It was in pain. She couldn't believe it was in pain. Bella took liberty in scanning out the patch where the bird directed itself toward. And in the brush, an outline in the shadows was made known to her. The girl looked closer, unbelieving what she saw, figuring an illusions of sorts. Under the willow, crouched, but taller than anything she'd ever encounter, was man, watching this bird hop toward him. A loneliness was engraved by decades upon lines of his faces, a long braided bread dripped over his chest, an axe in his hand.

He was over the fence. This thing was over the fence. He noticed the girl.

"Do you see that!" She pointed beyond the barrier.

Molly turned to her. "See what?"

"That man, look!"

And the redhead followed Bella's finger, but nothing save the crane was in the brush.

"There was a man there," claimed Bella. "He was sitting down. He was on the other side!"

Molly searched and searched. "Where? Where? I don't see him."

Bella jogged to her right to gain a better view. Her friend followed. They halted.

"He was right there, right where that branch bends."

"Are you telling the truth?"

Bella looked at her stunned. "Yes, he was over there."

Molly took one more glance to the reservoir, then back to her friend. She turned for the hill. "Let's go home."

"We need to tell the police! He can't be over there!"

"We're going home."

Bella watched her friend descend the dike. The switch in demeanor put her off. She scanned back to the tree line and reminisced about that man. There was nothing. Molly was serious. She started the vehicle. Bella made her way down, wondering to herself if she was crazy.

The drive home was quiet. Questions pressurized inside the girl's skull, yet she would not ask them. They arrived back at their establishment a few minutes later, an itchy and uncomfortable travel, however the stench had gone. Molly parked inside the garage this time. Kim's car was gone, and the pair wasted not a second entering inside and not a minute departing to their rooms. She wanted to know so badly, yet all the notion she got from her friend was "Good night." Through the girl's mute language, she wanted to resolve whether she was insane or whether someone had seen that man before. Bella changed her clothes and washed herself. She took to her phone in order to investigate her sighting. It proved to be in vain, and she was left scrolling her usual apps to forget. But she could not forget and was left with restless sleep.

Morning came too soon. Even Molly had slept in, or at least, Bella didn't hear her leave. Birds delivered a duller display today and appeared more often on branches than in flight.

The girl had woken on her own accord, prompted by no animal or human action. It was early. Sunlight crept through the always-closed blind. She wanted to check her phone and tore and arm through the nest and reached for it in her nightstand. Bella brought the device closer to herself and clicked the power button to the side. It didn't respond. Irritated and panicked, she checked around her, shifting the blankets around, and found what she sought. She pulled out her changing cord and threaded it into the phone's receiver. The girl was peeved and blamed herself for not plugging it in before. She folded her arms across her knees, forming a ball, and sat, waiting for a significant battery charge to begin scrolling. But as she sat there, a recollection formed from yesterday.

Bella didn't mind; she was used to getting overshadowed by Molly. Oscar seemed like a dick anyway. But it was horror to know that she threw up in public, the worst thing that could ever happen to someone, outside of being fired. The worst combination in her mind was to have thrown up at work, then getting fired for it. She shivered at the thought.

And then there was the reservoir. She had no way to convey if she had imagined the whole thing. However, her friend's response made her think that there was something, maybe not what she thought she saw, but something.

The girl checked her phone to see its percentage. It seemed adequate. She held the power button to restart the device.

Then came a knock at her door, just as she settled herself in.

"Come in," Bella said.

Molly stepped into the room wearing a soft-pink jacket that complemented her well, jeans with no holes, makeup done with sharp mascara, and her hair done up. She presented herself with a warm smile and a travel bag to her waist.

"Hey, how are you feeling?" she asked.

Bella looked at her. "Good. A lot better than last night."

"That's good. You were so sick. I didn't know if I should take you to the hospital."

Bella laughed. "I won't go there willingly."

Molly approached the bed and moved some blankets for a spot to sit. "The reservoir definitely helped."

"I think it did."

"You actually?"

Bella nodded.

A big smiled swept across Molly's face. "You know I tried to take Kim there during...well, I bet she told you, and she even said she liked it."

"Really? How'd you even get her to go in the truck with you?"

"Wasn't easy, but I really do believe there's something about that lake."

Bella put her phone down. "The Local's believe so."

"Yeah, that they do. And I think they're right."

"What about that guy?"

"What guy?"

"The one I saw." Bella adjusted herself to sit more upright. "You didn't seem to want to stay after that."

"I don't know if there was a guy," said Molly. "If there was, he was probably a Local. You know they still have ways to get their furs. Sometimes that means they got to get their hands dirty."

"How would he get through the barrier?"

"Beats me. They don't trust me enough to tell me that sort of thing."

"They don't?"

The redhead nodded. "I wasn't born into it. They think I'll rat them out. But that the furthest thing I could do!"

The last word lingered for a moment. Bella collected her thoughts. "What would you do?"

"Well...I'd join them.

"But you'd go to jail. It's breaking the law."

Molly edged herself toward the end of the bed. "I want to see what's up there. Is that a crime?"

Bella nodded. "It's federal land."

"You don't understand." The redhead stood up. "Maybe you'll get around to it once I show ya some more spots."

"I won't trespass."

"We're not gonna trespass!"

"Hey!" Kim shouted from the bottom of the stairwell. "I'm hungry! Let's get some of these shitty ingredients together!"

"Coming!" Molly yelled through the open door. She bobbed her head in that direction as well, without a word between them.

Bella sat up from bed and followed. She didn't even know what clothes she put on before she went to bed. She looked down and saw a purple hoodie and leggings.

Molly got to the kitchen, and Bella saw Kim in a flurry, collecting enough information to figure out what to cook. A flytrap mouth sat with a snapped-closed mouth.

"I don't know where I put shit," said Kim, her sleeve rolled to expose her elegant artworks.

Molly went to her side. "What are you doing?"

There on the counter sat a head of lettuce, onions, and a dozen eggs.

"I don't know! Help me figure this out."

"Burritos" said Bella suddenly.

Her roommates both looked at her.

"Let's make hot burritos."

Molly appeared puzzled. "You sure? It might…" And she circled her hand around her own stomach.

"That's a brilliant idea," said Kim. "I think." And she went to the fridge. "Yeah, there's some more sausage. We can do breakfast burritos."

"Sure," said Bella. "Do we have any peppers?"

"Yeah, I think Molly got some. Check the pantry."

"I'll get them," the redhead said. "Let's put everything in separate bowls though and roll them yourselves." And she went to fetch them in the pantry.

"What's the matter, Molly?" asked Kim. "I thought you loved spice."

"Well, I'd have it," said Molly, and she hesitated. "But I'm going on a date today around noon. I don't really want any issues."

Kim stopped what she was doing. She peered to Bella, then back to Molly. "A date with who?"

An obvious excitement lay within the redhead's voice. "There was guy from the bar who asked me out."

"What?!" Kim's eyes widened. "Was he drunk?"

"No. He acted normal."

"And you said yes?"

"Yes!"

The tattooed lady laughed, setting the meat down on the counter. "Well, that's great. I'm happy for you."

"You don't sound too pleased." Molly set the peppers.

"How'd he ask you?"

"He asked if I was free tomorrow and I said yes. Then, uh..." Molly glanced at the girl. "We had a little incident. Someone threw up next to us, and it caused such a stir. We moved away, and he asked for my number to establish things. He didn't say what we were doing, but he said it was gonna be fun."

Kim turned to the girl. She'd gotten a knife from a drawer. "This true?"

Bella nodded, grateful Molly didn't divulged her identity to be the one who chucked her insides all over the bar.

"See. Oh!" And the redhead also faced her. "He also mentioned a friend, Bellz. If you want to go, we could make it a double date!"

"I don't think it's a good idea," returned Kim. "He's your date. Don't get Bella involved."

"What do you say?"

The feeling in the girl's stomach returned. The thought going back into that world, nevertheless with a complete stranger, overwhelmed her.

"I don't think I can handle that right now," she said.

Molly appeared disappointed.

Kim stared at her, then moved to the oven to preheat. "What did he do to make you say yes, Molly?"

"What do you mean?" she responded.

"Oh, you know. You don't go on dates that much. Every time I see a guy ask you out, you've turned him down. How's this one different?"

"Oh, that's easy. He's a Pelt!"

"Oh, Jesus."

"What?" Molly watched her roommate cross to pick up the sausage and spatula.

"I think I would have liked to be there when he asked you."

At this, Molly's nose wrinkled and brow tightened "What's that supposed to mean?!" There came a response from Kim, busy orienting the pan. And Molly, offended, turned toward her product. She withdrew a board and began to chop potatoes, peppers, and onions. Halfway through, she returned to the tattooed lady. "What's that supposed to mean, Kim?"

Bella was afraid her friend might lose a finger. She did her best to do what needed to be done. Kim, she thought, would do the eggs, and Molly obviously handled the cutting. *Cheese!* she thought. The girl went to the fridge to retrieve a thick wedge of the produce and returned to the counter. She found her own knife and bowl and began slicing cubes.

Molly put all the items she chopped into distinct plates or bowls and set them over to where Bella had placed her cheese cubes. She raised a brow at the shapes. Kim took the longest, making sure there was no pink in the sausage. She then hurried with the eggs, scrambling them and scooping them out. She brought her component to where the others were. Together they made their food. A bitter feeling corrupted the air. Molly was still annoyed that Kim wouldn't answer her question. They rolled their food, while the redhead strayed away from anything spicy. They made one each, Kim with two, then walked over to the dining table.

Molly took the first bite, chewing fast and loud. Both girls started with her with expressions of surprise, the tattooed lady's devolving into a smirk. Her friend didn't care and asked again her question: "What do you mean you wanted to be there when he asked me?"

"You don't want to say a prayer?" Kim remarked.

Molly took another bite. "Answer me!"

Witnessing these felt like a regression, and the girl just ate. She wasn't gonna bother them in their feud.

"I just would like to have seen him," said Kim.

"Why?"

"To see if he actually looked like a Local."

"He was!" Molly almost threw her food down. "He knew about the Yudaku and the processes!"

The tattooed lady sighed. "What was his name?"

"Oscar."

"Oscar what?"

"Oscar Demitri."

"That's not a Local name," said her roommate.

"Your name is Kim!" Molly responded.

"Kim, Wheat."

The redhead appeared a bit embarrassed. "He still is a Pelt. I don't know what else to say to you."

Kim rolled her eyes at the adolescent's petty remark and sat in thought for a moment, then said, "This is what I meant when I said the knots make you a target."

"Well, how did dating start with Derrick, huh? Didn't you have to extend a branch to him? Didn't you have to have a little trust in him? Or were you always so jaded?"

Kim stayed calm. "We knew each other for a long time. We were friends first, then something a bit more, then to what we are now. He would spend countless hours with me, give me flowers. He even wrote me some poems. I still have it. Why do you laugh? Such a dork."

"And that's amazing, Kim," said Molly. "And so can't I have that? Why can't I have cute interactions like that? You had to trust him."

"Yeah, I guess so." Kim's voice weakened. "Treated Mason like a son."

Molly didn't want to look at Kim but did so anyway, her own face becoming marred by her friend's melancholy. "And...and that horrible thing that happened to him. But I can't have what you have with Derrick, without some sort of leap."

"Do you remember how Mason came to be?"

And at this sentence, Molly's chest caved in, a conversation she'd wished never to have again with her friend. "You told me."

Kim saw into the redhead. "Then please, don't be dumb."

"He's a nice guy. I'll be safe."

"Do you know how many guys there will be?"

"Well…that depends," said Molly. "I gotta text Oscar if Bellz is coming. Then it'd probably be just him and his friend."

"Good." Kim tossed her attention toward the pale girl. "Are you gonna go then?"

Bella had the burrito in her mouth. "Wha—?"

"Are you gonna go with Molly?"

And her eyes, they appeared so frightened, so different from how the nurse knew Kim. No sadness, no sarcastic grace, but fear, and it made Bella rush into her heart.

Go with her, she could almost read her roommate's mind. She knew that's the answer Kim wanted, but it was the answer the girl couldn't give.

"No. I'm not."

"Then it'll just be me and Oscar," said Molly. She looked over to the oven clock. It read 12:28. "I better go freshen up. I'll be right back." She stood up, leaving her plate in her wake.

The remaining girls watched her leave. Bella thought she said the wrong thing.

"I think she'll be fine," the girl said.

Kim ate without the slightest interest in talking to her. "I'm sure she'll be too."

"Maybe I can talk her out of it."

"You can do whatever."

Bella didn't want to stay with her roommate. She finished most of her food and decided to catch up with Molly. She left her plate and made her way to the modern art hallway, taking a single glance back at Kim, before ascending up the stairs. The girl felt she had disappointed her roommate, but Bella never asked for this date. She stuck by that notion and ascended. She reached the platform above, but to her surprise, she heard music. A small delicate sound with a mono-dynamic harp bell. It was pure. It was innocent. She approached the room. The door was left open and went toward the tune.

Molly brushed her hair and sat watching the thin table. One top, the immaculate box had parted, and what danced in the middle was a twirling ballerina in motion with the gentle cords. And what acted as its stage: the portrait of the rabbits, as the figure seemingly swung through dead time. Bella was filled with a childlike whimsicality, such care being put into a children's toy.

Molly heard her approach. "Hey, Bellz," she said with a smile. "You doing all right?"

Bella came into the room and sat beside her friend. The box jingled its somber tune. "What is this thing?"

"It's a music box. I like to listen to it every once in a while."

"It's lovely. Where'd you get it?"

The redhead straightened the rivets in her hair. "My mom gave it to me. I think for my..." She paused. "Sixteenth birthday?"

"That's pretty old," said Bella. "It looked like something you give a kid."

"I was still a kid."

"Well, teenager."

"I still feel like a kid now sometimes."

"You do?"

"Yeah," Molly said. "It's weird, but I don't know how to explain it. It's like I still don't have everything figured out."

"Weird" said Bella.

"You've never felt like that?"

"I guess I've always just felt like how I am now."

"That's sad," said Molly, and she went on to brush the other portion of her hair.

"Maybe I just never felt like I grew up," added the girl.

"Would you like the box?"

"No, I'm okay."

The song completed, and the music restarted along with the dance of the ballerina. It began to slow, the space between notes ever so slightly longer."

"You know, she thinks too little of me," said Molly. "We just got to this point where Kim criticizes everything I do. And I'm not here for it! She was just so condescending. I heard it in her voice just now. She thinks I'm not an adult."

Bella nodded.

"I know good people from bad. Hell, most people are good, for crying out loud! Like you, Kade, Amber, even that bitch down in the kitchen. They're all good! If everyone had a little heart for each other, maybe the world wouldn't be just a bad place. And you can count my soul on it."

The music faltered.

"You can't just shut everyone out and expect things to get better. You need to try and grab what you've been missing! Take it if ya need to! And if you think you can't, you're wrong. Eventually, you'll get what you want. Maybe you even have to lie to yourself that things will get better, that's okay, because things will. And that's what I want you to know. From this point own, I'll be changed. I just have a feeling, and if ya follow that feeling, just maybe listen to it once in a while, you'll be on top of a Giant!" She paused. "And I know what this is. I know it'll be different."

The music died.

"Don't think this is better than college?"

Bella bent her neck as usual. She would not look up for the remainder of their conversion. "Yeah," she said.

"You don't look that confident."

"It's just been harder than I thought."

"I know," said Molly, and she moved to do up her hair again. "But it won't always be hard." She finished and the clock in her phone. "Sure you don't wanna go?"

"It's your date," Bella corrected, her voice cold and scared. "I'd just throw up again."

The redheaded smiled. "Probably. We might have some more drinks."

"I figured."

"You gotta eventually get back out there, right?"

Bella said nothing.

"It's okay. We'll work on it. Maybe we can eventually do a double date."

The girl nodded. "I'll have enough time by then."

Molly moved over to hug the girl. Her arm went across Bella's shoulder, and the two embraced.

At that moment, the rumble of gravel led to a bounce on stone reverberating. A loud engine rowed with immense power and energy. The redhead went to the window and saw a decent- looking Mustang on the driveway. Her phone buzzed, and she reviewed a message from a static number: "Here." She then put the phone in her pocket and took one final look at Bella. "I'll see ya."

Bella gave her one last hug.

Molly then left her room. She exited from the front door, undoing its lock and stepping out to the porch. She expected someone else to redo the locks and walked toward the dark-tinted vehicle. The redhead never said goodbye to Kim.

The tattooed woman had ignored the commotion, hoping they would just leave. To her dismay, she heard a click and a creek, then a sudden slam. She sat in her chair and stared several seconds at the dry wood, not quite sure what to do next. She heard then whatever make she expected the vehicle to be crush the ground and accelerate off until mute. Her heart sank.

Bella watched them head off from Molly's southern window. A part of her was glad her friend had found what she was looking for, but the other could not shake the knot in the pit of her stomach.

Chapter

9

Bella was in her room. She enjoyed the silence, but eventually became bored. She hadn't seen much of Kim since Molly left. Her guess was that her roommate found herself busy caring for her plants. And the girl found satisfaction in scrolling through short videos, pictures of almost nude models flung by her finger along with handsome men acting in absurd mannerisms giving a life of about thirty seconds. When even that became dull, she switched over to an old game she'd download many months ago and began playing it. The game had numbed the girl's sickness, but was unable to kill the root of which she didn't understand.

Bella sat on her folded blanket mound when Kim entered. The tattooed woman didn't bother to knock and halted right to the end of Bella's bed.

"Hey, Bella," she said. "Have you heard from Molly?"

"No," replied the girl. "But she's probably busy having fun."

"You should send her a text. Just check if she's all right."

"Have you sent a text?"

"No," Kim approached the window. "She doesn't want to hear from me."

"I don't think that," responded Bella. "I'll send it if ya want. But they didn't leave for too long."

"I know. I'm just"—she breathed—"just nervous, that's all. I'm gonna be taking off here soon."

"Where you going?"

"Derrick comes back today. I'm gonna meet him at the airport."

"I'll hold down things here, I guess."

"Could you check with her once it gets dark?" Kim asked.

"Yeah, sure thing."

The tattooed woman withdrew a packet from her hoodie pouch and a lighter. "Do you mind if I smoke? Molly hates it when I do." And she pushed the packet to reveal tan-tipped cigarettes.

"Not at all," said Bella.

"Thanks. I really need one right now, too many things going on."

Her roommate stuck one in her mouth and lit its tail red. Ember erupted, and a cautious line of smoke trailed from her mouth and twirled in the yellow rays intruding through the blinds. The smell was all too familiar to the girl, and she watched Kim's demeanor relax to a normal state. She found it best then to prompt the question.

"How did Mason die?"

Kim inhaled deeply. She watched the gas rise to the ceiling. "We used to live further down. We were in a house just like this, about a mile or so east. I managed to keep Mason with me, even though you're not allowed to be in Planned Homes. Everyone kept a blind eye. But they told me to get rid of him. Everyone told me, so I kept him. He was my son, and I couldn't help who his father was. But he was my son." She took a puff. "Derrick would come over. He was just starting, and we would play with him. He loved Derrick. He'd laugh so much. And his favorite spot to play was the patio, especially in the spring. Sometimes a flower would grow through the fence, and he'd smell it, looking all curious with the colors. He'd pull and rip them to our side, even put them in his mouth!" And her voice soared toward a place the girl couldn't comprehend. "I looked away for only a second."

Bella didn't know what she meant, but sensed she should pry any longer. Her head was down. "We don't have to talk about it if you don't want to."

"And he was gone. Just gone."

"What?"

At this, there was no reply. Kim stared into the whirling smoke in a numb void, the cigarette between her fingers. There was no motion in her soul. "You remind me of him," she said.

Bella twisted her face. "What took him?"

Kim was looking at her. The tattooed woman stood with an ember dot an inch away from her. "You both don't know any better."

"Kim...what happened?"

Her roommate bobbed her head. "I looked back, and he wasn't there. The toy he was playing with and...and one of his shoes was. His little shoe..."

"Did he get up and walk away? I don't understand."

"No. He was gone. Not a trace of him. We searched and searched and searched, but we couldn't find him. The police came and looked, and they found nothing. Even our neighbors came and helped..." It struck the woman as if she was watching the scene unfold before herself. "Then the white collars came. They didn't tell us what they were doing. The police wouldn't even say. But they kept an eye to the mountains. They knew. They knew something. They wouldn't say, but they did, but they wouldn't say. And to this day, I can't tell you how much it hurts not knowing, not understanding how looking two seconds away killed my kid. But it did. And I'll never know what happened to him. And all they gave me was his face on that damn board." She hurried another hit of her cigarette.

The girl couldn't believe her ears. She doubted for a moment, but the anguish in Kim's voice stood as testament. A disappearance like this, no trace of the victim whatsoever, defied her concept of physics. "He couldn't just be gone. He couldn't." But not even the police prevailed in their search, as her roommate claimed. "I don't know what to say," she said at last. "I'm...I'm sorry."

"I'm still trying to cope with it," said Kim. "I hope ya didn't mind the plants."

"I don't. They're nice."

The tattooed woman nodded.

"Maybe tonight," said Bella, in search of a quick remedy. "You should spend it with Derrick."

More smoke whirled in Kim's lungs.

"You haven't seen him a bit," Bella continued. "And it might be nice talking to him about this."

Kim nodded again. "Yeah, I think so."

Bella's stare greeted its favorite spot. She didn't think she appeared genuine enough, but she was truly remorseful. No speech could express it, but she hoped Kim knew. A mirror reflected back in the tattooed woman's eyes, the red tips burning shorter.

"Thank you for letting me smoke," she said. "I miss him,"

Bella nodded and smiled and actually looked at her roommate. "I'll text Molly. I'll make sure she's home before I go to bed."

"I'd appreciate that." Kim turned to the hall.

"Goodbye," said Bella.

"Goodbye."

And the girl was alone again. She heard her roommate's steps change from the carpeted second story to the planked structure of the kitchen, and she descended to her room and back, which led her to the garage. Bella hated that she listened, but waited until she heard the popping of the heavy mechanical door, and the quiet enchantment of Kim's car. She decided it best to get up then. Maybe she should shower. Maybe she should. It was unclear what Bella thought to do next. She rose to sit on the edge of her bed. The girl had been unsettled. A little boy vanished, and the authorities appeared none the wiser. "How could this happen?"

Bella found herself downstairs within an instant. The sunlight cast sharp shadows that outlined the radiant yellow pouring in right before the mountain could block the sun's influence. It was getting dark, and the girl began to wonder when Molly would return. It wasn't a paranoid occurrence, but a casual notion as she skimmed through the kitchen to find something to satisfy, discovering how much she didn't want to cook. She found some apples. There wasn't any cracks or chips. She wasn't enthused, but she picked one of the red spheres up and sat at the table, putting one of her legs on a vacant seat. She pulled out her phone and filed through some artificial media. It calmed her.

Her eyes diverted to the screen and onto the patio, the small cement square and the sliver of lawn before halted by the fence. To think it happened there, somewhere identical. It disturbed her. She reclaimed her feet and approached the glass. She could imagine a little boy playing there, perhaps with a toy robot or stacking blocks. She could hear him laughing. She could see his smile, but then ceased, from what no one seemed to be able to explain.

She set foot onto the cement, leaving the slide door open, and walked to the edge of the privacy blinders. The girl stood close to the barrier. She looked past it, seeing the tall grassy field a ways before the ascent up the mountain.

They could build here, she thought.

Bella turned to her left and saw a myriad of copycat buildings all in the same accent. She turned to her right and saw the same thing, the only difference being what the residence had on their patios. Some had boxes, to what she assumed to be newcomers; and others possessed grills, hammocks, small children pools, and rocking seats. She noticed, far off in the distance, the plywood signature of a residence under construction. They were adding to the roof another story.

"How many could they add?"

The girl at last looked up to the mountain peak and how it differed from its siblings. She sat down and drifted to the corners of the patio. Against the house lay four lawn chairs, and in the other there was a large black bowl snug in its crevice. Bella turned back and produced her phone. She pressed a green icon, then scrolled until found Molly's name. She typed, "Hey, just wondering when you'll be back," and closed the phone. "She'll get back later," the girl said to herself. "Much later." And she understood why. They sounded like they were in love.

Her phone vibrated.

Bella checked the screen that read, "Won't be back until tonight."

She knew it and replied, "Okay," and slide the device in her pocket.

The girl took another bite of the apple. She wasn't the biggest fan of the taste, but it filled her. She believed this is all she would eat for dinner and set her sights on her bed. She entered back into the Planned Home and to her room. She positioned her blankets and lay back. Bella stayed there until the night chased away yellow, and she fell asleep.

The morning was still. No murmur came from the blue jay to the crow, and the robins all kept mute at the sight of the mockingbirds. No chants of grace to the rising sun echoed with the fowls. No sounds, save the wind rolling off the mountain pines.

Bella blipped from her unconsciousness and realized the void. It made it that much easier to drift back into the world without kinetic input, and her eyes sputtered shut. The wind grew wilder, hitting the northern side of the Home with malice.

A faint knocking could be heard. Not at her door, but somewhere else. Bella tossed and turned, wishing it would stop. Then the doorbell rang, then a second time, then a third. It had a cryptic tone, a cadence of the old days. Bella was angry to discover they had a doorbell and shuffled out of her nest and to the stairs. The sound had become a semblance of thumbing and eight-bit jingles. Bella descended closer to the front door. She noticed through the windows the morning's blue font, then faint incoherent sobbing. She thought who could want attention at such an early hour. A thump soon began. Her pace quickened, and she opened the door, undoing the lock. She brought her fingers to the knob and opened the front door.

In ruin, a girl stood in ruin. She slouched to her right side and possessed no footwear. Mascara ran from a beaten eye and strained purple cheek, red hair in a mess. Her pant button was missing, and her zipper was down, exposing a clump of pubic hair. Her knees bent toward each other as if bracing the pain of a hidden wound. The flaps of the jeans showed more battered skin under jagged rips. Her pink jacket had been torn asunder, her cut and bare breast kept close by an arm. She clutched something in her broken hands close to heart, a fine string that spiraled into ugly tatters.

"Help," she managed to say. Molly stumbled forward, Bella barely able to catch her.

Chapter

10

Red flashes and blue, the girl remembered them. The sirens melted with her friend's cries, leaving nothing to be conceived or considered. Bella remembered dialing the three-digit number, but merely rehearsing her address to the operator. Her speech was mumbled, inarticulate but did what she could comprehend. Then left the phone on while she held her friend tight, thinking it would keep her together.

She remembered the police cruisers filling around a Heartlake ambulance in the driveway. Officers arrived and asked questions, initially taking control over the scene. Bella could answer none of them and held tightly onto Molly. Their chief, a detective the girl believed he was, the trench coat and fedora signaling so, ordered his men to escort them to the ambulance. Two paramedics knelt beside them and gave the officer the okay to move the girls. A burly mustache man tried to lift them up.

Molly resisted with what little strength she had left and fell back to the floor. "Don't touch me!" Bella recalled her say. "Don't touch me!"

The girl heard the remarks of the policemen, their reactions, and their claims as well. She felt doomed to listen and unable to stand while holding her friend.

"God," proclaimed the man in the coat. "Get under them, get leverage underneath them!"

The officers did so, in unison this repetition, and brought the girls to their feet.

The redhead thrashed back, and Bella tried to keep her stable.

"It's gonna be all right," said the man in the coat. "Just calm down."

"Don't touch me," Molly's shouts turned into sobs. "Don't touch me."

The paramedics and the officer tried their best to de-escalate, but she wouldn't. She couldn't. They ended up putting Molly on a stretcher, strapping her down for her own safety, prying Bella from her, and she watched the redhead lifted into the ambulance.

"A fucking another one," the chief said under his breath. He turned to Bella. "Are you riding with her?"

The girl nodded. She kept her vision low.

"All right. Brigham help her on."

The officer extended his hand to Bella and pulled her onto the ambulance. Police vehicles stayed behind while others began to leave, discreetly, and the ambulance blared its sirens. Inside, they still tried to calm her. There was even a suggestion to drug her, which was dispatched quickly. Molly wasn't struggling much, her cries becoming hoarse. And Bella was to her friend's right, holding her hand.

What is this? she thought. She felt fear beyond reason, a dread that linger ever so deep in her torso, as if it sunk forever. She could barely recognize her friend like this. She didn't think about what had happened. She couldn't think. The officer next to her tried to ask her questions, but Bella's face remained still, unable to attend to him.

It was impossible for the ambulance to travel in quick fashion. The claustrophobic road left no room for flexibility, and people constantly blocked the way. It took the party longer than the girl's usual commute. But the vessel wound the infamous trials of the hospital, and she knew they were close.

A group of hospital staff escaped out of the emergency room. With help from Brigham, they brought Molly out and into her care. They examined her, and they escorted the redhead inside the facility. Bella close behind the group. The chief was not far from the group, his car in front of the ambulance, and halted the staff. Bella heard him say to the head nurse, "16. Private room." All eyes shifted toward that nurse, and an understanding among the men and women conveyed. They continued on, a shift in their direction. The girl kept her head down as they scrambled to a disclosed room. Molly still moaned. Many eyes were on her as they wheeled here through, mostly personnel, but some businessmen were aboard. Bella could tell from their shoes. The girl knew nothing of her surroundings, other than the always present tile built into every hospital. They went on for several yards until taking a sharp right. It was dark, and attendant flipped the light switch and led the stretcher beside the bed. Once static, the nurses aided the redhead in switching off the stretcher and onto the blush sheets. Bella tried to stay out of the way and watched the ruined girl switch to the medical bed. There was something wrong with her, an arm appeared limp. Brigham came in next. He stood near the girl and assured her the staff would take care of everything. But to his and the woman's surprise, most of the staff decided to leave in profile, stranding two nurses to tend to Molly.

They started evaluating her, describing the wounds and their origin. They were met with the same problem as the police. Bella shared no idea of what happened to her friend, and the redhead was still in hysterics. The nurses proceeded to tend to the wounds as they saw fit, right before a doctor arrived to perform precise medical analysis, immediately assessing the bruises.

"This part of your case?" he asked the officer.

"We don't know," said Brigham. "I hope you could tell us that."

He studied the girl. "Best you get out of here. We're gonna get her out of these clothes."

The officer nodded and nudged Bella. "Can you hear me? Do you need medical attention?"

She shook her head.

"Would you mind stepping out in the hall with me?"

She nodded. And Brigham motioned to the door. "Remember to inform Nelson," he said to the doctor.

"It's part of my job," he returned.

The stocky man led the girl out and pressed his back against the building not two feet from the door. A presently nervous officer presented over Bella. She glanced up to see his face and noted his orange hair receding backward, his moustache a hint darker. He stood twice the size of her, large shoulders and chest, and what appeared as somewhat of a beer gut. The uniform he wore was a deep blue with many symbols of the state and city sewn onto it, the most prominent being the country's flag and Heartlakes crescent eagle badge.

She brought her hand over one another and positioned herself opposite of the officer. The hospital kept a slow pace, discounted when Molly had arrived. She didn't expect the response they gave or now the tame demeanors of the staff. It appeared all too cycled, all too in a lockstep of routine.

They stood in their own little corner.

"Will you tell me your name now?" he asked, with a pen and a notebook in his grasp.

She collected herself. "Bella Tomson," the girl forced out.

"Good. You weren't saying anything for a moment there, and I got scared. My name is Officer Brigham. Everything was in a panic when we arrived at your home, and now you seem a little bit toned down. So while you friend is being evaluated, I wanted to ask you some of the questions and some new ones about Molly. It'll help us figure out what we're dealing with here. Is that all right with you, miss?"

Bella tottered her weight.

"Ma'am?"

"Yes. Yes, it's fine."

"Do you by chance have your ID on you?"

"I don't."

"Well, we'll just move on for that right now," said Brigham. "Do you know Molly's last name?"

"Needs."

"And you share a Planned Home with her, correct?"

"Yes."

"For how long."

"Couple of days."

"All right. And what is your relation to her?"

"We've been best friends since high school."

Brigham scribbled the last few responses. "Where did you find the victim when she arrived back at your house?"

Bella reimagined her first sight of the redhead. "Just on the front porch. It was still dark."

"All right, and do you know what Molly was coming back from?"

"She had a date all planned."

The office seemed surprised. "When was this date?"

131

"Just yesterday."

"Who'd she go on this date with?"

Bella answered after a pause. She could smell her own vomit form when she went to the bar. She recalled his face, his glasses, and his large mouth. "His name was Oscar Dmitri."

"Do you know this man?" the officer quickly asked.

The girl shook her head. "He approached us at a bar."

"What bar?"

"Drop Inn."

"Could you give me a description of him?"

"Tall." Bella blurted. "And skinny. He was in a grayish shirt and white pants. He had glasses on and..." His mouth came to mind.

The officer followed his pen until the witness faltered. "And what?"

"His mouth. He had a very large mouth."

"A large mouth."

"Yes."

"Like he talked a lot?"

"No. It was physically wide."

The officer failed to know how to interpret the information given and nonetheless jotted down the fact. He swiftly panned up and down his notes and returned to the girl. "Any other descriptions?"

She shook her head.

"Do you know if Molly took her own vehicle to go meet Oscar, or did he pick her up?"

"He picked her up." Bella shifted her gaze to the scenery around her.

"Did you see the vehicle?"

"No. But I heard it."

"Did you hear anything before you found Molly?"

"Nothing," Bella said without breath.

"No cars coming or leaving?" he asked.

"I was in bed. I'm sorry. I barely heard the doorbell."

"Do you have any idea of where they might have gone?"

"No."

The officer then put his pen and pad away after finishing. "That'll do, Ms. Tomson. Guess the doctor will let you know when he's done." He turned to his left to spy the chief approaching him, down the hall, seven uniformed men behind. He hadn't shaved in a while, a semi-gray beard took his face. He held tired eyes in his skull, with sharp knife-like tips.

Bella looked awhile and saw Kim by his side, appearing as if she'd been crying. She looked just how she did when she left the Planned Home. She assumed her roommate came back to the police investigating the porch.

The tattooed woman locked eyes with the girl and crossed to her. The party followed. The two girls hugged. The action surprised the girl.

"What's going on?" she whispered. "What happened to her?"

Bella didn't know.

"Did you get details?" asked the man in the trench coat.

"Yes, sir," said Brigham. And he produced his notes so the chief could read.

He skimmed over the writing. "Did you get confirmation from the doctor?"

"No, sir."

"What confirmation?" demand Kim. "What happened?"

"We're going to find out." The chief moved to the remote chamber's door. He thumped his knuckle on the broad board wood. The others followed, the group of police staying where they were. A nurse soon stuck out her head.

"She's not ready for all of you," she said.

"Send the Doc out," the chief said.

"One moment."

The chief backed away from the door. He checked the time and looked at the girls. Bella predicted he dreaded what he was about to say. He evenly spat it out.

"Your friend was likely sexually assaulted. We're having the doctor confirm it, but all evidence suggests so. I'm telling you this now because you're going to hear details that you're not going to like, but it's the reality of what happened, and we need to proceed." His vision rested on the tattooed woman.

Kim appeared as if she wanted to spit at the man.

"If you want to stay," he continued, "by all means stay. But you can go back to those officers right now."

"You need to get her family here, now," ordered Kim.

"We're working on that, ma'am."

The doctor stepped out of the room at that moment, and the chief directed his attention to him. He wore clean scrubs and a surgical cap, as if plucked from before going into an operation.

"Deacon," he offered his hand.

"Andrew," the chief reciprocated the gesture. "Why don't you give a briefing to the girls first."

"Did you pass that to the director?"

"They need some disclosure."

"Sharlet was admitted to these cases."

"They deserve to know. I'll talk to them later."

The doctor sighed. "All right." He moved over to the two women standing close to one another. He again stuck out his hand. "I've seen your face around here," he directed himself at Kim.

None of them shook his hand.

He retrieved his gesture. "My name is Dr. Cleveland. I'm the one they use to check these types of things. I won't sugarcoat it. That'd be a disservice. I've just finished screening your friend Ms. Need for a possible rape case. She was battered and bruised pretty bad with trauma around the head and neck area. It also appeared that the attacker must have dislodged one of Ms. Need's arms in his assault. Molly also received a bit of a wound on her right side, around her mid-abdomen, that's being treated for infection. And we found that the tissue in her vagina wasscarred."

Kim concealed her mouth. Tears swelled in her eyes. Brigham bent his gaze, the revelation not something he hadn't heard before. Bella still didn't know what it meant. She knew the redhead was beaten, but not the full extent of what her friend endured.

"Your friend should make a full recovery," Cleveland continued. "I don't see why she wouldn't. She's talking now, and we were able to get a couple questions from her on how it happened, but I'll leave that to the boys in blue here to fill in. But she will need psychiatric evaluation most likely, and I urge you both into taking some shifts for Molly. God knows Nelson won't be any more relentless."

"Can we see her?" begged the tattooed woman.

"Yes. You two can. I'll just be out here with the officers." He held open the broad wood for the pair.

Kim sped past the girl and the doctor, and Bella trotted a few paces behind. They saw the redhead lying on the soft medical cushions, gazing at the ceiling. A numb tint persisted in her irises, one barely visible through the purple swelling. She gently scratched the synthetic sheets. Blood stained on her abdomen toward her right portion in a half circle. They hurried to her side. Kim grabbed Molly's hand. Their friend looked over, dull, but smiled.

"Hey," she rasped out.

A combination of her voice and the beaten sight made the tattooed woman weep and placed her forehead on Molly. Bella hated to cry. The action made her feel so weak. She pretended the emotion brought on by her roommate; however, a wet glint appeared in her eyes. She rubbed Molly's leg.

Kim sought an explanation. "What happened to you?"

The two nurses operating within the space stood close to the girls, anticipating a tragedy that the patient would tell. Molly looked at them and then went back to Kim.

"Refuge looked nice," she said.

"Is that where you two went?"

Molly nodded.

"Is that where it happened?" Kim could hold back her tears.

Molly shook her head.

What was the action? Bella thought. *What was it?*

"I'm sorry," the redhead whispered. "You were right. I'm so, so, so sorry."

Kim squeezed the patient tighter. "Don't you ever be sorry. It's not your fault."

Molly laid back and tried not to regress into hysterics.

"What happened?" asked Bella. "What actually happened?"

Before the victim could respond, Deacon broke into the room. Next to him was Cleveland, and after the doctor strolled Nelson. His two locks of hair appeared damp, tempered. Sweat blotches marked his dress shirt and could be seen as his lab coat swayed in his march. He almost glared at the girls, but he kept the politeness of the situation in mind.

Bella and Kim both looked at the chief and the doctor who'd made their way to the base of the bed. Nelson stayed by the entryway and observed the scene from afar, directing his arms to his lower spine.

"How are you, Nurse Need?" asked Nelson.

"Good," she responded.

"A shame this happened. To one of my best ."

"You've been through a lot," said Deacon.

Cleveland agreed and brought a chair for both of the men to sit on. The chief produced a notepad and a pen like Brigham did with his witness.

"I don't mean to interrupt, but it is urgent I ask you some questions about the attack." And he looked directly at the two girls beside Molly's bed. "Can you get them outta here?" He motioned to Nelson.

"I'm not going anywhere!" yelled Kim.

"I need to question Ms. Need alone."

"She needs someone here!"

"Please."

"No," said Kim. "I'm not going. You're going to have to rip me out of this room."

Nelson then spoke. "Let the man do his job, Perry. You'll learn plenty from your peer once the chief has thoroughly questioned her and knows what kind of monster we're dealing with. Plus"—he beckoned them—"we're shorthanded. Both Tomson and Needs were scheduled today."

"Someone needs to be here when she's discharged," said Kim.

Cleveland interjected. "The observation unit can run with a couple down numbers."

Deacon gave him a nasty look.

"But these two are more than capable of helping," said Nelson. " Should I remind you were saving life? Did that cross your mind? I know this episode is not in the best taste, but the career you both chose requires extra. And I, as well as the others, need at least one of you."

"Both," ordered Deacon.

"I'm not going. You can fire me if you like, but I'm not moving an inch."

"That just might be what happens," said Nelson.

"Can't you call in anyone else?" demand Kim.

"You know as well as I do that we were short staffed."

"And whose fault is that?"

"Does this really need to be this hard??"

A pause overtook the room. Kim's stare pierced the grand doctors, and he clashed with hers.

"I'll be fine," said Molly. "Just go wait in the hall."

The tattooed woman turned to her friend. "Will you tell me what happened? Even if they tell you not to?"

The redhead nodded.

"Do you promise?"

"Yes."

"Okay." Kim detached from Molly's side.

"That's all I wanted," said Deacon.

"I still need someone to fill in!" Nelson shouted.

And the room once again fell silent.

"I'll take it," said Bella. She didn't know she even spoke.

"You're our only other option."

The tattooed woman faced her. "Thank you," she said.

"Let's hurry along now," said Nelson. "You have people relying on you."

Bella moved from the side of Kim and went toward the door. She knew this was the best way she could help.

"Wait." Her roommate stepped after and hugged the girl. This caught Bella off guard and returned to a frozen state at the gesture. "I'll make sure she gets back safe."

"All right." Bella smiled. She took one last at the room. Both the chief and the doctor appeared antsy to begin their procedure. The two assisting nurses followed out with Nelson, in rage to move the machine along. She then went to Molly and patted her shoulder. "I'll see you at home," she said.

"Bye," returned Molly.

And the girl parted into the midst of the hospital.

Chapter

11

Bella was provided a uniform. Not quite her size, a bit baggy at every twist, but she didn't seem to mind. Nelson was frank with her, a noticeable disgust in his voice. The incident had upset his order and could leverage his discontent to the faculty that served him. He repeatedly told Bella she wasn't going fast enough.

They made it to the elevator. The lift was awkward, and the girl thought if she even scratch her skin, Nelson would shout and condemn her, so she stood properly, like nothing bothered her. Bella noticed that some visitors had made their way to this floor, children giggling with their grandma and grandpa and adults swallowing the reality of what had failed their parents. Others were actual nurses and specialists, and in the farthest corner, a young couple argued with a doctor, they appeared to be Local.

Her boss funneled her into the rest area. It was beneath him to do such minor tasks, to manually fetch an employee for their shift, yet he would allow no one else to. Bella moved in paranoia and entered into the section. There were people taking their lunch break. One young man was dozing off, and two were talking by the table. Bella could only make out there shoes, those being of a lazy fit. She had no idea the order of which she was needed. Nelson entered there after here and turned to his magnificent scheduling board. The two coworkers lowered their volume. They seemed heightened by his presence. Bella dared a glance. One of them looked at the girl, and at last, he spoke.

"Where's Molly?"

Bella didn't respond.

"Did something happen?"

"Not your concern," said Nelson, finding the right place to drop the nurse into schedule. He walked over to them. "You two have a minute or so left on your break."

"Sorry, sir."

He looked down at Bella. "You're going to relieve Madison for now. She's been filling in your absent set. Room 329." And he pointed out the door.

The nurse nodded and went to where she was told.

Resentment harbored in her as she made her way down the corridors of the medical room. Disbelief struck that she was at the side of her ruined friend and then the next moment was off to work. Bella reacted to her environment, leaving with the tide and going where she must. She moved and only that, not comprehending what streamed past her. The beams illuminating were fake, for some reason, the notion came into her mind before anything else. Next was the threat of expulsion rather than a harsh punishment for the tattooed woman. But Nelson's word was law. She pressed on along through the walkways of the medical floor, taking sharp glances from the nurses on the stations. The girl received more nasty looks from the operators among the oval counters, the woman with long nails being the most stern. She did not follow the curve of the counter. Bella stopped halfway to her destination. The null of her knowledge struck her. She recalled what Cleveland said. *Why was there scarring? What did he mean?* Her stomach recoiled, and she grasped it.

A woman nearly bumped Bella as she walked by. The action reconditioned her, and she kept on her path. She saw some computer void of charts, not quite eclipsing the room number: 379. A yard or so in front of her, a larger but fair woman sat in a professional manner, typing on its keyboard. The girl walked closer, and the nurse must have felt her presence and turned around. To Bella's amazement, the woman exhibited no sign of bitterness and greeted her with a warm yet tired smile. She logged off the computer and vacated the spot for the girl.

Bella managed a smile back, though not expecting to. "I'm sorry," she said to fill the air.

"Oh, don't fret about it. I got some overtime." The woman laughed. "Mallory's been in and out of sleep. She mostly stays put. Just remember to give her meds"—she brandished a stock card near the window's frame—"and introduce yourself. She scared, just really scared." The woman turned to the glass. "Only seven ya know, but tough. She's a tough girl." She turned back to Bella and noted her unconventional demeanor directed somewhere else.

"Well, remember to finish your logs!" said the woman and laughed, then waved goodbye. And yet she remembered something important to say and turned back around. "Remember to check on room 319 and 309. Thanks!" She ascended down the hall, taking a right to the intersection where the elevator hid.

Bella watched her walk away, observing a slight limp buckling to her left knee.

She then panned her attention to the monitor and took a seat at her station. She felt the uncomfortable heat of its last user, resisting the reaction to squirm. Bella then logged on to the computer and opened the only app or icon present on the dull screen. It bore a basic shape of a spreadsheet with the emblems of the hospital.

Thereafter, Bella peered through gridded glass to check on her patient. There lay a small girl, blond in hair and soft in appearance, her frame reminding Bella of herself. The little patient, lit barely by the high-crested sun, lay on her shoulder toward a room filled with flowers and gifts and away from the revelation of her sitting nurse. String willowed from the artificial lights and was attached to plastic stars that Bella expected would glow in darkness. A rabbit with hard plastic crossed eyes leaned against the patient as if was safeguarding her, but not the game device on the bed's fluffy corner. All accommodations considered, Bella assumed they were implemented to make the young girl feel at home, knowing the visit would be long.

At first, the young girl reminded the nurse of Molly, who marked her heart with the deepest pity, the way she lay persisted through both individuals. Bella took the time to jot down on her notes and current timestamp observations and glanced through the glass slit. She considered the young girl asleep and typed in her log that the patient was "unable for greetings," a phrase he she figured would be used a

140

lot during the day. But as the keys clicked and the sentence midway finished, the child rolled to her other side, now facing the door, exposing an oxygen tube.

It did occur to her that she could write it off. The nurse didn't have to bear the weight of conversion. And knowing she was halfway through the opening note, Bella almost did, finishing her sentence as she intended and yielded, watching the girl for a moment. The patient almost had a stroke of red in her braids. It was part of her job. It was lying, stating the patient was unable to communicate to her. And if Nelson caught her...Bella checked her surroundings. The doctor was nowhere to be seen. And perhaps it was the guilt or maybe the fact that it was a child, but the nurse stood up. Bella softly cursed herself. She went to the door and twisted the handle.

With a deep breath and a push, she threaded the door frame and entered the room, shocking the young girl with a gasp at the sudden intrusion.

"Oh, sorry!" said Bella. "I just wanted to check up on you."

The young girl sprung up.

"I'm Bella," the intruder continued. "Or, well, Nurse Tomson. You can call me Nurse Tomson. I'll be watching over you for a few hours." Bella looked intently at the young girl and noticed a knotted amulet around her neck, the vestige that Molly still clutched.

The young girl persisted in her stare, averting her eyes only when they met the nurses.

"Um, well, Mallory," Bella continued. "H-how have you been feeling?"

"Good," the patient muttered. "How do you know my name?"

"There's a sheet outside that tells us about you, what you need at what hour."

"You know what's wrong with me?"

Bella stuttered. "Well, no...I'm just meant to watch. Nurses just watch. We aren't allowed to really know most things. But we keep you comfy!" She faked enthusiasm.

"Oh." Mallory reclined her head into a pillow.

"Do you need anything? Did you already have lunch?"

"No. Yeah, I had lunch. I had a peanut butter sandwich."

"Okay, well then." Bella looked around at the flowers surrounding the patient. "I like your flowers."

"Mommy gave me most of them."

"Oh? Are they all from your mom?"

Mallory nodded.

Bell felt satisfied from the conversation. "Well, I'll be outside in case you need me." Bella turned around to exit. "But I'll be back for your medication, all right—"

"Lady!" Mallory shouted.

Bella spun back around.

"You look like her," the young girl said.

"Who?"

"Your skin," she added. "It's pale like my mom."

"Oh." The nurse was surprised by her bluntness. "Is she from Haze?"

"What's Haze?"

"Just a city up north. Your mom must have been born there."

"Why?"

Bella stopped confused. "Well, you said she was pale."

"Oh." The young girl bolstered her head. "Does that mean you turn back to normal color?"

"What?"

"Will you stay pale forever? You look like a vampire."

"I'm not sure. People say I won't, but I haven't really notice a change. Has your mother?"

"No, she hasn't."

Bella tilted her head and leaned on the frame. "How long have you lived outside Haze?"

"I don't know where that is."

"Well, then, how could your mom be pale?"

Mallory stated, "When my sister got lost."

A familiar needle struck, and pathos flowed out to the child and to her mourning mother.

"She died?" Bella asked.

"I want to go home and see her," Mallory added, ignoring Bella. "I think if I were home, I could help her get better, but they won't let me."

Bella stepped toward the young girl. She approached the bed, and as she did so, the scent of vinegar became potent. She looked toward the source and found on a portable tray and next to some bunch of roses was a bowl of cucumbers in long sticks, a stinky glisten of oil on them. Next to the vegetable, tilted a picture of Mallory's family in a line: a man, strong and beard, a pelt near his heart; a woman, lean with white skin; a girl, identical to the patient; and a sister, a good height shorter then Mallory.

"How'd he get lost?" Bella asked, realizing the question might be too heavy for a girl as young as Mallory to answer.

Mallory shook her head. "She just disappeared. But she's gonna come back, and we're going to play again." She loosened her shoulders and lumbered into her pillows, then a spark flickered in her eyes, and she erected herself once more. "But she's lost right now, But that doesn't mean she will always be lost, because...because." And the girl made herself quite.

"Because what?"

"The Ghost is gonna find him."

Bella pondered. "The Ghost."

The girl nodded.

"Who's he?"

"He's gonna save my sister."

Bella changed her line of questioning. "Has it been just a few days? When did he get lost?"

Mallory shrugged. "A week."

This time Bella didn't respond. A dark realization struck her.

"L-let's grab your medication while I'm here," she uttered in an unsettled tone. She believed the patient to not be in the right mind and staggered to the cabinet to fetch the glorious orange bottles and poured a plump pill into her palm. "Is this ghost...," she continued. "Is he your imaginary friend?"

The girl shook her head.

"What is he?"

The patient fiddled with her hair. "My grandpa said that he protects people. He doesn't let people die out in the forest."

"Oh," exclaimed Bella, understanding what the tale to be. "That sounds exciting." She prompted the pills in her hand for the young girl to take.

Mallory frowned at the sight of the medication. "They taste awful."

"They should be tasteless. Would you like a glass of water?"

"Yes," Mallory responded and reached for the tablets.

Bella grabbed a glass of water for her.

She tossed back the pill and lunged for the liquid. With a repelled face, she swallowed and looked at Bella.

"Like plastic," she said.

The nurse concealed a smirk. Mallory was a welcome blessing of the day. Despite her youthfulness and energy, she noted her body to be worn, fighting a constant battle. Bella considered the medicine to be failing, but figured it must take more time.

Mallory faced the black television dangling in every room. She looked as if in meditation. All bliss had evoked from her, and she lay numb.

Feeling out of place standing at the bedside, the nurse directed herself to the door.

"Well, I hope you can get some rest, Mallory. I just be right outside if you need me."

But before Bella could reach the median of the distance between her and the station, the young girl cried out, "Do you think he'll find Lucy?"

"What do you mean?"

"Do you think he'll find my sister?" she repeated, keeping the same position.

"I don't think I know who you're talking about," Bella admitted with an uncomfortable laugh.

"The Ghost," she repeated. "Do you think he'll find her?"

"I'm...not sure."

Mallory nodded and slowly returned her sight toward the black square of the TV screen. The nurse feared she didn't answer correctly. Bella attempted to assure her everything was going to be all right, even though the odds were the sister was deceased.

"Wherever your sister is, I'm sure the police are looking for him."

The patient didn't respond. She kept her gaze fixated on the television, and her pupils shared no glare. Bella didn't want the conversion to end on a bitter note, but didn't know how to continue. The existence of her unfinished log materialized in the back of her mind, and she thought it best to end things here no matter how she seemed to the girl.

"Outside," Mallory muttered.

"What was that?" Bella crept to hear what she'd spoken.

The young girl repeated not and turned away from the nurse to her side and to the open window.

"I have to go, but I'll be right outside."

The girl kept silent.

Bella, leaving the room, took one last glance of pity at her patient. She then exited and closed the door behind her, not knowing what Mallory meant by the word "Outside." Bella returned to her desk, typed away in how she administered the medication and greeted Mallory as protocol.

An hour passed, and Mallory fell asleep in the room. The rest of Bella's time there became predictable and stale, unable to observe the strange local awake. She focused her efforts, precautions were taken place in order to cloak herself in the illusion of busy. And through this productivity, she discovered that most of her time was there behind a screen, taking notes on a fading girl. Bella wasn't treating her, only administering pills. A curiosity then set in off what disease actually had developed. She then thought she'd never know and kept to her duties. But as the nurse struggled to keep engaged in her work, a man, unnoticed by the nurse, approached the station. She didn't recognize him at first, but then it became apparent that it was Kade, a friendly smile and a warm cup of coffee in hand. He slogged along until he was within a few feet of the girl.

"How're you holding up?" he asked.

"Good," she said.

"Did you tell Nelson you were late?"

"He was the one that came and got me?"

"What? At your house?"

"No." Bella tried not to expose what happened, but perhaps her peer deserved to know. "From the emergency room."

"God, what happened? Where's Molly?"

Bell didn't look at him. "She…she was attack, I think, in some way?"

"What?" Kade exclaimed.

The nurse's demeanor only confirmed the statement.

"What do you mean she was attacked?"

"I don't know." Bella sought the floor. "I really don't know."

"How bad? How bad was it?"

"Bad. She didn't have time to tell me. The police booted us out. She could hardly speak, and she didn't have time to tell me before the police arrived."

"Oh my god." The man put a hand to his mouth. "Did something fall on her? Did she get in a car crash? God… What do you think happened?"

The nurse prepared a response, then realized she knew as little as her peer. Ideas of what occurred prompted in her mind. However, the girls shook her head and rejected her initial explanation. And with casting the intrusive ideas aside, Bella felt the desperate eyes of Kade longing for an answer.

"Someone inflicted an injury around…" And she motioned around her pelvic area.

The man squinted, unsuspecting what Bella had just inferred.

"She knocked on the door, and I found her—"

"Wait, wait, wait. What are you saying? Someone wounded her vagina?"

"I don't think Molly wants that to get out," said Bella, noting the volume of his voice. "I don't understand what happened, but Doctor Cleveland said she had scarring down there."

"But she is here? In the hospital?" clarified Kade.

Bella nodded as her stare remained static to the tile. She could see the man's weight shift from one foot to the other, a nervous motion she could recognize.

"I can't." He began to move away from the girl. "I'll…I'll get back to you."

"Wait," said Bella.

The man departed down the corridor and to the elevator.

She couldn't stop to wonder what Kade was doing. His body language reinforced what little information she possessed. She made her way in the opposite direction away from her station, curving the oval counter and the attendees forever casting stares. She pressed on to her next assignment.

She travelled along the progression of numeral metal slabs on wooden doors and soon found herself outside her desired destination: room 319. Another nurse, sitting and already stationed, was awaiting emancipation and wore sneakers similar to the woman Bella had previously encountered. However, raising her head, she discovered a thinner frame and an aged appearance.

The nurse grinned at Bella, as if she knew her; however, in the eye of the employee, there was a line of concealed resentment, or rather annoyance at the fact Bella was late to relieve her.

"I'm sorry," Bella spoke. "Nurse, um…well, Kade had me talking for a while and—"

"Don't bother." She then stood up from her spot and began stepping away from the girl.

"Wait, what condition is the patient in?"

"Read the slip," she said and kept on walking.

Bella didn't challenge the senior nurse, forgetting any inquiry.

With a sneer, the girl was left to tend the station, the former controller's footsteps fading into the commotion of the medical bay. Bella didn't watch her leave. The nurse wasted no time performing her mechanical task of logging to the computer. With a jolt, she peered through the slit-like window.

No soul slumbered in the bed. They were surrounded by a throne of metal stands all adorned with clear bags looped onto hooks that dripped toward the earth. The chamber was sickly bare. Everything appeared undisturbed, as if there wasn't even a soul in this room. And then, by the window, Bella saw the old woman, her chair slightly augmented to the side, and the woman herself looking past the window at the grand buildings of Heartlake. The nurse could barely make out a bag of sweets near her armrest.

The woman appeared awake. Bella murmured the thought of opening another conversation; however, the greetings with the previous patient went over smoothly. Her vigor only figuring the woman to be eighty in age and not much needed to be said.

Bella scanned the slip of poster material and stepped to the door, recounting to knock first. Through the crack, the odor of a deep, archaic, almost tingling scent hit her. She pressed herself over the threshold.

"Mrs. Rubido?" she announced. "My name is Nurse Tomson. I'll just be outside if you need me."

The old woman did not respond.

"Mrs. Rubido?"

The patent still ignored her.

Bella then approached the old woman. She was confused and cautious, worried something had gone wrong in the women's health. But as she neared, Bella heard music. It had no words. A melody was apparent, and the old woman hummed in time and in tune. It sounded pure. It sounded familiar. Bella now stood three feet from the patient, listening to her song, reminiscent of Molly's strange box.

From the city beam looming from the window, the old woman peered over her shoulder. She saw the girl standing in the encroaching shadows. Bella could see the deep lines in the patient's face, along with taxes chemo collected from a woman. Mrs. Rubido brought her hand to her ear, and Bella followed the action. The old woman spun the dial of a hearing aid.

"Forgive me, sweetie," she said. "I didn't hear you come in."

"No, it was my fault!" responded Bella. "I like your humming."

"Ha-ha, thank you. I have to admit you gave me a spook when I first saw you."

"Is your heart okay?"

"Ha-ha, no, no, it's fine. My heart's never been the issue, dear. I've been very picky with my diet."

"Really?"

"Yes, sweetie, no sugars or fats for me as a kid. When I got older, I even started taking those little gummies on the TV and ate mostly meats and veggies."

"That's great."

"Mhm, I even made myself stay active, mowing the lawn and planting my tulips. I even went off on walks so often." She then chuckled to herself. "My heart's never been the issue, dear. But you can see what good it's done me."

Bella eyebrows raised, and her mouth tightened.

Ms. Rubido laughed. "It's only a joke."

"That's horrible."

"Our sweet angel, dear." The lady gave a tired smile. "He'll take an athlete as soon as he'll take a smoker. It's just when, sweetie."

The girl was again brought to the suspension of local myth. She knew the woman was more than likely to further elaborate.

"I've heard of angels." She took a step closer to the patient. "Are you a Local?"

Mrs. Rubido scoffed. "Every church has angels. Every church has death in God's ranks, or at least at his whim."

The response took Bella by surprise. "Aren't angels supposed to be good?"

"He is, darling," the woman corrected. "But it's okay. You're young, aren't you? You don't really know him."

"What do you mean?" Bella laughed.

"You don't really know him. I can tell by the way ya look." Rubido pushed back in her chair. "Oh, I don't hold it against ya, dear. You're young! And it comes with age, and you can sometimes even see the angel do his work."

"I know people who've passed. It's in the news all the time."

"Ha! Isn't that true! You'll see him. You'll see him all around! But you never had someone close to you die, have you?"

Bella stepped toward the door.

"I don't think you have." She shuffled in her chair. "I'm old, dear. It's a great fear to outlive everyone, you know. You don't see the little details, that to see is unbearable. But as terrifying as it is, never think God's work is a bad thing."

Bella scoffed. "How could death not be a bad thing?"

"He leads us to new worlds." The woman gazed back to the city lights. "One of wonders! To change, dear. Change!"

"Um, well." Bella stood up. "Let move over to the bed." She extended her hand for the patient to clutch.

"Many of the greats met him. And we all will eventually. But I'm sure you're aware of the Ghost, dear."

Bella turned back to the woman. She noted a candling burning upon the open mantle near the woman's knees.

Mrs. Rubido kept her stare out to the window.

"Not until just a while ago."

"From who?"

"A little girl told me."

"He's a great tale for the youth to learn. I pity city folk. Such a great story."

The girl studied Mrs. Rubido. An aura of peace set upon her. She looked to where the old woman is staring and noticed the woman's gaze was not fixated on the city, but the dark mountains beyond its limitations.

"The Ghost can't meet the Angel," Mrs. Rubido continued. "At least not yet. A curse lay upon him. If you believe that sort of thing. It's all written stories and passed-down traditions. But it makes me wonder if there is something we must do before we can die."

"Why do you think that?"

The woman grew to a whisper. "I was saved."

Bella wasn't convinced. "F-from what?"

"From being taken, my dear. I can still remember it—and the clear path to the mountains."

The nurse thought the woman to be crazy, another example of local madness she'd come to know. There wasn't anything the patient said that assured her, her dementia ramblings, but knew an argument wouldn't be wise with a woman in such a condition. She decided to move on with her tasks.

"Let's move over to the bed, Mrs. Rubido," she said.

Mrs. Rubido declined the offer. "What did I do that made it okay for me to die?"

Unsure what to do, Bella looked around for something, not wanting to tackle the topic.

"I wasn't meant to die then, but I'm still not a corpse. Have I done it yet? Have I done what the angels want of me?"

The nurse shook her head then crossed over and took an IV drip line and rolled the plethora over to the old woman. She moved a coffee table out of the way and pulled the drip mechanism over to the side of the woman. Mrs. Rubido smiled, unfazed by the commotion. She began humming her song again, glancing over to the girl only when she got close.

"What were we talking about?" the woman asked.

Bella then prepared the right bag and the right needle for the dosage and began prepping Mrs. Rubido's arm for the injection.

"Just about the weather," she said. She pressed the tool into her.

"Thank you, sweetie," she said.

Bella focused on the IV. "This will get you hydrated."

"Say..." The old woman took interest in the girl's naked neck and saw nothing around her pale skin. "A Yudaku would suit you, dear. The local men would be lucky to have a sweetie like you."

Bella laughed. "I don't think so."

"Oh..." Mrs. Rubido went quiet. "Do you have a husband?"

Bella shook her head.

"Oh my...well, that is a pity. Where are you from then?"

"Haze," Bella looked at her to her skin.

The woman studied the nurse's complexion.

"It's the city with the smog," the girl continued. "You know with the dark skies and dirty streets, you have to wear a mask half of the year. I...can't recall. Is it a big city?"

Bella nodded, attempting to move along her unpleasant station.

"It must be nice then." She turned back toward the window. "My father would always tell me how great the city was, with so many lights and sounds. It is a blessing to see what he had labored so extensively for...I'm glad I get to meet him soon."

Bella finished with the IV bag, and the liquid flowed into the old woman's veins.

"Thank you, my dear," she said again. "Would you consider a Yudaku? I bet I could get you some?"

"No, thank you." Bella smiled at her.

"A young woman should brandish the knots."

Bella shook her head, an image of Molly clutching the necklace came to mind. "No, thank you."

"The offer is limited, dear!" The woman laughed to herself.

Shifting her stance, Bella glanced out the window and back at the old woman, who returned to her luxurious scene. "It's okay, you don't remember, just now you mentioned nearly being taken. What does that mean? What was trying to take you?"

"I can't recall what it looked like. I don't think I even saw it. I was playing with my family near the edge of town near the Giants... Heartlake was a town before it was this...and I remember going off just beyond the tree line to grab something. We were playing catch. My brother could throw far. And I went for, I believe, a far ball that went behind a tree. I then felt a gust of wind and a sharp pain to my side. And before I knew it, I was flying, travelling faster than even a car and..." She stopped talking. Her face stiffened by the remembrance of lost memory.

"You saw him?"

"I...I don't recall. But I stopped, somehow. Somehow I got to the ground, and I think I lost my breath. Then something picked me back up, but in a cradle not over the shoulder. I can remember that."

Bella didn't know what to make of the story. "Was it a man?" She moved her eyes to the door and back to the old woman. "Could it have been the same thing?"

"No, dear. I was carried by two different beings. I can tell you that much. He was...tall, and I think hairy. I can tell you they weren't the same, sweetie."

Bella kept a static expression.

Rubio continued. "He brought me back to my father and vanished into the brush."

"That can't actually be real." The girl looked out to the city and then to the mountains beyond. The Giants were shrouded in shadow and bore only a faint glint of sunlight.

"I have no reason to lie," said Mrs. Rubido.

"It's too fantastic." She sensed an argument. "I need to go fill in my charting. But just wave me down when you're ready for bed, okay? Have you had dinner yet?"

"Yes, I'm just about ready for bed." The old lady stopped, fumbling an inconceivable word to herself.

Bella watched the old woman's eyes shifting and searching for a name that was not imprinted in memory.

"Bella Tomson," the girl said.

The old lady smiled at her. "Thank you, my dear. Bella will do nicely." She returned to her peace.

The nurse smiled and stepped back from Mrs. Rubido. She walked out of the room and sat back down at her station. She watched the old woman from the slit of glass for a few minutes. When confident of Mrs. Rubido's stability, Bella started her entry in the computer's log. She found herself finishing without much to write down and posted ideally, brainstorming of ways to drag out its length. Clicking, clicking filled the median. It was all Bella could pay attention to, but for an instant, she swore she heard the hum of the old woman from the other side. The tune of the music box played besides it, and sorrow washed over the girl.

Another rotation underwent. Bella helped the old woman bed and saw it time to check on her last patient. A different personnel approached the girl to replace her. A man of middle height and of overweight body tapped Bella on the shoulder. In an instant, Bella flung her head up and moved over from her seat, apologizing and bowing to the tile. She worried of a stern response, but was parted with none as the man took his place without a word. Bella looked up at the man and found his gaze bent toward the earth, taking nervous glances at the girl. She nearly said something, but she reacted and pivoted away. Bella felt his gaze upon her as she descended for the hallway. She could pity him.

It wasn't long before the girl reached Evergreen's room. There was no sitting body behind the monitor, to which Bella responded by scanning the medical floor of a coming employee. There was none, other than the personnel behind the oval counter and their contempt. Having no other prompting, she performed what was mundane now, peeking, at last, into the chamber.

The old man slept to the droning flashes of a television. He drooled on his chest, and his belly rose and fell like a balloon. A half-eaten bag of pretzels dripped over the side of the snack stand. The girl noticed, like Mrs. Rubido, Evergreen had no gifts or pastime, other than his dreadful old book, and rationalized, they were likely forgotten about.

Her eyes unwavering from the book, the image of the creature crept back into Bella's mind. Fake or not, it disgusted her. She connected lines the old woman's story had drawn and thought perhaps Evergreen wrote about the Pelt myth or self-assured witnesses. It was all obviously nonsense to her, but she had to admit an admiration to preserve tradition, not having anything similar to speak about. It wouldn't be a lie if she claimed the patient to be asleep. She didn't have to step in the room. But Bella did lie to herself about fulfilling duty and entered the room.

Evergreen's loud snores provided coverage for the girl's footsteps. She crept to the man unnoticed on tiptoes. She stopped at the edge of the bed and looked down at the man. He fell deep in a world without troubles. Bella knew what lay before her but moved to the stand. She didn't know if the drawing was the only thing in the ancient pages, but an overwhelming desire to unearth swayed her.

She gathered herself as a thief. Her petite fingers brushed the weathering cover. Bella plucked the book from the stand and opened it to a random page. To her confusion, all that imposed, line after line, she could not speak, nor read, nor speculate in any way what they meant. It appeared related to English. It appeared to read left to right and composed characters that she could recognize; however, it was littered with semicolon and dashes that separated short phrases that were alien to her language. The presumed letters of the phrase or sentences were built of sharp lines crossed and connected to make up the bulk of the words. And among these sentences that the girl could not comprehend, the letter R could be identified and most prevalent at the end of words, and among the phrases. Arabic numerals could be understood. The key numbers being 25,772 or 26000.

She thought first this must be the native language of the Locals, developed from centuries separated by the Giants. But history didn't foretell of the Americas being divided in the Reorganization of Power. The Pelts always existed, toward the bottom of class, next to cripples and infected homeless. The numbers are a standard, though odd in the arrangement of the page. Bella thought Evergreen must have adopted the language of a faraway place in his journal.

Convinced in her assessment, she turned the page. In doing so, she discovered more of the sharp line language, more recognized numerals. However, now besides a sketch, there appears as observations and measurements next to the picture. Bella then looked at the image itself. A coyote's body possessed a raven's head, ink plumage combined with a mixture of fur covered it. Its pectoral limbs stressed saw-like claws, and its beak was full of teeth. On its side, the animal banished wings, too small to fly with. But looking closer, its feathers encircled pores that were scattered on their interior that oozed what appeared to be a powder. An arrow pointed to these holes and connected to a line with showed a sign and measurement: =40mg.

She flipped to the next page. There, sketched with memorable detail, the image the girl had witnessed before. But she didn't turn away, the horrid limbs and joints stretched to ungodly length. A familiar sick feeling returned to her stomach, but she forced herself back to the damned book. She followed the elongated limbs with hook-like nails until they reached its body, a thin leathery torso that wore gaunt flesh as molding paper, along with few pale patches of hair. The head was hardest to stare at, for the girl. It was proportional to its skewed body, but its eyes were missing, leaving dark pits in their places. Then its mouth, connecting where it shouldn't, caused the nurse to taste the inclination of her own vomit.

The book slipped from her grasp while the girl kept herself from spewing all over her patient. Her mind raced as she tried to fathom what was wrong with her.

"It's all fake," she rationalized. "Just drawings."

She eased herself back to an erect stance. She looked down at the old man, the depravity of one who would draw such a thing, but relieved to see he had not awakened. She shifted her weight, then clenched her fist. She looked back down at the book. The open page was lost and a new image revealed itself to her.

It appeared as a mere man, but once more, a greater deity. The sketch was depicted wearing a tattered coat of bear skin and wolf. He slumped a woodcutter's axe over his shoulder, bloody, with the same stick-like letters engraved in a column in the weapons handle. His hair, long and matted, resembled snow, a braided beard of waist length of similar color. Of his face, it admitted embedded rage, deep lines and deep eyes that of which bore only white spots. There next to him, an arrow pointed to him: a discernible number, then a measurement: 10 ft,? lbs.

Bella analyzed the estranged figure. She thought she'd seen him but wasn't exactly sure. She then remembered the lake, but that couldn't be possible. His appearance didn't cause any harm as the prior creature did, but she wouldn't call him a wonderful sight. It was as though she was staring at a king from history from a lesson school forced a passing grade. She picked up the book again and marveled by the ferocity in his face.

Thereafter, she noticed too late the lack of sound in the room, and the notion someone was looking at her.

"Enjoying my work?" sounded Evergreen.

Bella jumped in place. She darted to see Evergreen's open gaze. The old man burned his sight into the girl. He brushed his finger up and down his cast.

What color Bella possessed had left her. "I-I-I'm sor—"

"No no, stop. I don't want your apologies."

Bella bit her lip.

"What did you think? I know my stay would be bad, so I can't say I'm surprised. But rooting through my journal, the least you could do is tell me what you thought of it."

Bella said nothing.

"You going to say anything?"

Ideas raced within her. If the man complained, she'd be out of a job in less than two shifts.

Evergreen glared at the pale girl, who now was tossing scenarios in her head. He hadn't forgotten about the day before. His eyes then shifted to the book, then back to the pale girl. He sighed then, giving up on his anger.

"Well, can you tell me why you're snooping?" he questioned, this time sincere. "Did your higher-ups put you up to this?"

Bella didn't respond. She tried to find a word, but there were none.

"Don't ya realize that there's probably some things you best not know about a person? But I got you bastards good! You can't read it!"

At last she spoke. "No one wanted me to look."

"You're a bad liar."

"N-no, sir, I'm not."

"Then why root through my journal?"

"I was just curious, and I saw that creature the day before, and I just…wanted to know."

"Which creature?" he questioned.

The image came back to mind. "The large-mouth one," she said. "No eyes."

The man flickered through the book. "Him? You saw one of those?" His voice raised. "Where?"

"In your book. When we first met."

"Ah." A sense of calm rushed over. "Well, why him?"

She shrugged. "Just curious. Honest."

"I find that hard to believe."

Bella's stance firmed. "I'm telling the truth!"

"That's bullshit, and ya know it. No one's just curious," Evergreen persisted. "I won't be angry with you." He covered his elbow to cough. He endured the pain.

Bella took a breath. "I can't tell you why. I really can't. But…but it kinda looked like a man I saw." She stopped. "A part of me wanted confirmation."

"What man? What was his name?" the old man demanded.

"Oliver. His name is Oliver. He…he went out with my friend. They went on a date and—"

Evergreen's eyes widened. "What friend? Is she still alive?"

"Molly." Bella nodded. "Yes, but something bad happened."

"What was it?"

"I can't answer that."

"Can't or won't?"

"I don't know!" Bella yelled. She was surprised herself, and then afraid. Her voice coward after. "I don't understand. No one will explain."

Evergreens slumped forward as much as his contrast would let him. "Who won't tell you."

"The police...the doctor. They say it all weird and won't cough it up. I don't know what they mean. I wish they would just cough it up and say it. So I thought..." She hated herself. She wished she'd never come in the room. "I just put two and two together. It was a dumb impulse."

"What did your friend look like after the date?" Evergreen asked.

Bella could not think of describing her ruined break. She refused to retell that sight; he didn't deserve to know. But she knew the man to be a Local, and the sight of the ripped Yudaku came back into mind.

"He beat her," she said. "And her necklace was torn."

"The knots?"

The girl nodded.

Evergreen remained silent. He felt a different pain, one his aching body couldn't distract him from. He covered his mouth with his free hand, gentle tugging at his whiskers.

"It's a target," he finally spoke, but Bella did not believe he was talking to her. "Do-do you assume the man was the creature in my book?"

"N-no. It just reminded me of him. I know it's just fairy tales." She pointed to the book.

Evergreen looked at his journal. "Yes, you're right."

"You have very neat handwriting." She tried to change the subject.

"But don't tell anyone you saw it. You'll just look like a fool to the rest of the city folk."

Belle nodded. "Of course. I promise."

He smiled a dull smile. "Good. Do you know what my people call them?"

The girl remained still, then bobbed her head.

"Fann Draugr, that's the first European name, for it is the term I use way back when. Then Wendigo game from the Indian. Then my people started a name for it—Pale Things. The monsters are older than any culture. I'm probably one of the last men in Heartlake to know as such."

"How'd you learn?"

Evergreen pointed toward the ground. Bella followed his gesture to the weird briefcase that sat by his side.

"I've got just about every relic a Local could need in there." He shifted back to his place. "It holds what my granddad passed down to me."

"More books?" Bella asked.

"Yes, and little phrases to remember, brief words of advice."

"What do you do with all of that?"

Evergreen scarred at the black TV screen. "I don't know. I guess pass it down someday or have it buried with me."

"Do you have a son?"

The old man shook his head.

"A daughter?"

He repeated the movement.

"Oh," said Bella. "Maybe you could give it to a museum. That way your writing can last forever."

"The paper isn't what I'm worried about. There are things in my possession that our state won't find to tolerable."

"Like what?"

"Not too sympathetic articles about its abuse of power. You know, the basic claims a Local might make in court. Nothing too special. I like to call it family long discussions."

Bella worried the conversation would become political. She went back to her original topic. "What do these creatures do in your stories?"

"They take." He said it without hesitation.

"What?" The girl peeked from the tile.

"Everything." And his face rested to where Bella once looked.

Bella understood it may be a time to leave, studying his demeanor to be lost in recollections. She paced an inch. She wanted to talk to him more. Though inconceivable before, she enjoyed this conversation.

"I'll leave you be. I gotta start on my chart."

Evergreen nodded.

"I'll just be right outside if you need anything."

"You're pure," he said, and the phrase surprised the girl. "Be careful."

The nurse studied her patient. "An odd statement," she said to herself and went toward the on.

Evergreen reoriented his book as if it was never disturbed.

—ɯ—

Bella kept watch over the old man throughout the remainder of her shift. She jotted down many observations, but typed nothing about the conversation they had. She repeated her cycle until the very end of shift, where she sat once again outside Evergreen's door. The day had become night, and she expected the old man to be asleep. But as she peered through the glass, she saw her patient talking to himself, his free hand vertical and his vision bent. Bella stood up and was barely able to understand what the old man was talking about.

"How long, Lord? How long?"

Bella noted the edge in Evergreen voice. She felt like she should not listen.

"Why ravish your people? Why banish your Ghost?"

The girl shared a great deal of respect for the old man, and pity washed over her and brought her ear from the glass. She knew there was no cure for his lament. Bella returned to her station, not expecting a nurse to come and relieve her. She checked the time, then left toward the breakroom. There were still staff going about, trading others and filling in when they needed to be. There was no one behind the oval counter.

Bell turned and saw an orange-haired officer approaching her.

Chapter

12

"Ms. Tomson," Brigham started.

The nurse looked up. She stopped in the middle of the hallway with him. The officer gripped his vest on its straps. Bella observed an avoidance of eye contact, which she copied. Bella kept her sight on the officer's black boots.

"Your friend took Molly home, and she told us that you'd need a ride." He laughed a little. "Not much else is happening in Heartlake, I guess."

Bella smiled. "I guess not."

He rubbed his head. "So ya done for the night?"

"I think so." She looked to her side. "I just have to check into the break room for a sec to see if Nelson is there."

"All right, I'll follow you."

They started in the same direction. Brigham, a distance ahead of the girl, who was too intimidated to stand right beside him. The officer continually retracted his pace to that of Bella's, not confident in to which he led. The nurse responded by amping her strides, causing the man now to play catch up.

Not soon enough, they reached the break room. Bella strode inside while the officer positioned himself outside, scanning the hospital with folding arms and accusatory gaze. Upon entering, Bella could see no one within. She thought of waiting, but presumed the doctor to be busy with his well-oiled machine. She parted back out, and a voice sounded from the exit.

"Officer Brigham, right?"

"Yes, sir," responded the officer.

"Did you help discharge Molly?"

"Do you know her?"

"Yeah, I work with Molly on the same floor here."

Bella continued her approach. Out of the door she saw Kade, no mug in hand, conversing with the officer.

"I helped her get out the door, but that dark-haired lady took her Home.

"How'd she look?" Kade's eye's wandered off Brigham's to the girl. He bent a dim smile and waved hello Bella.

The nurse waved back.

"I can't give my opinion on that," said Brigham. "She was well enough for the doctor to let her go."

"Oh...good, good. I was going to offer if she had no one else, but I guess that's already covered. I could have seen Molly again if I did." He looked to Bella, then back at Brigham.

"You were close friends?" asked Brigham.

"Maybe just give her some air. Yes, we went on a couple of dates."

"Where'd you go?"

"Anywhere with a tree." Kade laughed.

"Does the name Oscar Dmitri mean anything to you?"

"No."

"Did you know Molly went out with a man yesterday evening?"

"I had no clue."

"Are you in an active relationship with Ms. Need?"

A lump grew in his throat. "No," Kade answered. "We never got to that point."

Brigham had almost pulled out his notepad. "So you had no idea what could have happened to Molly?"

Kade nodded. "I just wish.." He swallowed. "I just wish I was there. Maybe I could have done something."

"You probably would have. Not many people would just let this sort of thing happen."

"Yeah...yeah, I suppose so."

"Everyone around wishes they could have done something."

Bella nodded.

"Right…right," resumed Kade. "You know I could help you find who did this. I can take vacation off, and if you need some manpower, I could—"

Brigham almost laughed. "We have a good lead on who did this, sir. This should be over pretty soon."

Kade turned to Bella. "Tell me if she needs anything, please. And I'll do it."

Bella looked down.

"Just let Molly be for a while," said Brigham, motioning to leave. "Maybe send her some flowers."

"Did Nelson come back?" asked Bella.

The officer looked at her. "He was present, yes."

"He has a name for taking care of cases like this," said Kade. "But just to think it'd happen to one of our own—and to Molly of all people."

Brigham began walking. Bella watched the officer cross between her and Kade. Her peer flinched a little as Brigham neared him.

"I was nice talking to you, Kade," said the girl.

"Yeah." The man put his hands in his pockets. "Tell Molly hi from me. Do you think I could stop by to check on her?"

Bella shrugged.

"I'll get back to you on that. But don't let me keep you waiting."

Bella waved and went in line behind the officer, making his way to the elevator. She heard Kade's sneakers squeak to the break room. His actions only solidified the seriousness of her friend's encounter. He acted far too strange for the girl to ignore.

The officer waited for the nurse to catch up with her.

"He looked a bit shaken," he said.

Bella looked at him surprised. "Yeah, he did a little bit."

"Do you think he possibly knew Oscar?"

Bella shook her head. She initially changed the subject. "Did she tell you?" the girl asked.

"Yes," Brigham said. "She told Deacon the whole thing. Or I think she did. We haven't had a chance to rendezvous. I stood out by Kim. But when we moved Molly, she seemed to be doing a lot better."

"Was she?" Bella stopped in the middle of the hall.

Brigham halted and grabbed his vest straps. "I think she'll come out of this okay. It's just... hard right now. It's hard to know what this sort of crime does to a person. Cleveland gave her some sources, some groups she could get to for the mental part of recovery."

Bella studied the tile. She didn't ask what crime had been committed. "What was Nelson doing there?"

"I'm not sure. He grabbed Deacon and talked with him privately. It probably was something about the incident. He's done it with other cases."

"Has there been other cases?"

"Yes, but can you lead me out of here? I'm a bit confused around. I don't know how you guys function here."

Bella smiled. "It's this way."

A moment of silence filled by the bleeding footsteps led to a metal bucket held by steel. Bella led the way. She was amazed she didn't see the hordes of people crossing every which way to mundane tasks and fetch quests, and believed this officer walking beside must be a repellent. She wished he was with her more often. Brigham joined her, and the nurse pressed the button to the metal jaws closing. Down the basket went with humming a metallic creeks. The two did not make a sound between them, and the girl grew estranged and concerned, letting the conversation go silent.

Painful seconds pass, and the elevator doors reopen at the base floor. Bella took the lead and left the ancient basket first. Brigham followed scanning the hospital.

"Does it always look like this?" he asked.

Bella looked back to him. "What do you mean?"

"Stale," Brigham said.

The girl shrugged. "It's a hospital."

"I know, I know, but I'd think they'd make an effort to boost morale. I like the posters though."

"They can be fun."

"Do they help?" The officer laughed.

"I don't know." Bella laughed but didn't understand why.

The two continued several steps to the main entrance, passing the bright and joyful posters. Brigham glanced at each one.

"You mentioned there were other cases," said Bella. "Why did you say that?"

"Well"—the officer chuckled to himself—"in the same way more murders and robberies happen. It's part of the world we live in, I suppose."

"But...how so?"

"What do you mean by that?"

"I..." Bella fumbled out noises, none in proper English. "I don't know." She had a sense to know the correct question, but it slipped between her teeth.

"Have you ever seen someone come in from a gunshot wound? Someone stabbed?"

"I haven't."

"But you're a nurse."

"I work on the observation side," Bella said. "Not emergency."

The officer appeared surprised. "Oh, I see. That'd make more sense."

"Why?"

"Just how you talk."

The two walked in silence as they crossed the entrance of the hospital. Within an instance, the girl grew conscious of her choice of words.

"It's not a bad thing," said the man. "Just and observation."

Belle didn't reply, and the pair crossed the barren parking lot, a lone police cruiser perfectly parked within white parallel lines. The wind hurled across the cracked, and rubber filled pavement, and the night leaked over the hospital, with the gleam of the waxing moon shyly behind a cloud. All around were street lamps glaring down beams from old bulbs, some flashing, others burnt out. The man sheathed his hands in his pockets, and Bella retracted, hoping the officer would gain footing ahead. However, Brigham stayed beside her, scanning the empty lot and cars that fill it. The girl watched the earth pass by.

No words were spoken as the two got settled into the vehicle. Bella took the passenger seat, however wished to be in the back behind the plated bars. It appeared as a regular day to the officer, switching the car into reverse and pulling through onto the parking lot until traveling to the open road.

"Where too?"

"Left," Bella said.

Brigham listened. The car idled and accelerated to an exact speed limit. Traffic still littered the street, but dwindled in comparison to the morning rush. Sleepy clouds hovered above glinted by dime starlight of the slick night sky, a dense tempest faltering in the distance. This was unnoticed by the girl leaning against the police vehicle's interior. Molly welled in her mind. She would have to get the full story from her. Bella felt helpless. She didn't know how to make things right.

The officer noted her discomforted curl and tried to ignore her. "What on your mind?" He eventually said.

Bella didn't respond.

"If it's the crime stuff, then believe me, I understand."

"It wasn't that."

"What is it then?"

Slight hesitation warned her not to tell, but her lips parted anyway. "I don't think I can face her."

"Why do you think that?" the officer questioned.

"She asked me to go with her." The girl held her abdomen. "She said they could have made it a double date."

The murmur of the road became numbing.

"I-I-I could have gone." She tightened her grip on her abdomen. "I know you said wishing won't help, but I can't think I could've not done something. Maybe I should have discourage her more."

The officer listened while minding the open road. He never imagined a conversation like this between a nurse. "Could you have prevented this? Yeah. Could I have? Absolutely. But we were speaking in the present. We know what we could have, but there were no signs anything was wrong."

"I think there were red flags."

"Now you know what to look for in the future. Don't blame yourself too hard."

"What would you have done differently," Bella asked. "If you were with her."

Silence.

"Would you have struck the man? Would you pull him off her?"

"Something like that."

"Would you shoot him?"

Brigham glanced at the girl. She looked directly at him, unblinking.

"Look," he began, "it's like what I said to that fellow. Everyone wishes they could have done something to prevent this situation." He glanced at the girl in the passenger seat. "And yes, probably someone could have, but that person turned out to be a monster. The reality is she was more than likely surrounded by several men, bigger and stronger than her, outnumbered and overpowered." He sighed, doubting if he should say what came next in his mind. "Oscar didn't work alone. If you or I went with her, it wouldn't turn out too well for us. Not for this kind of rape."

That word, there was that word again. She knew not what it meant. But it's weight could be felt by the girl. The police officer didn't want to even say it to her. However, she still presented.

"No," she said. "I could have...I could have with a gun."

"It's not true," said Brigham. "If ya had a gun, it would have been illegal. And after if it would have fired, we would have to come and arrest you."

A spirit of protest manifested. "I would have stopped him though."

The officer quieted it. "You would have killed someone. Believe it or not, that's against the law too."

"What if I didn't kill him?"

"Two charges then—gun possession and aggravated assault. Maybe more but those two are off the tip of my head."

Again the numbing of the road rose. The two sat in stillness, worried of what each other thought of one. The girl could sense suspicion rising in the officer. She knew she couldn't stop what had happened, but she could still want to.

"I don't mean it," broke Bella.

"I know," said Brigham. "And I don't blame ya. It's an awful thing. You should have heard what your friend said."

"Kim?"

"Yeah, I'm not gonna repeat what it but you can guess what a woman like that could come up with."

Bella smiled. "She's crude."

"Again, it's all reasonable. The man who did this was a monster, and it's not like I can defend him. He deserves it, and we're gonna put him in jail."

"Do you promise?"

The doubt came as a shock to the officer. "Yes," he said. "I'm sure of it."

The girl shielded her face against the window. More dead air filled the space between the two. She remembered how he looked at her, where his vision drifted toward ever increasingly around the elegant dry knots. Bella unveiled herself and turned back to her escort. Brigham again flung a glance at her.

"The Yudaku," she whispered. "He was looking at her Yudaku."

"Oscar?"

The nurse nodded.

"Molly didn't mention any of that in Deacon's report."

"I saw him staring at the bar."

"Why wouldn't Molly mention it though?"

"He wasn't paying attention to where he was looking. She doesn't study people like that."

"All right, so you think there's some sort of religious angle to this attack?"

"Kim told me something about Yudakus being targets. I'm just wondering if that applies here. Take a right here."

Brigham turned and flipped his blinker. "Well, if what you're saying is true, it's one hell of a detail. Don't let me forget it."

Bella nodded.

"I'm kinda treating you like my partner right now." He laughed. "Bouncing ideas off one another, analyzing the scene, it's kinda crazy."

Bella didn't laugh, but sat there cold and hunched.

The officer shrank in response to his failed joke, but concentrated on the farthest north in the city. They traveled mute for a few seconds, which nearly killed the driver. He could feel the avertness in her gaze and glanced at her several times to prove his hunch.

"It's the next one right there," said the girl.

"Which one?"

She pointed. "No. 310."

Brigham turned in the Planned Home driveway. He stopped in the middle and turned to the girl. He parted his lips, but no words came out. Bella waited for a question or statement, then opened the car door.

"Thank you," said the girl.

"It's gonna be still tricky to talk about things," he finally said. "I wouldn't try and force anything if she's not willing. She had enough prodding for one day."

Bella nodded her head. She then pushed ajar the door and stepped out of the vehicle. "Be safe," she said. "Remember the necklace."

"You too," he said. "And I will."

Bella then closed the door.

Brigham made sure the girl was safely inside before he left. The front door appeared unlocked, and the girl stepped inside the building. He reversed then and took off into the night.

The lights were off and the blinds were all closed, making the house darker than the outside. Molly had always made sure the lights were on when she was home. Bella thought it would always be that way.

She crossed into the hall, a painting still on the floor, perhaps it was hit by her roommate or the police investigating the area. Bella entered the empty dining room. There was no traces of food nor anyone having even been there. To the right in the kitchen, she saw nobody, but to her left, through the screen door, she saw a primitive radiance, an orange glow and blazed from a black potlike grill. Molly was drooped down in a lawn chair, and Kim was sitting next to her. Bella's mind raced to the million things she could and shouldn't speak, to a desire and lust of being mute. She did her best to remedy the anxiety-ridden manifestations in her brain and made herself creep forward, creaking the floor board, with sickness stirring in her gut. Her eyes shined as she got closer to the redhead who was witnessing the fire and ember floating into the sky. She heard her friend talking and recognized it to be the tattooed woman talking in depth of a story with almost rhythmic-like structure. Molly seemed cured of the shock, or at least functional. Kim's voice had a tone of folly, like it was an old time spent in the infinite.

Bella reached the screen, the back of her mind tried to tug her away, testifying of guilt and shame that should condemn the girl to lock herself away. She almost believed and withdrew her hand from the door.

Kim had spotted her from outside and beckoned with both hands for her to come and join them.

Bella raised her hand to open the screen but stopped. Her fingers tapped the plastic handle. The mind was blank, but Bella wanted more time. She needed more time, to come up with a plan on how she would talk to her friend. Tears bit at the corners of her eyes. She felt ridiculous. Finally, with pressured breath, she slid the door open. Kim killed her story upon the action and turned to her. Molly still stared at the fire. Bella stood in a multitude of horror.

"I'm sorry," Bella said and covered her mouth. "I'm so sorry."

She went to the redhead and pulled her arm tight around. Molly hugged her, leading her head against Bella's.

Kim glanced at them, then into the fire. "About time you showed up," she said. "I spent all this time getting this fire ready and worried we would not all get to enjoy it. Would you like to take my seat?"

"No, I'll stand."

"You sure?"

"Yes."

Bella noticed how cold Molly felt in her arms. The redhead didn't possess the same strength as she once did. The girl loosened her grip and sought to gaze upon Molly's face. But her friend was positioned toward the blaze, and she would not look at her. The nurse noted no tears in Molly's eyes, only a long exhausted expression and hung lopsided with her bruises. The redhead then finally looked at, holding a tired smile.

"Are you still hurting?" the girl asked.

"I'm okay," said Molly.

"Are you sure? Do you need anything?"

"Yes, I'm good."

"I already got the fire going for her," said Kim. "We're technically not supposed to have one, but I think we can get away with an exception."

Molly wore fresh clothes, a hooded jacket and some jeans. Her hair was slightly wet and drooped along the back of the chair. Kim still wore her original clothes of the day, not bothering to change her due to the smoke. The girl figured she'd do the same.

"Did you eat anything?" she asked.

Molly shook her head.

"I've been trying to get her to," said Kim.

"It's okay, I'm just not hungry," said the redhead.

"What about an s'more?"

She considered it, but shook her head.

"Did you tell the police what happened then?" Bella questioned.

Taking a moment to respond, the redhead nodded. "Yes."

"How did that go?"

She shrugged, tapping her foot. "It went fine." A tremble was in her voice. "I told him how it happened and what I took, and how he"—Molly stopped—"what he did. I'm sorry you two."

"You don't have to be sorry," said Kim.

Bella went mute for a moment. She spoke what itched on the tip of her tongue: "What did he do?"

Molly looked past the fire. Her gaze was fixated in the dark mountain over the barrier.

Kim was appalled. "Bella!"

But the girl didn't reply to her. She waited for a response.

Then, reaching into her pocket, Molly produced the Yudaku, the ends of it torn from an unseen snap. The redhead peered at the necklace, afraid of what she saw. She showed Bella the damage. "This," she said. "This is what he did to me."

And Bella, her stomach ever turning, beheld the broken knot, the sacred furling rope bent in an ugly bundle upon her palm, how something so wonderful could be ripped away from someone. And the girl, somehow frightened at the sight, no longer questioned.

"I'll...I'll tell you the full story someday. I'm just trying to process it all." She then looked to the mountain. "But Kim was right." Molly pupils slashed to the embers and put the necklace back in her pocket.

Kim wanted to claim she wasn't correct in her reasoning, but knew it would be a lie. But Bella didn't believe so, but kept her objections within. Only the fire cracked while they figured what to say next, if one needed to say anything next. It estranged Bella to see Molly like this, but she held on to a notion that the redhead would keep her composure and no more fire would have to be made. The idea led to her to say, "How many people do you think see the smoke?"

"Oh, the whole block for sure," scoffed Kim. "There're probably all gonna make complaint to the station. The worst we could get though is a ticket, unlicensed burning."

"Haze had a protocol before I was born."

Molly shook her head.

"Yeah, most cities enact something like that. I learned before Heartlake passed its ban, there were a ton of bonfires. Led by the usual suspect, but it was still fun."

"Who told you that?" asked Bella.

"Guess what my family was," said Kim. "I guess still is. They're really nice people and all. My father thought this one could have used a different brain." She pointed to herself to try to be humorous. "But they were really nice people."

"You still talk to them?"

"No." Kim laughed and rolled up her sleeves and exposed her tattoos. "Not with these things."

Molly snickered. Bella noticed this is what Kim seemed to be going for.

"I think I was about nineteen when they fully cut me off."

Bella laughed. "Loving family," she said, being harsh to the woman who she thought would hit her.

"No kidding," said Kim. She kept admiring her tattoos. She scanned first her right arm, a grin still present on her face. Then switched to the left, but with witnessing the designs, her joy dissipated and her shoulder sunk. Bella caught a quick glance at the artwork before the woman rolled up her sleeves. The flowers were ever prettier under the fire's light. The girl then peered over to the redhead, noting how she kept herself almost completely covered, so far as to ball her fists inside her coat.

Kim's vision then crossed to the redhead. They reached for Molly, but the ruined girl kept a steadfast stare the night's abyss. Unknowingly, Kim watched her.

"Molly?" The tattooed woman tried to get her attention.

Molly turned back to the group. "I'm sorry, what?"

"It's not the only reason for my tattoos," Kim repeated. "My parents."

"Yeah?" Molly bore a twisted brow and contorted until she finally understood what Kim had meant. "Oh, right, yeah, I remember."

"You listened to me tell Mason's story millions of times."

Molly nodded.

"You helped me get through it."

"Derrick did more."

"You did a lot." Kim's voice was firm. "And that's what me and Bella are gonna do."

Molly shifted.

"We're gonna help, listen, take you anywhere you need to go, anywhere you want to be. Still be you, don't let that evil fuck win."

Flames kindled toward the tattooed woman, and Molly nodded. "He got what he wanted," she said.

Kim stood up. "Just know we're here. We'll do anything to help you."

Molly's eyes targeted the tattooed woman. The charred wood at the base of the flame cracked a flurry of sparks. The girls watched the wisp fade into ash. Kim then looked at Molly one last time.

"I'm gonna have to get ready now," she said. "But Bella is gonna be right here by your side."

"Wait, Kim," said the girl. "You're going in."

"Yep, not enough manpower. I picked it up when you left. I felt bad that you had to go when the old fart came back in."

"Are ya sure you wanna go back in? That a long while without sleep."

"I'll manage." Kim smiled and began walking toward the door but looped under the fire. The woman halted and bent to the redhead and hugged her. Molly only used one arm. Kim then looked at Bella, to whom nodded. Kim did the same, then separated from Molly, and walked into the darkness of the Planned Home.

Only two left, Bella sat watching the orange embers of the flame climb higher into the sky and disperse in the wind, sweeping through gentle streams tugging at both girls. Alone, Bella could convey a scheme to heal all the wrong. But words alluded her.

The girl's lips part, gathering strength to say anything; however, she was unbalanced by attention, looking deep into the mountains. Bella turned to where she saw, the moonlight almost gave sight of the peaks.

She couldn't help the notion of wanting to apologize, again and again, a thousand times. She redirected herself and thought in terms of actions, gestures, gifts she could give the utmost empathy one could hold, now only struggling with expression. All instances of her tongue failing her, all the conversions she couldn't save now crescendoed to the inability to comfort her friend. Bella never thought of herself as a good person.

Bella landed her gaze on the thorny barrier. Tall grasses stretched through the chain-linked diamonds, their dry exterior begging to be lit. Bella thought she could almost see something crouching in the far distance. The girl scraped the cement with the bottoms of her shoes and turned to Molly. The soft light of the fire warmed the redheads cheek and the private fence behind. Her eyes glinted wet. Bella almost spoke. Molly parted the quiet.

"I need to be up there."

Bella was surprised. "What?"

Molly pointed beyond the barbed wall and down the hill to the mountain's tree line. "There."

"On the mountain?"

Molly nodded. "Just away from the city."

"What about Refuge? Go see your family."

"No!" The redhead nearly leaped out of her chair. "They can't know! They can never, never know!"

The girl was frozen. "Okay."

"Do you understand me?"

"Yes."

"You can't tell them! Please you can—"

"I've never met them."

Molly lost her intensity. She exhaled and turned back to the Giants. "Right, right."

Bella looked at the sliver of lawn. "I wouldn't even tell them if I knew them."

"How did Kade know?"

"Did…did he come down?"

"Yes."

"I just told him that you were hurt!" Bella pleaded. "I didn't mean to."

"No one can know," said Molly. "Don't tell anyone anymore about me. Let's all just forget that this ever happened."

Bella watched her friend rub around her bruise, outlining the infected skin. She thought it must be itchy and observed her friend scratch her side, where the bite mark and a couple of stitches stuck out.

"I'm sorry," she said. "I wanted to stay with you! But...but Nelson wanted me to work. He wanted me to fill in, and I couldn't stay. I wanted to. I did. But he wouldn't." The girl's heart sunk when she heard no response. "I understand if you're mad at me. I don't mean to bother you by saying this. But I get it if you don't wanna talk."

"I'm not mad at you." The redhead brought the palms of her hand close to face. Faint weeping transformed into mourning. "I'm filthy," she could barely say. "I'm filthy, I'm filthy, I'm filthy, I'm filthy!"

"You're not!" exclaimed Bella, running to her friend's aid. "Stop! Stop it!"

The redhead began rocking back and forth, then slowly pressing into her skin so much that the tips of her nail painted crimson. "I'm filthy, I'm filthy, I'm filthy."

Bella tried to pry Molly's claws away from her, but her friend possessed more strength then she expected. She failed to outpower her.

"Stop! Stop! Molly, stop!"

"I'm filthy." Eventually, Molly pulled nails from herself and dug into her pocket.

The girl stared at the Yudaku, the ripped ends yearned for nothing. It scared her the way Molly looked at it, her color fading. She saw what her friend was planning.

"Forgive me," the redhead said. "Please forgive me."

Molly tossed the necklace toward the fire, but Bella intercepted, grabbing her friend's wrist before any considerable momentum could be generated. "What are you doing?!"

The fire shimmered as the wood within depleted. The Yudaku hit the cold cement.

The girls looked at each other. Bella could hardly recognize the woman before her, deep nail marks littered the redhead's face. Molly then dropped to her knees. The girl errored to catch her again, but brought her down easy. Tears fell next to the knots.

"Take it away," Molly said. "I don't want it anymore."

"I can't—"

"Please."

"Molly, it's yours."

"I can't stand the sight of it! Please…"

Bella looked down at the necklace.

"I don't blame you for what happened," said Molly. "I don't blame anyone." She stopped to cover her eyes. "I blame myself."

Bella was quick to counter. "It wasn't your fault! He did this to you! Don't…don't ever put that on you! I—"

"It was. It will always be. The signs were all there. I saw the way he looked at it." She looked to the mountain. " I deserved this."

"That's the furthest thing from the truth."

A crack in the flame relight another wave of embers into the sky. Bella scanned the ground and went back to her chair. Her mind sought the best way to encourage Molly, some way to rejuvenate her spirit. All while Molly lifted herself from the ground, keeping unblinking stares toward the peaks.

"I wish I could be up there."

"Where?" Bella asked.

"To the Elders," she said. "Next to Giants."

"I'm sorry." And she shook her head.

"I want to be away," said Molly. "Is that really a crime?"

"You'll feel better after some sleep."

"I don't ever want to close my eyes again." The redhead nodded and gazed back to the mountain, unwavering her dedication to the fibers earth.

Bella didn't know what to make of her friend's statement, but noted she could probably stay quiet. The girl looked down at the Yudaku and turned to the shadowy mass too, blinking, scanning around if she could spy something. All while the light of the fire slowly died as morning charioted the horizon.

Chapter

13

The bird's didn't sing. It was as if they weren't there, a late migration in the early spring causing them to flee, to the southern lands.

Bella reached for her phone. It read 6:30 a.m. It was too soon, recollecting her late night. She rolled over, waiting for a chirp, conning her ear, but was unable to find a relaxing position and turned again. The nurse had never thought she'd miss the volume and debated whether or not they would ever amplify their cries to annoy her. She then wondered why she couldn't tune out the noise. Not even a stray dog barked. Bella battled with restlessness for a couple more moments, the null sound being too deafening. She admitted defeat and sat up on the side of her bed, ideas of what to do to fill the time migrated in her head. Work wasn't early for her as it was for most, at least not for today. She thought of making breakfast, but she realized Molly wouldn't be up at least for another two hours. Cleaning became the rational idea next, anything to help the ruined girl. But she knew it would just get dirty again. And finally, she landed on the idea of showering, which she seemed to like, considering she still stunk of smoke.

The girl left her bed and made her way into the bathroom, quiet down the stairs so as to not wake Molly. She went down and didn't look out the screen door, turning to the hallway and stepping just before the dual chambers. Bella peered to her left and into Kim's room, seeing the queen-sized bed with many plants encircling it. It was like a jungle, but it made no noise, the tattoo woman presumably still at the hospital. Bella then went to the bathroom and opened the shower curtain, then turned on the water. She undressed as it heated up, careful not to look in the mirror at her naked body. Warm water ran down her when the girl saw fit a lovely feeling that made her not want to leave. She made sure to lather herself with soap and shampoo and condition her hair. She finished quickly, not wanting to take too much water, and brushed her teeth while patting her hair with a towel and applied cheap Chapstick to her lips. She withdrew the Yudaku from her jammie's pockets, and Bella exited out the bathroom wrapped in a white towel holding her clothes.

The girl stood on the platform that connected the three rooms. Molly's door was closed. A sigh of relief escaped her, figuring the redhead still must be in bed. She then crept toward the opening of her own room and got dressed for her shift, fitting in more properly sized scrubs she'd picked out months prior, knowing she would have to change into them eventually. Covered, she looked in her closet mirror. *Better*, she thought, and she sprayed some perfume around her collar.

She then went downstairs and through the thin hallway, accidentally stomping on a painting left on the floor. She stopped at what she'd stepped on, a blotch of blue mix with yellow crunched beneath her food. The girl didn't react, plucking the artwork from the tile and walking to the dining area. She set the canvas on the table.

When Bella looked up, she was standing at the center with the screen door, the fence wall, and the mountains behind it. The two lawn chairs were still out, along with the weird pot used for the fire. However, just above where the fire extinguished, rested a head of red curls. Molly still wore the clothes of yesterday. She was leaning against the barrier. She was kneeling on the lawn.

Bella didn't hesitate. She moved to her friend and slid clear the panel. Her bare feet struck outside. She shook the redhead. "Molly!" And again. "Molly!"

Her friend lifted from her state, and eyelids opened to the image of Bella coming into view, at first frightening, then a blank expression void of pain or pleasure. Molly forced a smile afterward.

"What are you doing out here?" questioned the girl.

"I…" Molly looked around. "I don't really know."

"I took you upstairs! Molly!. You could have gotten frostbite!"

"I came back down." Molly's face changed. "And it's warming up now."

"I saw you go to bed." Bella shook her head. "Now come on." And she grabbed one of Molly's arms. "I'm taking you inside."

The redhead pulled away. "No."

"You're freezing!" Bella protested.

"I'm fine. I had my coat."

The girl reached to feel her forehead, but even to that, Molly pulled away.

"Let me check!"

"Please don't," Molly said.

Bella recollected and sought a means to get her inside. She looked at her friend's chair and the slouching position it had adopted. "Will you please just sit down again?"

Molly didn't look at her. "I'm fine."

"Molly…"

"I'm fine!"

"Molly, the grass is wet! Look!" And she pressed into the soil to expose the moisture. "It's all wet!"

Molly turned to her. "It's not that cold."

"It's freezing!"

The redhead didn't reply.

Bella gained a grip on her friend's arm. "Please, just to your chair."

Molly hesitated, then nodded.

In one motion, the girl hoisted her friend up, and Molly brought her leg underneath herself. They moved to the chair. Bella used herself as a crutch for the redhead and walked beside her until she stood above the chair. She attempted to subvert and force her inside, but Molly halted.

"Just the chair," she demanded.

Bella nodded. "Okay."

They moved down together, the girl bent in order for her friend to sit down with much effort. Molly reached down to pick up the Yudaku she discarded last night.

Bella looked at it. "Are you hurt?"

"No," Molly withdrew the charm in her pocket. "Just trying to wake up still."

"It's okay, it's a big thing to do. Do you need anything? Do you want to make you some breakfast?"

"Well, it would be nice."

"All right," said Bella. "I'll make some eggs, and I'll bring them out for you."

"No," said Molly. "I'll...I'll come in in a bit. Just leave them on the table when ya get 'em done."

"Are you sure?"

"Yeah, I'm just about ready to go in."

"Why...," Bella began. "Why did you come back out here?"

The redhead didn't respond. She kept her gaze toward the mountain. "Molly?"

Again, there came no response.

Bella retracted herself from her friend's side. She admitted defeat and went toward the screen. She turned back for a moment. "I'll just be inside if you need me," and entered into the Planned Home.

Around the corner, Bella moved to the oven. She twisted the dials on the stove portion and waited for the black top to blare red. She glanced out the window above the sink. From there, she spied on Molly, checking if she resumed the same position. She couldn't believe the strength the redhead had to come back out to the barrier. She wondered when precisely Molly had snuck down.

And why? she wondered. *Had she been praying?*

Nothing made sense to her; and she resumed her mission, grabbing a pan from a cupboard, olive oil from another, and eggs from the fridge. She fetched the rubber spatula and began cracking the eggs, scrambling them as she began cooking. Every few seconds, Bella added salt and pepper to the eggs between stirring, and when solidified, she twisted the dial to Off. The girl then scanned for a toaster. She found it near the counter, then the bread nearby, and placed white slices into the tin slots and pressed the lever down.

"How long was she out there? Could it have been all night?"

A minute or so had passed, and Bella collected the two pieces of bread, then searched the cupboards to from plates. Thereafter, the girl distributed the bounty on two dishes, giving Molly's plate both pieces of toast and a generous amount of eggs.

Bell then set the plates on the table, next to the broken artwork, judging and critical. It was too bare, she concluded. The best she could do was fetch some water and perhaps the chocolate milk carton on the side. She swiveled to retrieve the parchments, but as her eyes zipped across the screen frame, Bella caught sight of a blur. It was quick, lighting fast, as so much as to make the girl question the very fact on which she saw. But she indeed saw something, gray but gone. What it was escaped her and dodged behind a patch of grass. Bella searched for it, swearing the color had manifested, out of the necessity to find what had eluded her. The girl could see her friend sitting in the lawn chair, but not a clue of anything else. She parted through the screen door, searching still, careful with her footwork.

She could only hear the breeze pass her by. Bella noted that Molly had leaned her head back and appeared to be falling asleep again. She tapped the redhead's shoulder. "Your food's ready."

Molly sat up. "Okay."

"Won't you come inside and eat?"

"I will, just give me a minute."

"I could bring it outside for you?"

"No. I spent too much time out here."

"It is getting nicer," said Bella.

"I guess," responded Molly.

The girl began moving back inside. Within two or more paces, she reached the door, before she heard the redhead shuffling as if moving to look at her.

"What?" asked Molly.

"Hm?" Bella pivoted.

"You said my name."

"No, I didn't."

"I heard ya."

"I didn't say anything."

Molly turned back around. "I thought ya did."

Bella laughed. "You definitely need to come in now," she joked.

"In a bit."

The girl stayed watching her friend, then eased her sight to the tall gras. She scanned as far as it led to the mountain's forest, then followed the pines up to the Giant's jagged tips. Her fingers crossed to her stomach, a familiar sickness returned. Bella cut back to her path and went inside the Home.

She could hear the neighbors' vehicles rev and garages open. The day began to come alive. The majority of people started to awake. She sat down at the table and looked back to Molly, still erect in the lawn chair, stunned at the whim of what she deemed the Elders. The girl nibbled at the precious mixed yoke. It wasn't longer before the nature events pestered her and baffled any conception of natural reaction to what affected the redhead. She wondered why Molly wasn't staying in the warm house or bed in the nice sheets and cushions. It didn't make sense to Bella why a victim wouldn't shield themselves up in their stead and rather be insistent to remain in the cold against the knife-like wind. *What is she thinking?* the girl thought. She then began to speculate on what the blur could have been. Her mind went to the painting, the ones she labored harshly over, of wildlife in all sorts of teeth. What had alluded her must have been neglect to all man, the culprit most likely a coyote, or even a deer.

The girl, confident in her conclusion, turned to her plate. Her fork penetrated the soft yolk, and she took in each bite one after the other.

"This must be what she thinks therapy is." Bella looked once again out the screen. She recalled the rain treatment and the pair's lake visit. It seemed likely, given the recent hell her friend endured. It must be a Local cure and rationalized some old woman wearing a brown robe told her the cure to all mental trauma is exposure to the weather. Bella shook her head. Her pity on the redhead bolstered more than ever before.

She knew the police would have more questions, or it seemed like they would. She wondered how long they would wait before they called, or even knock on their very door.

"Maybe Molly thought about this and was just bracing for another encounter."

An image of Brigham parked the street, tasked with watching her household, came to mind.

It would make sense, Bella thought. *He knows where we live.*

Having eaten half of her meal, she had the mind to go out and look for a police cruiser, but stopped herself, believing it nonsensical to act on.

She decided then to fixate on the modern splotch sitting lonely on the table. It was bound to the trash bin, and Bella wanted to dispose of it. She looked over at Molly, her hair dripped over the side of the lawn chair. The girl wondered if her friend had bought the piece of garbage, or maybe it was Kim. An insight would help, and she got up from the table.

Bella wanted to get rid of the rest, if she could get permission on the one she was carrying. Molly's food was losing its heat. The girl felt bad about wasting the good food, and so she stared at the dish for a while longer, thinking. She shot another glance at her friend, then back at the dish, noting a blip of gray.

Impeccable and distinct were the pops of a used home: Air-conditioning hummed, and the foundation settled. It was as if a curtain had been lifted over Bella's ears. She'd never noticed these sounds before and wondered as to why she could isolate them now compared to before. She grew wary at these vibrations because the sudden pluck of the veil had left her unsure.

A blur, her mind repeated. *There was another blur.*

A hollow tink hit solid.

She swore she heard something within her say, "Go," and another ordering, "Stay."

Bella felt her vein throb. This felt different. She forced her neck to obey her and turned ever so wary of what she might see.

The chair, vacant, cast aside as if blown over by the wind. Bella rushed onto the cement. The girl coward to the empty plain.

Chapter

14

Calls alerted the neighbors. The people came out when her voice tinted ever more grim, still wearing their sleeping attire. Some of them began aiding in the search; others stayed in the home. They couldn't find her.

Many called the police station. Hot rubbers burned against the narrow streets of Heartlake once more. Sirens were carried by the breeze, and the clouds joined and cast a dull hue on the land. The police hadn't expected returning to the Planned Home so soon. They made haste given the missing girl's name and description.

Two officers arrived there shortly and spied Bella hysterically calling down the rows of blinders and beyond the chain-link wall. They did their best to restrain the girl, and Bella did her best to calm down.

"What happened?" a short officer asked.

"I don't know!" the girl responded. "I looked away for only a second."

"When did you last see her?"

Many unfamiliar faces surrounded the nurse.

"Here!" she pleaded. "Right here! She was sitting in that chair."

The officers look. The shorter man scoured the lawn chair and the surrounding cement. He looked at the charred wood, and the campfire pot was still in. A sneer possessed him. "Can you give me a detailed description?"

His taller companion scanned down the urban alleys of thin grass. He checked both ways before peering out to the tall grass beyond the fence. A drop weighted his feted hat. He looked up.

"Don…," he said.

"What?" The shorter one looked at him, then to where he pointed. He squinted. "What is that?"

"I think…I think that's someone's skin."

Bella followed too, and she saw a shredded piece of meat with tethered clothing of blue jeans.

Some of the neighbors spied it as well.

"It can't…" Don positioned himself to get a better angle. A drop of blood fell before his eye and landed in a patch of grass that stained a drying brown. His heart raced. "Fuck," he whispered. "Do you think?"

And they stared out to the plane between the mountain and city.

And Bella could hear him utter, "We have to be safe. Get Tune"

"I'll call them in." The officer's partners snatched his radio. He put his mouth close to the device and muttered a four-letter code, then the address of the Planned Home.

"All right!" the man then boomed. "Everyone's back! Everyone back in your homes!"

Bella saw the short man whip his arms, pushing the small crowd of the residents back. She became puzzled and fearful, and the other officer ushered her inside.

"Get inside! All of you! This is now a crime scene!"

She kept hearing him shout as she was isolated and instructed to wait. She wasn't able to tell if the crowd obeyed.

"Just sit here," said the partner. "We're gonna have some come speak to you."

She could tell the man was nervous, but paid little attention. Bella sat, hand pressed between her knees and head to the tile. She wanted to dull herself, but it raced with unfathomability. She had only looked away for a second. It couldn't have been longer than that.

Distant sirens soon became louder. Several cruisers filled in one after another, and a large van squished into the driveway. They filled both sides of the street. Policemen filed out their vehicles and immediately went to work, some with bordering tape and others with forensic tools only seen in homicides. There were two men in white-collar shirts. They had badges and odd crests that the girl saw sparingly, but they appeared in charge of the operation, giving order to the lower-ranking officers. With them, they possessed instruments that appeared heavily expensive, and they were pointed to the mountains.

"What's going on?" were the questions of many bystanders.

To the response, the men threatened, "Get inside or you'll be detained."

Within a minute, the police had captured the small patio and outlined it with restriction tape. There was a moment when the police rooted through the chaos and brought order to their operation, discussing what they thought had happened between the high-ranking officers. Some of the officers went back to wherever else needed them, seeing that the crowd had been pacified and the area secured, but others did stay and kept the perimeter. Stupefied guards faced outward with their weapons ready, as the two white-collar individuals went to work, collecting a sample where the blood had fell with their strange equipment. One of which seemed to be setting his colleague off by himself, turning and walking toward the screen door. Bella noted his long face and spiky hair, but the badge calmed her nerves.

"Good morning," he said, crossing the screen. He pressed something in his pocket. "Agent Tune, FBI." He held out his hand. The two shook hands. Bella with a feeble grip. "I understand that you were the first one that noticed Ms. Need missing."

Bella nodded. "It was so fast—"

"When did you last see her?" he quickly cut in.

The girl paused. "Right before I started calling for her."

The man appeared puzzled. "Can you elaborate?"

"I looked away for a second. Then I looked back, and when I did, she was gone. I don't understand it."

"And you began looking for her as soon as she disappeared?"

"Yes?"

"Where was she?"

"On that chair." She pointed out. "I tried to get her in for some food. I made breakfast. But she kept saying she would come in. And she just stayed out there."

"So Molly never came inside," Tune stated.

"Well, for a little bit," Bella said. "When we went to sleep, she did."

The agent seemed a little surprised. "She wanted to stay outside?"

The girl nodded. "She wanted too. But I made her come in. She didn't like it, but I begged her, and she finally listened. And I even thought it was good from there on. But then…" Bella didn't know if she should tell this detail. She carried on. "But when I woke up, I found her out there. She was leaning against the barrier, asleep. It was like she was kneeling." The girl shielded her face. She felt tears coming on, but she could not shed them with this agent here. She would not.

"Just try to relax," said Tune. "Was she in any contact with a Local, or may have frequented any Local ceremonies?"

"Yes," Bella said. "She talked about them a lot."

The agent folded his arms. "Did she express any questionable views to you? Such as wanting to heal herself through water or perhaps wanting to leave outside the barrier?"

"I…" She thought for a moment. "Yes. Yes, she did."

"How long did you actually look away?" His tone was condescending and shot a glance to the barbed-wire wall.

"Just a few seconds," Bella said.

"Could you have thought it was a few seconds but it was actually a few minutes?"

The girl's brow twisted as she cast it to the floor. "I turned my head, then right back again. She was gone when I looked."

"Did you see anything disturbing the grass back there? Hear anything rustling?"

"No." She thought of the blur. "No."

"Did you hear possibly anything?"

"No."

Tune shifted his posture. The girl answered and seemed to have calmed a bit. "Was she doing anything else before she disappeared?"

"Just sitting."

"What was she wearing?"

Bella had to recall. "A black jacket with pants."

"Did she have a piece of fur on her?" the agent added. "Like dog hair or something?"

"No. She wasn't actually a Local. But I think she likes them."

Tune placed his hand in his pocket. The girl spied a nice watch in his wrist. "Do you know anywhere she might have gone?"

"She told me she liked taking walks along the barrier. She liked to watch the Giants."

"All right, that should do. Now, miss, I just need your name."

"Tell me," Bella interrupted. "Will you find her?"

Tune prepared a response, but as he did, his fellow agent tapped him on the shoulder and pivoted his attention away from the girl. He whispered something in Tune's ear, the recipient agreeing to what he heard. "Give me a sec, miss." And as they conversed, out of the corner of her vision, the nurse saw another officer carrying a ladder to which some more men helped lean it against the barbed fence. With pliers in hand, he carefully climbed to the top bar and plucked a bright flesh from the steel spike. He tucked the evidence into the plastic baggy and, with a gloved hand, zipped it shut, then descended down the ladder. The men all gathered to look at it. The girl could tell they were chatting among themselves of the origin. The officer then made his way inside to where his superiors still whispered.

The white collars turned.

"Go stop him. The girl's still in here," said Tune.

The other agent agreed and went to intercept.

Tune then turned to the girl again. "I think this is bigger than we think," he said. "Discounting you friends behavior, do you recall seeing anything usual?"

"No," Bella lied to herself. "Everything else seemed normal."

"That's okay," he assured her. "I just figured I'd asked. We'll start looking around ASAP." He knelt face level to the girl and brought a finger to his lips. "Be we need you to be quiet about this. This type of story will go viral in this town, but the press doesn't have to know until we can get more information. Do you understand? I'm saying it's best we find your friend before it all gets out. Better for us and, I assume, better for you. Give me a nod."

She did.

"Good. Now I'll give you a minute, but we need to get going." Tune stood back up. "Old Deacon wants to see you. I'm not sure, but I guess we're taking requests."

Bella looked up at the agent. He avoided her gaze. He possessed a guilt in him, a routine that molded him unfazed by what his career requests. Bella then spoke. "I have work today."

He studied the girl's clothes. "You a nurse?"

She confirmed.

"This won't take long," he said. "What time do you work?"

"Noon."

"We'll surely be done by then. Or he will at least."

"I also need to tell Kim."

"Who?" Tune questioned.

Her voice cracked at the last word. "She's my roommate. She'll be back any minute."

"We'll inform her then," said the agent. "Does anyone else live here?"

"Her boyfriend Derrick sometimes comes over. But I'd like to warn her..."

"No need. We'll touch base with them." The agent then altered himself to the screen. "We leave in five." Then he joined his partner out on the cement.

The girl tried to collect herself and piece together how wrong the morning had gone. It was only a moment did she look away, and despite the agent's doubts, Bella knew. Molly couldn't have walked away so fast unless she purposely hid, which was unlikely. The girl remembered as she checked and the neighbors checked, and they searched together. The redhead wasn't down the lanes, wasn't in any stranger's Home, not running to the road and down the street. She was gone, like the instant sound leaves a snap, gone in the brief switch of a clock's tick. "How?" She remembered the flesh dangling from the barbed wire. "Could she...?" It was intertwined fabric and vessels, fiber and fiber. "No. I looked away for only a second."

Tune then emerged from the sliding door. He ordered her to follow him and another officer to a marked police vehicle. Bella obeyed, following them to the vehicle. They had to cross the road, which was so narrow, it only allowed one lane for traffic to flow. The man who'd questioned her hopped in the passenger seat, and the thin officer took his place behind the wheel. Bella filled in the back, shooting glances at the two men behind the grated bars. The officer shifted into drive, and the cruiser rumbled to the pavement.

Bella held her head in her palms, a cascade of scenarios and explanations pleated her brain. It ached, and her body hurt, feeling as though a rift had stretched within her. The cool glass administered aid, but did little. She looked out to the passing world. Everywhere her eyes fell the thought as a possible place Molly could be.

"Why does he want to see her?" said Tune to the officer.

"It's for the George Grey case. He'll tell ya what's up when we get there."

"It's fallen in our jurisdiction. Didn't anyone tell him? Do you guys have any order whatsoever? He has no right to resume anything without our say!"

"I think Sharlet gave him the green light."

There was a pause.

"She did?" asked Tune.

"Yes," responded the driver. "Like I said, he told me to tell you he'd fill you in."

The agent folded his arms. "I wish he'd keep his nose in the political game."

"I'm afraid he doesn't like the smell of shit, sir."

The marked wagon burned to the police station, ultimately halted by the normal congestion of the city.

Bella paid no attention to the front-seat passengers. She replayed the mental frames of the redhead climbing over the fence. Her friend failed every single time. The girl would always turn before she was even halfway up or stall at the sight of the barbed wire, not having the will to mortify herself. And there was no noise.

"I would have heard something," the nurse kept saying to herself. "There wasn't any sound."

People seemed wary of the cruiser. No one dared cut the state vehicle off. Other's allowed the driver to turn where he pleased without much wait. The police station soon came into view.

Bella's mind grew silent. This was somehow worse. In the absence of the assault, it produced only one thought, a single bullet that had pierced skull. "Gone." She remembered the tattooed woman's child. Her soul grew apart. Bella fought against the notion, but there was no other phenomena that even resembled what had happened. It embedded itself. She could shake the idea, and the girl's body grew cold.

The car stopped. Both of the men hopped, and the cop opened Bella's door for her. She stared up at him. He would not look at her. She finally accepted it and stepped out of the vehicle, closing the door behind her.

Bella instinctively senses the pressure of a concrete jungle, tall buildings condensing into themselves. She went to where the agent guided, treading behind in a safe pace. It resampled an old courthouse but with modern paneling and fixes. A massive golden shield with ribbon around it possessed the phrase, "Heartlake City Police Station." It hung above the entrance and by two columns that reminded Bella of the Greeks. The parking lot was fairly sized considering the restrictions of the city, every lot was filled by state vehicles.

They journeyed closer. And as they did, Bella noted the variety of staff entering and exiting the facility. There were normal-dress individuals, men in uniform, others that appeared to work in officers, and, at last, the white collars with their black shiny ties. They all carried holsters on their dominant side. Bella checked Tune to confirm this. She was correct and stared at the pistol.

The agent and the spare officer stuck near their witness, passing by the columns, then the automatic doors. Inside she stood facing a long, polished desk built into the wall. The desk was separated in thirds by thick glass and three personnel behind each of them. Each section had a push box and a circular speaker mouth level with the recipient behind. Bella could spy a computer. The police brought her closer to the desk, where all three receptionists eyed the girl down. The nurse refused to be enchanted and peered elsewhere in the room, where she saw more golden shields of the station scattered along its new-age decor.

The men pushed her along the fine wooden planks and stood her in the front desk.

"Is Deacon in his office?" asked the agent.

"Yeah. He's stayed longer today, which is strange. He isn't happy. What's going on?"

"Nothing," answered Tune, and he flashed his identification.

He began to pull the girl in the direction of a well-lit hall filled with photographs of well- decorated officers and metal slabs below them. The receptionist merely watched as Tune funnel Bella down a hall of a couple rooms. The thin officer followed behind. They walked until they reached another chamber, this one possessing a great cast of honor. Many flags and pictures of great monuments, almost as museum displays, hung around the walls. A wonderful artwork incapacitated the dome ceiling: soldiers with muskets fight the decering fight to form the girl's country. To the left of the girl stood a dual door with the brass eagle above it, and to its sides, statues of war heroes were on guard, incased in perfect marble.

And in the opposite, two smaller versions of those statues were placed below a large board wheeled against a brick wall that almost touched the ceiling. Filler after filler was plastered on the board. Page after page of missing persons reports were stapled to its carpet surface, giving the board an almost paperlike camouflage to the white confines of the room. Bella couldn't not grasp a clean glance at the multitude of faces before she turned and stood facing the large dual doors of the commissioner's office.

"I'll take her in," said Tune barely above a whisper. "I'm sure there's plenty for you to do."

The officer looked down at the girl, then back at the other. "I think I'll wait for the chief to dismiss me. If you don't mind me staying."

"We'll be talking about sensitive subjects.. Sit this on out."

"I showed up at the original site. There's nothing you don't know about this that I don't."

"He requested me and the witness, not you."

"He told me to stand by."

The agent turned. "You have nothing to stand by for."

"Maybe," said the officer, and he motioned the board against the dentate wall. "Did you find them?"

The agent looked back to the board. Bella did as well, becoming weary of the conversation. He spun back to face the officer. "They're all open cases."

"And maybe an extra pair of ears may help find one in a goddamn while. I mean, for christ's sake, look at it!."

Tune shook his head. "They're open cases."

"They're all dead."

"What are you trying to prove here?" He glanced at the girl. "We can talk about these privately."

The officer looked at Bella, then back to Tune. "Okay. And I'll be dismissed by my actual boss, if that's all right."

Tune's face neared red. "I am your boss. Do you hear me? My clearance is technically above Deacon's."

The officer turned forward. He curled his fist. "Fire me then."

Tune read the man's name plate. This breath quickened. "Yeah, that can be done. I'll tell Sharlet about how Officer Davis refused to follow orders. You like how that sounds?"

He kept quiet.

"Is this really worth losing your job over?"

"I just figured—"

"Not so much as a smart move, is it? I can make sure you never work in law enforcement again. Do you hear me now? You'd be reduced to the most rural sheriff department and still wouldn't be able to snag a job. Wanna keep fighting about it?"

Davis looked defeated. "No."

"No what?"

"No, sir."

"Smart man. Now get the fuck out of my sight."

The officer passed an angry-swelled glance at the agency, then shifted his weight. He moved to the other hall on the outside of the grand room. Bella watched him go, a worry in his footwork.

"I apologize for that," said Tune. "He's just a petty city cop. Right this way."

The agent guided Bella to the entrance, knocking on the hard, stiff doors. A deep reverberation emitted from the thick wood. Tune then pushed them open to the sight of a deep-blue rug with the shield and bird of the station woven onto it. Bella stayed as his shadow and moved her line of sight from the rug to the triplet windows sheathing in augmented light from stained cyan glass. And, in between, lay the desk of Commissioner Deacon, polished yet simple, covered in file after file of past and present events, all separated from a detailed bottle of fine whisky and gin, brushing up to a pristine cup. Behind the desk sat Deacon, guarded by the flag of the country and state, his trench coat and hat the same as the day he first came to Bella. He didn't see the agent and girl walk in, and only looked up when Tune's tall frame came into his angled view. The commissioner peered up, pen in hand. He stood up.

"Good morning, Tune." The chief shook the agent's hand. "And to you, Ms. Tomson." He copied the same gesture. "I'm sorry we had to drag you along in this. But you were the last on to have seen Molly."

Deacon told Tune to grab one of the velvet chairs from the edges of his office. "Get the door too if you will." He asked Bella to take a seat.

She did, a nervous tremble in her leg.

"This situation involving the sudden disappearance of Molly, well, it doesn't come as a shock to tell you that we've dealt with these cases before. I got to work early this morning when 911 calls started to come through. It's not unusual, but it's apparent that we have a chat with the witnesses before the press can get involved." Deacon poured out whisky in his glass. "Need something to calm ya nerves?"

Bella shook her head.

"All right. Tune, are you taping?"

"Yes," answered the agent. He hovered near the desk, his arms crossed.

"Good," said Deacon. "I assume you've already given a description."

"A dark coat with blue jeans," said Bella. "Her hair was down."

"Did the coat have any designs in it or a designer brand?"

"I was Black Label I think. She got it from Refuge. It's her hometown."

"Does she have family there?" the commissioner asked. He hooked on Tune. Bella gave an impression of certainty, which made Deacon question a suspension. "Right," he said after. "We'll have someone notice them. Do you have by chance have their numbers?"

"I don't," answered the girl.

"Right, we will find a way to reach them." And he turned to a paper on his desk.

Bella spied a name of the page. It read, "Jessica Manning."

"Now, could you describe what you were doing when Ms. Need disappeared."

"I already told that man," said Bella.

"Just say it again," said Deacon. "It won't hurt."

"I had just finished making breakfast. I was sitting down eating."

"Where was Molly?"

"Just outside. She was sitting in a lawn chair out on the patio. I kept trying to get her in, but I couldn't. She just…she just really wanted to be out there."

"Anything suspicious about the night prior?"

"Yes. And…and I told him"—Bella directed herself at Tune—"about what happened."

"Summarize."

"She didn't go to bed. She came back out and slept against the barrier."

"When did you notice she was missing?" questioned the chief.

"Two seconds after I looked back," said Bella. "I turned away for two seconds, and she was gone."

"Are you sure about that time frame?"

"Yes! Why do I have to keep saying it?"

"We're just being sure," said Deacon. "A lot of the details can get blended together in this sort of thing. We just need to clarify."

"I don't think you believe me." The girl stopped, knowing what she'd say would get her in trouble. "You all think she climbed the barrier."

"I don't know what to think yet."

"No, no. I know what you think. He had me answer questions about if she was a Local. She slept in the fucking cold!" She covered her mouth, realizing her outburst. "She couldn't have enough strength."

"There's a lot of things that could have happened," rationalized Deacon. "And we're going to explore them." He glanced at the agent, then to the wooden door behind the girl. "Is there anywhere else she would have gone?"

"I don't know."

"Do you know any other residents that she could have snuck off to?"

Bella shielded her head. "I don't know. I…I remember her looking over to the mountains. But she couldn't—"

"Ms. Tomson, are you aware of the phenomenon of disappearances we have in Heartlake?" Deacon leaned forward in his chair. "Many families and communities have grieved over the unexplained deprivation of their loved ones. We're saying she went over the border. I guess the main reason I wanted to bring you here is to brace yourself."

"She has to come back," said Bella, tears forming. "She has to."

"We're going to look. But I can't guarantee we'll find her."

The girl's gaze fell to the square dotting of the floor. "She has to be out there. She can't just be gone."

"Again, we'll search."

The feeling returned to her stomach. It made her arm and legs feel numb. Images of the chunk of flesh caught between the barbed wire oozed into her mind. She couldn't control herself, so she began dry heaving.

The chief jumped to assistance. "God," he said, quickly looking in this drawers for something to catch any excrement. "Go get some water!" he shouted at Tune.

The agent scowled at his tone, and the two locked eyes. He then walked out in the hall in search of a water fountain, taking a cup from the chief's desk.

The girl kept gagging. She cried between each heave, struggling with each breath, and it became harder to resist. She couldn't stop it. She had to let her body's reaction flow its course. She fell down to the ground, kneeling. Deacon came to her side. He held a small paper bag.

"It's all right," said Deacon. "Just take it easy. You're feeling okay."

Bella made herself nod. She convulsed again. "You need to find her."

"It's not that simple."

"Please. She can't be dead."

The agent returned with water in a small paper cone. He gave it to the chief and stared down at the girl, his hands in his pockets.

Bella then regained a hold of herself, quickly taking the liquid. She swallowed it and refused to look up. She clutched the paper cup.

"Before she was gone, I saw something."

"You saw what?"

"I don't know, but it was a sudden movement, a blur almost. Can… can that help?"

"Can you make out any details? Was it a man or an animal?"

"Pale. It was pale."

Tune rolled his eyes. "Probably was just a coyote. Chief, I think we've got all that we from this."

Deacon stood up. "Would you like some more water?"

Bella shook her head.

The commissioner then returned to his desk and sipped the whisky he had poured and looked back at the girl. "Is there anything you'd like to add?"

"I'll help you look."

"There's no need," said Deacon. "You did your part, but there's actually one more thing you can do for us." He searched for a particular article and withdrew a calendar. "Could you write down your number for use. We'll most likely be speaking again."

"Will this stop the investigation into Oscar?" Bella asked with baited breath.

"No." And the chief caught himself before he spoke and redirected his thoughts. "He'll face what's coming to him."

"Could they be linked?"

"I hope not."

Tune then spoke up. "I think that's enough time we have for Ms. Tomson," he said. "We have quite a bit of work to do, wouldn't you say?"

Deacon then turned to the agent, then the girl. "I suppose you're right. I'll have someone drive you home, and again, we'll inform any close family and friends involved with the victim." He possessed a monotone voice, the same dulled speech she'd heard from the agent.

She wouldn't not lift her gaze from the odd squares. "Can you ask if Brigham would take me?"

The chief smiled. "Yeah, I'll see if he's available. Man might become your personal chauffer through all of this." The commissioner revealed his phone and pressed a seven-digit number.

"Do you mind if I wait outside your office?" asked the girl.

Deacon nodded.

Bella wanted to leave the moment she stepped into the building. Tune watched her squirm out of the commissioned officer. She checked down both hallways before carrying on straight. She stopped alongside the foot-high stone statue and peered up to the fliers. Some were tearing, made before the girl was even born, and in obvious distress. Her frozen hands reached up to the contents of the board in hopes to reach them. Enshrined almost, not from the fanatics, stapled reports and old photos of people from every color, class, and party. The faces of both men and women littered the board, young boy and young girls too. Some bore titles that date the 1950th year, others before the State was reformed. The sight concaved the girl's heart. A group of three, they were a few weeks separated. . Bella looked closer and recognized the triplet of women. They were movie stars. They were pretty. One individual stood out: Anny Botly, which she knew from a show she'd seen online. The other two were not as familiar: Thruid Lessner and Janis Grant. But the girl felt as if she had seen them before in some sort of film. Then, at last, she moved her sight until she saw a little boy. The image was in black and white, but Bella could still tell his eye resembled Kim's.

The girl could feel herself becoming weak again. She moved to a bench on the outer side of the grand hall. She covered her face. None of them have been found.

Chapter

15

The girl carried on to work, assured by the officers there was nothing she could do. Brigham drove her to the hospital and gave her his number so she could alert him when she needed a ride home. The girl took it and estimated she'd be done around 10:00 p.m. She barely conversed with him. Bella could tell he wanted to share something, perhaps details he had discovered, but the nurse couldn't maintain talking, or even the fact she rode to her job on the day her friend went missing. Guilt pestered her mind throughout the cycles. She spoke to no one and stayed properly behind the keyboard. The only time she left her chair was to administer the patient's medication and to change Evergreen's bandages. She remembered what he said to her.

"She's gone," said the old man. "Isn't she?"

Bella didn't reply.

"You have that look. You saw something snatched right under your nose."

"They're gonna look for her," she argued. "There gonna find her."

Evergreen looked down at his exposed scabbing pins. "They won't go beyond the barrier. I'm afraid it's time to best start forgetting. Nothing is going to save her, I'm sorry. I tell ya this not—"

"You don't have to tell me anything. I don't…I don't really want to keep talking."

"I understand, lass. I'd do anything to trade places with her. Honest."

Bella spoke without a voice. "I would too."

"God bless you," he said. "May he show mercy on your soul and Molly's."

The girl was able to finish the wrapping without another word from the old patient. He was involved in his book and bothered the nurse no longer. When Bella went back to her station, she almost cried. The girl held so desperately her will. She wouldn't not break down. She wouldn't right now.

Bella managed to rotate through her list of care, spying Mrs. Rubido and Mallory through their corresponding windows. The woman didn't raise her attention to the nurse as she was given medication, but the little girl asked what was wrong.

The nurse responded, "Nothing, I'm just not fun today."

To which the little girl understood and left her caregiver to her own devices.

Bella continued these rounds until the moon basked the city with its presence. None in the hospital cared until a digital clock signaled their period to leave. The day seemed never-ending, until a fellow colleague said to her, "Hey, you know you stayed thirty minutes late, right?"

Embarrassed, she exited the hospital. She moved down the elevator and through the spacious hallways. She called Brigham on the main floor. He told her he'd be there in a couple of minutes. Their call ended, and a sigh escaped her. She found a seat, a corner of a waiting area, and reflected on the visage of imagery sight: Molly resting by the barrier, then disfigured, the vacant cement in front of the chain-linked wall.

Brigham's police maneuvered Heartlake. He turned exactly, paired with acute acceleration. They bantered with the "how are yous," and "good, how are you?" Not much was said beyond small talk. The cruiser reached Bella's home with no errors or setbacks and rolled into the driveway. Brigham shifted the vehicle into Park, and both of them exited the cab, which surprised Bella, preparing a "Thank you." Darkness perched in every direction, and he walked her to the front door, stopping a few feet away from the porch. Bella halted, noting the officer had left and turned back to him. Brigham stood there contemplating whether to say what he thought would help. At last he could not withhold it.

"We made way in the investigation," the officer said.

Bella continued to stare.

"The assailant," he explained. "I have a pretty good idea who it is."

"Who?"

"Do you watch *Irresistible* at all? It's that sitcom from not so long ago."

Bella's expression changed little.

"Well, it turned out"—Brigham stiffened his shoulders—"there's a lot of steam involving George Grey. I think it's our guy." The officer caught his tongue before he continued, the girl's expression unchanging. "It's just surprising," he said. "I just thought you would know him. Everyone does."

Bella almost turned back around. "He said his name was Oscar."

"Turns out there is no Oscar Dmitri in Heartlake. None that we could find anyway. We expect he changed his appearance just enough so he wouldn't get recognized."

"How do you know it was him?"

"One of his boys ratted him out. It's…it's a bigger problem than we once thought. But he gave his real name. I didn't believe it at first, but this witness and others put someone of similar built seen with a curly redhead the night Molly was raped."

"Who's this guy?" Bella questioned.

"I can't tell ya."

"Where did the rape take place?"

"Well"—the officer shifted and jogged what he knew about the case—"presumably George took the Southeast quarter, on Turner's drive, then maybe have went to Main Street, then to the Canyon. You've ever been in the area?"

The nurse's demeanor changed. "Why down the Canyon?"

"I think they may have went to Refuge."

Bella shook her head. "God…" She rubbed above her eyebrows. As a singular movement, the girl sat down on the step. She put her head into her hand to shield them from the prying officer, shamed but not knowing what else to do. Brigham gave her a moment, then approached and sat next to her on the slab. He appeared unsure of what to do next.

"I'm sorry," he said. "I thought it might help to have some closure."

"It's all right," Bella responded. "I'll be all right, I think."

"We're going to find her," the officer said next, much to his surprise.

"How do you know?" Her words were hollow.

"I think she may have gone back to Refuge. I think mostly this phenomenon surrounding the city is just people wanting to leave another life, not counting the child cases. I'd stay awake in case she comes back to her truck."

"But she was gone in an instant. There's no way she could have hid from everyone."

"It's unlikely, but it could have still happened. But there's no evidence anything took her." He then added. "George can't do any more harm."

"But..." She thought about protesting the officer's assumption of the disappearance. She wanted his vision to be correct.

"We're gonna get him," the officer said.

"Good," Bella huffed. And she raised her head, her cheeks tear stained, and she stood up nodding and motioned for the door.

The officer did the same but stopped her rotation. "Just don't tell anyone about George," he said. "Until a jury can see him, we have to keep quiet. But I think it's right that you know."

"You should tell her family," Bella replied. "They need to know everything."

"Yeah." The officer rubbed his head, alluding that he knew more.

Bella caught this detail.

"What?" she asked.

"Nothing," he said.

"No, wait, tell me!"

"It's already been a hard enough night," he exclaimed. "Let's leave that for another night."

His words made Bella ill on the reminder of repetition. "Why not now?"

"Well, partly because I can confirm my details yet." He then continues, "You should get some sleep, it's been hell for you anyway."

"I don't think I can do that," she said. "Will you tell me once you know for sure?" the girl smelled a lie.

"Well..." The officer stopped to think. "Yeah. Yes, I can."

"Thank you." Bella nodded and turned back to the door and walked toward it. She knocked three times. The officer eyed her, puzzled.

"Don't you have a key?" he asked.

"No. Everything got in the way of that."

"I would wait in the car if you feel unsafe."

"I'll be fine." And she managed a smile. "Thank you though."

"I'll get going then," he said, smiling back. "Call if ya ever need anything." He waved goodbye and left for his cruiser. He looked once more to Bella, seeing the tattooed woman open the door. The girl entered, and the officer ignited his engine and reversed out of the driveway.

Bella's smile then dropped, and she went inside the Home. Kim locked up tightly. The lights were off, and the girl didn't bother to turn on the cheap rays and traveled down the wall by ruined paintings on the floor, guided by moonlight. She glanced at the ruined artwork before reaching the table and sitting. She put her elbow on the surface and brought her head to her hands once again. No tears followed.

Kim came in after. She stood for a moment, shaking, then took a place across the portable table. Her twitching thumb broadcasted her anxiety. There wasn't an motivation to speak. Under the silver light, Bella could see the gleam on Kim's cheek. Inexpensive mascara loosened and dripped. The tattooed woman stretched a hand across the hard surface in order for Bella to take. The girl clutched it, wanting to voice a "Don't worry," only to quench her friend's mourning, but guilt swelled reason, and what else could she say to another other than, "It's my fault."

Slowly, Bella began to regain herself, but Kim couldn't sheath her sadness. She pulled away to wipe her face. The girl held her in the best regard she could, but she was unworthy to be a supporting pillar. Nothing around her got better, and she was left feeling out of place by touch and the aspect of one needing her. She knew this emotion, but never this potent, no experience great enough to pull from her past.

She waited for Kim to stop. Her roommate managed to lower the volume, the lament for Molly was still heard. The girl found confidence.

"They'll find her," she said. "They're gonna try. They're gonna look in Refuge."

"They never do, Bella," said Kim. "They never do."

"She has to come back. How? How could she just be gone?"

Kim remained mute.

"It has to be something else," continued the girl. "Even if she managed to climb the fence, she can't just have vanished!"

"They told me they'd find Mason," said Kim. "They told everyone on that damn board, 'We'll look,' yet not one single fucking person has ever come back!"

"Why?" Bella exclaimed. "Why would they do that?"

"Because they have to. They have to say they'll look because it's part of their job, all while they actively piss on the Board and get away with it!"

"Deacon said there was no guarantee, but Brigham was confident. He said Refuge—"

"It doesn't matter what he said." And she swallowed and looked to the mountain. "He's a dirty liar, all of them are." She tried to hold herself. "That police chief, he said he would look, about...about five years ago. Said it with such confidence. And my Mason's still gone, right under his momma. And that bastard has the audacity to say that same goddamn thing to every family to that godforsaken board!" She appeared ready to cry again. "We'll look. Don't worry. We'll look."

Bella covered her eyes. She fought fiercely to believe Molly was still out there. "How? Just how?"

"I wish I could tell you. I wish I could take this away from you."

Bella looked up at her.

"All of this," continued Kim. "And I wish...I wish there wasn't any wishing. Everything should just be good. It should be good. But something hates us." And she pressed into her skull. "I don't know what we did to deserve this."

Bella claimed, "We did nothing."

And her cold eyes set on the girl. "Do her parents know it yet?"

The girl shook her head.

"I don't know how to do a funeral for her. But we could."

Bella clenched both of her first. She couldn't accept it. The sickness in her gut instructed otherwise. She shook her head.

"Bella..." Kim outstretched an arm again, beckoning the girl.

"She can't be."

"It's okay."

"No," she spat. "No, it's not."

"It's the only fact that you can trust."

The girl stood up. She bit her tongue and turned to the front door. She pressed her lips and rushed to the hallway. She wouldn't look at the tattooed woman.

"Wait!" exclaimed Kim. "Where are you going?" She chased after Bella, stepping on the loose painting on the floor. She stopped at the bottom of the flight. "Come back down! Please come back down!"

Bella dashed into her room and slammed the door shut. She covered her mouth and slid her back against the hardwood until her legs buckled and she fell to the carpet.

"Bella! We need to talk about this."

The girl began to shake. She tried to stop. She closed her eye and focused on her breathing.

"Bella, please! Don't hide! It's okay!"

The nurse covered her ears. She began to weep.

The tattooed women kept calling Bella. Over and over she wailed from the stairwell. Once more she tried before admitting different things. She left to her own room, awful and worried.

An element of hyperventilation presented itself within her breathing. Her heart sunk deep within her chest, as if it plummeted forever, as she waited. For what she waited for, not even the girl knew. She feared moving but crawled to the center of her room. Her mind spiraled while she faltered and lay motionless. She was forced to recollect. She managed to position herself on her knees and brought herself to almost a bow. Bella prayed, though she did not know how.

Tears still fell. Bella refused to look up. Time blurred and merged in the unending present, now would not yield. Yet a tick was cast, an authority illusion toward her right. It hit again, and manifested itself as a single note. It caught the girl off guard. A measure then concluded. The girl peaked in the direction it sounded, wondering if she had gone mad. Then the song continued, and Bella rested her gaze upon Molly's music box, sitting on her nightstand.

How the item ever left her friend's room and managed itself in her chamber alluded Bella, as she wouldn't expect anyone to move the toy, yet alone to place it in her room. But there it sat, more beautiful as the last time Bella saw it. The girl rose and walked across to seized it. As she studied the box and the key used to prompt the song, she was bewildered on how it played. She brought the toy back to the center of the room, as if escorted, and knelt once again, analyzing the box. But she couldn't solve its mystery by looking. The song ended, and she rewinded the key.

It repeated its childlike melody composed of somber bells, lifting the room and Bella's sunken heart as if power could be strung into notes. She caressed its delicate surface and the labored art. Memory soared when Molly and her would laugh, telling stories and sharing meals, the snarky comments and the well-intended jokes. Bella could even smell the same air back to those small moments that made all the difference. To have it void was unthinkable. Then, not knowing if it was her own fruition, she felt her head rise up to the window to an emerging glow.

The music box slipped from her grasp.

Small but righteous, a single light dotted the dark mountain face. A heavy wick on the Giant's back cut through the pale shine of the moon and pierced her Bella's soul. The orange, so bright, cleaved the chaos of her mind and the mourning of her heart. The girl's mouth was made ajar. A warm aroma then surrounded Bella, as if embraced by tender arms.

A moment, for instant, Bella belonged alone to the light. And they then came out their Planned Homes, walling with chronic limbs and fatten wastes, the neighbors to the side of them and their neighbors until the very edge of the border. Bella looked down near the base of the barrier and saw the people confused and frightened, others angry or taking photos. More civilians came out of their homes to witness the shining wick. Even the tattooed woman stood in awe at the blaze. Bella looked directly below to see Kim on the patio and quickly ran out of her room and down the stairs. She whirled through the hallway and threaded out the screen door. She nearly trampled her room, yet the tattooed woman shifted and caught the girl.

"It's her! It's her!"

Kim looked at Bella, starstruck and tear stricken.

Here, the murmurs of the crowd became apart, a great number of them appeared uneasy at the sight. They bickered about what it was, many of them fearing and reacting to call the police. None seemed happy, all except the girl.

"It's Molly! It's Molly!" she spoke.

The tattooed woman did not respond and stared into the light.

Bella called on her friend last time to listen, but she would not respond. The nurse then turned to the light once again. It somehow burned brighter than when it first revealed itself. And through the confusion and intimidation sirens in the distance, Bella praised the mountain.

Chapter

16

The rage simmered with the break of dawn. The Light had been snuffed by what the birds foretold. Those who saw it told the ones who didn't and the ones who didn't passed it onto the ignorant. By morning, everyone had at least heard something about the orange shine. The girl's phone ran wild with notifications, many fake men and women claiming that light to be whatever benefited them most. Officials attempted to restrict the view of its glory but were foiled by how vast the sight was seen and arriving too late to set the appropriate blockades. They merely held the gleam, as well, and forced their way and their strange instruments to the forefront next to the barrier. White-collar men drove the operation. All eyes were on the mountain, but whatever revealed itself now hid.

And the men sought immediate means. Bella witnessed the agents stay, still searching all morning long, spying them from her window corner. They administered a station on her neighbor's back patio, with equipment and retracted from the Planned Home to the insult of its residents, packing information to unmarked vehicles that constricted the street. The ones who stayed monitored their instruments and pointed them at the tree line. The girl notice another group of agents were three houses down and another, to her right, two or more. The panned back to the particular group of men that stayed on her neighbor's property perched with their telescopes and cameras all set up, tool boxes filled with accessories and briefcases with closed components. Bella believed they expected what she knew to be true, albeit impossible.

Soon Bella caught the notice to speak with the agents. She wanted to know if they would say anything regarding the light. She flirted with the idiom, to even brace for conversion, but as she prepared to consult them, the resident of the adjustment Home stepped onto the patio. He appeared distempered, a round citizen wearing shorts and a tank top, a wire tattoo around his left bicep. He didn't gesture outward hostility to the white collars. He took a careful approach and motioned to the cement while speaking. The men turned, vexing him, shouting, forcing the man back inside, one of the men daring to bash him with the butt his handgun. They brandished their authority, and he was quick to move inside. To this, an agent withdrew a key from his pocket and locked the owner from his own backyard. He then returned to examining the mountain side.

Bella wondered if they possessed a key for her Planned Home. It then occurred to her that the locks were all the same.

The girl sat watching the Giants before she heard a loud spatter outside. A helicopter roared over the homes and entered into her vision. It stopped, hovering above the grassy clear way beyond the barrier. Not a moment later, more joined, four in total, or as Bella could see. The men watched it and spoke into small devices. Bella watched soldiers ready for a war propelled from the aircrafts, all in forest mimicry as well as weapons the girl had only seen in movies. When all boots landed on virgin grass, they divided, forming squadrons, setting off in predetermined positions. Some forged a path straight to the approximate source of the light. Others assumed more of a flanking role, curving under and bending toward the mountain. The girl held her stomach at the sight of the men slipping into the trees. It didn't appear as an arresting force.

She moved away from her window. Her eyes twitched due to her restlessness of the night prior. She felt like she shouldn't have seen those soldiers. Her mind then went wondering if her neighbors had seen the same thing. The agent didn't seem to mind the exposure. She paced, then went back to the glass. She saw the helicopter scanning over the thickets, fanning out in all different directions.

"All of this for Molly?"

She determined that she couldn't stand the sight anymore and parted for the stairs, developing a dry thirst anyways.

Bella carefully kept by the open door of her friend's room, a chill escaping from it. She looked inside, everything in its exact spot since it had last been occupied, except Molly's music box. The girl looked back to her room and found the item to be placed on her nightstand, a glint of sunshine radiating one of its silver corners. She clenched her jaw and descended the stairs.

Having been strung by the line of repetition, Bella passed into the kitchen from the hallway of ugly paintings. To her surprise, the first sight was of Kim, peering from the screen door to the agents, a cigarette in her hand. She turned back, hearing the girl approach, first having no words but then admitting, "This is new."

"She's alive," said Bella. "I don't know how I know, but that was her on the mountain."

The tattooed woman breathed deeply into her poison. "I don't know if we should believe that," she said.

"You saw the same thing as me. Who else could it possibly be?"

"If it is"—Kim took a pause—"it'd be better if she just died."

At first, Bella was paralyzed giving reply by her roommate. She could then feel the heat bubble in her face. "How could you say that?"

"If she tried to come back, it wouldn't be a life worth living."

"You lived," protested Bella. "You lived after Mason."

Kim turned away. "I wasn't talking about that." Another inhale from the red bud. "I wish I was dead."

"Why?" Bella's voice almost growled. She shook her head. "You saw that light. We both did. I'm guessing you saw the soldiers and them going out to bring her back. How is that a bad thing? How dare you see that as a bad thing."

"Why do you insist on them saving her?" Kim answered calmly.

"What else would they be doing?"

"No rescue party, ever, has used assault rifles when looking for someone. Why do you insist they are saving her? Their assets. Thugs. They're going to kill her."

"Why? Why would they kill her??"

"Because no one crosses the state. Because you don't start a fire on the property and get away with it. Because she wants to be Local."

"That's ridiculous. She might get jail time, but they don't know it's a girl who's lost her way and wants to come home!" Bella paused to recollect herself. "You don't know what you're talking about. Those men...those men are good. They're here to help. I'll even ask Brigham. And they're going to bring back Molly, and this whole thing can go away."

"Can you hear yourself right now?"

"Yes, I do."

"You just have to trust the process?" Kim puffed from her cigarette and looked down at the kindle. "What will you do if they don't find her?"

"They will."

The tattooed woman stared at her with a blank face.

"They will," repeated the girl.

"Are you prepared if they don't?"

Bella didn't respond.

"I've seen people lie to themselves before," said the tattooed woman. "But this...you're terribly, terribly scared of everything, Bell. Molly noticed it, and I do too. You need something to attach yourself to."

The girl shook her head.

"I'm just being honest. Did your mom or dad ever tell you to be strong?"

Bella glared into her eyes.

"You deserve more," Kim continued. She walked to the sink and snuffed her cigarette. "I'm doing my best, I really am, but I'm not her."

Bella watched her roommate. "Don't turn this on me. It doesn't matter what you think of me. This is about Molly."

"If she is alive, she should run. She can't come back to this."

"Stop. Stop saying things like that!"

Kim looked at her, a moist glint in her eye. "I'm sorry, but it's true. She's better off dead."

"You can't tell me that you didn't see that light!"

A helicopter drowned the conversation. The two girls hushed for the craft to pass by.

"You think they'd use that many choppers?" Kim then asked. "Yeah, I saw it. And I'm terrified. They're not going to just let her walk back to civilization. If they don't kill her outright, they're gonna make her pay."

"We're going in circles," said Bella. "When did you become so hopeless?"

Kim looked out the window, then to her inked arm. The girl witnessed an old mourning in her eyes. Bella's inside's clenched. The tattooed woman then looked at her phone, then back at the girl, a cold glaze overcoming her. "Go get ready for work."

"Kim—"

"This is the only time I'm doing this. You're gonna have to find someone else to drive you. They're gonna be no talking, no mentioning, not ever a remark of this conversation. If you do, you're walking the rest of the way, and Nelson can fire your ass. I've had it, Bell. I'm not dealing with this shit anymore."

"Kim, I'm—"

"Don't. Don't bother. I'm done. Go get changed or I'm not taking you."

Bella stood motionless, not knowing what to do, not expecting Kim to leverage her of what she rationalized her only means of transportation. "I'm sorry." She then complied, carefully moving backward, then turning to the hallway.

Kim watched her leave and, not a moment later, withdrew another cigarette from her pocket.

Their drive was quiet, with the usual slug through Heartlake traffic and the occasional jump from a wheel slipping into a pothole. Every time the tattooed woman tensed behind the wheel, Bella leaned as far as possible from her roommate. Kim knew she was hated, and Bella knew she hated her. But the older nurse kept her persistent expression and didn't appear bothered. The girl would sometimes look at Kim, but eventually stopped, focusing on the mountain flashes over the inconstant roofing, wondering where Molly was now. At one point, she spied on one of the helicopters and wondered how many soldiers were actually out there looking. A familiar feeling took root.

Many turns and they winded their way through the maze entrance of the community hospital behind another employee of the hospital, but instead of navigating to the employ reserve stalls, Kim swung over to the front of the facility, and Bella looked over to the main entrance of the building.

Bella looked at were with a slight squint. "Okay," she said, and opened the car door. The girl then bent down after her feet hit right before the curve. "Thank you," she said with her head inside the vehicle.

Kim looked surprised. "You're welcome." And she smiled. "And if you need a ride back…"

"I have a ride." Then she shut the car door and stepped up the curve onto the cement and toward the entrance with haste in her step. Kim drove off, and the girl entered the hospital, scarcely observing the customer service desks and pressing onward. And even as she passed the two customer service stations, the girl felt eyes upon her, whether it be from fleeing glances from those passing her by or from the ones at the back burning holes in her head. She grew cautious. And from what she rationalized in her own self-paranoia was shattered by her own account of the people, and unlike what the mind manipulates, the expressions on these bystanders were mostly sympathizers, not of judges. But they nonetheless looked, and Bella hated being in their view.

She pressed one, trying her best to ignore their glances and stares. Bella managed to get within a few feet of the embedded elevator before noticing a man on an intersecting path before her. She recognized him. Kade wore a similar face as the others to those. And so she waited for his approach until he was within speaking distance.

"Is it true?" he asked.

"What is?" Bella responded.

"Everyone's talking about it. It's all of the news, Internet…I can't get away from it." He paused. "They say Molly jumped the border."

Bella couldn't speak at his tone, but her reaction confirmed his suspicion.

The nurse bent his head. "I can't believe it."

"She's alive," said the girl. "Isn't that a good thing?"

"She better be off dead," he said without hesitation. "I know she was into the Local stuff, for god's sake she had a Yudaku, but crossing the border? I bet one of those cultists told her to do this, some bullshit about how it would save her soul. My fucking god."

"I'm...I'm gonna be late for my shift," Bella said and motioned to the elevator.

Kade blocked her. "Did you even try to stop her?"

"What?"

"Why didn't you stop Molly? Instead some fanatic got a hold of her and brainwashed her into practical suicide!"

Bella looked around, then at him. "You said you would do anything for her."

His heart stopped for a second and fell.

"There wasn't any fanatic," she battled. "I don't know how and I don't know why, but all that matters is that she's alive."

Kade shook his head. "As a Local? She's better off not coming back at all." And he removed himself from Bella's path.

Bella watched as the man ventured back to where he came, crossing the room in a timid bleak fashion. She searched the floor and figured why Molly and he never worked out. She panned up the slab and pressed the button on its panel. She could hear the metal cab descend down its cable thread. The door opened, and the girl stepped inside. It reversed itself and ascended, Bella pondered her interaction with Kade and went on when the basket stopped and the metal doors opened.

To her surprise, the joining floor possessed a scarce amount of people on it. She stepped out and couldn't see the crowds that had one annoyed her. However, few employees still did walk the hallway, glancing over at a shell-shocked nurse. Bewildered still, but continued, she walked to her own footsteps in beat with a singularity, otherwise unmobbed. It was as if her scalp had been left ajar, and she rounded the corner into the break room. She hurried to a spot and sat, calming herself. Muffled but an embossing voice still barked lectures. Bella's gaze found its way by the coffee maker, and saw Nelson's square figure with his chin held high, a clipboard in his grasp, instructing two nurses who at best will be insulted or at worse be fired. Bella approached him. The doctor must have caught a glimpse of her and angled ever so slightly toward the girl. He then shooed the two nurses away and waited for Bella, a usual frown across his face.

"How are you doing today, Tomson?" he asked.

His question felt genuine, but Bella didn't believe him. "I'm fine," she said, looking down at her sneakers and his church shoes.

"Good." He nodded. "It's good to see you."

Bella nodded.

"Check the chart to see who to switch out. If I remember correctly, it was by Nurse Thornknock. Shouldn't be any different than your first couple shifts." He paused for a moment. "I expect you to stay longer today. I'm interviewing a couple of ladies, but in the meantime, the others have found it hard without Nurse Need. I can' attest to that."

Bella nodded.

"It's sad. She was a good employee. Never thought once she'd—"

"She's coming back," interrupted Bella.

The doctor appeared surprised by the interruption, scanning his workers if she even harbored the courage to cut him off. He glared at her and deduced she wasn't being sarcastic nor comedic.

"Is she now?" he continued.

Bella nodded.

"I must send someone down to the penitentiary to officially dismiss her then."

There was no hiding. If Molly was to live, she must do so behind bars. Bella accepted this.

The doctor then moved the center of the floor. "Keep an eye on Evergreen Seager," he continued. "Ever since this whole light fiasco, he's been acting suspicious."

Her boss's words felt wrong to the girl. "You mean ill?"

Nelson nodded. "Yes," he breathed. "I fear his health has been altered due to this mania."

"Should I check on him first?"

"No, go change who you need to." And he called the names of those he'd been instructing,

Bella left him to his business, parted into the main room, checking what notes required her. She made her way past the oval counter. They kept their stares about her, and Bella quickly passed by them, a stern glint in their eyes. She wondered what was wrong with Evergreen. Thereafter, she found the correct door and the correct fat woman currently behind the observation desk, peeking her name tag to make sure, and tapped the woman's shoulder. The woman flinched at the sudden touch but quickly calmed after seeing Bella's small frame.

"You scared me!" she said. "You're quiet! Let me just finish up this log."

Bella gave a weak smile. The woman, who seemed familiar but her name escaped her, carried on in a hurry, long pace, pecking away at the keyboard.

"And there, all done. Sorry, I-I just fell behind."

"No, it's okay."

"Yeah, I just sorta spaced out if you can believe. There's not a lot going on with her."

"That's okay. When's the last time you gave her the medication?"

"Not too long ago. I'd say around like eight o'clock?"

"You say?"

"No, I'm sure it was around like eight. You'll be fine keeping watch. Maybe give her a snack. She has been nothing but sleepy."

"All right, well, thank you."

"Yeah." The fat woman stood, and there began a shift in her tone. "Did Molly really cross?"

Bella took her seat and began to log in.

"Serves her right though," the woman continued. "I ain't gonna cry for a fanatic. I feel bad for you though."

The girl didn't respond.

"I guess give a holler if ya need anything." And she left her, walking to her next painter with heavy steps and little breath.

Bella turned to watch her. She hit the tile with her foot. She then spun back to the monitor and thought of the chance she saw in her peers. She recollected that everyone seemed to have shared support for Molly in the attack, and when she was missing, at least the officer sent their regards. But now Molly was coming back, and they all hated her. The girl stared off in the corner of her eye and pondered the reason but found none that sufficed.

She viewed the observation window next. There lay the little girl snug in her dark tomb of pillows and stuffed animals, the blinds shutting the sun, new trinkets littering the floor and new flowers starting to wilt. Bella studied Mallory and in the painted-eyed looking hypnotized by the rays reflecting in her eyes. The nurse panned on the TV station on. She failed to see what was airing, but caught a headline on the bottom of the screen. It was the afternoon daily brief, but as she watched, she could only make out one word on the headline: "Pelt." And it shifted to another short line: "Trespasser."

Bella rushed into the room, scaring the little girl half to death. She quickly seized the remote, dialing the volume up.

The host, a slick man in a suit and gelled hair, spouting on next to an image of the mountain, arrows indicating vague positions on certain levels. The full line read, "TRESPASSER STILL AT LARGE."

"Investigators say," voiced from the TV, "they've narrowed down the search considerably, that being the Elder's mountain trio toward the northern quadrants. Questions arise as to whether the suspect, Molly Need, chose to cross jump boundary or cut her way in another location. Critics are pointing out the barbed wire would have made the scale nearly impossible. However, experts claim that it wasn't impossible for Local to find a way around the defense, and the undoubtable piece of evidence that it was here was a campfire that was seen yesterday evening. I want to point out how absurd it would be to say, to all those fanatics out there, that this is a Taken case. We have every right to assume that Ms. Need, indoctrinated by Locals, or Pelts, became extreme and would endanger herself on state land and possibly risk a wildfire. Now we know how dangerous Local traditions can be, and this woman had clearly joined some sort of occult pagan task to spend a night in the Giant. Hell, we shouldn't even call them that. That's the name these extremist have given them, and to keep calling them is to incentivise these religious fanatics. James Rook is hear now—"

"Are you okay?" asked Mallory.

Bella turned to face the patient, the news anchor and his aforementioned guest still bleating.

"Yes," she said. "I'm fine."

"You look angry," said Mallory. "I can tell when people are mad." She points to a balled first toward Bella's side. "My dad does that every time he talks to any of you guys. He says you don't know anything."

"We don't," the nurse admitted. "We're all lying." She turned back to the screen, which was now showing an employee photo of the redhead while the two talked about her crimes. "How, how'd they get this?"

"Hey, I know her!" the little girl shouted.

Bella looked back.

"Where has she been?" Mallory continued. "I wanna hear more stories."

Bella's eyes darted. "She watched you?"

"Mmh. Why are they saying those things about her?"

The nurse went to find the remote. She found it lying by the crest of Mallory's bed. "Who turned this on for you?"

"The last lady. She watched it for a bit."

"We're not gonna have this on anymore." And she changed the channel. "Do you like cartoons?"

"My mom doesn't let me watch cartoons."

"Why not?"

"She says they'll mess my brain up. You could just leave it on this."

Bella looked back to the screen, then to the girl. "What if I told you a story?"

"Like Molly?"

"Yes, like Molly."

"I don't know," said Mallory. "She told really good ones. Mamma said not to listen to other stories."

"What do you mean?"

"I'm not allowed to. I don't wanna get in trouble. I'll just wait for Molly to come back."

"What trouble would you get into?"

"I'll just wait for Molly to come back."

"I don't think she is coming back." The words escaped Bella. Saying them made her stomach clench. "Everyone in the world seems to want her dead. They're going to jail her if they see her. Do you know that big fence surrounding the city?"

"We live by it."

"Oh, well, Molly crossed it, and they hate it here for it. And it just seems impossible, almost like I didn't do it at all. Something's wrong." The nurse held her abdomen. "I feel sick—all the time." She then looked at her patient who, upright, looked at her. "I'm sorry," said Bella. "You don't want to hear that. I feel silly."

"I don't feel sick," said the girl.

"You don't?"

"No."

"Well, do you want anything, a glass of water maybe? I feel like that's all I can get you."

"Sure."

Bella moved to the sink and withdrew a cup from the cupboard above. Water came from the spout motioned by the black sensor at its base. The nurse then delivered the cup to the girl who stared at the television. The men droned on about the trespasser, but Bella paid them no mind and turned to Mallory.

"And it was the lady before me that turned this on for you?"

"The fat lady." The girl nodded. "I don't know her name. She never says anything. What your name again, miss?"

Bella smiled. "Nurse Tomson."

"What's your real name?"

"That is my name."

"What's your first name?"

The nurse understood and gave way. "My name is Bella."

The girl smiled. "When Molly took care of me, she said her name off the bat."

"She isn't proper."

"She's the best."

Bella nodded. "She was."

"Are you sure she won't come back?" asked Mallory.

The nurse's vision collapsed toward the earth. She didn't know what to believe and shrugged.

"Can't...can't you do something?" the girl continued.

Bella shook her head. "No."

"Can't you tell them to let her go? She did nothing wrong!"

"She did. Apparently. She definitely did. But I don't see problem, I can't for the life of me see it. " Her mind went into a flurry. . "Maybe I did see her."

The patient did not care for her nurse's ramblings. "But how's that bad? Momma told me about the Giants. She said their holy! They baptized people in the lake!"

"Just myths."

"But Molly would tell me them."

"Yeah. She's a wannabe Local."

Molly stared at the nurse, confused by the choice language. "What's a Local?"

Bella twisted her head. "Nothing. It's just another name for your people" She quickly sought a means to change the topic. "When Molly… when she told you these stories, did they just include, um, baptisms?"

Mallory shook her head.

"Did they involve going on the mountains?"

"Mhm."

"And crossing the border?" Bella quickly asked.

"No," said the patient. "They were about the Ghost."

"The Ghost?"

"Yeah! And where he's been all this time. You said you saw something. Maybe it was him?"

Bella couldn't help but smile. "No, I'm sure it wasn't. Probably a bird or something scared."

"Well then, it doesn't matter." The girl stared emotionless.

The nurse thought long and hard for a moment, then responded, "What does the Ghost save people from?"

The girl pulled the covers up to her mouth. "Bad things."

"Like what?"

Mallory kept still.

"Animal?" suggested the nurse. "People?"

"Bad things."

Bella paused for a second and recounted Evergreen's book. Image of the creature crept into her conscience.

At this point, the argument befalling the television became too much. The nurse turned back and clicked the device. The news channel closed and revealed a black screen, whose reflection encompassed Bella staring into its mire.

"Thank you," said the nurse. "I'll just be outside if you need me." She sat the remote down by Mallory's leg and began leaving."

"I wish you weren't," said the girl.

"What?" Bella turned on a dime, hurt by her comment. "Why?"

The girl didn't respond.

"Mallory, why? Why don't you want me to stay?"

The patient turned over, eyes glossy. Her lips quivered and her brow bent. "I want the other nurse," she said, but the subject of the words sounded foreign to the little girl, but at the same time, something she knew or at least a version of relatability or a shared longing for a taken soul. "I want my mommy."

Bella thought to comfort the girl but stepped to the door. Seeing the crying child, she left in a single motion. She now stood in the hallway, strangling her emotions. She prevailed and sat down flat. A flash of anger involved her, then dissolved, then a bubbling over confusion, which led to a road block. She thought about what Mallory could have understood from the channel and how it could have affected her just now. The girl's a Local, Bella knew this, but she couldn't help that the patient understood from the disgendered channel. And the notion of unseen things resonated in her mind, she'd best to forget it, discredit herself upon which could have been fabricated, however Local it may have seen. But the girl could not. She clung to the fact, held it close to her. A dreadful idea grew. Of that brief sprint, Molly didn't leave; she was taken. "With what evidence? But the curling of your own stomach." Bella covered herself. She felt naked.

She shoved her superstitions down within her. The nurse resumed with her tasks and pecked away at the keys, leaving out details that she feared the facility would take special interest in. No matter what her job compelled her to do, she excused any mention of Molly and of the Ghost, checking for the square-faced doctor who would have no problem sniffing out mines beneath mundane lines on a workspace spreadsheet. Nevertheless, she wasn't caught, but kept her composer until the rotation demand her to switch stations, leaving a dull-haired nurse to her own chair and following suit to her next assignment, not a name but a number: 319.

She made the commute, dodging the equipment carts and personnel, until she stood outside the room with the black marking 319. Bella approached the male nurse sitting there, a lofty man with a timid face and an undangerous demeanor. He almost left without a word before the girl caught him with a question.

"How is she?" Bella asked.

"Mm?"

"The old lady here." She said the word before noticing a new patent under the covers.

"Died yesterday. Not sure why," he said. "His name is Edward, and he's nonverbal. I wouldn't even introduce yourself, save some of your time." And he walked away before the girl had a chance of processing the information laid before her. Bella's mind instantly went to the old woman who told her about the angel. She couldn't remember her name. She damned herself, for she couldn't remember her name, only fathoming what the lady foretold of forgetting and an angel's hand in that motion.

Why can't I remember her name? she thought. *Margret or Mattie. Opal or maybe Becca.* She possessed no clue and sat in dismay. "How could it happen so fast?" Bella reminisced what the old woman foretold, but the speed at which never crossed her mind. She then looked inside the room, to which she found no IV pouches, only a twisted limb man in the bed facing an empty room. It appeared the old woman was wiped from existence. Bella hoped someone could remember her. "Rubido. That was it." Her mind caused her heart to race again. "Is she dead?" Her eyes swirled around the floor as the motion made vomit present itself in the back of her throat, causing her to gag. "She couldn't. She'd fight them off. She'd find a way to win. She'd survive without a shadow of a doubt." She got up from her chair and charged through the patient's door and blazed past him to the sheltered view behind glass. Through the window, she yearned for the peaks sticking out behind the condensed city. She sought the sight that had warmed her, that fire that had lifted from her worldly state; but from the pines, no light was seen, save the sun in its high throne. And the girl, left hand clutched, parted back to her place, among the most agony she had ever endured.

However, before she could pass the patient's bed, unbothered, Bella heard a sigh and delivered a look on the man in bed. He was disabled, permanently, limbs linked as dead spiders, bent beyond recognition, palms and soles facing completely opposite directions, hips slightly off mast. He's eyes were incredibly sunken, and hair nearing baldness, gray patches that didn't appear as his own attempt to fill, doing more than a fair job. More unsettling, Bella beheld his jaw, the man's wide and uneasy jaw, far too stretched. At first, he stared, without motion, but as soon found he had the girl's attention, he dispersed his lips from his teeth, unsheathing a wicked grin. Bella stepped back in repulsion. The yellow ungodly smile of the man spread wider and wider beyond humanly possible, and drool began to form at the bottom of his lip. It mocked her. It laughed. It knew what she had lost. It knew that beyond that fence lay the dying corpse of the victim not even out of her twenties. Its voice possessed all hearing.

Not sure of whether to strike the visage or flee, Bella stood trembling. She didn't realize she took a step toward the door, and as she did so, its limbs began to stretch and swirl and loop like never before into masses of unknown shapes and volume. Petrified, the girl ran, as she never did before, as hard as her legs to carry. The door flung, and she quickly shut it. The whole floor looked at her. All eyes from the oval counter to the far quartet were beaming on her.

Bella flung herself to the observation window to see if it was still there. There sat a disabled man, laying on his side, drooling, a slight smile on his face. She was in disbelief. The nurse turned back to the peers behind her. One woman came up to her side and asked, "What happened?"

Bella found a response. "I just scared myself."

"Well, don't do it again. Goddamn." And she left with a judgment glare. All the others slowly returned to their duties, leaving the girl unseen at different times. Bella gripped the edge of her desk, finally breathing.

One inhale after the next exhale, Bella dissociated her breath and slithered down to her seat, hands still staking, the monitor screen still on the log-in application. She brought her hand, fingering consecutive pattern of her password and located her logs. Struggling to know what to put down, Bella put, "Patient was asleep," and left the sentence be.

Bella stared at the floor. She couldn't muster another line, and for the next minute to the next hour, sat in turmoil until her session was over. The same dull-haired woman came over to relieve her, tapping the girl's shoulder, shocking her out of the self-made trance. She bolted up to see who had disturbed, fearing it was Nelson. She then left when she saw the dull peer, without saying anything, paying no heed to her concern.

Redundancy moved her, while fear pressed on her heels. She avoided everything with her head down, and to her next assignment she went, avoiding the eyesight of the nurses and personnel that had more reason to look and mock her. She managed like clockwork to find Evergreen's room and went to relive the nurse on duty, yet only found when she looked up there that there was no one present. She scanned the premiums for an early nurse fleeing but found only the usual bustle. Bella sat down, obedient to routine, and looked out through the observation window: There sat Evergreen, television's glow in the reflection of his glasses.

Bella didn't bother signing in to the computer. She went forth into the room and approached the old man's side. Evergreen glanced over to the girl, quickly, pitifully, and ticked back to the screen, to the same station Mallory's room had been playing, this time only, the anchor was conversing with a bitter woman with thick, ugly spectacles.

"There's simply a threat to democracy," she claimed. "There isn't really any other way to put it. There is an uneducated class that has a tendency to vote for problematic officials, well, you get people who do this sorta thing. We as citizens can't afford to let this keep happening, and the fact that they are even able to vote scares me, Mike. Scares me to oblivion and I have a right to not be scared, Mike, I do."

Evergreen turned to Bella. "I've been watching all day. They were just showing where Molly could have gone, where they think that light lit up. Now I don't know what the hell they're talking about."

"She's a troll," said Bella, staring still at the television.

"She's just doing her job. Same as you, she's just paid to be upset."

"They have no right."

"You're right, but they need someone to pin this on."

Bella turned to the old man, and she met his wide eyes, showing more life in her short time knowing him.

"Did you see it?" he asked.

She knew instantly. "The light?"

"Yes, my dear. You must have."

The nurse nodded.

A tender smile swept Evergreen's face. He turned toward the window, then back to the girl. "Do you have any idea what this means?"

"It means she's alive. But they're going to kill her."

"Yes, it means she is, but, no, no! There not going to kill her! Don't be stupid, girl. What it means is that he has found her."

Bella rolled her eyes. "The Ghost?"

Evergreen agreed. "Did someone tell you already?"

"Yes," Bella responded. (supposed to be behind above line) "A kid." The nurse turned back to the television.

"No, no, don't you do that, missy! Don't discredit her because she was raised right! All that we teach the youth is real!" He reached for his briefcase. "You've seen my journal. You've seen the figure."

Bella glanced at the old man struggling. "Let me help you," she said. "I saw a lot of things in the book that I wished I didn't."

"But you looked!" He brought the briefcase on the side of his bed. " Now he'd be the one with the long braided beard. You saw that one, right."

Bella nodded.

"Good, good, so you know what to look for."

"To look for?"

"He's the one keeping her safe. That light, his campfire, the one he made for her. It's a single."

Bella shook her head. The mere idea made her frown break into a smile. "You must have a fever." But then she saw the man's eyes, brimming with rejuvenated life, nearly willing to break out of his casts. "You're crazy. No, that can't be true, sir."

"Why not?" he asked. "You know of the light. You know of the Ghost. We both know that sweet innocent girl didn't go willingly. She couldn't climb the barrier. Anyone with a brain could tell you that. She'd been torn to pieces trying to jump over. And all that is a lie, a flat-out fucking lie that they keep pinning on the Locals here. There is no ritual for running out to the forests. Any sane Pelt would be terrified of it. No one would tell her it would bring peace."

Bella cleared her thoughts, shunned about the clarity her first instance brought. "Can you tell me what happened then?"

Evergreen scoffed. "You'd know better than me. I'm assuming you're the eyewitness. I watched a man on here claim you saw her climb the fence."

"I never saw that," Bella yelled.

"What did you see?"

The girl bit her tongue.

"There's nothing to prove to me. It's the same every time. It's too much work for them to research, so they say she was one of us. She won't be counted as missing, but everyone has always see something before..." He turned the page of the journal until it rested on that elongated figure that had haunted the girl.

Bella turned away. She refused and kept her gaze at the floor.

"Look," he said.

"I can't."

"Look," he repeated.

Bella disobeyed.

"You eventually must see."

Slowly, she wavered toward him and beheld what nightmare witnessed days ago. She fixated into the dark chasms for the eye. And the image spoke truth to her. Details, buried, began to reveal themselves.

"You must know evil," he continued. "If you will face it."

"Are you sure? Then we must call the police."

"No police." He cut off the girl. "They won't believe, but they will tell their masters. And it's them who would kill him and her if she's with him."

"That, that can't be true..."

"Maybe not for all of them. I'm sure there are kind white collars. But there's enough that will. Don't ever, ever go to the police for your problems. Not for this kind of problems. You must fix them by your lonesome." He turned to the girl. "You must fix them."

"How could I?."

Evergreen coughed and cleared his throat. "Listen to me now, It doesn't matter to you individually or personally. Everything up to this point has been a coincidence. That light isn't for you individually, but for anyone what would heed it. I wish I could go. I wish I could go and do something worth my sins in weight to bring her back, to bring all of them back. But I'm broken. I have no sons or grandson to go, and finally, my body has failed. I've been cursed with my choices. But yours...yours hasn't. You see that light the same way I do. You can see it high in the Giant's eye. I know you did, and your first thought was of her. You can go."

"This...this is..." She stopped herself. "I'd lose everything."

"Is what you have really worth keeping?"

His question stung her deeply.

"How could I even do this?"

"Stay outside on duty for now. Keep doing what you do, until nightfall. Come to me, then drive back to your house. Do this quickly."

"I...I can't drive," she stated.

"What?!" he nearly jumped out of his bed.

"I never needed it!"

"My god." Evergreen brought his hand to his head and sought a solution. "Is there anyone you can trust? Anyone that wouldn't say a word, without a shadow of doubt?"

Two people came to mind. Bella chose the latter. "Yes, there is."

"Is he a cop?"

"No," she answered.

"Good." Evergreen kept firm lips then admitted any control he had over the situation. "Go choose how to get here, just get here. Please. We don't have a lot of time. Please come as soon as it gets dark."

"I'll try." And she made a motion to exit the room.

"This is real," he said. "Believe me."

Bella nodded and left the room. Starstruck by what the old man told, she took her seat behind the observation window. A tremble had managed to stagger her breathing, enforcing a stillness with her skull, and numb fancy clouded as she stared into the blank screen of the monitor. Some people passing by noted the lack of accomplished work. But the girl paid no attention to their refracting sneers, only whether or not to trust Evergreen. Reason stuck her, along with worldly law, and inner doubt: "You can't." However, as these ideology attempted to ensnare her, the undying thought rose once again of that notion that she did see what the patient showed. Again her own doubt and vexation wanted to corrupt the thought, but reality of the fact then showed through: "It must be true." And she knew pulled her own hair at the conclusion. "It must all be real." Her blood pressure raced at what she must do.

"Busy?" a voice boomed from behind Bella. The girl jumped and looked at its producer. There stood Nelson, arms folded, cheeks expanding due to a clenched jaw." You sure look it," he continued.

In an instance the girl flipped around and started logging in to the computer. "I'm...I'm sorry, sir."

"What have you been doing? You're at least twenty minutes into your rotation and not a single line on your log.

"Just checked in with Evergreen."

"Did he say why he was acting strange?"

"I'm gonna check in with him again."

"See that you do." The doctor turned and strolled down the hallway, making sure his perfect building was whole.

Bella watched his leave and turned back to do her work, but failed to press any letters. From the black, she looked into her own emerald vessels, a twitch in their corners. Instead, the girl turned to the floor and saw every nurse behind every computer. They were not giving aid, they were not providing care, all of them watched and recorded whomever rested within their quarter. She saw some who were young, some in the crisis of their life, and the old. They could all be replaced by robots. And the dead seemed better off to the girl, for this can't be called living, nor is it exactly death. And the help the nurses administered was far from her aspirations and knew the opposite of health. Bella then stood. She made direction any which way she desired and followed suit, glancing in every slit that frayed from vision. They were all sick. Never getting better, less staying alive.

She found herself in the break room. She looked and beheld no one. Bella checked the time. It was hours since she had left her seat. She watched, its painstaking hands delivering slowness unto her.

Nelson found her there. He seemed damped by the sweat of anger and baffled by the idiotic action of his employee.

"What are you doing?" he yelled.

Bella turned to him, then began walking past the doctor.

"Get back to your station!"

She stopped in the hallway and looked back at him. He stood in the doorway.

"What am I here to do?"

His brow furled. "You're here to monitor the patie—"

"Too help them?"

"Excuse me." His voice dropped. "Don't ever interrupt me. You have no authority over me. You will not speak when I am speaking. Okay? That's what's going to happen."

Bella didn't answer.

"Now what you're going to do is get back on that computer and you're gonna chart everything he said to you and vice versa. Then write the correct date and time and hit fucking send. Do you understand?" He pointed. "I don't want to have this conversation again."

"You might have to," responded Bella.

And the doctor was struck dumbfounded. "What?"

"You would have no way of knowing what me and the patient talked about. You can't so bluntly spy on people."

"Spy? That's not what—have you lost your mind?" He now stood over her.

"I was never a nurse, was I?" Bella looked up at him.

"I don't even know how to begin to address that statement. You are in a hospital, you wear a medical uniform, you give—"

"Medicine that doesn't work."

Nelson pressed his lips together. "I won't repeat myself. You're lucky we were so short staffed. Get back to work." And he tried to get away from her.

"But I could lie," she said. "You'll never know what we talked about. It only exists between me and the patient. Does that make you upset?"

"How do you think this is a good argument, stating you can lie? Never in my years have I heard such nonsense. If you lie then and I can prove it, you'll be let go."

"But you'll never know."

"What is this? What are you trying to do?"

"I will never tell you what we discussed."

"It's almost like…like you wanna be fired," the doctor spat.

Bella nodded, she did not waver. "Please," she said.

"Why?" Nelson tried to wrap reason in the plea. "Why would you want that?"

"Give me nothing left to lose."

The employer stood in awe. His collective years could not guide him on what to do next. As for the first time in a while, he couldn't move, paralyzed by audacity and nearly resulted in profanity. "Are you crazy?"

But the girl, staring up at him, meek, little, but unrelenting, backed away without so much as a second, third, or fourth rebuttal, glance, or care. She descended down the hallway, becoming even smaller and smaller, until she obscured from sight.

The doctor shouted for her, but she would not come.

Chapter

17

The curve felt cold. Cars passed by, picking up family members, escorts at their side, wealthy-dressed men and women coming and going. A few yards away, Bella sat in her dismay, uninterrupted in the dull revving rays of a skinny street post. Her head rested between her knees, and her arms bared over, a mimicry of a cradle. Her phone, held ideally in her hand, showed up on its screen a white background filled with gray boxes and green of a conversion. The screen then went black, but the girl still clutched the device and did not move from her stance. Her demeanor endorsed nothing of economic certainty but rather queer, a calm, not a terror, shook within her bones. No questions to whether she made the right decision, no qualms to which anxiety could extend past its faint reason, no insufferable murmuring of inner conflict, but by its lonesome: a calm. Peace, as if she believed she had made the first correct choice in this fine mess. Though she did shiver, for the curve felt cold.

Cars flowed with drive through. The day had revealed a soothing approaching night, with crystallized dazzling of a bright sliver moon to the blue dimming sky, and through its bliss, a police cruiser went on course to the hospital's ground, gently steered. It made its way through the paved maze and turned approaching the main entrance. Bella identified its sound and looked toward the source. It parked then in front of her, and Brigham exited. He wore casual clothes, slacks and a T-shirt cozied by a leather jacket.

"Hey!" he said, smiling at the girl, who stood up in response, whose pearly whites greeted him back. She then, in a burst of speed, ran up to the officer and hugged him. The motion stunned the man, who tenderly reciprocated the gesture yet confused, meeting his arms to her lower back.

"You all right?" He laughed.

"Yeah," she said. "I just got fired."

"Fired?!"

The two separated.

Bella nodded.

"Good god," said the man. "That's terrible. What happened?"

"It's not really important. I really don't know what is going on. But the doctor got really mad, and so he let me go. But it's not really important."

"Well, it seems important. He just up and fired you?"

"I'll...I'll tell you, but first I gotta get some things from my..." The girl hesitated. "Locker. I think that's where my stuff is."

Brigham tilted his head. "Did it just happen?"

"Yes," she said.

"Good god," he exasperated. "Want me to go to the park?"

"No! No, just stay here. I'll be quick."

"You sure?"

"Yeah, yeah, they're lax here." She began moving again toward the main exit. "I'll be fast I promise. I just need to grab..."

"Yeah, yeah, I'll wait here then." And he smiled.

She then smiled. "Thank you." She turned around, speed walking to the open door, but then spinning around yet again to wave to the man, to which Brigham replied with a simple gesture of his hand.

Bella kept her speed till crossing the threshold of automatics, then after she broke sight of Brigham, she hastened her pace and darted a glance to the presiding employees who gave direction to a family of four. The girl used the opportunity to sneak past, expecting the nurse to be Nelson's bouncer, and began her way down the prime alley to the cryptic elevator. Of the little personnel scouring the lower level, there was none, so to the glances of physicians and operators began glowing perception counters, paying little mind to the former nurse stealthy navigating the hall.

Then arriving at the elevator, she pressed two swift buttons and the casket rose to her previous future and opened to a catacomb. Here she had lost the calm she'd had before, upon seeing the reflections of workers on the tile.

She strode one single step, then another, once more another though uncertain. Bella possessed no explanation to why she'd returned to her peers. She couldn't be stuck in a conversation. They knew she owned nothing for they own nothing. Someone would suspect, and she knew her plans would be suicide if revealed.

"But what plan?" she uttered to herself. Another step was taken. She hugged the wall to see past the decorative window to the main floor. It appeared her former boss wasn't there, but Kade and a few other recognized faces flouted around on, of course, the oval counter that no one alluded. The girl shared not aspect of who Nelson would have gossiped about this ordeal too. She needed to avoid the doctor the most. Anyone else, she concluded, would just alert him.

Bella knew she could only peer from the window a few moments longer before someone spotted her or someone needed to enter or leave the floor. She then chose to gamble the odds, and step foot onto the floor, walking fast and focused, as if nothing was wrong.

"Where ya been, Bell?" a passerby asked, a face recognizable but name forgettable.

"I was on break."

"Oh, I see, I saw ya talking to Nelson. What was—"

"Nothing." And the girl eclipsed the distance in order to hold conversation, traveling steadily to Evergreen's room, now in view, void of any personnel monitoring, the old man. However, still she felt eyes all around her, focused and pressed. She turned her head toward the oval counter and saw in direct eye contact an operator lift his phone.

Urgency struck, but Bella tried to keep her calm, keeping step in line with the next until she reached Evergreen's door. She opened it, entered, and quickly shut it, pressing her back to the hard wood and sighing. Her next sight was of the old man, his suitcase and his book on the bed closest to her, and the man himself fiddling with rope that fed through the odd groove of the case attached to an unknown object.

"Finally," he said. "We can't waste any more time."

Bella eyed the rope. "What are you tying?"

"It's for your safety. You won't stand a chance in hell without it."

The girl paced toward the old man, her eyes fixated on the scarred suitcase. Slowly, beyond the lifted lid, she caught a view of what lay waiting for her: first the nozzle, then the body, then its rest. Her stomach soared as she saw the rifle seemingly in slumber on the cushioned interior of the scarred briefcase.

"A gun?"

"Yes," Evergreen answered. "My father's."

"You had that in here this whole time?"

"Long before you. This is how you load it." The old man took from one of the pockets and within its place, a case of bullets, shining in the artificial rays. He then pulled back a tiny notch on the base of the rifle and revealed a small empty slit. The man then inserted the bullet and pushed back on the notch, which in an instant closed with a sharp metal snap. "It's easy, even babies can do it." He then pulled the notch back again and removed the bullet, setting it down and returning to his work on the rope, which he did with one hand. "We made these, chemical composition and all."

Bella's attention now moved to the armrest of the weapon and beheld a dense ring around the end of its wooden buck. From this, the old man wound an intense knot, one that seemed impossible to tear.

"I don't understand," the girl attempted. "What do you expect me to do?"

With one final tug, Evergreen finished the knot and looked up Bella, a glint of worry in his aged eyes. "For your safety," he said. "I'm not sure what you'll find." He grabbed by the side of the rifle his book and opened to the page of that giant man. "You need to find him. Follow the fire. He'll surely light it again. She'll be by it. But you can't make yourself a burden to him while he defends Molly. That's why you need to take this with you."

"I…I've never held a gun before."

"Hold it."

234

"How am I supposed to get it out of here? You can't even have a firearm! How do you have it? I can't—"

"Hold it." And he gestured to the weapon.

Bella hesitated, but gave in, arms reaching down touching the cold metal first, then the polished wood. She then seized it by the body in both hands almost as a balance beam, moving it upward in an awkward direction."

"Come here," said Evergreen.

And the girl timidly slid to where his arm could instruct.

"Jam the buck into your shoulder."

"Like this?" The girl listened.

"A bit. Bring it higher. Yeah, that's good. Is that your dominant hand?"

"Yeah."

"Good, now set it in here.

Bella did as the old man told, placing back within its case.

"Give me your hand." Evergreen patted by the edge of the case.

"Why?" the girl asked, but obeyed nonetheless.

"It needs to be tied to you at all times." And the old man began tying a well-fitting rope around Bella's wrist. "It is too dangerous not to. Could you hold the rope here?"

She held a certain part of the tie. Bella eyed the rope back down the armrest of the rifle. She then darted to the odd grove on the side of the briefcase, with the fact that could be undone with one hand.

"The case is to hide it," she exclaimed.

"Yes," answered Evergreen. "But also to hold any other tools you might need along your way. You'll have plenty of ammo. Us Pelts, we became crafty little devils. We used trick after trick and new tricks when they figured out the old tricks. You might come across as suspicious, but as long as you hurry, no one will bother you."

"And you made all of this?"

"Take the interior out. I don't need your other hand any more, the entire cushioning comes out."

Bella grabbed the hard fabric and pulled one side up, revealing a wire cutter nudged between a barrage of loose bullets and spare paper.

"We made everything. Once you reach the barrier, fill your pockets with bullets and take the cutters. Leave the case shut on the town's side or in your house would be better." He stopped tying for a moment. "No, that won't work. Take the case with you. Get rid of it in the forest."

"Are you serious?"

"In case the police get to your house before you. And remember what I showed with reloading! You…you shouldn't have to use it, hopefully. He should be distracting it. I wish you had more time…Do I need to show you again?"

"Yes, please."

Evergreen finished the knot in a final motion and took the weapon again, levering it against the bed and demonstrating again how to administer a round into the rifle and unloading it quickly with its metallic clicks echoing the room. "Now you try."

Bella examined the interloping rope around her wrist. She then did so, picking the rifle up rather fondly but still displaying amateurish hesitancy. She peeled back the metal chamber and fumbled a bullet at an awkward angle into the gun.

"Keep your finger off the trigger," Evergreen said. "Raise it higher on the wood."

The girl moved her finger upward. "Sorry."

"Just a bit of gun safety for you. I wish it had more firepower, but it'll do. Like I said, the Ghost should be keeping it away."

"What exactly is he keeping away?"

He looked at the girl with dreadful eyes. "This journal isn't fairy tale. It's a notebook. Every group has a different name for it. Pale Thing is ours. What it is isn't exactly so obvious. I've tried all my life to figure out what makes these demons. I think they were once people, but could strive from hell, wherever that may be, could be spirits or both, or simply just animals from long ago. What is undeniable is their hunger. Local myth puts it as pure desire. Insatiability turned into being. I've never seen one, to be honest with you Suspicions and things I swore I saw." He stopped for a moment, seeing his broken figure. "I'm sorry it had to be you."

"It doesn't matter anymore," replied Bella.

The old man nodded. "Listen for the crickets chirp. Listen for the night birds. If they begin to fade, or if the forest becomes deafening, run as fast as you can to that light. Do you hear me?"

Bella nodded, heart sinking.

He began to gather his things and set them underneath the interior, his personal journal included. "Set it in here." And the girl cautiously laid the rifle with its case, leading the rope onto the groove. Evergreen closed the lid, and the rope hung outside still attached to the rifle and Bella's wrist. He then handed the girl the briefcase, which she slumped to her side.

"You need to get going. It's nearly dark."

Bella stayed, unable to legitimize what she was about to do. "I'm scared," she said.

The old man smiled. "Sacrifice attracts the Lord. He will protect you if all else fails."

The girl shook her head. "I don't think I can believe in that one."

"This whole ordeal may just rely on belief. You're as prepared as I can make you, and you're the most trained you can be."

Bella nodded. She turned to the door and desperately scanned out the window for any one that would be waiting outside.

"God bless you," said Evergreen as he surrendered his head to the surface of his pillow. "And God speed."

"I'll bring her home," said Bella. She turned to meet the door and carefully analyzed the area outside. No one paid attention to her side of the sector. Bella gripped the handle, her heart nearly beating out of her chest, then quietly and acutely, she pulled the handle and entered the floor.

Evergreen returned to himself.

Bella scanned to see if anyone noticed; but a few of her peers, with only quick glances, heeded her. She parted, considering the old man's words, and began to hurry her way back to the elevator, quickly moving pretending she wasn't strapped to the scarred suitcase, not noticing the gaze behind lock onto her. By miracle, she passed the break room, nearing the edge of the medical floor. She picked up her pace, delighted that she had avoided every fool. She gained speed toward her destination. It was within a few feet. Bella frantically pressed the button. She could hear it ascending. Her hope grew. Shouts then made themselves present. With the speed of a demon, she bolted to the side of the elevator, the case banging on the worn cement. The bucket finally rose, and stepping out of it is Nelson. He stepped out and yelled to his phone. She saw her chance and took it, entering after their departure and jamming her fist to the first floor.

But as the elevator's gate closed, from the exit swung out a motion that captured the girl's sight. With panic and fury, the doctor turned to see Bella. The door closed. The doctor ascended Bella's sight, and the former nurse looked as if caught in winter.

She knew she'd been caught, or at least found out. She knew security would be upon her in seconds if she delayed for even a moment.

The instant the casket leveled and the moment a sliver in its gate, Bella dashed forward, the case flinging to her side. Her footsteps squeaked on the tile floor as she rushed, seeking escape. But as she passed into the main hall, turning, nearing a fall, a voice yelled, "Stop!"

All eyes were upon her from the counters and the sides, as down the hall toward her right a guard ran fast. Bella stumble to gain her footing, gaining her balance after a several clumsy step forward. She knew she need to move forward.

The guard, yards away from the girl, shouted once more. "Stop! Stop running!"

But the girl, with the flight of a devil, with each frantic stride made her way closer and closer to the exit.

In the straight way, another guard approached her, sprinting, with an idea to cut her off before she reached the exit. She pushed hard upon realization, navigating to the cusp of the exit before him, however only by several feet. Now, in view of rising moonlight, the girl found that the attendant had moved to block her way through the automatic doors.

Bella had no space to stop and designed within a tick on an ivory face that this nurse would not stop her. She brought the case up and, like a battering ram, bashed into the side of the attendant who, in a vain attempt, tried to smoosh the girl into the side of the glass and grasp any morsel of her that she could. It all failed but the grab, the attendant pulling her arm for the approaching security.

However, the girl managed to slither her arm from the woman's thick finger, and her big size now impeded the guards. Bella then felt the thwack of the sidewalk before any other sense could be processed, passersby twisted to the dilemma. The nurse saw the police vehicle, miraculously still parked beside the curve as if the girl thought she'd have to marathon all the way to her own home.

She began waving to the cozy Brigham. The girl came a bit closer and yelled, "Let's get going!"

The officer heard a muffled version of her words and looked over to see the former nurse rushing toward her. He squinted toward the tied rope and the suitcase. But then he saw the security pursuing her, gaining ground.

He initially started the vehicle, then reached and flung open the passenger side's door. In came the gallivanting Bella, almost flying over onto the driver's seat. She slammed the door shut then shouted.

Brigham cranked the steering wheel and stomped the gas. The two security guards were perplexed, seeing a police car driving off. They looked at each other for leadership, finding none, and the onlookers to the event watched on as the lone police cruiser drove on.

Chapter

18

"It's not yours, is it?" The officer drove steadily.

The hum of the road soothed Bella and rested her. "No," she said. "Not really."

"Did you steal it?"

"It was given to me."

"And it's tied to your arm..."

"I didn't mean to wrap you up in this." The girl fiddled with the case's latch. "It's nothing bad, I swear! A patient wanted me to have it. He was really keen on it."

"Why were they chasing you?"

"Who knows?"

"They had to have had a reason to."

"Maybe to confiscate it. We're technically not allowed to accept gifts. I just got scared, and I ran. There's nothing in it but books."

The officer side-eyed the scarred case. "Why wouldn't they allow gifts? If you could call it a gift."

"Can't have any real relationship with them," said Bella. "Just enough to make them feel less scared."

"Again, seems a little odd."

"I know. I guess it's just how Nelson likes it."

"He's your boss?"

"Not anymore."

"Ah," reposed the officer, without any more to add. He remained in his usual state of clarity and serenity. The girl not noticing an ounce of malice toward herself in his tone but subconsciously expected as such. She feared she caused harm to him.

"I'm sorry," she said. "I...I don't think anyone noticed you, even if they do report what I did. No one noticed you."

"Oh, ya don't need to be sorry, Bell." He smiled. "Even if they did report some, I wouldn't mind. Me and the Deacon aren't the best of friends right now."

"Why? What happened?"

"I'll tell ya, but first. What's in it?"

"What do you mean?"

"The case or whatever. What's really in it?"

"I told you, books." Bella searched for a quick response and clung to the first possible thought. "And some drawings."

"Drawings?"

"Yeah. The patient was a painter. He would draw things for Molly and some of the other nurses. Well, she wasn't one to be told what to do, and she actually cared about the people she looked after. And so Evergreen, that's his name, would draw things for her. And well, he said that I could take them, so I meant to take them. Just as a sort of memory of her. Something physical helps a lot."

Brigham looked at the knot around her wrist. "I guess that makes sense. I still don't understand what they mean to stop you."

"He's a Pelt," said Bella.

The officer lit up. "Ah, I see."

"He was also paranoid."

"Yeah, no, I get it. Actually pretty smart in the inner-city streets. Not too sure about the hospital though.

Bella rested her head back onto the passenger's side window. "What's wrong with you and the station?"

Brigham sighed. "Ah well." He scratched his head. "I don't know how you're gonna take this. But they took me off the George Grey case."

The girl erected herself once more.

The office nodded. "They took everyone off. And when I asked for an explanation, they failed to give me one, or well, a convincing one. By they I mean the agency. You see those white-collar guys walking around?"

Bella nodded."

"Yeah, well, their big shots from the federal government. They kicked everyone off. I can do jack all about it." He turned to Bella for a split moment. "I need to be upfront with you. It doesn't sit right with me if I'm not. Now that it's in their hands, I don't see him getting caught. They…they just…I don't know why they want anything to do with him, but apparently, he's of value to the state. That puts us with a firm block. And Lord knows Deacon won't push back at all." The officers looked over at the nurse once again, pity within his heart. "I shouldn't have promised. I thought I really could get him. Everything points to that man, and we're letting him slip."

Bella said nothing and viewed the passing houses.

"I know it's not the news you wanted to hear. And no one's more upset than I am about it. There's just, just nothing can be done."

"It's okay," responded the girl.

"You all right?" asked Brigham. "I understand if you're upset. I'm furious."

"Just keep driving." And Bella gripped the suitcase till her knuckles bleached white. The rope went tight around her wrist.

Brigham once again shot a glance at the girl, then back to the road. No more will I bother her, the officer made the decision. The air grew tense around them. He abhorred the girl's disdain. And the gentle murmuring of the road was all that the pair heard on their way to Bella's Planned Home.

The ground leveled, and loose minute pebbles popped and juggled as well-kept tires rolled up and onto a cement driveway. Bella and Brigham both exited the vehicle, the former clutching the sacred suitcase as if it were a kin. The latter appeared worried. The officer then proceeded to escort the girl to her doorway, bending with the swirl of the walkway, and up the hard steps to a plank porch. There was haste in her steps. She made her way in front of him.

"I'm sorry," he said. "I wish there was something I could do. But they could fire me."

"Why would doing a good thing get you fired?" Bella asked.

"Because it's their problem to handling now. He might face charges but when they're done with him. Who knows when that will be."

"I want him to pay." The girl said this without rebuttal.

"I know…I know. What he did was evil, and he deserves to spend the rest of his life in jail."

"That's not good enough."

This phrase stunned the young cop. He then blurted, "What is?"

A waver presented itself with Bella's voice. "Don't let him get away with this."

"What is?" the officer repeated.

"Death," she almost ordered. "He can't get away with this. He can't keep doing this!"

"You can't just kill him, Bell!"

"Then catch him," Bella pleaded. "Please just catch him."

The officer folded his arm. He looked out to the dying day and back once again to the small- framed girl, standing up on the porch over him. "It's not like I want to go, not like I don't want to stop this monster…I have bills to pay. As much as I want, I can't afford to go after him."

"Maybe you should lose it."

"What?" The officer was surprised as the bold response.

"Is a job worth keeping if it stops your morals?" the girl questioned.

"Depends on what you count as good."

"I lost my job today because I'm about to do something finally right, and that isn't just waiting around for someone else to do what's necessary. And I don't care about the future, and I'm terrified of it. I only know what I can't ignore, and what I should."

Brigham staggered a little. "What should you do?"

Bella scrambled. "What I did. Sorry, I meant, what I did."

"Right with quitting."

"Yes. With the case." Bella glanced down at it and rubbed one of its silver hatch locks.

"What's in it?" the officer asked again.

"I told you," she said. "Just drawings."

"And books," he added.

"Yes." Her mind blanked. "Yes, of course."

Brigham scanned the girl. The blue sky shaded into black. He looked at her form and at her hands, and then her eyes, who escaped his own. "I'll try and find anything I can do. But I can't make another promise."

And before he knew she had moved, Bella flew down the steps and hugged the officer maneuvering the case to not bang his knee. Brigham was caught off guard, but gave in and made way his arms. And with a low tone, Bella voiced the line, "That's all I ask." She broke up the hug. Brigham stared with scrambled thoughts. She gently waved, stoned face, and slipped up on the porch and stopped at the door.

Brigham walked back to his vehicle. He looked back to see Bella sitting near the wood's edge. He hollered, "Want me to wait?"

The girl shook her head. "I'm just waiting to be let in!" she shouted back.

The man remembered and entered the cab. The car started, and he rolled back into the street. He went off toward the right, and Bella watched him far off into the road.

She made sure he vanished from view, then Bella peeked to the side window a few inches from the door. Bella checked her phone, a message from Kim ran across her screen: "Hey, I'm gonna be out with Darrick, lmk when you need a ride." The house was vacant. The girl stood there for a moment, thinking, then peeked again at the window. It possessed no net.

Bella wasted not another second. She checked one more time to her surroundings, then plunged the end of the case through the glass. She brought it forth with all of her might. It took two swings to break through and a few more to knock the accompanying pieces off. The glass shattered into a million pieces. No emotion circled her face. The girl ceased her moment and jumped through the frame. In a flurry, Bella strode up to her chamber and hooked into her closet. She search for a warm fleece and found the leather jacket she came to Heartlake wearing. It possessed the undertones of Haze and appeared a relic from her past, but it was the warmest clothing she could find. She unracked it from his hanger and went to put it on. Her right hand fitted freely into its sleeve, but the left, shackled to the rifle, provided an issue. It wasn't possible to fit the case nor rifle through the sleeve, so instead, Bella lifted the left side of the jacket over her corresponding shoulder, her exposed wrist unsheltered. She moved to the corridor between rooms and, in the corner of her eye, caught sight of the simple box upon the nightstand. It yielded the girl. Her grip grew tighter.

Wasting no more time, she flung herself downstairs and through the connecting hallway. Bella grew swifter, bolting into the kitchen, decking a chair with the case and opening the screen door. The cool evening air, dripped from the mountains, forced a deep breath. Bella succumbed to a pause, but under urgent acclaim, she pressed forward. She darted to the fence, setting the case down on the patio and unlatched it. The rifle still shocked her. To her, it was the most deadly weapon one could hold, but again, she refused to delay. Bella seized the gun. She then placed it on her lap and removed the soft interior, exposing the shiny man-made bullets, the journals, paper, and the wire cutter. The girl packed a handful of brass inside her scrubs' pockets and few more within the jacket's zipper crevices. She then removed the wire cutter, large and rustic. Finally, she shut the case and moved it to the side and gazed upon the giant barrier. Bella looked up, pondering how even a creature could make such a scale through nails and barbed wire. She bent her knee, setting the rifle on the cold ground, and primed the cutter, lifting both handles apart, rearing its blades. It felt heavy in her hands. Bella begin low, touching a weed that poked through the steel and began snipping. With the first incision, the wire wined. Bella spun around to the neighboring homes to see if the small noise had alerted them. Silence assured her. She grabbed both ends of the cutters again and continued her snipping, unyielding as the fence succumbed to the tool's pressure. She'd planned to shape a half circle at the end, but at her first few cuts, she found the fence lengthened far beneath the soil, a few attempts unearthing the steel made these clear. She decided then to hack a line and slice just enough to get thrown. Bella acted carefully until she finished her crime, peeling back a square just big enough to crawl through. The girl then pushed the bent and angled the wire to the side of the wall.

Bella sat there on her knees, looking through the incision. A dandelion slumped forward, and the girl reached and touched the yellow petals. The weed felt soft, fragile to her power. She then lifted her gaze and scanned for the light. It proved to be shy, but the sky still harbored an ounce of blue.

The girl continued with the old man's plan. Bella pushed the case through, then bent down on all fours and placed her right hand through the crevice. Her palm crashed down on the virgin vegetation, a feeling that alienated the nurse. She then placed the other and pushed herself to manage one foot in, mindful not to scrap on the sharp ends left by the tool. She pulled through her other. Now grasping the rope, she pulled the rifle and reached back to grab the wire cutters, probably stuffing them back in the case.

Bella then turned to the uncluttered view of the mountain range. Dumbfounded, she stared at the daunting Giants. The clear emerging night shadowing the dark forest yards away, the faint rising moon highlights the cusp of a pine ridge needles mass. She took one step instinctively, the other hesitantly, then a third back to her beginning. Exposed in this field, and the girl felt naked once more.

Bella regained her lost ground and kept her eye on the darkening Giants, searching for the light. The girl kept a timid pace, humbled by their sheer size and glory. She stopped once more in the middle of the field. The girl needed to see it. She needed to know what to follow. The nurse panned over areas she had panned before, again and again, seeking for anything that would allure her to that beckon.

Seconds added over into minutes, and still, the girl watched in the open field. As she felt time slip past her and the night's ever-growing shadows, Bella lost control over her breathing, unstoppable, swallowed by what she recounted the most. Her mind spun on what to do next but forever stuck on notions of the encroaching darkness, the silver moon providing little in the volume of the voids of the forest.

It became harder to stand, and so she sat, next to dried grass and mole hills. Bella fought with the urge to curl within and wallow in her own dread, forcing herself to stare and stare until she felt the mountains themselves looking back at her.

A single spark then flashed. She turned to whatever verge position the blip spun from her peripheral. Another stuck. Near the mountain's peak, toward its northern side, a small patch of uncluttered forest began to glow. Bella rose to her feet. It became more intense. Each spark eventually culminating into the fiery light. Bella smiled, looking up and drying her eyes.

The girl hesitated no longer. She found her wits and drew a mental line between the beckon and herself. The best plan she could recite. Bella planned to follow this line, relying that if she found herself lost, she could always peer to wicks of the flames from the trees. Confident, she discarded the case near under the grass and brought both hands on the rifle. She took one bullet from her pocket, sliding open the chamber. The girl then placed a bullet within the space and did as the old man told, poorly, sheathing the chamber and rising up toward the pines. The girl marched the rest of the field, cracking over the vegetation, until she stood near inches to the first layer of trees.

A primal remembrance whispered to her. It foretold the girl of the unknown land, and her own wariness must be her saving grace. A deadly stench allured past the bark and twigs and mixed with the arid scent of pine, telling that this wasn't a holy place, but perhaps, out of reach of God's hands. She found hope in a slight chipping of cricket somewhere deep in the brush.

Ear and eye primed, Bella claimed a step within the forest, her leg extending past the first of many ancient trunks. Her right leg followed. Instantly, she kept her posture fell to a hunch, making herself appear as little as she could; for as the next step solidified, a rash reaction that begged her to leave. She ignored it and kept the mental projection of a line that connected to the light, obscured now by the tendrils of the mountain.

Her belief fell upon this fantastical line inexpertly figured. She carried on, the best thing she knew how to do. Eventually, the girl transformed her jolting steps into a more natural walk, her loaded rifle brought close to her chest and fingers stiff on its trigger all together in the same low profile she entered with. She expected herself to be as weak as a rabbit, understanding the paranoia and fear would keep her alive, and a careful and balanced frame treading on loud and uncertain ground, realizing one snap of a twig, one uneven crack of dead leaf could result in her being found; and she dreaded with that unutured knowledge, the most useful of genes begging her too. By these forces, a whisper to continually scan the fauna, searching and marking any error of the pine's flora that could hide any threat. Pupils dilating vastly to compensate for the dark, her ears followed suit and opened wide to hear in an attempt to catch even slightest rustle or breathing of this ungodly place.

The pines gave no reassurance. Old and unforgiving, their ruff bark casting illusions on the girl's mind, resembling faces that watched her ever more closely. Dried needles covered the forest floor, along with cones and severed branches. Bella tried to keep attention to the earth below and the area in front of her, careful not to trip, along to the back and to her sides, each producing their own angry blank stares that linked as masses of dark green.

Bella kept her trail clear and pace steady, comforted by the sounds of the crickets playing faint violins with strung legs. This she could rely on, for the creatures of the forest do not conspire together, recounting Evergreen's knowledge on keeping the insects within hearing. But not only did the crickets chirp as she went further on, the girl could now listen to the tune of night birds, their occasional hoots and strange songs. Even bats, appearing out of their homes to feast on the midnight banquets, screaming added to the tune, all allowing the girl to loosen her grip of the weapon upon the sweet sound of the nocturnal. Now she could not see, save the piercing rays from the moonlight, fragmenting the underbrush in faint crystal beams. She girl continued. She kept her march unyielding, however still bending, as she began to feel the ascent of the mountain.

The girls fought an increasing slide, adding not a chorus. A growing concern established itself when going forth present no wicks of fire that the girl could see behind the trunks, but Bella kept in mind and trialed on the semi path with her estimated target and inclined with the rising mountain. She began tripping and fumbling, making noise. She struggled to manage, then began using the weapon's muzzle as a blind man's walking stick, feeling for unseen hazards. The revelation worked wonders as she maneuvered trees large and small, walking steadily. Bella eventually felt something she could not feel around and raised up her arm to behold what she assumed to be a rift slide messed with dirt and exposed rocks. She saw no other way and tried climbing in the near darkness, feeling for roots or stone for grips. She let the rifle dangle, pulling herself up a few feet. Using all her upper and lower body combined, the nurse found the edge of the rocky and a relatively flatter space compared to what was below. The girl made a reach for it, but overestimated the sway and the weight of the rifle and stepped where a root was not and slid down the brief, scraping her side and landed onto the forest floor. And earth-shattering pop followed next.

Bella froze, her ears ringing. Not that she was injured, but because of that sound, which rang out and could be heard several miles away. She knew not where the bullet rang toward and waited for any reactionary twitches toward her mistake, but all that dampened were the song makers, which presumed after the noise had left. Bella rose to her feet at first notice of the chirping and brushed herself off, noting a changeling at her feet. She squatted to feel what it was and was met with cold metal with a sharp point. It was the bullets. They had fallen from her jacket, to which Bella frantically stuffed them back in, not knowing the exact number which should be in. She felt back toward the cliff, tossing the rifle up, having no fear of a misfire. The girl was careful not to pull the rifle back down, the rope at the end of its length. She had to grab high with her left hand and searched again for the footholds, finding them, bringing herself up to the lips, and with one final push using as much power her upper body could muster.

Bella managed to lift her torso onto the edge and rolled over her legs to be fully on the new level. Exhausted, she lay there for a moment to recover. She felt more brass leak out and quickly scooped them back into her pockets. She arose once more and guessed to where the line would have passed through. She loaded the gun, struggling in the near blackness, shines of moonshine helping little. Loaded, she continued on her way, searching for any flickers of light.

It grew colder and colder as she ascended. Bella was thankful she brought the jacket, but the breeze that passed seems to move past the leather and into her frail bones. She began switching off hands to hold her weapon as she warmed the other, desperate to not be slowed by the lowering temperature.

Again she utilized the muzzle, bumping into what she could tell were rocks and branches, pine cones or full trees, and followed round them all, keeping that mental line projected in her mind. But now, as she has traveled further, her eyes sought desperately for the light.

Bella could see more of the forest, yes, the moon rising to a more luminous position, yet still visibility was low, and she could not find the flame. This fact she obscured, but it began to wane on her conscience, urging her along to almost a jog, lifting the rifle up as to mainly avoid trunks. She knitted between obstacles, but still found not even a fragment. Upon this point, she knew not where she was, not even if she still followed the mental line.

The girl became frustrated, unable to piece together her next move. The more ground she covered, the less likely she'd see it, wishing she could have flown toward the beckon from the field. She thought she was going the right way, but now nothing was certain. It was impossible to know. She needed a sliver. She waited in the silver.

Bella estimated the direction. At least, she knew she needed to keep going up and figured a slight diagonal angle would help. She kept, paced herself, keeping herself calm. She traveled what she presumed was a good distance and the closed roof needles gave way to more beams, causing the underkeep to be seen, and Bella brought the rifle back to her chest. The girl was confident in what she could make out, yet at the best of her intentions, she failed. And at the base of the neglected bush, her shoes unearthed something, catching between her legs.

The nurse fell, this time not firing, but banging her knee and rifle on the ground. She looked to see what had caused this and set a hand to retrieve it. To her surprise she didn't feel like any natural material, but plastic, then smooth metal, then rough bumps. The nurse brought the object to her vision, moving her hand across it to gravitate toward an idea. She saw a handle, a scope, a barrel and ammo, a sharp fragment poking her finger. She discovered the object was a gun, the same the soldiers carried into the forest days ago.

Bella sprawled to get up, and in doing so kicked another item. She looked and realized it was a radio, appearing crushed, as if by a heavy boot. The girl tossed it, walked around the bush before touching something else, this time a pair of binoculars, their lenses shattered. The tools presented a suspension that hollowed the girl, for she knew a soldier would not be so careless as to leave these equipments behind.

She let the rifle hang low, the rope lethargic on the mountain soil, and looked behind, several feet to her right, another weapon and gear scattered among the understory. And she noted, these items were not so in a pile, but a staggered trail that ended as if nothing further could be dropped.

All of the sudden, the girl was all too cold, and the chill seeped down into her heart. She began to shake, half shivering, unknowing whether it was from the sight or the temperature. An overwhelming feeling, as though she would die here in this unnamed place, became glaring. She loathed the fact that death could take her before her task. Bella bent and fell to her knees, slowly resisted less and less until her chest pressed against the dirt and rifle rested. She realized she was so unbearably tired, the distance she had traveled escaping her.

Yet she remembered the sound of this place, the woodland cricket strings, the night birds and bats humming. And that chorus caused her to lift her head in another resistance. And she lifted her head as if guided by the gentlest of hands, a wick, a wisp, a fragment of a shard shining from the dark underbrush struck her eyes to behold it. The magic and glory, she managed to push herself from the yearning soil and slipped one of her legs underneath herself. Bella began to walk, awestruck by the whips of fire leaking through the ancient wood. The girl brought the rifle to her hands. She panned her head, tilting it from all angles for the absolute certainty it was real. The wick stayed and beckoned her, and she moved closer.

Bella ran, emboldened by the highlighted understory, stumbling, not wise with her steps, but unstoppable. The forest became brighter and brighter, warmer and warmer. Her breath nearly could not keep up with her speed, the sounds of the lung flailing against her rib cage filling the forest.

"Molly?" she said just above a whisper. "Molly?" she called again, but louder. The forest filled with an orange glow, and she could feel her heart pounding that she had made it, all while confirmed by the assurance of the chorus that never lost its tune.

The girl pushed harder and harder, until her body had to yield. The flora swept by, as if she cared to look, but then slowly stopped, the girl panting still deep under the canopy. She smiled at her destined target.

Then a foulness filled her lungs, a smell rotting and fly producing lingered in the area where she stood. Her nose wriggled, and her stomach dropped into sickness. She looked down to find the source of this smell. A body, sliced, dismembered, laid inches away, gore leaking from his entrails that were dragged from his anatomy. The girl nearly vomited. She dry heaved and looked back. The body wore military grade gear, a petrified face behind lifeless black beastly goggles. It then forced her. She regurgitated what little she had eaten, the action moving her to view another body lying, its entire inner system pulled inside out. She turned and turned and turned, seeing limbs and severed heads, hearts, and lone livers. The girl was forced into dry repulsive curls when no more could come out.

And the crickets then did cease. The night birds were hushed, and the bat no longer snickered. The night had become dead. All at the same moment, Bella felt as if in view, as if someone's eye watched from out past the cruel pines. A breeze passed, moving the branches and trees, save one, out in the distance. Paralyzed, the girl wanted to move but couldn't, terrified to even breathe.

"Bella?"

She did not move.

"Bella?" It was spoken as if near, as if someone stood face level to the girl, but was meet with darkness. It sounded with the hint of many but distantly that of her best friend's voice.

"Bella," the forest called again. "I'm here. I'm here. I can't get up!"

The nurse gripped her weapon.

"I...I need your help! Help me! Come over here! Please! I need help!" It began crying. "Please."

She managed a step back toward the light.

"It's severed. I think it's broken."

She managed another, eyes filled to awakened horror.

"I can't feel it. It hurts."

The girl turned sharply with speed surpassing all that she thought capable of herself.

"Bella!"

The air grew denser. The unseen specter began to fade, but lighting, as if rabid,sounded behind her, chasing after the girl, appearing in an instant and fading. Thereafter, the crash of breaking wood thundered out to the left of Bella, perpetual running dash, blazing where she was. And whatever creature pestered her stopped and ventured to the right, rustling only the pine's sharp needles.

Bella feared. She ran harder, not giving way to features as the voice became almost nonexistent. The loud footsteps cut off, then sound again, then disappeared once more. Bella didn't care for the odd mannerism. She knew they would come to her and sought the beacon, the heavenly fire, without doubt knowing it would save her.

She tasted blood. Her heart thrust against her rib cage. Bella kept the pursuit, pushing the last distance. The trees receded, and before the girl knew it, she entered onto an open patch of the forest, the beacon illuminating evening unto a crackling orange until its eventual tree line border. She struggled to stop, but found leverage in the odd rocky ground, then drawing her rifle. The girl shot glances in every direction, not sure what she was looking for, but found the source of light: a large bonfire blazing into the sky. Surrounding it, a circle of bare land and a stump next to a pile of firewood. Further toward her and rooted on a mound of rocks and clay, glimmered a hawthorn tree in the beacon's full light.

Uncertain, Bella kept notice on the pines, searching for something that would leap out and began heading for the hawthorn, the only landmark of note. Watching the surroundings, she hardly noticed the change of texture on the forest floor until her foot chilled and sunk in a white powder. She pulled it out, avoiding not the oval marking of snow, and heading onward and in search of Molly.

Her eyes then fell upon a queer object at the base of the hawthorn. She wondered what it was and noticed the fur were from various animals tucked in a cylinder notion, as well as several herbs and berries, all staggered and warped around branches that threaded the furs.

Bella grew closer, the scent of lavender and sage became strong. She brought the rifle down, now fixated entirely on the wrap of furs, now appearing more to take shape. The girl stood within a meter of it, and it appeared a body was lying inside. The girl passed over wooden stakes, bloodied bands and torn clothes. A coat Bella spied next to her shoe. She turned it over: black and purple with letters that spelled "UNIVERSITY OF HAZE." Bella looked to the fabric, then to the queer mound.

No further could Bella's heart fall. The nurse dashed to the side of the mound, now understanding it wasn't as such. The rifle fell to the ground as well as the girl to her knees. She ripped the pelt that covered what appeared to be a face. Utter despair struck the girl. There on the cold ground lay the redhead.

She whispered, "Molly?

There came no response.

"Molly?" she said this louder and nudged the furs, gently then firmly. She then began to shake her friend hoping she would awake. Bella pressed her knuckles into the sternum of her friend and began to rub, digging deep into her skin. She felt no heartbeat. She brought two fingers to her jugular vein. She felt no pulse. Tears, shining in the fire's light, fell upon the palace of fur and herb.

"You'll be okay, you'll be okay. Don't worry, I'm here now."

Bella brought her trembling hands to behold her friend diaphragm. She pushed hard, breaking ribs to give the corpse air. When it proved in vain, the girl continued, begging aloud, "Please." When nothing came of it, she then shook Molly by the sides, shouting to the clear sky.

Her nails dug into the fur and felt something wet on her palm. She retraced the arm and saw deep crimson. Bella jumped to the responsible side of Molly and saw blood breaching the pelts, near her ribs. She then started ripping off the branches and opened the folds with the furs connected. She beheld Molly's naked body and massive chunk stolen from her side, the raptures in her flesh as teeth would to carrion. And within the wound were special leaves and root material, some in front of makeshift stickers.

The girl's sorrow rained. She covered the wound and shook the corpse, praying for a soul to be sent back down. She plopped her face into Molly's chest and mourned. She began to shake, a pit in her stomach eclipsing into a chasm. She begged, "Please, please come back," and repeated with the fire's breaks.

Bella retrieved her head and looked at Molly's face. It possessed all the beauty of the living, her skin still none the wiser, fair yet pale. Her closed eyes merely appeared as if she was dreaming.

"You can't go. You can't."

There came no response.

Bella retired her head to the fur. She tried all she could to bring the body back to life, pleading to the night to give her friend back to her. Her arms were brought together, her palms greeted on another. And she cried a psalm to those who were lost.

"Please, please come back."

And the pines returned with laughter.

Bella shot up, her cheeks tear stained.

Another voice joined the jeering. Traversing the air, a scream, sounding like a little boy, echoed in the distance, then morphing to an old woman's crackle, then an adult man's. It shape-shifted and tuned into different cries and screams, high and low until it settled upon the one: Molly's voice weeping.

Bella clenched the fur and peered toward the tree line, believing it resonated far beyond where she looked, but still sought a figure. She took a glance at the back of Molly, and to the rifle, finally toward the great blaze behind her. She then kissed her friend's forehead and promised to the dead. She stood, gaining strength, and grasped the rope-tied rifle. Bella turned toward the laughter and woe. She returned to it a scream, a horrendous, broken note.

Complete deafening silence, then a murmured twig snap in the undergrowth.

Bella, drawn to the iron sights, walked over to the edge of the light, staring into the forest.

Chapter

19

It passed the crosshairs of her rifle. It crouched down on all four, lurking close to the earth until it erected itself behind a pine's shadow. Bella's aim caught up to the figure. It appeared to have once resembled a man. Its arms and legs were stretched beyond the limits of mortal limbs. Its bones showed through its pale leathery skin, with gray tufts of hair sticking in patches around its gaunt form. Black stains showed upon its chin and lips, saliva furling from its large hinge-like jaw, connecting far back in the throat and to each missing ear. It smiled an elastic wolflike smile, with gore-infected human teeth that lined up straight through its grin. No eyes bore within its sockets.

Death's scent sweeps through the patch of land. The creature stayed in the shadow, watching the girl, one arm curved around the tree, the other dipping down past its knee. It dwarfed her, standing double her height.

Bella stepped forward, her iron sight's dead set on the monster.

The creature gaped its maw, motioning back and forth. Bella heard no noise from the figure. It was all but mute, save a few seconds later a sound that a sound echo far beyond in the distance, a faint whisper of Molly's voice.

The mere sight of the Pale Thing sent her concept of life and biology into contradiction. Her bowls sickened and tied, her muscles locked and contracted, her eyes stuttered and her heart trembled. But she willfully kept her stance. The rifle unwavered, her finger itched on the trigger.

She forces a step, then another, from the light, keeping sight of the demon.

The Pale Thing kept still.

Rage accumulated. Nothing was left. And all that remained was the fact she would kill this god-defining beast. She drew a single breath, uniting her body. Her finger then pulled. A shot rang out across the land.

But she did not see the creature fall, nor feel the repulsion from the fire firearm. A quick jolt of motion bush around her, Bella experienced pressure wrapped by her waist. Then the sudden descent of scenery escaped her, view of the light obscured. The wind streamed through her hair, and the ground beneath her listened, and the pines had never rushed past her so violently. The rope went tight, and the rifle flailed. The girl didn't understand, her arm followed with the momentum. She began to quickly grow nauseous from the galloping motion. She found herself adopting, enduring sharp turns and buffers. She was moving, that she knew, but at speed she couldn't comprehend. The girl sought a view at the ground, a white streak interrupted the strict dirt every, a blur of pale.

Bella stretched to peer over her shoulder and found herself looking at the creature's occipital. She then understood what many others did on their way to meet the angel. She felt its long arm and shoulder blade jammed into her skin, like a python to its rat. The Pale Thing carried here through the forest's underbelly. The nurse tried to struggle, twitch and kick, shaking in every which way imaginable, but the creature grip constricted. It was unbelievably strong. The way to break free seemed impossible, but she tried again, and again before arriving at that conclusion. But she would not accept it. She began lunging to bite the beast on the arm, but she couldn't reach.

Adrenaline clouded her mind. If the monster arrived to where it sought, Bella knew she would join her kin in paper, hanging on a police board. Thereafter, vision of the rifle crossed, the weapon whirling with the extreme speed. An idea begotten, schemed from that old man and his ancestors.

The nurse brought forth her free hand and pushed into her trapped pocket between her waist and Pale Thing's shoulder blade. She plunged her hand, squirming at the feeling of its unclean flesh, but bypassing her revolt, unzipping and thrusting into her jacket pocket. She recoiled and produced a piece of brass. Next, she struck the bullet between her teeth and pulled on the rope and brought the rifle to her. She held it with the other and attempted to insert the bullet, but failed, a sharp turn loosening her hold, and the brass lost to the understory. She tried again, scratching rotten meat, grabbing yet another round and trying to place the bullet within the empty chamber. A jump had caused it to fail and to fling past her to fleeting vegetation. Again, she stuck more desperately than the last, feeling the creature readying to slow. Her hand between her and the beast, this time the creature clenched harder and pinned the girl's limb to its body. She turned and brought her hand past it, baring all the strength she could call upon. The struggle gave way and from her pocket she retrieved a bass carriage. They broached near a cliff side. The Pale Things angled up to a sheer wall. The brass in her mouth, she prepared the rifle, gripping tightly. With cautioned resolution, she carried out arming the weapon as Evergreen taught, managing to load the bullet within the empty chamber and sealing it closed. The girl arched over as much as her spine would let her. She aimed to where the blurs grew fatter and tempered its pace.

Its right leg moved.

A boom roared, then a wet crack.

The world spun around. Bella barreled into the rigged mountain floor, contouring her left side with an anguished pop. The beast tumbled close, having dropped the girl a few feet away. It hit the rocks harder, bringing its long and gnarled fingers to the wound through its hamstring. Many voices did seethe out of the boundaries of pines.

Bella studied the condition of her adversary. Upon observing it in agony, she attempted to stand, collapsing all of a sudden to lightning-flared pain that circulated through her battered side. She cried out to the night. The girl made a motion to lift the conflicted portion, but her leg stiffened and her arm hung low to her chest, the rifle nesting to the earth.

Bella attempted to push away from the beast using her nondominant hand, her working leg kicked against the soil. The girl checked her surroundings, finding herself under more blankets of unnamed forest.

She noticed more patches of snow here, gripping the white powder, uncaring the cold. She crawled with all remaining might.

Lifting her gaze, Bella saw what directions her body pointed to and beheld the sharp incline of the Giant and a small incision in front of her, an indented cave in the cliff. The silver moon shone, and as the girl looked within this small shadow hole, she witnessed eroded cryptid bones scattered within and out the incision, all different sizes of human origin. And with them, newly stacked men in military gear.

Bella shrieked and turned away from the den, trembling among the dirt and weeds. She called upon that same strength, but only lasted a minute set of inches. A faint scream whispered in the girl's ear, foretelling the Pale Thing to be miles and miles away, ever soothing her to stop fighting. Yet Bella turned.

The creature stood over her, its jaw partially ajar. Black blood oozed down its injured leg, its weight shifting to adjust. Its eyeless sockets stared past hers.

Bella sprawled away.

It grabbed the rifle and lifted her up. Bella felt the rope around her wrist go tight and felt herself risen by it. She cried again to the night, the pain overwhelming, resulting in her only good leg to fury at the beast in an attempt to cease her agony. The Pale Thing stared, unaffected, and lifted the girl even higher until its maw leveled with hers, grabbing her torso with its other limb. Its snickers echoed from the edges of the forest. It grinned, and saliva pooled down its lips onto its chin.

All was quiet. No fight was left in the girl. Her head went limp, and her leg stopped kicking. And, in that moment, she found herself praying to the God of the hated, the one spited and thrashed against, the one she counted along with myth. All things, right and wrong cultivated through her mind, wishing if he was real, that he would at least understand she tried.

The Creature unhinged its jaw, a wide and never-ending mire. It enveloped the girl's head, its impatient teeth hovering over.

Bella felt as if knives began to pierce into the base of her skull, but she would not cry. And all that was said in the uncaring and nameless patch of wood, moonlight trickling through sharp needles was a single word against the silence. Closing her eyes for the last time, she muttered aloud the forever-bastardized word, "Amen."

The Pale Thing lashed, its teeth going further.

But submission hindered. The force of the beast stalled, a pine head into the skull of the girl, as if by maledict means to draw out an execution. The pause conserved now further. She felt the creature trembling, as now she thought the Pale Thing attempted to bite down with all its might, yet unable. She became aware of an object touching close to her ear and her hair, its own mysterious weight pushing down against the maw.

Its mouth began to shake. The creature's grip became meek and tender. The pinprick indented into Bella's skull leveled. She bore witness to the faint mournings in the distance. The girl then fell from the embrace of the creature, dropping to the forest floor between the breast and two massive fur-coated feet. She crawled away in retaliation between the entities, fathoming strength out of the confusion and raised her attention to the fray.

There, Bella saw a man, equal in height to the creature, prying its jaws open with his large stubborn hands. A gray beard, heavily braided and knotted, bloodied by the Pale Thing, hung down his deadly face. White hair that reached his lower back. Hateful, revenant, unwavering eyes set aimed at the monster, who screamed and flailed both thin limbs at the man. Her eyes fixated on the figure, covered in animal skins and ropes, then an axe, jeweled and silver, tucked by a self-made belt, baring strange runic inscriptions.

The false voice lamented, resonating behind the veil of trees. Every slash struck forward, the man made no response, no recognition of pain as he continued to pull the Pale Thing's jaws apart. Maroon blood oozed down its gaunt skin into the weeds, coughing to the face of the man, yet he yielded not, pushing its mouth further and further.

Its maw broke.

The winds rushed, and trees howled. The creature clung to the man, its emaciated and mangled jaw dangled by decrepit flesh. The man shoved the beast to the earth and drew his silver axe. It rebounded and fled, crawling on all fours to make its escape, unearthing plants and stone, but the wound inflicted by the girl dampened its incomprehensible speed. It could no longer run; and the man, in several paces, caught the Pale Thing and stood over it.

Again, the pines shrieked, and the monster brought its arms in defense, hindering on a blanket of snow. Never flitting, no emotions surpassing, the man unhooked the axe and brought the glorious weapon to the sky. It shined in the lunar light. Bella stared at the scene, fixated upon his wrathful glare, teeth grated as if he had felt everything, seen all sin undone before him, and what had snuffed out purity. She knew she witnessed the Ghost of the Mountain.

A noise escaped him, a godless yell.

And the ax crashed forth, embedded itself between the beast's sockets.

The forest went silent. The ax's head had broken off into the Pale Thing's body, and it bent backward and buckled toward the ground, gore lashing out to the white snow.

The Ghost sheathed the hand under his leather belt and knelt to the monster's corpse. He checked for breath, pushing the blade deeper before retrieving it from the Pale Thing. He stood, looking at his work, then wiped the maroon on his pelt. The Ghost then turned to her.

Bella bowed her head, half in reverence, half from fatigue. She then succumbed to her own weight and lay lonely on the dirt and weeds. Her heart grew conscious of how her eyelids yearned to be shut, but the girl managed to keep them open long enough to see the man step toward her, his expression shifting from malice to a dull shade of compassion. The girl lifted an outstretched arm to him, unable to fathom what thoughts lay behind his empty eyes. He bent a knee and accepted the girl's hand, the man's palm dwarfing the girls. Bella looked up at him wanting to speak, but was unable to. He examined her battered arm, gently prodding it with his middle finger following along up the bicep to the shoulder. He then set the rifle upon the girl's lap and moved her good arm to hold it. Bella didn't know what he wanted, her vision beginning to fade. She felt one massive hand slip underneath, being swept underneath her legs and another under her torso. Bella felt once again lifted to the height of the trees. She then finally succumbed to exhaustion, and the corners of her vision stretched into black.

Chapter

20

Dream delving from dream into terrors that flirt with reality, which in itself currents on unfathomable tides. Conscious to nonexistence, mingling with the other as they crash and resign as fluid waves in a tired sea, the state of which begot an eternal ever-rocking vessel that all set sail in sleep.

Bella remembers the tittering, the rise and fall, suspending in the damn air. She could at times glance the rolling image of ancient flora passing by, pain be this cause, appearing and fading, and at other instances, she floated beyond her body and watched herself from the canopy viewing the tall man carrying her through the forest. And while she could sometimes see, crickets chipped and filled the mountain breeze. She could feel him touch her, addressing her wounds, but with what, she did not know.

He carried her though bends and curves, over streams and deep wells, over lands not seen by the human eye for centuries, some places she thought she spied old cabins. There were inconsistencies to the rhythm of the scenery, finding smaller trees and tender soil, as if they were treading on forgotten farmland, and areas completely void of all, save dry grasses. And the moon reflected its last light, tucking itself over the Giant's range to the far west.

Blue had returned to the sky, bird's reclaimed the morning. She didn't remember being sat down, but lay motionless upon grit sand, propped up by a hawthorn. The man's presence left the girl's, leaving with little more than an exhale, and a fresh wind touched Bella's face.

She cracked her eyes and witnessed a bank she was on, a clearing uncluttered by needle underlined by the sweet noise of water rolling onto the sand. The reservoir brimmed with waking life.

Bella slowly began to move, twitching her shoulder left to judge its damage. She twisted it freely without pain. She was expecting pain. Under her shirt, she then peeled back her collar to a bruise, but her arm still held within its socket, and within it found an unknown juice spread across. She went to her leg next, nudging it, the response tender but fine and found again the same treatment.

She sensed that she'd seen this place before, and she began to look to the edge of what the foliage would allow. It didn't take her long to spy the gray metallic wired wall not even a mile due toward where she imagined Heartlake resided. It's sight, a diseased one, reminding the girl of a future not certain.

She drifted with the tide, and the lake whispered to her, seducing each muscle into stupor. "What can I do?" She tried to steady her eyelids, yet they closed again, so vainly tired. And she looked out to the lake's waters seeking immunity from the evil comprehended. "What can I do?" She'd failed. What her mind conjured seemed rational, as her next step was in the lake. It was Molly who she thought of last, ashamed she wasn't faster, for she knew if she'd heeded the first light, her friend might have survived. She emancipated her liquid consciousness, and her lungs filled without the slightest anticipation.

She could feel her idea of oneself bleed into the murky green, as everything crept into the reservoir. Bella remembered sitting with her, the girl and Molly's useless conversations of the day and atonements of the hard to drive. And the melody of her friend's music played.

A flash of dryness, then the girl folding back to the rough bank sand. She was sopping wet, her gun still attached by rope. Bella then spewed out inhaled liquid. She peered up to the figure that had plucked her from the water. Standing in the tide, the Ghost looked down at her.

He stared at her as if he understood, but Bella sprung back to the lake.

He again intervened. The sound "Eigi" escaping his lips, responding to her action.

"No." Bella grew more violent in an attempt to get past him.

"Eigi."

"No, no, no, no, please, you don't understand. I can't live anymore. Please I'm begging you. I have nothing left."

At this, the man picked up the frail girl and set her back upon the sand. She screamed and kicked and failed and fought, pleading, all the while sobbing. The man kept her from the reservoir, preventing her from gaining any space or inflicting any injury to him or herself. She begged with all her heart for the man to let her drown, yet the Ghost kept his head down.

"Aldrei." This word he said, and it commanded Bella to cease.

He then looked up, and Bella met the man's aged eyes, tired and poor, worried vessels that ordered stillness within her soul. However, she couldn't, not after what she had seen. She lamented for what innocence was lost, for that she could not live without.

Yet the girl stopped her thrashing, and the man let go of her arms, her battered limbs relieving soreness. Upon this, Bella brought her knees over her head and curled within a ball. And the Ghost watched, standing for a mere moment before setting himself beside her, observing the shifting water glimmering in morning rays.

Bella was surprised he didn't leave her. There were trails made by the girl to cease her tears, catching them in her hands like raindrops, but when she did, there were always more that fell. The Ghost gated the way to see her.

The man waited a minute longer, then reached a pouch near his belt. He entombed it within his large knuckles and reached toward Bella's fist closed face, tapping her. The girl scanned his cut and worn hand, and within his palm, he let the girl see: a small necklace made from knots. Bella's mouth went ajar, and she looked to the man and to the reverent object. The Ghost ushered Molly's Yudaku, and the girl first thought it couldn't be as such, and then examined it further. Instinctively, she thought the man robbed it from her friend's corpse in a savage display, and thereafter she looked toward the ends to see their damage, but to her astonishment, the ends possessed no signs of tear, no uneven texture, no signs of malice. Bella stared closer and saw the repair of sick strands of rope begot by the forest. She was in disbelief, for that which had been its severance, now woven together, creating beautiful spirals that awaited now a neck to be laid across.

He motioned for Bella to take the Yudaku, but Bella pushed against his hand. She shook her head. Yet the man persisted and did not withdraw. Bella looked in his eyes and saw a notion, appearing as if century after century built upon it, and his ancient form spoke of a more memorial lineage of man who would not let their dead so easily be forgotten. She took his resolve and hesitantly looked upon Yudaku and clung it close to her chest.

Then the Ghost rose, standing as tall as the hawthorn, and went toward the forest.

"Wait, where are you going?" Bella asked.

He entered the tree line and promoted the girl to wait. He then left into the dark mountain forest without so much as a sound.

She stared into the edge, then glanced to the lake and finally to the border. What would happen seemed unfathomable, possibilities swirling in innumerable variations, none of which would end in a result desirable outcomes. She didn't plan for any of this. The only thought after seeing Molly's was to kill that Pale Thing, yet she only wounded it. The girl didn't know what to wish for anymore, other than to see her friend again before she is put to soil. Nevertheless, what thoughts would not delve from her from, the banks from the lake did not sway her back within the waters. Bella held the Yudaku and pressed to her heart as close as she physically could and felt the essence that had brought her here, in the radiance of the wind, those notes from the music box.

Bella could hear sirens in the distance, disrupting the tune; but the girl, still unknowing, found comfort in what had incited her, and rested her head to the ground, and stared up at the free blue sky, the rifle by her side and the knots upon her chest.

She was graced again by the birds, wondering how he could ever spite them; however, a scraping of branches alerted the girl. It was the man, returning from where he'd disappeared. With him, strange sages, to which he motioned to the wounds of the girl and ushered a rubbing motion. He stepped on the sand before silence fell, and his ear perked.

A machinal chatter sounded in the air. A helicopter looped around the lake and scanned the perimeter. The Ghost hid within the trees, but Bella stayed near the lake. She looked up at the aircraft and waited till it circled back and had her within its sight. The helicopter stopped high above the reservoir.

Eventually, the Ghost dashed from the covered forest and seized Bella, snatching her out of the pilot's vision, setting her back down in the brush. He glared at the craft. It hovered for a moment, scanning over the nearby forest and the bank, then flew off in the direction, loud blades blaring.

He moved Bella again further into the forest. Bella expected they were looking for her. The Ghost attempted to usher the girl along, yet she stiffened. He looked at her, and she looked at him and pointed to the direction of Heartlake and the barrier. The man trailed the direction she pointed and rebuked her, shaking his head. She persisted in her stance. She could not run. He hesitated for a moment, seemingly thinking to himself, then sighed. He bent down to pick up the girl. Bella didn't expect this, and they headed west through the understory.

Thunder initiated throughout the vegetation as the Ghost carried Bella with incapable speed, not a match to the demons, but swift. The rifle and rope lay across her lap. The girl wondered what they would do to her, what punishment would be required, not only for the actual crime, but for the prepotent she broke, the norm she snapped. She closed her eyes, for it seemed imaginable now, and what she'd endure would be just, but for now she possessed the amulet that inspired her criminality and kept her insanity stable. Jail was a popular theory, but how harsh her sentencing would have eluded her, but out of the radiance of hope, maybe she'd be let off with a warning.

They made their way near the border. Hiding in the flora, they could spy the chain-link barbed wire wall. But behind it, police vehicle lines up. White-collar men popped out, shouting among themselves, ordering, stratifying their next move and what their options were. A SWAT car then reared over, and out poured men in riot gear and many other methods of crowd dispersal. The officials were all parked in a crude manner, swearing and navigating to the wall, and at their head, a spiky-hair agent with a taut tie.

The force stood where Molly and Bella had after their night out, which seemed but wasn't to the girl having taken place weeks ago. She panned just before the border and saw the u-shape patch of mud and gravel on the opposite end where she had seen the Ghost that night, the land appearing more savage from this point. She scanned to see if she might catch a glimpse of that beautiful crane with the wounded leg.

He let go of Bella, and the girl swung her feet under herself. She glanced at the Ghost whose sight aimed through the fence and at the white-collar men.

Bella touched the giant's arm and stepped forth, exposing herself to the stark lighting of the day. The Ghost turned his attention toward them as she stopped out of range of the forest's coverage. He remained there, watching. Bella walked toward the border, grasping tight around the rifle, unsure what they would do.

One officer saw her and bumped his brother in arms. He saw her, then the cop next to him. The information made its way to the leading agent, and he spun toward the forest. All went quiet upon viewing her approaching out of the shadows and crossing the thin bog that separated the border from the lake. The bystanders began to form, and some officer forced them back, but phones went up and captured videos of the girl in hospital scrubs, a leather jacket, and a rifle by her side walking to the police.

The officers all look at each other. Tune squinted and ordered them to draw their weapons, as he did. Tune stood bewildered for a moment, then gave the order to cut through the wire.

"Drop the gun!" the officers said in variation.

Bell froze upon hearing this order, clutching the rifle.

The blue-uniformed men worked on breaching the barrier. And Tune lingered over there, shouting at them to hurry.

Some of the men ordered, "Keep your hands in the air!" while others commanded her to move forward. Few in the group recognized her, Agent Tune being one of those and called out to the girl.

"Stay where you are!"

The other synced there commands with the agent, and the wall was finally opened by the men. Tune ordered a handful of officers to accompany him, and they flooded onto the bog, firearms all drawn.

"On the ground!" Tune order. "On the ground now you piece of shit!"

Bella felt stiff, but she did as she was told, bending toward the ground and paralleled to the mud seeping through clothes and onto her face.

They all encircled her.

"Hands behind your back! Don't you move!"

Bella did as ordered.

Tune made the arrest, drawing his steel handcuffs and fastening it around the girl's wrist.

A knee burrowed into her back.

"Why is it tied around you? Why is this fucking tied to you?" Tune beckons to a nearby officer. "You, get this off her and the rope."

People stopped to the police-car traffic jam. Their peering inquisitions made their way into the barrier.

"Block their view!" Tune yelled. "Get them away! Block 'em!"

And the men in riot gear secured the area as instructed by their commander, yet people still snuck photographs of the girl in the mud.

Bella resisted not, closing her eyes as she began to taste the wet earth. And when she was hoisted up, clumps of the bog fell from her face. The men pushed her to their inscession.

"Get her out of her," said the agent, turning toward the forest, looking for something. Some of the other officers stayed by him, scanning as well. Tune followed the tree line with his sight, scanning the waves to roots to then a fur boot. He froze at the recognition and lifted his vision. Obscured by the forest, two wrathful eyes peered behind a tree.

"There! There! He's right there!"

And all the men spun to where the agent pointed.

They all aim for the collective target. Thunder sounded from the pines.

"Shoot him!" Tune commanded in a hysterical yell. "Shoot him!"

Bullets fired blindly into the dark veil. Bella, deafened, gave a last cry out to the Ghost, before being ushered into the city.

Chapter

21

Arrest processed to the station. Bella rested her head on the steel barrier dividing the driver from the criminal in the back seat. A sense occurred that she was not the first one to translate through the barrier, perhaps the Locals and their felonious ways landed them in similar scenarios, and Bella wondered if others even dared and were arrested for crossing. Her eyes shifted from the officer to the white-collar agent, the vehicle stinking with repulsive cologne.

I know nothing, she thought. *I know nothing*. And she waited for the car to eventually stop, bracing for what she expected ahead of her.

Tune brought her in, shivering and dirty, still abjuring the scars of yesterday. They stripped all possessions, including the Yudaku. Many other agents surrounded her. But sunlight was wrapped, and before she knew it, the girl could see nothing, remembering being carried, rushed, attempting to cry out but gagged by a taut rag around her mouth as she entered onto what she conceived as station grounds. Her cheeks were tear stained, and her mind occupied by what was to come next, senses firing to gain a trace of her surroundings. Her hosts showed little sympathy, seething at each stagger she made while transporting her into that pit. There was shuffling, chopped language, and the hum of appliances, the first recognizing sound being the squeak of hinges. She could tell then she was being transported through a door. She tried to scream when they tossed her, or rather tried to, thrust upon what felt like a metal chair. They didn't care what their action induced. They quickly shackled her to a smoothed surface that leveled to her height, her wrists not bought but imprisoned together. Little more could she uncover of her environment, other than a faint humming beyond her confines. The air, through whatever was over her head, smelled moist; and the floor felt smooth to the touch of the heel of her shoe, and also a cracked cluster rivets as she shifted in her deprived throne.

Bella clung to these facts, divining physical truths that cannot be shrouded in falsehood, darkness peering eyes began to bend and mystify fake parlors and shapes that curved and devoured into statice and folly. Her hosts had failed to keep her entirely null, and for that, she smiled and glued her heel across the smooth cement beneath her.

That pride then dissolved. No, her captors had not failed. She was in the place they wanted her, unable to resist, shackled to the metal chair and to their whim. So with void claims to the environment, she waited and anticipated for any alteration from the static that slithered and contorted, ready for what they deemed fit for her crime. And so she waited and waited, the passage of time seemed like a tick. Here pupils expanded the best they could, did aching from the confines of this placed in, and eyelids fell for remedy. However, there were no better than when they were lifted. At one point, the girl believed but discredited herself, that she heard muffling, yelling of the sort, but blocked by whatever presented itself in front of her. And then the waiting continued. Her blood pulsed in her veins. She was convinced time had stopped, until what she feared materialized.

A click, then a low cry, then a whine. A bleak ray of yellow rays hit the girl, outlining a figure under a doorway. The silhouette paused within the boundary and with rushed heavy footsteps made its way to the nurse's side.

"Bella!" a male voice cried.

The girl felt an outstretched hand grab her a material near her face and fling something onto the ground. The incoming light was harsh on her sight, but she soon recovered and looked and saw the shaded figure. Relief swept her body. In blue uniform head to toe, bordered by the yellow rays which Bella understood to be hallway light, and a golden badge that bore the crest of the city of Heartlake, stood Brigham, his burly body and red mustache completing his warm face. The girl drew an exhausted breath.

"Are you okay? Are you hurt?" The man knelt down and undid the gag around her mouth. "I didn't...I didn't know they'd bring you here. How could they?"

Bella looked up at the officer and relieved in a broken voice, "Brigham...what's going on?"

The burly man hesitates, then replies, "I...I don't know, but all this...I mean look at you...By god, my god, you look like you've been dragged through a swamp. This is heinous even for them." Brigham glanced at the hallway, anxious he would be heard. He turns back to Bella. "But...but I'm gonna get you outta here."

"Where am I?" Bella presented.

"An old room. We don't use it ever. I don't understand..." He looked around to the four corners. A portable table erected itself in front of the girl, two chairs opposite of Bella, and a long mirror what went the length of the wall, against the left side. "But...maybe we have."

"How'd you find me?"

"It's everywhere. Deacon told me where he thought you'd be. I didn't believe him. I got rid of the guard for now, but Sharlet is gonna slit his throat."

The world seemed open now, and the light highlighting the officer seemed ever more welcoming.

The officer saw the glee in the girl's eyes, and his heart turned inside his chest. Hesitating no longer, he spoke. "I just need a few minutes to regroup with the chief. We can get you in another room. Not this hole in the ground.

The pit shrunk. The light that passed the officer felt cold and artificial. Bella's smile evaporated.

"Don't leave me here," she said.

Brigham winced from the girl. "I...I have to," he said. "I don't know much time before they come back. I'm sorry." And he stood up, nearly turning the table. "It'll be quick. I'll come back, and I'll get ya out of here."

Bella clenched her teeth, the man shadow interrupting the static yellow beams. "Then why did you come at all?" she spat.

"Shh! Shh!" He went forth to silence her. The officer turned attentively back to the open hallway and listened for any notice that

Bella's noise was heard. There came no reception. He turned back to the girl. "You gotta keep quiet!" he said in an almost identical manner. "I needed to make sure you were alive," said Brigham. "I couldn't live with myself if something—"

"If they killed me?"

The officer lowered his head. "They won't kill ya, but they'll make you wish for it."

"Who are they?" Bella demanded.

"The men and women in the white collars," he replied. "They won't say who they are. When you'll be questioned, they'll say they're from the FBI or CIA, but they're not. They have special links to those agencies, but they are high, high up on the government ladder. Their assets are covered. They barely exist."

"What do they want with me?"

He chuckled to himself. "Who the hell knows? But you apparently have something to do with what the PRA are very interested in. This whole case involving Molly hasn't gone without the least bit of supervision. These are the same people who took me off George Grey. And whatever happened to her or is going to happen with that monster will only be known by then, and whatever happened on that mountain, they're gonna want to know."

"I won't tell them," she stated.

"You gonna have to comply until we can move you."

"I won't."

"Bell—"

"I'm not! They should just shut me in jail for crossing the border. I broke the law, but I don't have to tell them what I saw."

"That is not all you broke. They're going to make an example out of you."

"Can I call a lawyer?"

He shook his head. "There are ways to get around rights, and right now you're considered worse than a terrorist. You won't get a lawyer for at least a few days. What happens in this room doesn't exist, do you understand? What they do won't get put on any record or there isn't a camera in this room. They could kill you, then say it was suicide."

"Unless you unlock these," she said, raising the shackles to Brigham's face.

"I—" Brigham stopped. He honestly pondered Bella's proposal, then spoke again. "I just can't rip you out of here. I need Deacon's backing, or they might as well shoot me. I'm…I'm sorry. It's not right, it's not, but I promise you, I swear, I will come back."

The officer scanned Bella's face for a response, but she would not look at him and instead sought the cement. He drew a solemn breath and got off his knee.

"I promise," he said again, then walked toward the open exit of the room.

"Wait," blurted the girl.

Brigham spun around.

The poor girl stared into his eyes full heartedly. "Did you see the light?"

The officer nodded.

"Then you saw her."

Brigham fathomed a response "Who?"

"Molly."

The officer nearly voiced another question, but the sound of footsteps descending toward the room alerted him, and he peered down the hallway. He looked to his left, then back into the room, staring into the poor girl's eyes. Bella kept her sight on where the officer stood as the door swung back into its frame, gently bracing the thick wood before it met the metal latches. Never did Bella ever long a speck, an ounce, a morsel of radiance to crawl beyond wood. But the barrier denied her, and no light leaked past.

She would not be freed. Bella lowered her head back to the cement floor as she listened to what sounds of Brigham made walking away. They were chased away by sharp footsteps that clicked on the unseen floor's hard surface. She could discern two separate pairs walking toward the door, but nothing more. They continued to grow with each step, step, step. Bella thought they were being deliberate in there torture, drawing out there arrival, driving her mad; however, she couldn't prove this malice and continued to listen to each step, step, step. And as if she couldn't help it, she began to hum. A soft song, one of youth but not of her own, the notes shaking and chiming. The room echoed her melody, dampening it slightly making her lament audibly to only her own ears as it drifted through the empty space of the accused pit she was wallowed in. The tone soothed her as it did from the moment as it left the box, but beyond the door Bella heard the voices that drove Brigham off crescendo, stomping out her hum as they made their final step, step, step.

They stopped dead outside the door.

There was an instance of quiet, then a click from above and then a sudden flash that over took the girl. Bella snapped her eyes closed. Blinded, she could only hear the door knob twist and its hinges creek. In stepped two pairs of footsteps—one bleeding sharp, the other flat. Bella's eyes soon adjusted. At first, she noticed the static white light illuminating the concrete floor to which she faced. Then, but not wanting to, she followed, with her sight, the floor up to find that the white light ended in a ring that encompassed her, no more than a few inches from where she sat. She raise her head and her gaze passed the ring, scanned darkness between, then found a familiar yellow ray from the hallway, then two pair of silhouetted shoe—one in the shape of men's formal wear, the other of the shape of elevated heels.

"There's the little shit," a familiar voice slithered.

Bella followed his formal shoes to his hidden face. A man, slender and tall, with a spiked head of hair that glistened under the yellow rays of the hallway, stood before the girl. He held a black bag. "Who took off your bag," he continued, a hint of worry in his voice.

Bella's eyes then shifted toward the frame besides the man. A lady, straight in the spine and overall thin, with a tight bun and frail glasses, possessed a clipboard and a pen.

"We'll manage." She spoke with the evidence of experience. "What we must first do is to apologize." She perched, reaching the threshold of the white light. Bella could now see the age of her face, dark shadows endowed by the wrinkles of her in her skin. She wore fragile metal-framed glasses that focused her dark, dark eyes behind, complemented with elegant white fleece along with a black dress. "This is an unconventional way of being detained," she continued. "Not every criminal, no matter how dangerous, goes through and not a sweetheart like you would go through. And you must have been so very much afraid." She reached the table. "I can't imagine what was going through your mind. I must apologize, my dear."

She sat down in one of the chairs opposite Bella. Tune neared the other spot.

"So let's start over. My name is Miss Sharlet." The lady out stretched her hand to the girl.

Bella looked at the woman's long nails in disgust. She did not reciprocate.

Sharlet withdrew her favor. "But you will understand and understand it well, every measure taken, every resource spent was worth it, less the safety of our great country be compromised. Do you praise the state?"

Bella left the question unanswered.

The man then copied the woman and crossed into the confines of the light. His face is healthy, and his hair stiff from over use of gel. He wore a simple white collar shirt with black pants and a tie, with a gun on his waist and a badge on his peck. He set the black bag down beside his seat. Bella glared at the man. He stared back. Both of the individuals sat in their metal seats across from the sight of the soul between them.

Sharlet, noting the lack of reply, smirked, regaining a friendly shroud again.

"You're a trespasser," she said. "And on federal land, I can't imagine how your sentencing would go."

"You ought to get use to a place like this," said Tune.

Bella steadied her gaze on the two agents.

"But you're a guest here," Sharlet stated. "No crime has been committed in my eyes—yet, and surely not in yours."

The girl glanced at the lady who kept her smile and leaned into Bella, changing tone. "Unfortunately, you are a part of a bigger picture. However, it may not be all bad." She erected herself straight. "Destiny is a strange thing, a Local belief. But when I find myself alone at night, I start to believe in strange things. Surely, you do. I need you just as much as you need me."

Bella kept her silence.

"So," said Sharlet, "let's begin."

Tune reached down into his pocket and pulled out a strange black device, catching Bella's attention. It took a second for Bella to realize it was a recorder. It took Tune less than a second to switch it on, a red glow resonating in beats along its side. Sharlet then placed the clipboard down she held in her hand and slid it across to her confidant.

The man cleared his throat and turned the first page of the clipboard. He then read, "Today's date, May first, 2024, Wednesday. This is Agent Tune speaking along with Director Sharlet Questioning witness Bella Tomson, Heartlake. We'll be processing as a protocol. Miss Sharlet?"

The lady studied her questionnaire, gauging what thought sprung through her head, then said, "Continue, Tune."

"Yes, ma'am," replied the agent, flipping the page of the clipboard, pinning it against the table and the weight of the board. He then focused back on the suspect. "When we found you, Bella, you were within restricted state land in front of the Heartlake reservoir. Is that correct?"

The girls saw no use lying. She nodded.

"I need a yes or no response," said Tune, motioning to the black box.

Sharlet made a quick glance to Tune with a smirk upon her face, then swiveled back to the girl across from her. Bella returned this look. She felt as if somehow Sharlet wasn't blinking.

"Yes," Bella replied, directing a lowered head toward the man.

"Good, and in your hand, or rather tied on to your hand by and old rope, you possessed a firearm, is this that correct?"

"Yes."

"Good," Tune said again. "Least, you're cooperating." The man checked the clipboard and plucked a small square photo from its vice. Tune then slid it across the table toward Bella. "Now, tell us about this."

Bella peeked up at the photo. It was a picture of the weapon laying on the grass. Around the butt was a small but thick ring and an inch or so from the ring was severed rope, bent with strain and appeared to once have a magnificent shape. She slid the photo back to the agent.

"It's a photo of a Brook Knot," clarified Tune to the recorder. "And a rifle on the ground."

"I didn't know," asked Bella. "I just tied random things."

Tune gasped the photo back and stuck it into the clipboard. "Well, why did you tie it in the first place?"

"I'm crazy," stated the girl. "I was scared I might lose it."

Bella looked over to Sharlet, who watched her like a undying cat, in search of a response that would explain to her. None came, only the reassurance.

Tune then leaned forward. "We're not stupid. This is a knot used by Pelts. And you're not exactly the type to know how to do this, so there must have been someone that taught you."

Bella leaned back. She still gave no response and, in avoidance, turned to the gray room's walls. Bella could see now, with the white light on, the dim outline of individual blocks that made up its composition, each single unit having a role in the construction.

"Did you learn to tie this knot? Or did someone else tie it for you?"

The girl remained silent.

"Bella," said Tune in a dry, firm voice, "answer the question."

The room grew quiet. Sharlet and Tune both stared at the lone girl, anticipating a response. Bella inhaled deeply. She turned back to the man.

"Molly," she replied. "Molly taught me."

The agent squinted. "She did?"

"Yes," replied Bella.

"When did she teach you this," asked Tune, frustration sounding in his words to the answer he wasn't expecting.

Bella shrugged. "Before she was taken."

"Before she did the same thing you did and crossed the border?"

"She was taken."

The agents bit the inside of his lip and continued, "So she taught you to tie this before her disappearance."

"Yes," Bella replied.

"We have eyewitnesses stating that you left the hospital with a quote 'suitcase tied to her wrist.' Was the rifle in that case?" Tune asked.

"Yes."

"Why was it there?"

"Molly hid it for me in the hospital."

"Why there?"

Bella shrugged. "It was where we spent most of our time."

Sharlet just stared.

"Where did she get it?"

"I don't know." Bella's soul was cool as morning dew.

"You'll be asked these same questions on a later date," Tune continued. "And in your mind you obviously think Molly has been taken over the border against her will. Does it in any way stemmed from recent sexual assault? Did this in any way motivate you to cross into the border?"

Bella nodded.

"Yes or no," the agent pestered.

"Yes," Bella said.

"To which one?"

"They both had a wide mouth."

He paused for a moment. "Who did?"

"George and the Pale Thing."

Tune glanced at his superior. "George Grey?"

"You know," the girl replied. "I heard her was a very famous man."

"Yes, he is."

Bella nodded. "I let my friend go on a date with that monster."

Sharlet interrupted, "And what do you mean by Pale Thing?"

"A long jaw."

The interrogators were confused.

"In which," stated the man, "is in Mr. Grey?"

Bella nodded.

"But this Pale Thing. What was it?"

"I'd rather not say," she said.

"Why?"

"I don't want to relive seeing it."

"Well, for the sake of record, could you? A brief overall description."

The girl thought for a moment. "Skinny. Tall. Pale with a large mouth.

The agent rolled his eyes. "Guess that'll do." Then he looked back at his board. "Do you know any Locals that she was in contact with? Any homestead boyfriends that she could have taught her the Brook knot. Any neighbors, elders, little kids that she would have talked to. Anyone?"

Bella shifted in her chair and averted her eyes from the agent, to the door between her interrogators. "I don't know," she said dryly.

"You don't know, or you won't say?" Tune stated.

"I think there's more valuable information here, Tune," said Sharlet. "Please, about this thing you saw when you hiked up the mountain, what was it doing?"

"I bet you have an idea," said the girl.

"What is that supposed to mean?" Tune contested.

"I saw your men."

"What men?"

"The ones you brought in on helicopters and set them down just outside the wall. My entire whole street saw them. They all were dead when I saw them."

Tune peeked to the old lady still staring, a faint smile on her face. "So they were in military equipment?"

Bella shook her head. "You know I'm not dumb either," she said. "I know they were from you or some other branch."

"How do you know that?"

"They wore our flag."

"And these individuals were deceased?"

"Yes."

"Did you see any cause for mortality?" the agent asked.

"Why does that matter?" Bella replied.

"We just need that information."

"Go up there and look. They're probably still there."

"The creature, Tune," said Sharlet. She began a line of reasoning herself. "This Pale Thing as you described, Ms. Tomson, were you able to see more official features, besides it's frame and wide mouth you mentioned."

"I couldn't tell you," she responded. "It all happened so fast."

"But when you were up there, did you see it again? Was it around?" Bella froze, then nodded.

"Yes or n—" Tune voice lifted, then suddenly cut off.

"Quiet," the old woman said. "Did it have no eyes?"

Bella nodded.

"Long limb?"

The girl confirmed.

Then Sharlet smiled. "We don't have to play these games any longer. I'll be frank with you, my dear. We know what they are. We do not play this game any longer. They roam as far down as Molly-Mason to as high to the base of Haze, or rather. They love the Giants, and only venture down to prey upon our sweet Mollys of the world. They are controllable and incredible. I don't think evolution nor a god would claim these Things. They are an unpopulated species, if that, and don't like competition with others. We don't know how many or how they came to be, but if the number of nationwide unexplainable disappearances correlated with known cave systems, we estimate their population must be hundreds. But of all of their known habits, there is one thing they do not do, Ms. Tomson, and that is build fires."

Bella looked at the woman, whose smile slowly waned through her words. The nurse quickly came up with a response. "Molly taught me how to make the fire."

"Ah, you mean the second one?"

Bella nodded.

The woman grinned again. "That's quite the accomplishment for a girl born on misty streets."

"Molly taught me."

Tune spoke next. "Then who made the first?"

"The news says she did it." Bella hated herself for speaking the phrase.

"And that will stay the official truth," said Sharlet. "But if they only knew what we know, dear. They can lie all they want, but we both know, that young lady would have never gone over the barrier. A Pale Thing took her, and yet she had no means of getting away, no tied gun around her wrist. And those beasts don't let people go so easily, I think we both know that. Someone had to intervene."

Bella was silent.

"Describe what you saw, Tune. Maybe that'll refresh her memory."

The man cleared his throat and directed his attention to the black box. "When I arrested Ms. Tomson, I noticed something from the tree line on the southern end of the reservoir. I looked closer, and I saw what appeared to be this large hand wrapping around one of the trees. I stepped closer, and I saw this figure. He resembled a man, but far larger, not like how we said the Pale Things were. He was, for the lack of a better term, complete. I couldn't see all of him, but I swear I caught a glance of his clothing before he ran off, which was clearly some animal skin, and I saw a part of his beard. That's all I can report."

Bella glanced at the agent, then lowered to her to her muddy shoes. She chewed on her hair. "Maybe you're the crazy one."

Tune scoffed. "You came out of the part he was standing. How could you ever not see him? We have officers that will tell you the same thing."

"I didn't. I'm sorry."

"It's in great interest that we know, my dear," said Sharlet. "You couldn't believe the risk of having someone like that unchecked within our borders. It's a liability. You mentioned before that you saw our men on the mountain, or at least what was left of them."

She remained still.

The lady licked her lips. "This man isn't a saint or a god, or whatever your Pelt friends must have told you. Our soldier we sent out, they all had body cameras, and some of them were taken by the Pale Thing, but most capture this same man Tune describes. The detail is admittedly hard to make out, scatter, but you can clearly see men being thrown around, limbs being pulled from their sockets, and their gunfire, having no effect. Now do you think hiding this man is a wise thing to do?"

"He's good."

"So you admit seeing him."

The girl turned away.

"Look at me. Look at me, my dear."

Bella didn't obey. And Sharlet, seeing her command unfulfilled, stood and walked to the nurse's side. She then grabbed her hair and forced Bella to turn.

"Believe me when I tell you this," the director continued. "The good you'll do for your country will be momentous. The slightest smallest detail can help, bringing us that much to securing a loose end. Wouldn't that be great? We could even talk about lightening your sentence. Anything you could want, dear."

"And who'd kill the Pale Things?" Bella asked.

Sharlet let go of the girl. "We will. We will always protect you."

The girl braced herself. She wouldn't give up the slightest notion. "I'm sorry," she said. "I don't know what you're talking about. And I'd…I'd like my phone call now, please."

Tune looked at the old lady. Her face was null, and her lips pressed as she spoke from crooked teeth.

"Out of all the liars," she began, "that I have ever had the misfortune to question, you must be one, stupid." She hovered back over the nurse. "As a student, and from a college no less, you have a duty to the state that funded you. And we have an abnormal honor to fulfill." She struck the girl with the back of her hand.

Bella recoiled. She bent into her shoulder to shield herself.

Sharlet grabbed her hair and slapped her again and again, until pulling the girl's ear close to her mouth.

"Where was he going?" The director reached for Bella's cuffs and held her hand. She then kissed the top of her head. "You're not a bad girl. You're not. You seem lovely, tender. Maybe a bit misguided, but that's nothing he can't be corrected." And when Bella didn't respond, she continued. "We just need to know about him. The Giant. You can atone for your trespasses, and we can move on."

The old "just tell me about *him* and the traitors who taught you."

Bella dared not move.

She shifted her stare toward him. "Open the bag," she said. "She'll explain herself, won't you, dear?"

Tune hesitated for a moment, then did as the director wished. "What do you need?"

"Get me wipes." Sharlet turned from Bella and walked back to her chair. "Then come hold her."

The agent glanced at Sharlet, her steel-trap eyes locked on the questionnaire, then surrendered any notion of a conscience and accepted the new angle his superior provided, rummaging from the black bag a container of what looked to the girl as alcohol wipes. Sharlet then went to her left side.

"Hold her tight," she ordered.

The man did so and pressed the united shackles to the table. "Hold them arm," Sharlet then said, and he did so. "Extend them."

Tune brought her arms back until they straightened.

Bella remained calm, her face not conveying any terror she possessed. The eyes of the interrogator pressured her already broken mind. She inhaled deeply, not knowing what the two personnel would do to her. She held fast.

"Take as much time as you need," said Sharlet. The director pulled back the girl's sleeve and dug her thumbnail into Bella's triceps, right between the muscles, pressing it harder and harder until crimson ran down the girl's dirty skin.

The interrogator waited, still watching Bella for a response. She gave little more than gritted teeth, and Sharlet then began to turn her nail inside Bella's flesh. Tune looked away but fastened his grip on the unresting nurse. A seething whisper escaped from the girl as she resisted. Bella felt liquid oozing down her skin. Sharlet, however, bore no signs of meekness and, with machine-like composure, pressed the rest of her nails in a half-circle shape, contorting her finger in a strange image, then pressed down. Bella struggled, the strength of the woman was impressive, for the girl could feel the full length of the nails skin into her muscle. The nurse let out a wail.

Sharlet then yielded, a visage branded on Bella's arm. "This is what you did," she said. Then motioned to the agent. "Give me the needle."

Tune let one hand go and searched through the bag, fetching the instrument to his superior's pleasure and passed it to her. The director thereafter brought the sharp icy metal to the girl's bicep.

"Make her watch," she muttered next.

And the man forced Bella to look down her afflicted shoulder, clenching her hair and holding her shackles. Bella attempted to free herself, but her constant proved to be greater. Sharlet plunged the needle into her arm, then resurfaced it. The woman then began slicing, brushing, then little marks, starting around Bella's shoulder, and going down the length of her arm, harsher with her strokes. The girl closed her eyes, feeling every little cut, nick, and scratch down to her wrist and even upon her knuckle, each growing with more pain. The woman stopped.

"Tell me," Sharlet said. "Tell me about the Ghost."

Bella refused.

Then the director began again, starting at the girl's shoulder, and going unto even Bella's forearm.

"Did he say anything? Tell you anything?" Her cuts drew deeper.

Bella refused.

Sharlet started again. "What did he look like? What did she have to do with him? Where will he go next? Say something!"

Bella refused.

The scratches became lacerations, and blood dripped down on the floor.

"Tell me," Sharlet ordered. "Tell me!"

Instant, every moment, second, Bella felt there in the chair and the nerves wincing with each flick of the metal instrument. She only wished for the Yudaku and felt interchangeable with grains of sand, trickled down as from the hourglass. Bella gave a slight bobbing with her head. The broken girl gathered herself fully. She didn't think she could resist any longer, but she did. Mixed with the wallowing agony and the temptation to tell, to ease all suffering, she swallowed, and the idea was no more. She wouldn't give one word that would harm him. Bella raised her head to meet her eyes. No longer did she even flinch.

Sharlet stared down, her frustration boiling to the point of madness. She rose the needle, ready to force it deep into a vain. But out of all the hallway, a heavy chorus.

A click, then a low cry that whinnied in front of her. Yellow light froze the scene, and in stepped two police officers, with two more men in suits that stood as if guarding the far wall.

Brigham came flying to Bella's side. "Stop it! Stop it!" He pushed Tune out of the way, almost knocking him down. Sharlet stepped back to the shaded part of the room.

Deacon stayed in the doorway. He stood appalled at what he saw, staring at the gore on the portable table. He then spoke. "What could you possibly want that's worth this?"

"We need information!" Tune shouted. "It's not your business!"

"This is torture! How could sane people ever condone this?"

Sharlet then answered. "There is no torture, Mr. Loch." And she walked to the officer, her heels striking the concrete. "She received these wounds from her trespass. She came to us whoring and will be leaving us whoring. Do you understand, Detective? This didn't happen."

"It's chief," he replied. "And this…this won't ever be happening again. She as in our community, not yours. You won't lay another finger on her as long as I'm here. Brigham, get her outta here."

She scoffed. "Do you understand what you're doing?"

The officer yelled to Tune. "Give me the key. Give me the fucking key!" And the agent put his hand out to stop the advancing officer.

"Hold on, big boy." Tune pushed against him. "Keep going and see what happens." His hand rested on his gun.

Deacon caught sight of Brigham readying for a fight. "Hold on there, Brigham." And he directed back toward the lady. "The Heartlake Police Department will be conducting its own investigations into these disappearances. I won't stand for another second of your goddamn stench stinking up my city."

"What you need to do is what we need to do," Sharlet stated. "We work for the same state."

"I'm not too sure anymore, not after this."

"That's an odd response, Loch. What do you mean to do?"

"I can't prosecute you," he said. "It not like I even know your real name. But what I will do, Sharlet, is to use the utmost edges of my power to keep these obscenities out of Heartlake."

"All I've done for the people. But if you wish, we'll see how much a police chief can actually do."

"I can give this poor lady a bandage and some water. And if you will, you're no longer welcome here. Please leave."

"You'll be a target," said Sharlet.

"I don't have anything else to say to you. Please go," Deacon said again.

"What will the police chief do?"

"Escort you out, if it so costs me my job." And the man's face was of winter.

The woman scoffed. She looked into the eyes of the chief, but saw into his every soul that he spoke the truth and meant every syllable that filled the space between her and her passive subordinate. She then turned to her other and instructed him. "Hand them the key." She then walked over to the table and began cleaning her bloodied hand by the stinking cleansing wipes left out on the table's surface.

Tune dropped the key into the officer's hand, and Brigham returned him a dark glare, quickly spinning to Bella and unlocking her constraints. He helped her to her feet and press his hand into her skin to stop the flow.

His force stung, but she understood the protocol, doing the same to another wound further down her arm. "Thank you," she said and leaned against him. "Thank you."

Brigham looked to Deacon. "We need a first-aid kit."

"Is it lethal?" The chief looked past the lady. "Do we need to bring her to a hospital?"

And to the mere thought, Bella winced too.

"Don't worry," said Sharlet. "We were professionals." And the director finished cleaning her nails and turned to the door. "Come along, Tune. We'll need to sort this out." And she pushed past Deacon and into the hallway, the sharp striking footsteps echoing as she departed. The agent followed next, keeping her head to the floor, avoiding both Brigham's and the Deacon's gaze.

Deacon then took off his jacket and wrapped it around Bella's afflicted arm. "Let's put pressure on those." And they began escorting her out of the dark chamber.

Chapter

22

And the halls did hustle and the rulings of which she was brought up and moved, she did not recall. The voices, the surroundings, the caregiving were all interloping within seconds to which she sat ever so stiff. Bella sat on a bench in a molded cell. There was illumination from the corridor to her right, a steel hanger separating her from those baffled on what will become of her. A toilet dish was tucked kitty corner to her, and a mattress dead on the floor next to it, all on stones that resemble granite. Bella rubbed her arm, a bandage covered it, tiny inks of drying maroon bleed through the white material, but the girl didn't appear to care to her recent wounds, save for grazing where the gauze intertwined and undercuts and to where it never reach, to which she felt scaring underway. Oh, how she missed her friend's sacred knots.

The nurse sat there, looking up to the dark heavens through iron bars of the window, passing clouds under phantasms of the moon, a Giant's dark peak outreaching its hand to the mythic sky.

"Bellz?" Brigham called out from outside her cell, outpouring inches away from the bars.

The girl smiled, then waved, but stayed where she was and turned back to the mountain.

"How you feeling?" the man asked.

"Like a bad dream is over," she said.

His mustache curled. "I'm glad to hear that."

Bella got to her feet and walked over to the officer. She extended her functional arm out to the man, the other wouldn't budge. They stood in silence, awkward glimpses of each other, the man to her wounds and the girl to his solemn face.

"Does it hurt?" he asked.

"No, the Tylenol is helping a ton," she said.

"Good, good." But a shape of guilt returned in his face as the air grew quiet, saving the inner machines of the building's pumping heat and comfort into the facility.

"I don't blame you," she said. And she touched his hand.

The officer now stared at the covered arm. "I do." He gently moved his hand from the girl's. "It seems obvious now, a place like it wasn't for everyone to see. It was made to get answers, no question to how they left you."

"You needed the calvary."

"If I actually did." His sight deepened on her arm.

The girl cupped his hands and brought her arm closer.

"God, she did a number on you," he continued.

"I don't blame you," the girl so clearly stated again. "I just hate them, just them. Not you.

"You should hate me too."

"You got me out of there," she argued.

"But I wasn't quick enough. You got hurt. Gray got away. When I mentioned Molly, no one would say a word." He gripped the metal barn and looked to the title floor. "You saw the memorial, you saw what their investigations lead to. I was put on so many incidents where the white collars took over. Molly has to be the end of that. Whatever is happening, this mist of questioning keeps changing. No one can keep a promise." He removed himself from the bar, and took off his hat, and brought the item close to his chest. "Do you remember, when we were little, how all of the grown-ups would ask you what you wanted to be?"

Bella nodded.

"Did ya tell them 'nurse'?"

Bella smiled. "Yes. Where are you going with this?"

"You can imagine what I told them. I think we bothered to do what I think most people want to do and help others but"—he looked into Bella's emerald eyes—"I've rarely done that, it seems. Rarely solved a missing person case without them or whoever they claim to be covering it all up. Rarely put to ease a family, and that's what I aimed for. I promised people I would find them, and then the white collars would say their gone and never coming back. I won't make a promise anymore, but I promised you..." His hand clenched the prison's metal once again. "You should hate me. I'm a liar, and you should hate me."

"But I don't." She reached for the officer's burly hand. "I can't hate you. Not when you did what most men wouldn't have."

"And what's that?"

"You saved me. That should be reason enough to at least like you."

He smirked and shielded his head one more with his hat.

"But it's not an excuse," she said, and she closed the distance to the bars. "We'll never stop blaming ourselves for what happened. We'll never not be haunted. I don't expect us to ever forgive ourselves. And we'll be forced to continue, forever, but maybe that's how it should be. We're not supposed to forget."

Brigham nodded his head. "Grey won't get away."

"Did Deacon mean what he said? About the Department taking things back over."

"It sounded like it. It's gonna be a real pain, but I reckon we can make a plea if we agree to stay within the border. Let them want what they want with their land, and we'll keep the peace in ours."

"Will that work?" Bella asked.

"I don't know," Brigham said. "But we're overdue for some change."

"Don't do anything rash." She smiled.

He laughed. "Not taking advice from you."

And the scene grew quiet while the man formulated his next question, a morbid want of truth stemming from him.

"What...what did you actually find on that mountain? Was Molly up there?"

Bella backed away from the man. She surveyed a response, but none were drawn, and she was self-standing, smiling in the pale moonlight that dripped from the cell window.

"It's okay," voiced the officer. "You don't have to tell me." And he turned back open corridors and railings of the jail. "I should actually be getting back. Me and Deacon need a little pow wow. But..." He fixed his hat and rubbed his hand, warming them from the cool metal.

He then slipped his fingers down into his vest pocket and retrieved a wonderful sight. There, in his palm, lay the Yudaku her captures had stripped away from her. "I'll see you again, probably sometime tomorrow. Give you some company so ya don't go crazy."

Bella approached again. She reached for the knots and seized them and brought it close to her heart. Then she panned up to the officer. "What's your name?"

The officer grinned. "Lewie."

She smiled. "Never thought I'd meet a Lewie."

He rolled his eyes. "Don't get too cozy in there." And he turned toward the walkway.

"Wait!" Bella yelled. "Can you call Kim? She deserves to know what happened."

Brigham stopped in his tracks. "You never got a phone call, did you?"

She shook her head.

He returned to her. "You can use mine."

"I don't know her number," she admitted. "I just was thinking if you would call her, it would be nice."

He nodded. "Yeah, I'll touch base with her. She's gonna want to have a sit down with you though."

"I know," she said.

Brigham smiled. "Just get some rest, we'll get this sorted out."

Bella's cell would let her see. The guard came inside the room and withdrew his phone.

"I plan to."

The officer waved goodbye and began walking down the railway corridor. Bella watched him descend.

Bella then returned to the window and graced the sight of the summits, barely seen from the tall buildings suffocating her. She needed only the Locals to understand. She didn't think anyone else would believe her and wondered if she'd ever see Evergreen and a chance to apologize. Molly was what she had found next, and her failure morphed into determination.

"No, this place will not be my grave."

And her eyes to the same angle before the officer had surprised her, and gazing to the Giant's peak. "There will be no rest." And she schemed. Worldly things died as her heart thumped a steady beat. Her life, the schooling and the council, the tests and the arguments all came as a steady passing, as if she saw a tumbleweed tumble past her. But she did not flinch.

The Giants now shouldered the moon and kept it enthroned. Silver ray's soothed her.

Nothing could convince the girl what so absolute happened not. Even myths could be true, the most radical spender might exist, and she would be called their Local whore. Yet it would be a lie, but she would know fully the nature of the things on earth and what desires lead them to debauchery. And those lost, taken, stabled on forgotten boards, revenge will be cast on the souls of the wicked, and for them rests a worthy place in hell. And fire, fire of the wildflower.

And Bella heard music, and grabbed the Yudaku ever tighter. A gentle tone carried her ear, and guided Bella to catch an oddity on the summit. She got to her feet but bowed to her knees. A sense of relief washed over her as her body felt clean for the first time in days. Orange wicks shone. They bore witness to the single light against a dark mountain face.

End

www.ingramcontent.com/pod-product-compliance
Lightning Source LLC
Chambersburg PA
CBHW030958260626
47169CB00002B/589